Just like back in the day . . .

"Incoming!" Arsenal was shouting to the lingering press hounds, but Green Arrow had his own idea about crowd control. As Arsenal took down three flying meta-soldiers in quick succession with his crossbow, Green Arrow shot a fog bomb into the civilian crowd, obscuring them from the view of the arriving mercenaries.

"Now they'll just target on us," he explained as he turned back to face the water again, notching his bow.

"Gee," Arsenal drawled, "great plan, G.A. . . ."

DC UNIVERSE

INHERITANCE

Devin Grayson

WARNER BOOKS

NEW YORK   BOSTON

Cover illustration by James Jean
Book design by Stratford Publishing Services

Warner Books
1271 Avenue of the Americas
New York, NY 10020

Printed in the United States of America

First Printing: June 2006

10 9 8 7 6 5 4 3 2 1

*This book is dedicated to
Denny O'Neil
with reverence, affection, and gratitude.*

ACKNOWLEDGMENTS

The creation of a super hero comic is very much a team effort. Many of the characters in this book were created long before I was born, and their rich histories are in large part due to the contributions of literally hundreds of creative people working both independently and in teams over the past sixty years. I cannot name them all here, but do need to thank Mort Weisinger, Paul Norris, George Papp, Ramona Fradon, Mike Grell, Marv Wolfman, George Perez, Phil Jimenez, Neal Adams, and, of course, Bob Kane and Bill Finger for some of the key decisions that shaped who these characters have become.

The creation of a super hero comic and story writer also involves many people, and to that end I want to warmly thank Scott Peterson, Darren Vincenzo, Jordan Gorfinkel, Steve Korté, Devi Pillai, and especially my patient and enchanting editor, Chris Cerasi, both for his encouragement and kindness, and for unwearyingly correcting the spelling of the word "toward" 137 times.

A special thank you to Dennis O'Neil for his immeasurable positive impact on both my life and the life of many of the characters featured in this story.

Thank you, too, to Mark Waid, for his friendship, knowledge, and generosity, and for always being willing to read my manuscripts at any crazy time of the night.

Thanks to Bill Turlock for the generous donation of his time and expertise.

Thank you to my new online friends who so graciously came forward to talk to me about Navajo, Romany, and circus culture. I am particularly indebted to the writers Raymond Friday Locke, Alan Wilson, Jan Yoors, Isabel Fonseca, and Bruce Feiler for sharing their insights into these worlds. My gratitude also to all the scholars and brave survivors who created such clear and honest accounts of the aftermath of the atomic bombing of Hiroshima and Nagasaki, particularly Toshi Maruki, Michael J. Hogan, and Hideko Tamura Snider.

Thank you to Emily Diamond and Zoe Cohen for keeping me healthy and strong during the process of writing this, and of course to my amazing friends and family for their biased opinions of my writing and their continued loved and support. Mom, Frank, Jessi, Max, Linda, Schuyler, Ollie, Georgia, and my dear Auntie Bree, you're what family is all about and I'm grateful for you all. Kaye Jarrett, Moira Kate, Janean Langlois, Dave and Sam Segale, Dave Kinel, Eric Rhodes, Tonya Bowman, Jay Faerber, and Brian K. Vaughanily Vons Moore III, you guys are my Titans. Thanks for having my back.

Special thanks as well to Arnold Feener for tirelessly going over this plot with me, and for keeping Scott busy while I finished this.

Last but not least, thank you, Dad. You've always been a super hero to me, but even Batman, Green Arrow, and Aquaman could learn a thing or two from you about parenting. I love you.

Devin Kalile Grayson
October 2005

FOREWORD

This book is a work of fiction. However, some parts are more fictional than others.

Please allow me to explain.

When working with licensed characters, a writer often has a long, detailed tradition of character depiction and fictional "facts" upon which to draw. In the comic books, which are published as serialized monthlies, we refer to this as "continuity." In a book like this one, in which I am telling an original story about established characters, its often called "status quo," and it can get very confusing.

You probably already know that Batman lives in Gotham City. That's a well-established pop culture "fact" (and by fact, I of course mean fiction). If you're a fairly loyal comic book reader, you may also know that the name of the specific Gotham suburb in which Bruce Wayne resides is Bristol. Until reading this book, however, you could not possibly have known that the doorway to Wayne Manor, in the Bristol suburb of Gotham was marked by a cast aluminum doormat—because I just made that part up.

In the interest of being fair and clarifying the background of this story, I'd like to mention that the Quraci characters (Dabir and his family, Mahbi, and the few members of *Mutawwiin* that we actually meet), the officers on board the fictional USCGC *Herron*, and a few of the members of Great Frog are pretty much the only characters in this book for whom I can take complete creative credit. There really is, in the DC Comics atlas, a place called Qurac, which really was bombed by Cheshire who really did have Arsenal's baby who really is named Lian (and by "really," I of course mean fictionally).

I mention this now because our country is currently in a nonfiction war with the nonfiction country of Iraq. If I were to have invented a new Middle Eastern country for this book, I certainly would not have given it a name that conjures up so much contemporary political baggage (unless, perhaps, I wanted to tell a story that would take into account and comment on our actual conflict there—this is not that book). Moreover, despite the name similarity and the neophyte democracies, it would be incorrect to think of Qurac as a fictional Iraq. Qurac is more like Saudi Arabia crossed with Japan—its relationship with America when this story opens is respectful but distant, and its capital, Abu Dhabi, has endured the same atomic horror suffered in the real world by Hiroshima and Nagasaki.

I believe that we use fiction to explore truth rather than reality. The reality here is that Qurac and Iraq have absolutely no connection. The truth is that any discussion of war, allegorical or real, is not complete without an acknowledgment of human suffering on both a mass and personal scale.

Devin Kalile Grayson
October 2005

DC UNIVERSE

INHERITANCE

PART ONE

Dabir closed his eyes and tried to imagine the light. For every day spent in Gotham, he found his memories of Qurac becoming increasingly intangible. Though he could still feel the satisfying burn of the cardamom- and saffron-spiced coffee his grandmother called "qahwa" scalding his tongue and throat, he could no longer precisely recall the smell or taste of the drink. The sound of sand crunching underfoot could not seem to survive in his memory alongside the cacophony of Gotham's droning car engines, screeching subway train brakes, and taxi horns. Even on the American Coast Guard ship his father had arranged for their primary transport, the heavy, vertical shadows of Gotham City's financial district crushed all sense of grandeur from the bay, transforming one edge of the Atlantic Ocean into a queasy, polluted puddle of dull brown water that no longer even knew its own history well enough to smell of brine.

And the dusty, rich, warming light of home . . . Dabir began to wonder if such undisturbed beauty had ever truly existed. Gotham's skyscrapers thrust themselves into the heavens, obliterating the stars with a flat, neon glare, plunging everything below them into cold, leaden shadow. Dabir had never imagined such darkness. Even in the terrible glare of summer, the shadows stretched and shifted with the changing light of day, but never fully released the Gotham City pavement from their tyranny. They were present even at night, offering no relief from the heat, but hovering grimly behind lighted storefronts and collecting with blinding solidity in every small street and alleyway. In their all-pervading ambiguousness, Dabir found the city shadows nearly as terrifying as the freeze-framed specificity of the light-autonomous ghost shadows permanently flash-burned in white onto the seared walls of Abu Dhabi.

He refused, however, to show fear, fighting against the oppression of Gotham's shadows with the entire force of his fifteen-year-old being. He held his head high and kept his posture proud. A composed young man even at home, in Gotham Dabir became cool and deliberate. He was unfailingly polite to every person to whom he was introduced and diplomatically without interest or complaint concerning his family's travel itinerary. When the dominating height of a building or the chilling inscrutability of a badly lit pathway threatened to overwhelm him, Dabir turned his attention inward, faithfully tending the smoldering coals of rage that burned constantly in his stomach.

The American servicemen on the 270-foot Cutter avoided Dabir's eyes when he passed them on the deck, but Dabir nodded to them anyway.

"They will help keep you safe," his father had asserted with absolutely no trace of irony as he had sent his son off to board the USCGC *Herron*. Safe? Dabir barely understood the word, except as an antonym for the predominant condition of his life. "Safe" had been annihilated, along with 1,026,039 lives and over forty-six square miles of Qurac, in the space of time it took for the international terrorist known as Cheshire to drop a stolen Russian nuclear missile on the capital city of Dabir's homeland. The atomic bombing of Abu Dhabi had not even hit its fourth anniversary, but already the world seemed eager to forget. The global community had roundly denounced the attack, the United Nations had sent monetary aid (actual relief workers were not permitted into the country for months due to radiation contamination), and eventually the American government reported Cheshire's arrest and reluctantly turned her over to Quraci custody. By the time the blast zone had been cleared, Dabir's father had been elected as the president of Qurac and the small Middle Eastern country seemed to pump out sycophantically indebted international ambassadors in even greater quantity than the radiation-tinged oil for which they were so famous.

The event quickly came to be spoken of the way people discussed the unfortunate wreckage of a building at the hands of a rampaging super-villain, or even the unintentional destruction of private property triggered by a desperate super hero seconds before his final victory. Foreigners would frown in soft embarrassment and pick invisible lint off their clothing when they noticed the small glass pieces permanently embedded into the left side of Dabir's skull, or when his father calmly listed Dabir's mother and older brother among the dead. "At least it wasn't like Hiroshima," a low-level British royal had blurted out to Dabir during a lavish dinner party in London the year before.

"That is to say, at least no one was actually at *war* with you."

True. There had been no war. In fact, Dabir had read that the terrorist Cheshire—whose ultimate goal had apparently had something to do with blackmailing the world's more prominent governments with her missile cache—had chosen Qurac as the place to demonstrate that she meant business precisely because she assumed that no one really cared about it.

"One must understand the difference, politically, between protest and protestations," she had told an Internal Security Agency operative in one of her early debriefings. For a short time, the American tabloids had been full of her calmly tragic photos and of speculations about an undercover Central Bureau of Intelligence agent with whom she purportedly had a baby. Over and over again, she was described as "beautiful," "stunning," and even "captivating." Though most articles also referred to her as "coldhearted" and "without apparent remorse," they spent more time detailing her long, ebony hair and the exotic cast of her half-Vietnamese, half-French features. Her "real" name, the Metropolis *Daily Planet* finally reported, was Jade Nguyen.

Dabir, however, found her unreal, even implausible. She was impossible to make sense of. How could one woman be so powerful and so wholly unaccountable? She was photogenic, charismatic, brilliant, and, if the stories were to be believed, also an assassin, a martial artist, a sociopath, a former slave, an orphan, and the mother of a young daughter. Though she was universally despised in what remained of Qurac, to Dabir she was nothing more than an illusion—an intriguing poster girl for a disingenuous political attack. The idea of one woman dying or spending her life imprisoned to atone for the obliteration of Abu Dhabi was unsatisfying. Dabir didn't care what happened to her. He had his own ideas about who was truly to blame for the calamity that had befallen Qurac, at least insofar as it affected his family.

"Dude! Unclench!"

Dabir was startled out of his brood by the familiar voice of his cousin, Rashid. Though two years older than Dabir, Rashid's lanky, sloping frame and easy grin frequently made him appear younger than his more compact, impassive fifteen-year-old cousin. Dabir let go of the safety railing of the flight deck, which he realized he had been white knuckling, and turned to face Rashid.

"You become less intelligible every moment we stay here!" Dabir snapped in perfect English.

Rashid blinked slowly, momentarily caught off guard by Dabir's hostility, and then he smiled again, placing a sweaty hand fraternally on Dabir's shoulder.

"Relax, man, I'm just practicing my American slang. I want to impress the chicks at the dinner tonight."

Dabir sighed, looking searchingly into his cousin's angular face.

"*I* will do the talking," he said firmly.

Rashid nodded. He understood this to be the natural order of things. Politically and within the hierarchy of the family, Dabir was Rashid's better. There had been hints of this even when they were younger, both playing under the benevolent and watchful eye of Dabir's older brother, Amin. Dabir had always been so curious, so smart and funny and full of ideas, charmingly and inevitably leading his older cousin into lighthearted mischief. But now, without Amin and without Amin and Dabir's mother—without, too, Rashid's mother, father, and sister—Dabir's political and intellectual prominence over Rashid was secure.

Rashid sometimes felt the burden of Amin's absence even more keenly than Dabir did. Though he felt great loyalty and gratitude toward his uncle Hatim—Dabir's father—for taking him in after the loss of his own immediate family to the Abu Dhabi bombing, Rashid often wondered if Dabir could see, as he so clearly could, the pained look of resignation on Hatim's face when the Quraci president surveyed his new, post-apocalyptic brood. Rashid, who called his uncle Abu Amin (father of Amin, a title of familiar respect), was a poor substitute for Amin, and after the bombing Dabir had in many ways become a poor substitute for Dabir. Rashid literally had not seen his cousin smile since that day nearly four years ago, and felt he would have done anything to coax back, just once more, the affectionate, laughing, long-lashed playmate of his childhood. It was as if in the absence of Amin—who with his handsome face and princely social grace had made even the staunchest Quraci politicos nostalgic for the days of Middle Eastern royal families—Dabir had found it easier to become his brother than to lose him. Rashid, though older, could only rush to fill the void then left by Dabir. He embraced his new role as mischief-maker and family clown wholeheartedly, barely stopping to mourn whom he might have become on his own had he not been forced to help repopulate the thinning family ranks of the Abdul-Hakams. The reassignment of identity was not uncommon in the war-ravaged land of his birth, and Rashid was helpful and compliant by nature.

"Listen, the thing tonight's right by Robinson Park. What say we ditch the dessert course and go find out what Gothamites do for fun after dark?" Rashid hoped to tease enthusiasm out of his cousin, but instead Dabir glared up at him with an even darker frown.

"Don't be stupid. Safwan would never let us go."

"Not if we *ask*, but . . ." Rashid stopped as he watched his cousin squint and then rub the temples of his forehead as if fighting off a bad headache. "Dabir, are you all right?"

Dabir glanced up at Rashid with a slightly startled expression and then nodded, his mouth tightening.

"I'm fine." Dabir held Rashid's gaze for a second, then turned back to the view of the Gotham Tricorner Yards.

"There's supposed to be something like two hundred people there," Rashid continued. "Safwan's going to have his hands full just answering questions about your dad. Even if he did notice us slipping out, he wouldn't be able to bust out after us without causing alarm. We could find a video game parlor . . . maybe even a disco or something!"

Dabir's back was to Rashid and his voice was low, his shoulders hunched as he leaned his forearms against the ship's railing. "If you want to go, I won't stop you."

"Come on, it'll be fun! Who knows when we'll be in a city like this again –"

"I said no!" Dabir had whirled around suddenly, his eyes flashing at Rashid.

"Okay, fine! Forget it."

Dabir, who was looking over Rashid's shoulder, narrowed his eyes suddenly and Rashid craned his head to see what had caught his cousin's attention. Rashid turned the rest of the way around and together the boys stood up straighter and silently watched the approach of Safwan.

Safwan was President Abdul-Hakam's best friend, chief military adviser, and de facto bodyguard. An imposing man physically, Safwan's musculature and height were backed by his keen intelligence and resolute faith. He usually wore a traditional white *thobe* from shoulder to ankle and was never without his crocheted skullcap in rich hues of red, green, and black. Neither Dabir nor Rashid had ever been able to figure out his exact age, though both guessed it to be closer to fifty than forty. It was not the fine lines around his dark eyes nor the smattering of silver in his otherwise shiny, cropped black beard that suggested this, but rather the stories he told and the font of wisdom from which he pulled that had always signaled to both boys that they were dealing with a practiced and seasoned elder. Everything about Safwan demanded respect, and most people gave it instinctively without ever consciously deciding to do so.

"*Salaam alaykum,*" Safwan said formally as he approached them. His voice was deep and rich.

First Dabir and then Rashid shook his large hand, both murmuring, "*Wa alaykum as-salaam,*" in unison.

"There has been a change of plan," Safwan announced evenly, turning toward Dabir. "As you already know, the president was delayed in Qurac and sent the *Hijra* ahead without him. The ship is still scheduled to arrive in Gotham Harbor as planned, but your father was able to break free of his entanglements sooner than expected and boarded a flight early this morning. He will meet us tonight at the reception."

Rashid's expression brightened. "Aren't you going to retrieve him from the airport? We can get ourselves to the event, no problem."

Safwan shook his head, smiling faintly at Rashid. "I will be escorting you. The Americans can deliver the president safely to the reception. It would be hugely embarrassing for them if anything were to happen to him. But we are leaving early so I can properly secure the room. Please attend to your grooming now."

Dabir immediately nodded, squared his shoulders, and began walking past the Law Enforcement Detachment officers who quietly shadowed the family's every move. Rashid headed for the ship's main passageway after his cousin, but was stopped by a strong hand clamping down on his shoulder.

"Were you and your cousin quarreling just now?" Safwan demanded, pulling his hand back to fold his arms across his muscular chest. Rashid watched Dabir until he disappeared belowdeck, then forced himself to meet Safwan's questioning eyes.

"No, sir. I mean, yes, sir, but it's—we're all right now."

Safwan raised an eyebrow at Rashid. "Gotham is not a safe city, Rashid, and we'd do best to stick together. I require you to keep that in mind at all times."

Inwardly Rashid cringed, grateful Dabir had not been present to hear this remark. Dabir seemed to go ballistic anytime anyone expressed concern over his personal security.

"I will," he said to Safwan, offering a single nod. "I was just trying to . . . you know . . . loosen him up a little."

Safwan's expression did not change, but he offered a brief nod. He stood beside Rashid for a long moment, watching the bay, then he turned and briefly placed a large, reassuring hand atop Rashid's head.

"We leave in just over an hour," he said quietly, and then he turned and headed back toward the stateroom.

Rashid lingered on the flight deck looking out toward the city, enchanted by the idea that behind the darkness and the twinkling lights, thousands of human dramas were unfolding. Gotham City held the world's richest and poorest, the famous and the anonymous constantly rubbing up against one another in the overcrowded avenues and underground subways. The arts and sciences were advanced during casual conversations in badly lit neighborhood bars, and the fate of nations regularly decided in boardroom meetings held forty stories above sea level. The stories in Gotham were not just historical, they were alive. Anyone standing on a street corner in the city had the right to expect to be included in one at any second. Rashid had memorized a list of resident movie stars and politicians that he hoped to meet during his visit, and had also boned up on Gotham's legends and myths. His favorite was the one about the city's vigilante crime fighter; a strong, fierce, and unforgiving half man, half demon known to Gotham's criminals and true believers simply as "the Batman."

Dabir had combed over his memories of the Great Terror, as the day came to be known in Qurac, more than a thousand times. They were supposed to go to the beach, all of them: Dabir, his father, his mother, and Amin, who was going to start teaching Dabir how to windsurf. Dabir had been looking forward to it for weeks.

But he woke up that morning to the familiar sound of his mother and father arguing.

"I am not a mere office manager, Ghaliyah! I cannot just tell these men that I have other plans and 'Sorry, please come back next Tuesday'!"

"You cannot tell them that you are a father and you care about your boys? I cannot take them myself, Hatim! You *promised* them!"

"They understand how these things work. You are the only one who gets hysterical."

"How would *you* know that? When do *you* see them!?"

"They are proud of their father as you should be of your husband! And shame on you for raising your voice to me! Honestly, sometimes I think that I am too free with you, Ghaliyah."

"*You* are too free with *me*!?"

"Look . . . I am nearly out of *oud*. Take the boys and go to that new mall in Abu Dhabi you've been telling me about. And buy anything you need for the house. You have my permission. Just . . . go."

Dabir sat up in bed and glanced at the clock on his bed-side table: 9:43. He'd slept in late, again. Ever since he had turned twelve, he'd had a hard time getting out of bed in the morning.

There was a gentle rap on his door and then his brother pushed it open, already washed and dressed in a clean, white *thobe*.

"The Crystal Palace Mall, Peewee! Aren't we lucky?"

"But what about windsurfing? You promised you'd teach me!" Dabir knew that the disappointment welling in his heart wasn't Amin's fault, but he couldn't keep his voice from sounding petulant and accusatory.

"And I will, but not today. Believe me, I'm just as unhappy about this as you, but there's no point arguing with Dad when he gets like this. Something came up, some kind of official business. At least I'm not getting dragged to that."

"But we're getting dragged to the mall?"

Amin sat down on Dabir's bed and reflexively smoothed the covers over his brother's bare legs. Dabir watched his brother's intelligent, golden eyes as they inspected the bedspread for wrinkles. "I'll go to the mall with mother. You should study. And then when you're done, you should take advantage of the fact that no one will be here, and you should take the Bentley out for a little drive."

Dabir's pulse quickened and he threw off the covers his brother had just smoothed. "The Arnage? But I'll get in trouble!"

"Less so if I've stolen the keys and you only take them from my room." Amin winked and rose from the bed as Dabir jumped out of it and ran to begin dressing. "Be good, little brother. I love you."

Dabir meant to reply—to tell Amin that he loved him, too—but by the time he'd pulled his nightshirt off from over his head, Amin had quietly let himself out of the room.

Bruce Wayne had barely stepped foot onto the cast aluminum doormat of his family mansion when the grand front doors were swept open by his butler, Alfred.

"Welcome home, Master Bruce," Alfred drawled, his voice marked by a soft British accent that had managed to overcome more than thirty years of living in Gotham. The barest suggestion of a smile flickered across his thin lips and tipped one end of his pencil-thin mustache up as he reached out to relieve his employer of the burden of his briefcase. Though at least a foot taller than his butler and capable of carrying approximately four times his weight, Bruce had long since stopped arguing with Alfred about the practicality of carrying his own items indoors.

"Thank you, Alfred." Bruce nodded, surrendering the case and already striding past him into the manor's luminous Great Room. Of all Alfred's qualities that he most admired—and indeed there were many he had no idea how he might live without—it was his old friend's talent for speeding along the tedious routines of daily life that pleased him the most. Over the years they had worked out a sort of shorthand pantomime of standard living that included both the necessities of daily care on which Bruce was grudgingly still dependent and also the niceties on which Alfred insisted, but which rarely, if ever, interrupted Bruce's ability to concentrate on the weightier matters ceaselessly pressing down on his broad shoulders. "Alarms?"

"None, sir."

Bruce continued down the marble hall toward his study, back strong and straight, confident that Alfred was fast at his heels.

"Calls?"

"The usual. I took the liberty of rather forcefully dissuading a reporter from *The Rich Life Magazine* from calling the house, accepted a subscription to a new local newspaper, and assured your dentist that you would make your cleaning appointment on the fourteenth."

Bruce entered his home office and headed straight for the neatly stacked pile of opened mail on his mahogany desk, thumbing through the sorted papers with a soft frown. Alfred came in behind him to place the briefcase neatly on the burgundy carpet beside the desk, then waited patiently for his master's overcoat, which Bruce began to shoulder off impatiently.

"Mail?"

"Just what you see before you: several bills I've already attended to, requiring your signature on the indicated lines, and a bank statement I've cross filed by account and month."

Bruce, who wasn't fond of sitting down, handed Alfred his overcoat with his left hand while producing a pen with his right. Alfred folded the overcoat over one arm and watched as Bruce hulked over the elegant writing desk, rapidly signing his name on the indicated checks.

"Don't they make rubber stamps for this?" Bruce queried, half jokingly.

"There's one to your two o'clock, sir," Alfred replied dryly. Bruce, still scribbling out his signature, looked up at Alfred with a quick wink. His stone-gray eyes held more humor than most people realized, and more pain than most people knew. "May I remind you," Alfred continued, "that the Gotham City Police Department fundraiser begins in just over an hour? I've laid out suitable clothing for you upstairs and prepared a thermos full of

Albóndigas for you to take along this evening, assuming that you will not return home for supper."

Having finished with the bills, Bruce turned his attention to a large, antique grandfather clock standing majestically against the north wall of the study. He deftly pulled open the Scottish walnut and glass door that protected the gilded dials and began to carefully move the minute hand with his index finger.

"No food at the fund-raiser?" he asked, his back to Alfred.

"There will be some catered refreshments and an open bar, but nothing suitable for an evening's repast."

With the dials indicating 10:47, Bruce somberly took one step back from the clock. With a soft clicking sound, the entire timepiece swung open like a door to reveal a dark, stone staircase winding down into an apparent abyss.

"Any other social events of note?" Bruce asked, pausing on the top stair.

"There's a bachelor party for a famous Hollywood actor down on Cape Carmine that promises to be quite rowdy, and a U.N.-sponsored Quraci Embassy party at the new Daggett Industries building near the park which should be attended by Quraci president Hatim Abdul-Hakam. There are also two new restaurant openings, but I'm familiar with the work of both chefs and predict nothing more exciting than a few dozen cases of mild salmonella poisoning."

"Remind me not to schedule any dinner dates at either one, Alfred."

"I shall, sir."

"I'm going to run my own risk analyses for the evening, but I'll be up in time to change."

"Of course, sir."

Alfred stood at the edge of the study with Bruce's overcoat folded carefully over one arm, watching the shape of Bruce's back as he descended the stone staircase until the grandfather clock snapped neatly back into place of its own accord, hands already resynchronized with the atomic clock. Only the slightest dip of his head gave any indication of how sad it always made Alfred feel to observe his friend's nightly descent, and it would have been hard to note even that much, such was the speed with which he turned and walked briskly back down the hallway, conveying the coat to its proper closet within the perfectly ordered labyrinth of Wayne Manor.

The thirty-second floor of the Daggett Industries complex by Robinson Park was slated to house an upscale seafood bistro, but during the time it took for the menu to be finalized, the space was frequently used to host lavish business and society events.

Dabir had been in extravagant banquet halls and the sumptuous private homes of royalty, but the ornate geometric splendor of Gotham's art deco-based opulence was new to him. Trying to focus on the dark, polished curves of the oversized maple bar, he found his eyes wandering up the spidery veins of silver inlaid onto the pastel walls. The magnificent urban view, showcased by 360 degrees of floor-to-ceiling windows, softened only slightly on the east side by the green of Robinson Park, was reflected back a thousandfold by hundreds of shimmering mirrors lining the interior walls. The ceiling glittered with multifaceted crystal chandeliers and the carpet beneath Dabir's new dress shoes was frantic with rose- and gold-colored looping swirls. Every available inch of space that wasn't teeming with shifting tuxedos or the alluring flash of female skin framed tenderly against the satin sheen of an evening gown held a spindly green potted plant or perfectly maintained ficus tree. The cheerful clink of glasses could just barely be heard beneath the roar of laughter and increasingly alcohol-infused conversation that solidly dominated the occasional jazzy lilt of a distant saxophone.

Hesitating just in front of the elevator in a vain attempt to calm his assaulted senses, Dabir felt the steady pressure of Safwan's warm hand on the small of his back.

He made his way into the crowd with Rashid at his side. A glance at his grinning cousin confirmed that Rashid was as electrified by the surroundings as Dabir was overwhelmed by them.

"Drinks!" he saw his cousin mouthing, and then Rashid was gone, darting freely off into the crowd. Dabir moved to follow him and was immediately blocked by a sea of tight smiles and extended hands, his father's bulky shoulder suddenly pressing in tightly against his own. Though he had removed his hand, Dabir could still feel Safwan's reassuring presence behind him as he began to nod greetings and shake hands next to his jubilant father, who was trying to whisper a personal greeting to Dabir as an aside. Dabir forced himself to smile at his father and endure a quick sideways hug. Inwardly he braced himself just in time to avoid flinching at the repeated references to his dead mother and brother that seemed to fall compulsively from the lips of those too uncomfortable to ever reference the cause of their deaths.

". . . growing up to be such a *handsome* young man . . ."

". . . if only your mother could . . ."

". . . considered your brother a dear friend . . ."

". . . wanted to meet you ever since I heard about you losing your beautiful mother at such a young . . ."

". . . met Amin when he was only six years . . ."

". . . so glad about these improved relations between Qurac and the United . . ."

". . . remember Amin used to love big band jazz . . ."

Dabir lowered his head, teeth clenched, only to have his father reach over and pull him closer again, laughing as he affectionately mussed his son's hair. Dabir pulled away with a frown, earning a mock pout from his father.

"You are too big for this now, I am sorry. Do you remember Ambassador Biladeu, Dabir? She came with a Red Cross team after the elections."

"Very nice to see you again," Dabir mumbled, unable to look the woman in the eye. The sense of being inundated was giving way to a sense of building fury fueled by his father's toadying bows and smiles.

"My goodness, but don't you look *just* like Amin," the woman told him brightly, bending down slightly to bring her face closer to his, her voice scented with expensive scotch. It wasn't true. Dabir looked nothing like Amin, except for perhaps the thin bridge of his nose and the expressive dark eyebrows he habitually lowered over his smoldering brown eyes. Amin's eyes had been touched with gold, and had always noticed when Dabir was uncomfortable. With a shiver, Dabir realized that he did feel eyes on him, but not the lovely golden orbs of his dead brother.

For just a second, he wanted to run.

"Dabir!" Dabir had turned backward in a panic of emotion only to bump into the unyielding chest of Safwan, who gently grasped him by the shoulder and spun him to face his cousin, who was calling to him from just beyond the welcoming crowd that still surrounded his father.

"You can go now," Safwan said quietly, bending over to direct the comment precisely into Dabir's ear. He extended an arm into President Abdul-Hakam's throng of admirers, magically clearing a path. Dabir walked toward Rashid in a daze, grateful when his cousin thrust a drink into his hand.

"What's this?" he asked, just to get Rashid talking.

"It's a chocolate martini," Rashid answered, grinning. "I've already had two! Come, you must see this view!"

Dabir was not supposed to drink—both because of his age and because of his religion—but he took a long swallow of the ice-cold liquid and felt his mouth fill with the flavor of candy and gasoline. Rashid had grabbed his arm and was dragging him toward the east wall.

"Robinson Park!" Rashid enthused, gesturing grandly at the windows. Dabir swallowed another gulp of his cocktail and fought a strong sense of vertigo as the horizon dropped away into a sudden expanse of green at least thirty floors beneath them. Turning his back to the window, Dabir had a sudden sense of exposure. The crowd had thinned slightly and Dabir did not believe for one second that the windows would stop him from falling should someone push him firmly backward.

Standing less than a foot away from his cousin, Rashid wasn't sure what happened first. It seemed to him that

Dabir's martini glass shattered at his feet half a second before the floor-to-ceiling window behind his cousin imploded with a spray of glinting glass. Two hundred gasps and screams competed with the hot, swampy air outside to permeate the wounded room. The panic seemed especially keen near the elevators, which Rashid suddenly understood had ceased to function. The call panel was crackling and smoking, a bullet lodged firmly between the "up" and "down" buttons, much to the amazement of the nearby crowd.

Rashid's chest was tight as he turned swiftly back to his cousin. Dabir was holding the outside of his own left arm, pinning it to one side, and he looked oddly pale. Rashid called to him and was about to grab him by the front of his shirt when Safwan's muscular back suddenly blocked Dabir from view. Within the space of one breath, Safwan had gathered Dabir up like a small rag doll against his chest, one large hand reaching out to grab the back of Rashid's collar. Rashid gave himself over to the focused force of Safwan's will and felt himself dragged across the room toward the elevator banks, where two uniformed guards were trying to kick open the door that led to the fire exit stairwell. Rashid was shoved into a corner near the blocked door, where he found his uncle's trembling arms reaching out to him.

"My boys, my boys," Hatim was crying, "Rashid, are you all right?" Rashid felt his uncle's hands checking him for injury but his own focus was on Safwan. The bodyguard and military adviser was lowering a wide-eyed Dabir into a sitting position on the floor, and the front of his white *thobe* was red with blood. Hatim seemed afraid to even look at Safwan or Dabir as he spun Rashid around to confirm that he was unharmed.

"He's been hit," Safwan said loudly, as much to the nearby guards as to Hatim. Rashid felt the Quraci president's hands release him and knew that his uncle was finally turning to observe Dabir.

"I'm a doctor," insisted someone behind Safwan. The woman was in her mid-forties with long, straight, dark hair like Dabir's mother had had, and dark kohl lining her eyes. She swiftly pulled the tuxedo jacket off the man standing next to her before coming to kneel by Dabir. With Safwan's help, she removed Dabir's jacket, exposing a bright red stain on the teenager's left arm.

Rashid knelt down by his cousin and placed a hand on his shoulder, trying, for the younger boy's sake, not to tremble.

"The bullet just grazed him," said the woman who had identified herself as a doctor. She gave Safwan the jacket and instructed him to hold it against the wound, applying pressure. Dabir watched her in a daze, a familiar ache taking hold of his chest. The woman's brown eyes stared into his for a moment and then she gave him a soft, private smile. "You'll be all right," she told him calmly. Dabir closed his eyes. She smelled like gardenia.

Above him, he heard his father bellowing. "Someone tried to kill my boy!" Hatim was moving as if to leave the safety of the corner into which Safwan had herded him. Every so often, Safwan would calmly reach out and place a hand against the president's chest, checking his movement before he could storm off.

"Stay," he commanded quietly after Hatim's fourth

attempt to leave, and Rashid was not surprised to see the president obey.

"Dabir?" Rashid whispered, moving his own face closer to his cousin's. "Dabir, are you okay?"

Dabir's eyes flashed into Rashid's and slowly focused. He swallowed and looked to Rashid like he was about to cry.

"I'm not dead," he said with something close to incredulity in his voice. "Rashid, I'm not dead . . ."

"I know," answered Rashid, tears springing into his own eyes as he smiled at his younger cousin with relief. He grabbed Dabir's right hand and gave it a squeeze. "I know," he repeated. "All praise the will of Allah."

Just past them, the building guards forced open the emergency exit doors and the party attendants began to stream down the metal stairs like an unfolding bolt of satin.

The Bentley handled like a dream. Glistening bronze in the midday sun, it was literally dazzling to look at and intoxicating to drive. Dabir blasted the air-conditioning and unreservedly strained to reach the pedals on the softly carpeted floor. He hadn't meant to take the car out as far as An-Sufwat, but he figured that he was safe as long as he could see the stacked crates and sweaty vendors of the dusty, outdoor souk. He could always find his way home from the teeming marketplace on foot without difficulty, and the route would be that much more quickly traversed in the car.

He stopped for an older man leading camels across the hot road and figured out how to use the emergency brake to make the car still without having to slide all the way out off his seat to press down the brake pedal. The camels

halted in the middle of the street suddenly, as if st
and Dabir instinctively closed his eyes and ducked his
head under the dashboard as the midday sky overhead lit
up with an enormous, blinding flash. The man in the street
had an arm thrown across his face and was trying to catch
the camels that were frantically pulling away from him.
Dabir jumped out of the car to help and immediately heard a
thundering explosion from the northeast. The noise elicited
a few startled screams, but mostly people turned toward
the capital city of Abu Dhabi in shocked confusion.

Later, survivors described a wave of destruction racing
out from the city concentrically, almost like an air-tsunami
flattening everything in its path. Dabir, however, had focused on the thick column of white smoke rising from the
center of the capital. He had seen photographs of Hiroshima and Nagasaki and tried with all his might to stop
imagining that the massive, cloudy tower was going to
bloom into the shape of a mushroom, but that's exactly
what it did. Dabir barely even had time to be sick to his
stomach. The second the horrifying shape had registered
in his mind's eye, he was thrown off his feet as the blast
pushed through the souk and continued rushing outward.
Crates in the souk were flattened, their contents hurled
across the desert. The windshield of the Bentley exploded,
spewing glass. Children were wailing and everything on
the ground seemed torn from the earth itself, objects and
parts of objects swirling madly in a blinding thermal wind.
Dabir managed to grab on to the Bentley's front bumper
and clung to it for his life. He imagined he could feel the
radiation seeping into his skin and poisoning his very
blood.

stand again, he searched the north- capital, but could see absolutely no . It was gone . . . the entire city seemed ed. But the horrible mushroom cloud re- ble, even as the sky around it began to clear. Parch nd bleeding profusely from the left side of his head, Dabir began to stumble home.

There was nothing else he could think of to do.

Gotham City Police Commissioner Jim Gordon frowned at the spray of broken glass covering the eastern part of the carpet on the thirty-second floor of the Daggett Industries complex. The bullet that had shattered the window had been linked by his forensics team to a shell casing on the roof of a building across the street from the Daggett complex. This meant that someone had shot at the window from the opposite side of a four-lane boulevard, managing to hit the elevator call panel halfway across the room, disabling lift service to the floor, while grazing only one fifteen-year-old boy in a crowd of 214 people. Even the best sniper on his prize SWAT unit couldn't have dreamed up such a shot, much less executed it. It was superhuman.

With a sigh, Commissioner Gordon walked the six meters that took him back to the elevator bank and let himself out the emergency exit door, which had apparently been rigged shut from the outside prior to the shooting. Stepping carefully over a forensics detective busily trying to collect prints from the door, Gordon pushed his glasses farther up the bridge of his nose and climbed the interior stairwell to the building's roof to let himself out into the sticky, dark heat of the night.

"How's the boy?"

The voice that surprised Jim from the dark was a hot, menacing growl. If he hadn't heard it hundreds of times before, it would have made him instinctively reach for his service revolver. As it was, he had to catch his breath and calm the increased beating of his heart before he could answer.

"He'll be fine. We took him to General just to be sure, but it's a light graze above his left bicep. Mostly he's just scared and confused." Jim smoothed down his white mustache in an unconscious gesture of self-calming.

"He was marked."

"Marked?" Jim knew better than to try to locate the source of the voice, but allowed himself to turn part of the way around when he heard Batman drop down from the roof's water tower into nearby shadows.

"The sniper wanted someone to know that the boy was his target."

"But he missed. The kid, that is—he got the elevator panel dead to right." Interested in the direction the conversation was taking, Jim realized he had turned the rest of the way around and was now facing Batman. He swallowed and took a step back without meaning to. Even though he knew the masked vigilante considered him a friend and would never hurt him, he couldn't completely quell his instinctive response to the man. The eyes that met his from the darkness were fierce, white slits, demonic and inhuman—probably just an effect of the dark cowl that covered everything but the man's mouth and strong jawline, but a good one. The form that began to suggest itself in the water tower shadow was solid and tall, the dark cape flowing from shoulder to heel doing little to conceal the raw, muscular strength of the man who wore it. Jim trusted and even regularly depended on the formidable intellect and discipline he knew to inform the man's very core, and yet there was something dangerous about him that could not be ignored—something animal, feral.

"He didn't miss. Every inch that bullet traveled was perfectly calculated. He was sending us a message."

"Don't know many people who could make a shot like that," Jim conceded.

"I know three. This was the work of Slade Wilson, better known as Deathstroke."

Jim opened his mouth to respond and then shut it again, realizing there was little he could add. Batman was, as usual, several steps ahead of everyone else.

"What kind of security do you have on the boy?" Batman asked, pulling something out of his belt. Jim guessed that it was a grapnel rope.

"He's got his own bodyguard—usually on the father, but I imagine they're switching focus. The family's already being watched by a Law Enforcement Detachment on the *Herron*, but beyond that they're refusing to accept any additional security. I offered them a detective detail, but . . ." Jim trailed off, sensing that he was once again alone. Sure enough, as he squinted into the long shadow cast by the water tower he found no evidence of a human presence.

"Talkin' to yourself again, Commish?" Detective Harvey Bullock was climbing the fire stairs to the rooftop access doorway, which Jim had left ajar, already pulling a pack of cigarettes out of his vest pocket. Harvey was habitually eighty pounds or so overweight, and Jim guessed that the climb hadn't been a pleasant one for him. To the detective's credit, he did not appear to be winded.

"What would you say if I told you I knew who the shooter was?" Jim asked, turning to Harvey with a wry smile. Harvey pulled a cigarette out of his pack, tapped it three times on the cardboard carton, stuck it in his mouth, and then answered as he began to fish through his pockets for a lighter.

"I'd say you should stop putting so much stock in guys who wear extra ears on top of their heads." Finding a lighter, Harvey lit his own cigarette before offering the pack to his boss as an afterthought.

Jim shook his head. "Thanks, but I quit."

Harvey took a long drag, shrugging. "Yeah, but only once."

Jim smiled, patted Harvey on the shoulder, and turned back to the rooftop access door. He was about to head back down the stairs when his expression sobered and he turned back to his detective.

"Harvey, you ever heard of a guy called Deathstroke?"

Harvey's eyes widened slightly behind the glow of his cigarette. "As in Deathstroke, the Terminator, Death-stroke?"

Jim nodded grimly, not liking the look on Bullock's face. It spoke volumes about the kind of man they were now tracking. Harvey continued.

"He's one of those costume freaks—you know, a meta or whatever. Super reflexes, super smarts . . . basically some kinda murder machine. Mercenary for hire, as I understand it. Supposed to have a conscience, but with a kill list like his, I'm not seein' it." Harvey paused to take another drag off his cigarette. "That our perp?"

"So says the guy with the extra set of ears."

"Great." Harvey tossed his half-finished cigarette down on the gravel of the rooftop with a dark frown and ground it out with his shoe. Jim noted that in spite of Harvey's all-too-frequently vocalized distrust of Batman, he did not for a second doubt the vigilante's word.

"What!?" Oliver Queen had to yell to be heard above the din of the Seattle bar and even with one finger already firmly jammed into his free ear doubted he had a chance in hell of hearing the person on the other end of his cell phone. "Wait, just—hold on a sec, will ya? It's a little loud in here . . ."

Tapping his foot in time with the beat of the live cover band behind him, Ollie stuffed the cell phone into the front pocket of his jeans and, still lounging comfortably on his bar stool, smiled roguishly at the young, muscular blond tending bar, signaling him over.

"Refill?" the bartender shouted, smiling back at him and indicating his still half-full pint of amber stout. Ollie shook his head.

"Keep that warm," he bellowed, indicating his bar stool before pointing at his beer. "And that cold!"

"What?" the bartender shouted back, still grinning cheerfully.

"I'll be right back!" Ollie tried. "Gotta take a call!"

"Round for all?"

"Call! I've got a call!"

"You got it!" The bartender turned away and began

happily filling beer glasses from the tap, presumably for everyone in the bar.

"Oh, well. That works." Ollie slid off his bar stool and gestured broadly to the room as a whole. "Drinks on me!" he hollered gamely before fighting his way across the press of the dance floor to a side exit. Once outside, he took a deep breath of fresh air and admired the twinkling lights of Capitol Hill before remembering to retrieve his cell phone from his pocket.

"Oh, yeah—hello?"

Nothing.

Ollie shrugged to himself, ran the thumb and finger of one hand over his blond mustache to check for beer residue, and was about to head back in when the phone vibrated in his hand. He flipped it open again.

"Queen here."

"If you're not going to wear your communicator, you should at least learn to use your cell phone."

The voice was unmistakable. Ollie grinned and took a step away from the bar back into the alley.

"Batman! How ya doin', big guy?"

"You're not in Star City."

"Nope. Visiting the old haunts in Seattle. You think that place was loud, you should hear the crowds over in Pioneer Square. All tourists down there these days, but when Dinah and I lived here, you could still slide in around happy hour and get—"

"I'm looking for Arsenal."

Ollie frowned thoughtfully and turned his gleaming green eyes back toward the bar. "Roy? Hm. You checked with his band?"

"Roy hasn't been with Great Frog in nearly ten years, Oliver."

"Really?" Ollie was genuinely surprised. "He's a good drummer; he should get back to that. Kid's got rhythm. Though the guy playing here tonight, lemme tell ya—"

"I need to know when he last spoke with Cheshire."

"Oh, well I know where *she* is—"

"Yes, so do I, but she's unlikely to be cooperative. Your ward is a better bet."

Ollie stroked his goatee thoughtfully, trying to remember the last time he'd spoken to the orphaned kid he'd taken under his wing all those years ago. Of course, the kid wasn't a kid anymore—he was a twenty-something . . . father of a little girl, even. Ollie was pretty sure she was four, but he might have missed a birthday or two. Cute kid, though, that girl. Lian was her name. Where had he last seen her?

"New York!" Ollie remembered with a jolt of satisfaction. "I think Roy and Lian are in New York."

"Oliver." Batman's voice suggested that he had reached what was evidently the last little bit of his patience. "How do I *reach* him?"

"Commit a crime and wait for him to show up?" Ollie shrugged into the dark. He was proud that the kid had kept up the hero thing. When he had been training him, he'd called him "Speedy" due to the kid's fast arm—even at thirteen Roy'd had the best bow reload time Ollie had ever seen—but now Roy called himself "Arsenal" and practiced some kind of martial art form that allowed him to use any object in his vicinity as a weapon. Due to his killer aim, though, he still primarily relied on a crossbow, which pleased Ollie. That just seemed fitting for a kid who had grown up with Green Arrow. "What's this all about, Bats?"

Ollie had continued wandering down the alley as he talked on the phone and could now hear the other man typing on a computer keyboard.

"The teenage son of the current Quraci president came under attack in Gotham earlier this evening. I believe Deathstroke's been hired to assassinate him, but I don't know who's behind the contract. I doubt Cheshire is still interested in Qurac, but due to her past strike against that country, I haven't formally ruled out her involvement. I was hoping Roy could tell me if she ever mentions the Middle East anymore. Though he's not supposed to have any contact with her, I can place him at her holding facility three times in the past year."

There was absolutely no trace of humor in Batman's voice, but Ollie laughed anyway. So, the kid was still sneaking in to see the terrorist who had given birth to his daughter? Good for him! Ollie had no affection for Cheshire, but he was a romantic at heart and always championed young love. And if it took a complicated woman to hold his ward's attention, well, Ollie could understand that. He preferred the heroines to the villainesses himself, but that hadn't made his love life any less treacherous.

"So is the Quraci kid still in danger?" he asked. He had reached a brick wall that signified the end of the alleyway he'd been pacing, so he turned to walk back toward the bar, one hand in the pocket of his jeans, the other holding the cell phone to his ear. It felt good to be outside after the cloying heat of the bar, and listening to Batman, he was starting to realize that vacations were overrated.

"Yes," Batman replied. "His family has a bodyguard, and while in Gotham they're staying on a Coast Guard ship with a USCGC LEDET. But until I know who it is who wants the boy dead, no one will be able to adequately protect him."

"You think Deathstroke will take another shot at him?"

"That depends on how quickly I can unravel this."

Ollie could hear from Batman's tone and from the amount of activity he seemed to be engaging in on his end of the call that the only reason he hadn't hung up was that the phone conversation had become mere background noise to him. He was already busy with his next bit of business, having at some time during the conversation dismissed Oliver's potential usefulness to him. Ollie might have been galled, but he knew that Batman was an admirable multitasker, and not one for idle chatter. He also tended to take on what Ollie considered to be entertainingly dangerous cases.

"Tell ya what. I'm not doin' anything here but drinking my way down memory lane. I'll try to catch up with Roy, and we'll meet you in Gotham. I can help you with Deathstroke while you do all the detectivey stuff."

"Not necessary. I'll have Nightwing track down Roy."

Nightwing was Batman's former ward—or maybe Batman had actually officially adopted the kid at some point, Ollie wasn't sure. Either way, Batman had been the first one to take on a kid sidekick, an eight-year-old orphan he had immediately begun training as his partner, Robin. Ollie thought the kid had been too young in the beginning, but had to admit that he'd grown up well—he was respectful, easy to get along with, and trained to the teeth. And unlike his own ward, Batman's charge had never gotten involved with drugs or accidentally impregnated an international terrorist. He had, as all the kids seemed to do, eventually thrown off the mantle of Robin in favor of taking a new, slightly more grown-up hero name for himself, but Ollie was sure that he still came to Batman's aid anytime Batman called him, and probably showed up for Sunday night dinners, too. Ollie knew it was more his fault than Roy's that they didn't have that kind of relationship, and maybe, as Roy sometimes suggested, they'd had more fun back in the good old days anyway, but he did sometimes envy Batman the apparent orderliness of his life.

"Aw, come on! Two heads are better than one!"

"Not always."

"Great! See you tomorrow, then!" Ollie grinned into the phone, cheerfully ignoring Batman's refusal of help.

"Oliver—"

"Listen, I've gotta go, but don't you worry about Deathstroke. I'm on it. See ya soon, friend!" Ollie clicked his phone shut and strode the rest of the way back to the bar. A proper adventure was exactly what the week called for, and he was glad Batman had thought to call. Mercenary assassins, endangered kids, seedy Gotham docks, Coast Guard boats . . .

. . . Boats!

Ollie flipped open his phone again with a smile and then frowned at his call contact list. What the hell was the area code for Atlantis? And where *was* his Justice League communicator, anyway? Ollie let himself back into the bar from the side door hoping he hadn't put the communicator through the wash cycle again.

Arthur saw the light of his JLA communicator flash and promptly began to swim toward the surface. From the depths of the Pacific Ocean, the light of the moon was an almost indecipherable transformation of color in the slowly brightening water, then a soft glow, and finally fractured beams of diffused radiance tempting him into a whole new world.

He broke through the water surface into the night with the muted mixture of anticipation and uneasiness that still attended such visits, and turned his attention to the communicator on his wrist. The thinness of the surface world air always left him feeling slightly exposed, as if just released from a reassuring embrace. Shaking water droplets from his cropped blond hair, he opened the airwave frequency.

"Yes?"

"Aquaman! What's up, pal?"

"Green Arrow." Arthur offered a polite acknowledgment of his summoner and waited to be informed about the surface world's latest emergency. He moved his strong legs slowly underwater, easily keeping his broad chest and head out of the sea.

"You busy? Batman's got this thing going down in Gotham that I thought you could help with."

Arthur scowled slightly, his vivid blue eyes narrowing, as he watched a tanker make its way slowly across the water in the distance. "Is this official JLA business?"

"Nah. Just something to do."

"I understood that these communicators were to be used exclusively for Justice League business."

"Yeah, well, I told a bunch of sturgeons in the bay that I needed to talk to you, but they pretty much ignored me."

"Sturgeons are freshwater, Ollie."

"Yeah, so?"

"I'm in the *ocean* . . ."

"Well, there you go. No wonder you didn't get the message. Anyway, there's a boat involved."

Arthur looked up at the stars overhead and sighed. "I can't communicate with boats, Oliver."

"I know, but maybe some barnacles heard something or . . . I don't know. Look, it'll be like a party—might even end up getting the kids involved. And with Batman on the case, what's it gonna take? A couple hours?"

Backstroking languidly in the general direction of the East Coast, Arthur allowed his friend a slight smile. "Where's this boat?"

"I dunno. Gotham Harbor, I guess."

"Tricorner? Dixon Docks? Port Adams?"

"Uh, meet me on the south side of Sprang Bridge."

"And after this will it be all right with you if I get back to, you know, this little matter of ruling the Seven Seas?"

"Whatever flips your switch, man."

Arthur chuckled, switched off the communicator, and dove back underwater where his powerful physique felt more fully utilized to him despite the superhuman strength he enjoyed on land. He was perfectly aware that he had been summoned as a companion for Green Arrow more than as a hero, but he didn't mind. Batman would hate having them tag along, but it would be good for him.

Surface-dwellers in general, and Batman in particular, often underestimated the importance of community.

Arthur smiled at the pleasingly rhythmic hammer tapping sound of a sperm whale identifying herself several miles away, and then caught the brilliant flashing of a large school of herring moving up ahead. He hurried his pace to join them.

The ocean, like the surface world, was no place to be alone.

"We must consider cutting the trip short." Dabir had not said much of anything since the shooting, and so it was Safwan who argued with President Abdul-Hakam over the boy's safety. "There is no way to know whether or not Dabir was truly the target, and if he was, then he will not be safe here."

"Believe me, Safwan, I do not want to lose another son! But we are better protected here than we would be even at home." Hatim gestured toward his cabin door on the USCGC *Herron* that was under guard by LEDET personnel. "If someone wishes Dabir or myself harm, we have no choice but to find and punish them! To run would only demonstrate cowardice and leave us grossly exposed."

Watching the exchange, and also the silent, brooding figure of Dabir, Rashid could not keep himself from interjecting.

"But, Abu Amin, why would anyone want to hurt Dabir!?"

Safwan turned to the seventeen-year-old with a raised eyebrow, displeased with the interruption, but Hatim only sighed at his nephew and sank into a wooden chair by the stateroom writing desk.

"It could be an attempt to get to me, a racially motivated strike . . . even a symbolic gesture meant to express some unhappiness with any moment or decision in our country's entire history. And it could just as easily have been a mistake—some utter madman aiming for anyone within range."

Rashid crouched down next to his cousin, who was sitting in a large maroon leather chair, unsmiling.

"Does it hurt?" he asked with concern.

Dabir roused himself as if his thoughts had been very far away and slowly shook his head. "Not much. Just burns a little. Nothing like the glass . . ." Dabir gestured weakly to the left side of his head. Though far enough from ground zero on the day of Qurac's bombing to avoid the radiation poisoning that had slowly killed nearly half of the blast survivors, Dabir had been standing near the Bentley in the outer circumference of the detonation waves. Heavy crates filled with produce and clothing blasted apart and came rushing toward him at an inescapable speed, but it was small particles of windshield glass that had imbedded themselves in the left side of his skull as he tried to turn away. Even four years later, as his skin naturally sought to renew itself, small chips of glass would work their way out of one side of his head, needing to be pulled, sometimes, like splinters, and other times causing days of itching before they could be safely extracted.

"You don't want to go home, do you?" demanded his father. Dabir turned toward him with a slow blink and again shook his head.

"We'll just pretend it never happened," Dabir said, his voice very low and quiet. He folded his arms across his chest and lowered his head. "Just like everything else."

Safwan frowned and moved toward Dabir, stopping to kneel in front of his chair.

"I will not forget," he said gravely. "This I promise you."

"Safwan?" Dabir lifted his head to meet the older man's eyes, curiosity suddenly animating his features. "The bullet that scratched me—was it the same one that hit the elevator buttons?"

Safwan nodded. "There was only one bullet fired."

Dabir pressed his lips together thoughtfully and visibly sank back into his brood. "Good," Rashid heard Dabir mumble to himself almost inaudibly.

There was a brisk knock on the stateroom door, and Safwan stood and moved to open it. The ship's yeoman stood outside between the two LEDET guards who had been posted to guard the stateroom.

Nodding to Safwan, the yeoman turned to address Hatim.

"Mr. President, the C.O. and the electronics technician have requested your presence in the wardroom."

Hatim nodded and stood, smoothing out his *thobe*, as Safwan turned to Dabir and Rashid with a frown.

"Both of you stay put," he commanded. "I'll be back in time to escort you to your appointment with the Health Services technician. Understood?"

Rashid nodded, even though Safwan's last comment had been directed to Dabir. Dabir remained seated in the large leather chair, but his eyes flashed up and met Safwan's long enough to satisfy the bodyguard's inquiry.

Rashid waited until the yeoman had escorted Hatim and Safwan from the room, then turned eagerly to his cousin, smacking him lightly against his uninjured arm.

"Come on, we've got work to do."

Dabir looked up at the seventeen-year-old boy with a frown. "Work?"

"Yeah, dummy—we've got to find out who's trying to kill you!"

Dabir gave up counting corpses after 230. His throat was so dry he couldn't swallow. Even more frightening than the burnt, lifeless bodies on the ground were the scorched and bewildered walking dead. Bleeding from one side of his head with his *thobe* badly torn but not burned, Dabir was in better shape than many of the people he passed. He saw a man trying to get up from the sidewalk who couldn't seem to understand why his flesh was dripping off the bones of his arms and legs. He saw a woman sitting by the side of the souk so charred that he hadn't been sure she was human until she blinked her eyes. He saw three schoolgirls crying as they searched for someone in a ruined restaurant, their faces stained a raw, painful red.

A small gray cat ran into the road in front of Dabir, apparently unharmed, but mewling as it wound around his ankles. He picked it up and started to cry, thinking about radiation poisoning, and how he didn't know what to do to save the tiny creature. He carried the cat for a mile and a half until it suddenly leapt out of his arms and ran for the shade of a half-smashed house. Dabir kept walking, ignoring the few running cars that blasted past him as panicked Quracis fled the area. Dabir couldn't imagine going anywhere without his mother and Amin.

When he got to where he thought his house should have been, he stopped, exhausted, and sat down in the middle of the street. Palm trees had been ripped from the ground and were strewn about the pavement like broken toys. Fires were raging in every direction he turned, and a large, mangled heap of black metal he slowly came to recognize as a piece of his driveway's front gate was all that remained of the home he'd woken up in that morning.

Fading in and out of consciousness, Dabir felt sure he was dreaming when Safwan's strong arms lifted him out of the wreckage and carried him to a car that sped away from the country faster than anything he had ever attempted in the Bentley.

The teeming din of the ocean became increasingly anthropogenic as Arthur neared Gotham. The crackle of snapping shrimp was slowly drowned out by the low hum of shipping freighters, and the cheerful echolocation clicks of distant cetaceans were replaced by the rhythmic inquiries of military surveillance sonar.

By the time he reached Gotham Harbor, the water had become so polluted that Arthur pulled himself up onto the Dixon Docks and walked north the rest of the way to Sprang Bridge. Though many of the people he passed stopped to point or watch him with interest, some of them recognizing him and others merely intrigued with his powerful stride and the bright green and orange of his attire, a surprising number of Gothamites ignored him completely. Arthur didn't mind either way. As the former King of Atlantis, he tended to attract a lot of attention underwater, too, and was used to going about his business under both heavy public scrutiny and shunning disregard.

Green Arrow was, not surprisingly, nowhere to be seen once Arthur reached the appointed meeting place. Arthur leaned against a bridge tower and settled in for a wait.

"Aquaman?"

The voice that came out of the dark was not the one he had been expecting. Arthur looked up and saw a lithe young man dressed in form-fitting midnight blue and black hanging acrobatically from the shadowed bottom of the bridge deck. His dark hair was tousled and he wore a small black mask over eyes that Arthur knew to be a blazing azure. As always, the young man's voice was infused with respect and his entire being radiated vitality.

"Nightwing," Arthur said with a smile. "Good to see you, son."

The young man untangled himself from the support beams with an elegant midair flip and landed in a crouch near Arthur's feet. Rising swiftly to his full lean height, he offered a smile and a handshake, both of which Arthur accepted.

"You shaved," Nightwing blurted out. Arthur, who had been concentrating on not crushing the boy's hand in his own during the greeting, looked up just in time to see a sheepish smile flit across Nightwing's clean-shaven face. Perhaps he was embarrassed for having noticed, but Arthur didn't find the observation odd. For one thing, Nightwing was a trained detective whose life regularly depended on noticing subtle shifts in details. For another, Arthur had worn his hair long and sported a full mustache and beard for years. Though to him it was merely a matter of returning to an earlier personal grooming habit, to the young man the new look must have seemed a significant alteration.

"I thought it was time for a change," Arthur answered with a smile, running his left hand self-consciously through his short blond hair. Nightwing's attention darted to the hand that, though perfectly formed to the rest of Arthur's body, was made entirely out of enchanted water. "Lost the hook, too," Arthur acknowledged, holding out the new appendage for Nightwing to examine. The young man's eyes widened in surprise, then narrowed with curiosity.

"What does it do?" he asked enthusiastically.

The young crime fighter's manner was marked by an irrepressible inquisitiveness Arthur had always found pleasing. Arthur frequently had to remind himself that neither Nightwing nor his mentor Batman was superhuman in the technical sense of the word. Arthur, with his ability to communicate telepathically with sea life and his new enchanted hand, was exceptional even by water-breathing Atlantean standards. On terra firma, he possessed tremendous strength and fortitude as a direct result of his body's ability to move so quickly underwater and withstand the immense pressure of the deep sea. Nightwing, on the other hand, had started life as a completely normal surface-dwelling human, but even as a child—then known as Batman's sidekick, Robin—the boy had demonstrated remarkable intelligence and dexterity, traits that Batman had seized upon and further trained. Batman—also merely a human under the fancy armor and cowl—was considered by the entire super hero community second in impressiveness only to Superman, and Nightwing was widely regarded by his meta-human peers as one of Earth's finest guardians and team leaders. It seemed fitting to Arthur that two unembellished surface-dwellers should win such high ranking among the collection of aliens and biologically enhanced beings comprising Earth's super hero population, and he was proud to know them both.

Nightwing's presence also made Arthur think of his own ward, a young Atlantean Idylist about Nightwing's age named Garth, whom Arthur had rescued from abandonment and dubbed Aqualad. Garth now went by the name Tempest, and was good friends with Nightwing.

"Truthfully, I'm not yet entirely sure," Arthur admitted, pulling his thoughts back to Nightwing's question about his hand.

"How do you wash it?"

Both Arthur and Nightwing turned to the bridge's south cable, where another young man—this one clad in black and red with nothing but a four o'clock shadow and a wisp or two of his own red hair obscuring his handsome face crouched by the cable anchor, grinning.

"Arsenal!" Nightwing sounded both pleased and confused, and Arthur watched as the two young men approached each other, punched each other in the arms, then embraced. Arsenal was Green Arrow's grown-up sidekick and wore Oliver's charismatic, easygoing attitude just as evidently as Nightwing modeled Batman's discipline and discernment. Arthur again found himself thinking about Garth, wondering if his ward took after him, and if so, what that might look like.

Nightwing pulled back from the embrace and lightly

touched a gloved hand to Arsenal's chest with evident concern. "You still healing okay?"

Arsenal shrugged and flashed a sardonic smile that looked so much like Oliver's it made Arthur do a double take. "Eh, you know. Takes more than a bullet through the heart to slow *me* down."

"That-a-boy!"

No one was surprised when Ollie himself, magnificent in his Robin Hood-inspired Green Arrow garb, dropped down under the bridge to join the conversation. Nightwing and Arthur both smiled at him while Arsenal endured a quick, paternal mussing of the hair with a small measure of embarrassment and an even more evident degree of pleasure. It would have been obvious to anyone looking on that the men respected each other and enjoyed one another's company, and also that to disturb them would be a poor choice. The friendly grins and shoulder pats might have made them appear approachable, but there was no disguising the amount of sheer collective muscle mass they shared, nor the likelihood of hidden weaponry backing up Green Arrow's displayed bow and quiver and the crossbow Arsenal wore on his back.

Nightwing, enjoying the camaraderie, let the small talk go on for a full four minutes before he cleared his throat and turned his mask-hidden gaze on Green Arrow.

"I hate to cut the festivities short, but . . . I suppose we're all wondering why you gathered us here this evening?"

Green Arrow snapped his fingers and nodded forcefully, as if glad to be reminded of his hosting duties. Before he could speak, though, Arsenal shot Nightwing a smirk.

"Actually, *I* was wondering where Garth was."

"We'll get him," Green Arrow asserted. "We'll get any-one you want. We're here to help Batman."

Nightwing's eye mask did nothing to hide the sur-prised and doubtful look that crossed his face. Green Arrow barreled ahead to ward off any protestations.

"Not that he asked for it, of course. But I've got a feel-ing he's spread too thin."

"Did you actually coordinate with him, Green Arrow, or—?"

"We've got to find Deathstroke!" Green Arrow's proc-lamation once again cut off Nightwing before the young man could defend his mentor's solitary nature.

"And there's a boat involved," Aquaman interjected dryly, rolling his eyes at Green Arrow.

"Right!" Green Arrow continued enthusiastically, un-daunted by the obvious misgivings reverberating through his haphazardly assembled team. He realized too late that it might have been a mistake to involve Nightwing, whose loyalty to Batman was actually the only thing Ollie knew of that ever slowed the boy down. He had to get him mov-ing before he spent too much more time thinking. "Bat-man's got the boat angle covered for now, though. What *we* need to do is ferret out Deathstroke's location, and I know just the place to start!"

He began striding confidently forward, heading south, back down toward the Dixon Docks. Arsenal, either out of habit or boredom, immediately fell into place behind him, and Aquaman heaved a slightly annoyed sigh before pushing himself up off the tower he'd been leaning against and began following as well. Nightwing, however, re-mained firmly rooted under the bridge, raising his gloved right hand to his face, clearly about to hail someone on the communicator expertly integrated into his gauntlet. Green Arrow spun around toward him and growled his best Batman imitation.

"Dick!" he barked, using the young man's civilian name. "Are you *coming*!?"

The transformation in Nightwing was substantial and immediate. Like a soldier caught napping, the young man snapped to instantly, his posture aligning perfectly a millisecond before he obediently started after Green Arrow. Arsenal shook his head derisively, then caught Green Arrow's victorious wink.

"How high?" he mouthed to his former guardian, mocking Nightwing's predictable response to martial orders.

"Works every time," Green Arrow mouthed back. Arsenal smiled and then dropped his eyes, suppressing the desire to add "not for me." Dick only responded that way to older men, and only if they were being deliberately unkind (or, in Batman's case, chronically impassive). Arsenal couldn't think about it without instantly recognizing the complex relationship between Batman and Nightwing that made it so, and the deficiencies in his own relationship with Ollie that had left him free to question authority, but also fundamentally forsaken and insecure. There had to be a happy middle ground between Batman's authoritarian protectiveness and Green Arrow's benign neglect, but Roy didn't know what it was. He only knew that he both envied and rejected his friend's more militant upbringing. He didn't think he would have been able to endure the grueling training and emotional torment Batman had put Dick through, but he also knew that in a pinch, he'd rather leave his own daughter with Batman than with the man who was ostensibly her grandfather. It wasn't that he thought Ollie would do her any actual harm. He just didn't quite trust his former mentor to attend to her most basic needs. It was probably an unfair concern, but Roy couldn't help it. Every time he thought of the hell he knew Dick had endured to become the exceptional hero he now was, he also thought of the crippling solitude and desertion he himself had experienced at the hands of Ollie's more laissez-faire theory of sidekick-management and child-rearing. Were those the only choices? An awesome but domineering Batman or a charming but usually wholly absent Green Arrow? Roy stole a peek at Aquaman, striding alongside him, and wondered again about the whereabouts of Arthur's ward, Garth. There was safety in numbers, and as much as Arsenal admired the older generation of heroes, he found solace and amity in the companionship of his remarkable but hopelessly messed-up peer group. He slowed his pace until he was walking alongside Nightwing.

A few paces ahead, Aquaman had caught up with Green Arrow.

"Your boy's looking good," he commented, both because it was true and because he was making an effort to honor the role he had assumed as Green Arrow's chief entertainment.

"Yeah, he is, isn't he?" Ollie sounded pleased. "That kid's always been a looker. They all are. No wonder people like to speculate."

Arthur frowned slightly as Ollie laughed.

"I meant he looked healthy," Arthur clarified.

"Oh, yeah." Ollie was undaunted. "I meant the hero-sidekick thing, how everyone assumes we're doing dirty things with these gorgeous kids in the—"

Arthur used his most regally authoritative voice to cut his friend off. "I *know* what you meant."

"You never got that as much. Guess the whole breathing underwater thing is freaky enough. But Bats, man! Well, look at that kid, no wonder."

Arthur sighed and gave up. Oliver knew either that Roy's health was significant due to his past history with heroin and his recent close call with a chest wound, or he didn't. There was no point trying to explain.

"We put the children through a lot," he said finally, glancing over his shoulder at the two young men following a few steps behind. They both looked fit and energetic, and also cheerful as they traded compliments and friendly insults in equal quantity. "We're lucky they're still on our side."

"Well, they weren't gonna grow up to be criminals!" Ollie chortled. "Not on *our* watch! I think we did a pretty good job, considering we kept havin' to go off and save the world and stuff."

Arthur made no reply. His mind had carried him back in time, leaving his arms aching with the remembered weight of his two-year-old son just moments before he'd had to surrender the tiny corpse back to the sea.

Dabir let himself be pulled along by Rashid, who seemed to be virtually on fire with purpose. Though impressed with the small miracle of having slipped past the LEDET guards outside the stateroom door, Dabir would have rather stayed in the stateroom until the next scheduled offshore excursion. Where Rashid was going, and how he thought he was going to get anywhere on a ship swarming with Coast Guardsmen, was beyond Dabir. But Rashid proved surprisingly adept at sneaking around the hull of the cutter unnoticed—or at least disregarded—and with minimal effort, Dabir found himself in parts of the ship he had not yet explored.

"Rashid, we're not supposed to be here. We're going to make someone angry," Dabir protested.

Rashid was undeterred.

"Don't you want to know who's trying to kill you?"

Dabir shook his head. "What difference does it make? Besides, you heard Safwan—maybe it was an accident, and I just happened to be in the way. Or maybe it was you, Rashid. Maybe you hired an assassin to get rid of my father and me so that you could rule Qurac. You'd have a lot to gain."

There was nothing accusatory in Dabir's tone, but Rashid took umbrage anyway.

"What are you *talking* about, Dabir? Qurac's a democracy now—even if you and Abu Amin *were* slain, it would do nothing for me but leave me homeless!"

"The sympathy of the Quraci people would be with you. You could rise politically. And I'm sure Father will leave you money, maybe even the house. You could turn the country around, make it independent again."

Rashid stopped and frowned at his cousin. Dabir sounded more hopeful than hostile, as if weaving a pleasing plan instead of hypothesizing about a conspiracy to end his life.

"I don't want to be president," he said flatly. "And anyway, where would I get the money to hire an assassin?"

They had come to a door in the main passageway marked CIC, and Rashid stopped to spin Dabir around to face him, one hand on either of the young man's shoulders.

"Listen, there will be someone in here, but I know him. For once, let *me* do the talking, okay?"

Dabir nodded glumly, feeling suddenly sure that both he and Rashid would be gunned down the second his cousin crossed the next threshold. Instead, the door opened into a narrow room thick with radar screens and electronic sensor readouts, and lit by the strange green glow of several computer monitors. Dabir was awed despite himself.

A black-skinned American man in his late twenties slipped a pair of headphones off his ears and turned to Rashid with a friendly smile.

"Hey, 'Sheed. This your cousin?"

Rashid nodded and started the introductions. "Dabir, this is Electronics Technician Fred Billings. E.T. Billings, this is President Abdul-Hakam's son, Dabir. We need your help."

Dabir thought Billings looked more amused than concerned, but the man nodded respectfully and turned to gesture to the vast array of equipment spread out before him.

"What can we do for you, gentlemen?" he asked readily. Dabir realized that the man was including the sonar equipment in his offer of assistance.

"You have no doubt heard about the incident earlier this evening, in which my cousin here was hit by an assassin's bullet!"

"Grazed," Dabir corrected, instinctively placing a hand over the gauze-covered wound. "It was just a graze."

"Grazed, yes." Rashid seemed momentarily thrown off by the interruption, but then regained his momentum. "It is possible, of course, that this was an accident of place and time, but I believe it would be foolish to proceed under such an assumption. If there is a plan to harm Dabir, then it has not yet been completed, and we can expect a second strike."

Rashid was directing his speech toward Billings, as if presenting a legal brief to a seasoned judge, and Fred was nodding thoughtfully, encouraging Rashid. His expression made Dabir certain that the officer viewed his cousin as a child, and was merely playing a game with them.

"So, you see, it is imperative that we discover not only the identity of the assassin, but perhaps even more importantly, the identity of the person who *hired* the assassin in the first place."

"Agreed," Billings said with a nod, after Rashid had been silent for longer than ten seconds. "So what's your plan?"

"First, we need to know if anyone from the outside has contacted anyone on this ship about Dabir. We need to search incoming, um, *communications* for the name 'Dabir.'"

Rashid looked at the electronics technician expectantly, but Fred just laughed.

"All right, well . . . to do that, you'd need the help of the O.O.D." Fred turned to Dabir with a helpful smile. "That's the Officer of the Deck. He's usually on the bridge."

Rashid looked crestfallen. "You cannot procure those for us?"

"Not with the radar, buddy. Not unless your 'communications' are sailing toward us hidden behind the cruise liners."

Fred had gestured toward a complicated-looking radar

monitor, and Dabir could tell by the expression on Rashid's face that his cousin didn't know anybody on the bridge.

"Come on," Dabir urged quietly. "Let's get back to the room."

"Do you have a list of suspects?" Fred asked Rashid. "You know, at least a working record of anyone who might have something to gain if young Mr. Abdul-Hakam is hurt?"

"We were talking about that on the way down here," Rashid admitted before thumbing toward Dabir with a roll of his eyes. "He thinks *I* did it."

"I didn't say that," Dabir said softly, his eyes lowered. He was unwilling to let his cousin's honor be impugned in front of a stranger. "I just said you'd have a lot to gain."

Fred's eyebrows went up in lighthearted interest, so Rashid tried to explain.

"His father took me in when my own family was killed," Rashid said calmly, without the surge of emotion that always seemed to overwhelm Dabir when he tried to speak of his mother or Amin. "Since my uncle is so powerful, I guess Dabir thinks I'm somehow in line to inherit his . . . position . . . were anything to happen to him and Dabir. It might be true that Abu Amin would leave me some money—you know, try to provide for my future if he couldn't do it himself. My father was his brother, after all. But he's an elected official. It's not like Dabir gets to be president if something happens to him, or I'd be next in line if something happened to Dabir."

"But Amin was," Dabir whispered into his shirt, almost inaudibly. Fred seemed to feel the emotional charge in the small room and was quiet as Rashid glanced at his cousin with a pained, slightly worried expression.

"His older brother," he said softly for Fred's benefit. "He also died. In the, you know, bombing. He kinda had . . . I don't know, political aspirations or something. We did all think he'd run the country one day." Looking more closely at Dabir, Rashid added, "But that was different."

Dabir raised red-rimmed eyes to his cousin as Fred leaned back in his station seat and tried to shift the conversation from the already dead to the slightly less sobering potentially murderous.

"How about that bodyguard you guys've got—the military dude who's always following you around?"

"Safwan?" Rashid asked with incredulity. "He's the one who *protects* us."

"Well, yeah, sure, that's his job, but maybe secretly he thinks Dabir is some kind of threat to his presidential access. You know, like he has the president's ear, but would even more so without the guy's son around."

Rashid, though taken aback, looked impressed. Dabir turned an angry, contemptuous glare on the electronics technician. Fred shrugged.

"Or maybe President Abdul-Hakam's got enemies, and they're playing dirty—goin' for the family, you know, below the belt kinda thing. You guys must have political enemies."

"Yeah," Dabir growled. "Like the *Americans*."

Fred put his hands up in mock surrender. "Hey, not us, kid. Qurac and the U.S. have been allies since after that bombing. Why else would we be risking our necks to guard you guys now? Believe me, if there were hostilities between our countries, I wouldn't be lettin' you anywhere near this ship, let alone this room." Fred cast a quick glance at the radar screen behind him and then turned back to the boys. Dabir was standing sulkily with his head lowered and his arms folded across his chest while Rashid was carefully leaning against the console. "What about that terrorist who did the bombing in the first place? Cheshire? Would she have anything against your family?"

Rashid cast a glance at Dabir, but when his cousin said nothing he shook his head. "I don't think so, but it's an interesting idea. You probably know more about what actually happened with her than we do. But it was always reported like it was pretty random. Like she chose our country because she considered it *in*significant, not the other way around."

"She doesn't know anything," Dabir snapped, still looking down at his shoes. "She's a dead soul and a dead end."

"Maybe one of the other guys on that plane with her, then." Fred swiveled in his chair to face the radar screen again, and started to lift his headphones. "The point is just to think about obvious suspects. See if anything kinda clicks."

Rashid turned to rouse Dabir, feeling it was time that they left Billings to do his work, but Dabir had already lifted his head and cocked it in Fred's direction.

"She was on the plane alone," Dabir asserted. His whole body was leaning forward toward Fred with panicked attention.

Fred smiled and shook his head. "That what you heard? Nah, there was some undercover CBI guys there, and this other criminal, a mercenary by the name of Deathstroke the Terminator. We're pretty sure the bomb thing was all her idea, but you don't go out on a Tu-22 all by your lonesome."

Rashid thought that Dabir was beginning to look dangerously pale and decided that it was time to get him back to the stateroom. "When's your appointment with the Health Services guy?" he asked, gently taking his cousin's elbow and tugging him toward the door. Dabir didn't answer, so Rashid thanked Billings and led his cousin back down the main hall, this time with nothing more elaborate than a nod to the servicemen they passed.

Dabir walked out of the funeral by himself, right in the middle of the final prayers. He knew that the bodies of his mother and brother had never been found; either they had been incinerated on the spot like most of the people in the capital that day, or they had been burned in one of the huge, collective pyres used to clean up the city once the search for the living had been called off. Safwan had all but admitted that the service at the temple was for "closure" and to help advance Hatim's political career.

"Your father is on the verge of global prominence," Safwan had told Dabir that morning. "Qurac will become a democracy, and your father will be its leader. He will do great things."

The only great thing Dabir wanted anyone to do was bring his mother and brother back from the dead. He hated politics, he hated Qurac, and more and more he hated his father. Every handshake and smile and patriotic sound bite made Dabir's teeth ache. He was told over and over again how lucky he was to have a father who was making something good happen out of such a tragedy, told over and over again that he was the son of a visionary, a leader, a pioneer.

Later that night, he endured his father's tirade as Hatim berated him for walking out on the service.

"We have lost too much not to fight for what we can have now, Dabir! What do you think Amin would say if he saw you acting out in public like this? Your tragedy is a national tragedy, Dabir, you share it with all of Qurac! Honestly, you could be dead, do you realize that? Sometimes I think you have absolutely no idea whatsoever of how very fortunate you are!"

Dabir stared at his hands and then the carpet beneath his feet. His father was right.

He had absolutely no idea whatsoever of being fortunate at all.

"Where's Lian?"

Nightwing and Arsenal continued to keep stride behind Green Arrow and Aquaman, and had eventually fallen into a quieter, more intimate conversation than the joking fraternity in which they had initially indulged.

"Got a new nanny," Arsenal answered with the slight, incredulous smile that always warmed his features when he spoke of his five-year-old daughter. "He's great with her."

"He?"

"Yeah, well, you know—I had a couple female nannies first, but . . ."

"You slept with them."

"I slept with them."

Dick shook his head, laughing, and Roy smiled at his friend, failing to point out that Dick's amorous track record was rapidly catching up to his own, albeit for completely different reasons. For Roy, sex was an almost compulsive ritual of self-sustenance. He genuinely loved and respected women—enjoyed being with them, flirting with them, touching them—but even more than that, physical intimacy was the only thing that kept him connected to the rest of humanity. Without it, he felt adrift, inaccessible, and forsaken. Lian was the only person on the planet—with the possible exception of her mother, Cheshire—with whom Roy felt he could share any emotional intimacy. Heroin had briefly, defectively, horrifically obliterated his need for it, but now that he was clean, sex was the only place he could go to get warm. He knew that some of this was the direct result of being orphaned at such a young age and enduring several major upheavals during his early childhood, but he didn't like to dwell on any of that. All he knew, day to day, was that he felt unendurably cold.

Dick, on the other hand, was a tried and true romantic, and also, Roy had come to realize, a contact junkie. As intelligent and analytical as he was, everything for Nightwing generated in and eventually distilled back down to the physical. It was the plane he lived on, the language he spoke, the doctrine he heeded. Roy didn't even think he could talk to Dick about it. The former acrobat lived so firmly entrenched in his own skin that he probably barely recognized other ways of being. Though Batman's chief power was cerebral, he had always been able to back his ideas up physically, and it was as a physical presence that he continued to dominate his adopted son's emotional life, which seemed to Roy to be a rapid-fire series of covering ground, kicking ass, and falling in love. It didn't seem to matter to Dick whether he was kissing someone or kicking them, as long as there was contact. And the only person or thing that could distract him when he was physically engaged was Batman. Roy had grappled with Dick on more than one occasion and had never failed to be blown away by the intensity of it. It was difficult for him to even imagine being so engaged with the corporeal world.

"She'll be pissed that she missed seeing Ollie," he continued, turning his thoughts back to Lian. "But maybe I can drag the old man back with me for a quick visit whenever we're done doing whatever the hell it is he's getting us into."

"I'd like to see her, too," Dick said, with evident affection.

Roy nodded. "She'd love that. She still swears you dish up the best hide-and-seek game in town."

Up ahead, Green Arrow and Aquaman had stopped a few feet in front of a truly squalid-looking dockside watering hole. Roy watched as Dick's face lit up with recognition.

"Oh, *this* place," he said enthusiastically. "This is a *good* bad place."

"Kinda place Deathstroke might hang out?" Arsenal asked doubtfully.

Nightwing shrugged. "Ollie said he had a lead, right?"

Roy turned his head away from Dick just in time to hide his smile. A few feet up the dock, Green Arrow was signaling to Nightwing.

"Okay," Green Arrow said with practiced authority once

Nightwing and Arsenal had caught up to him and Aquaman. "Nightwing, I need you to check for back exits—"

"There are two." Nightwing interrupted Green Arrow with a courteous smile. "One in the back at exactly twelve o'clock from the front door, and one that opens up into the alley between the bar and the warehouse, off to the side at ten."

Arsenal again turned his head to hide a smirk, this time away from Green Arrow. How could Ollie have thought Nightwing wouldn't know the exits leading out of every dive in Gotham?

"Good! You're on top of it. That's what I like to hear." Green Arrow moved seamlessly from surprise to praise and Arsenal's amusement abandoned him as swiftly as if it had been blown away by a hard, cold breeze. He thought he saw Nightwing's chin jut up ever so slightly in response to the approval and frowned down at his own boots with a familiar emptiness gnawing at his stomach. He hated Nightwing for hungering for praise as desperately as he himself did; he hated Batman for being the cause of Nightwing's starvation; he hated himself for the tremor of envy that ran up the back of his neck at the sound of Ollie praising Dick; and he hated Ollie for so lightly wielding such a dangerous weapon. "Go guard the back! Don't let anyone out."

By the time Arsenal looked up again, Nightwing had vanished into the shadows and Green Arrow had turned his attention to Aquaman.

"You get that side door he mentioned."

Aquaman nodded and stalked off toward the indicated post. Green Arrow watched him for a moment and then threw an arm paternally around Arsenal's shoulder, beginning to lead him toward the bar. Arsenal wanted to lean in to the embrace, wanted to shake himself loose of it, wanted to punch him.

"As for you and me, Speedy ol' boy"—Ollie was grinning as they approached the front entrance, speaking to Arsenal with the exact same casual affection he had used when Roy had been an impressionable thirteen-year-old boy racing after his heroic mentor—"we're gonna start a fight!" Green Arrow stopped in front of the heavy oak door and winked at Roy before kicking it in with an undeniable flair for the theatric.

The door splintered open with a resounding crash, flooding Green Arrow and Arsenal in the orange-tinted glow of the bar's interior lighting, guaranteeing them the full attention of every man inside. Arsenal grit his teeth and realized his fists were already balled half a second before the left one cracked into Green Arrow's jaw.

"No problem," he smirked. "Consider it started."

He stepped over Green Arrow, trying to ignore the bewildered look on his former mentor's face, and headed straight for the bar, signaling for a drink. It wasn't hard to find a seat. The joint, already half-empty, rapidly began to clear as the half-inebriated patrons took note of the two costumed bow-bearers who had just burst into their midst. Since Green Arrow was getting to his feet by the front door, most of them were heading toward the back. The two brave enough to try to slip past Green Arrow were immediately tossed back. Arsenal had only tasted his first swallow of beer when the throng testing the back exit came sailing back in with Nightwing's boot prints on their chests. Roy didn't know whether or not Aquaman actually enjoyed fighting, but between Dick and Ollie, the poor suckers in the bar were in for a long, painful night.

Still hunched over his drink, Arsenal followed the bartender's alarmed gaze to the jukebox. Green Arrow was crouching on top of it with his bow out, reaching back into his quiver for any one of a hundred inventive trick arrows. Nightwing's gloved fists and Kevlar-covered elbows occasionally darted out of the darkness toward the rear of the bar, connecting, every single time, with someone's face, and just to round out the mayhem, a full body would intermittently sail over the tables near the side exit, tossed by Aquaman as effortlessly as Roy might have tossed one of his daughter's stuffed toys.

Arsenal sighed and turned his attention back to his beer. The four of them could have taken on an intergalactic army of fully armed meta-humans with fifty-fifty odds—the skells in the bar, beefy as some of them were, were sorely overmatched. It was almost embarrassing. When the bartender came up from under the bar with a scowl and a shotgun, Arsenal took him out with a well-aimed flick of a toothpick. It never failed to amaze him how sensitive people were about their eyes. He was just about to rouse himself up off his bar stool to get the shotgun when one of Ollie's arrows whizzed by his head and firmly attached the bartender's trigger hand to the wall behind the cash register. Roy figured that gave him plenty of time to drain his glass.

Nightwing, though, was determined to get the shotgun unloaded before anyone else thought to pick it up. There was only one handgun, one switchblade, and one pocket-knife between him and the bar, so he moved forward in one fluid press, grabbing the gun-bearer's arm and twisting it into a jujitsu lock before leveraging his own weight off of his captive's. An unwilling accomplice, the man with the gun nonetheless made a secure fulcrum as Nightwing's booted feet left the ground, swinging first into the taller man with the switchblade and then forcing him, switchblade and all, into the smaller man with the pocketknife. Landing in a crouch to one side of them, Nightwing let the momentum of his flip surge into his arms before releasing his lock on the gun-wielder, snatching the handgun away with his free hand before sending its owner flying into the other two men. Satisfied with the groaning pile they had formed on the floor, Nightwing tucked the handgun into his boot with his right hand while cartwheeling onto his left. When his right hand wheeled down again, he pushed off the wooden boards toward the bar, landing in a crouch next to where Arsenal smacked down his empty beer glass.

"Having fun?" Arsenal asked him dryly.

"No sign of Deathstroke," Nightwing answered, jumping down behind the bar to grab the shotgun and unload it.

"No kidding." Arsenal leaned forward across the bar to refill his glass from the tap, and Nightwing was just about to hop back over the counter and try to determine if anyone was still conscious when he felt a presence obliterate the space immediately behind him. Simultaneously, Roy's beer glass hit the rubber mat behind the bar with a soft thud. For just one fraction of a second, Nightwing closed his eyes and exhaled in time with a hot release of breath on the back of his neck, synching his breathing to the presence behind him almost instinctively. Even after all these years, the strange feeling of protective danger that ran up the back of his spine when he unexpectedly found himself in his mentor's shadow thrilled and overwhelmed him.

"What are you *doing*?" The voice was dark and thick, and the question, though spoken less than two centimeters from Nightwing's left ear, was directed at Green Arrow. The entire room fell silent as all eyes turned to Batman. Only Nightwing remained with his back to him. Batman was standing so close behind him that Nightwing couldn't turn around without bumping into him. Batman had learned years ago that it was the only way to keep Nightwing still.

Green Arrow rubbed the back of his neck and grinned up at Batman sheepishly. The only two men in the bar who were still on their feet took the opportunity to bolt for the back door.

"We're looking for Deathstroke. You know, following a lead."

Nightwing didn't have to see Batman's face to know that the cowled eyes had narrowed.

"*What* lead?"

Green Arrow shrugged lightly and turned toward Aquaman. "Arthur, didn't you say somebody saw someone here who might have seen someone who saw him or something?"

Aquaman folded his arms regally across his broad chest and shook his head, smirking slightly.

Batman gave a brief nod in his direction. "Orin."

"Batman."

Green Arrow frowned in confusion over the brief exchange and then turned back to Batman with his arms open and his most charismatic grin firmly in place.

"Well, obviously he isn't here. But since you are, and

since I've got this great little gang assembled, what can we do ya for?"

Batman turned with a frown to the moaning bartender fastened to the wall behind him and pulled the arrow out with a quick jerk of his gloved hand. The bartender went pale and passed out from the pain.

"You can avoid terrorizing Gotham's citizenship."

"He had a shotgun," Green Arrow countered with a shrug. Nightwing felt the space behind him open up again and filled his chest with a slow inhale as he locked eyes with Arsenal. Roy was standing absolutely still by his bar stool but inclined his head toward the door and raised an eyebrow when he caught Nightwing's eye. Nightwing pressed his lips together and gave one quick shake of his head, but Roy failed to look deterred.

Batman had moved to stand in front of Green Arrow, his back to Nightwing and Arsenal. Arsenal, ignoring Nightwing's subtle warning signs, slid one foot silently toward the door and shifted his weight. Unusually alert to projectiles, he did hear the Batarang whistling toward him but wasn't sure where it would land until he almost tripped over it. He stared down at where it was planted just past the toe of his boot, wondering if he could have thrown something that precisely and that fast.

"Pay for the beer."

Arsenal knew that Batman was still halfway across the room, but he would have sworn that the terse command was articulated directly into his ear. How the hell did one guy get so scary? He fished a five-dollar bill out of a pocket hidden into the underside of his belt and tossed it across the counter.

"Right, there ya go. Okay, well, nice seein' you all . . ."

"I need to speak with Arsenal." Batman's tone was commanding. Nightwing watched Roy's shoulders sink in resigned acquiescence. "The rest of you can go."

"Not so fast."

Nightwing turned, slightly surprised, toward Aquaman. Though the Atlantean's voice was less chilling than Batman's, it was every bit as regal. Watching him in the low light of the bar, Nightwing realized that he'd never seen Aquaman look intimidated by anything, not even by Batman. That particular type of self-assurance was a quality that Batman almost always rewarded with respect. "I know that you're anxious for us to get out of Gotham and let you continue with your work unabated, Batman, but I also know that Green Arrow isn't going to give up until he feels as though he has lessened your burden. The kids will be easy to sway in that regard as well, especially your boy there." Aquaman cast a glance toward Nightwing, who suddenly busied himself with a bit of imaginary lint on the front of his costume, and then turned his attention back to the demonic figure of Gotham's self-appointed guardian. "Perhaps you would do well to give us something to do, if only to keep us out of your way."

Batman's frowning, impassive expression did not change, but Nightwing thought he saw an almost indecipherable shift in his posture.

"Nightwing, you take point on Deathstroke. You've fought him before. Take Green Arrow with you and conduct a *systematic* inquiry into his whereabouts."

Nightwing nodded his compliance to Batman, who was still looking at Aquaman, then turned toward Green

Arrow, who was giving him a triumphant thumbs-up. Batman continued.

"Orin, see if Garth's available and team with him on security for the Coast Guard cutter until I return. Put him on a teenage boy by the name of Dabir Bin Hatim Abdul-Hakam, who must be protected at all costs. I want you to secure the ship and as much of the bay as possible. Our primary suspects are still those closest to the boy, so don't turn your back on anyone."

Aquaman nodded, an understated smile softening the severity of his features.

"Arsenal, you're coming with me."

Nightwing smiled reassuringly as Roy turned to him with a pained expression, hands held out to either side in a gesture of entreaty. "You'll be fine," Nightwing mouthed, nodding encouragingly.

Roy sighed and turned around to follow Batman, but suddenly could not find him in the dimly lit bar. He turned back to Nightwing with a shrug, but Nightwing was thumbing toward a narrow open window behind the bar.

"You gotta be kidding me." Arsenal squinted up at the window, cast baleful eyes on Nightwing, and finally turned and sauntered out the front door, fully anticipating the strong, gloved hand that reached out of the darkness to grab him by the back of the neck the second he cleared the threshold.

PART TWO

There were two good things about having Batman as a partner. The first was that, no matter what, you were safe. Batman took it personally when anyone he was working with was threatened, and Arsenal knew that such an inclination would encompass even him. Secondly, there was the Batmobile. Between sidekicking for Green Arrow and working for the government, Roy had seen some pretty cool vehicles in his day, but nothing, *nothing* matched the all-out awe factor of Batman's armored car. It was beautiful, tremendously fast, and filled with surprises. Being in the passenger seat made him feel like the baddest vigilante on the planet. He folded his arms behind his head and leaned back in the Nomex-covered seat, admiring the dashboard and wondering which little button turned on the radio.

"You're not wearing a mask."

This, for Batman, was downright conversational. Roy, who knew better than to even bother asking where they were going, turned to the intimidating hero with a speculative smile.

"No, uh . . . I don't really bother with the secret identity thing so much these days. It didn't seem like it was making a difference."

"What about Lian?" Batman was referring to Roy's five-year-old daughter and, Roy knew, a strongly held personal belief that heroing endangered one's family and loved ones. Because of his close friendship with Nightwing, Roy actually knew Batman's civilian name, but he also knew what a closely guarded secret it was.

"I thought about it, and I tried, but to be honest with you, whatever was gonna happen happened anyway. She's been kidnapped, threatened . . . at this point I just feel like, look, you're gonna go after my daughter, you're gonna look me in the eye."

Batman frowned. "Once your identity is public, you can't take it back. How can you be sure you won't regret this decision someday?"

Roy shrugged. "Maybe I will. Wouldn't be the first time. But I still don't really see what difference it makes in my case. So the world knows that Arsenal is Roy Harper, so what? Who the hell is Roy Harper?"

"Lian Harper's father."

Roy scowled at Batman and wondered if the man ever got tired of being right. Turning to look out the window, he saw the outside world whizzing by so fast he couldn't get any sense of where they were. The thrill of the speed rushed suddenly from his groin to his throat, transforming along the way into a familiar strangling emptiness. Roy shifted his jaw and decided to pick a fight.

"I was thinkin'," he started, still looking out the window. "When Lian gets a little older, maybe I'll start trainin' her, you know. Like my sidekick." Roy snuck a sideways glance at Batman, but the detective's masked face was impassive as usual. "What d'you think?"

"I think you'll do what you deem best for her," Batman answered with maddening steadiness. The calmer Batman was, the hotter Roy's blood seemed to boil. The Dark Knight never modulated his shadowy pitch, never took his eyes off the road. Roy felt like a teenager in his presence; impulsive and agitated.

"So what do you think's a good age to start?" he demanded. He knew his tone was confrontational, but he couldn't help it. "Five? Six? I mean, Dick was what? Eight? Don't you wish you coulda gotten in there a little earlier?"

Batman turned his head and looked at Roy for a brief moment before turning his attention back to the road. Roy realized that identities weren't the only thing face masks hid. With the cowl on, Batman's eyes were menacing white slits, impossible to read.

"The last time we had this conversation we were both under the impression that Green Arrow was dead," Batman said darkly. "I allowed you some leeway because of your grief."

"Oh, so now that I've been proven wrong and it turns out that the guy who raised me *isn't* really dead—even though no one saw or heard from him for over two years— I'm not allowed to criticize your parenting? Is that how it works!?" Roy realized he was yelling and also that he was jonesing, a sickening physiological aftereffect of his drug addiction that he more and more frequently found himself able to keep at bay. Yet getting near Green Arrow—or even, apparently, Batman—brought it all back. He forced himself to take a deep breath and tried to stop digging the fingernails of his left hand into his right wrist.

"Under those circumstances, I was a reasonable parental substitute for you to vent to—"

Roy was aghast. "*You*? A parental *substitute*—!? If you think for one *second* you can hold a candle to Ollie—"

Batman cut him off. "But now, don't you think you should be airing your concerns to *Oliver*?"

Roy knew the answer to Batman's question but he charged ahead. "Oh, believe me, I've got plenty to say to Ollie, but Dick's my best friend, and I've got the same question for you that I had before!" Roy felt himself building toward an emotional eruption and was surprised to feel his energy drain out of him all at once, leaving him slumped against the passenger seat, his voice a husky whisper. "What were you thinking, man? Taking in kids . . . What the hell were you guys thinking?"

Batman made no reply, and Roy was grateful for the silence. It gave him time to try to collect himself. He couldn't believe how much of a mess he was sometimes. He couldn't believe how far he'd come. Half the time he couldn't even believe he was still alive.

But he was. And not only that, he was a father. And Lian—she was more than he ever would have dreamed of asking for: funny, sweet, beautiful, way the hell smarter than he himself was, and, where he was concerned, totally, endlessly forgiving. Roy closed his eyes and let the ache for her slowly flood over the heroin jones. He'd sworn over five years ago never to go near heroin again, but Lian . . . with any luck he'd be tucking her in before her next bedtime.

With a jolt, Roy opened his eyes and sat up straight again. He'd just realized where they were going. Batman wouldn't request his assistance unless he planned to deal with something Roy might have more insight into than he would. And since there was no chance that they were going out to jam with a rock band or score heroin, and a visit to a Navajo reservation seemed equally unlikely, the Batmobile had to be speeding toward Jade Mei Nguyen, better known to the rest of the world as the terrorist Cheshire.

Roy was not sure that he remembered his father. He'd been told about him, even seen a photo once, and sometimes in his dreams there was a voice he thought he recognized, or a dim cottage interior he thought he knew. The soft, muted gray of the forest ranger uniform, the smell of pine resin and smoke, the sticky mess of aphid honeydew all over the Jeep windshield, the feel of the word "*Coconino*" rolling off his tongue—these were all Roy had of the man once known as Will Harper.

He knew even less about his mother, but he searched for her scent on the flesh of every female he touched and imagined he could feel the cool of her hand against his hot forehead on the rare occasions he found himself laid out. He wasn't even sure what her name had been, or what she had died of. Maybe he had never known her. Maybe his entry into the world was also her exit. He wished he had someone he could ask.

What he did remember, vividly, was turquoise and shell and heron's feathers, white corn and sand paintings, the taste of fresh squash, the flash of silver bracelets in bright sunlight, high blue skies and the sudden bursting speed of a rabbit racing across the valley, cottonwood and the jutting red mesas, sheep skin drying by the hogan fire behind the trailers. Past the shadow of the white spruce mountain, under the rock that is rough, northwest from the rock with a hole through it, and just west of the canyon within the rocks, he remembered *Ch'ínílí*, the place where the water flows out.

And he remembered Raymond Begay, the Navajo medicine man who had raised him as one of the Dineh from the ages of three to thirteen. Ollie insisted on calling him "Brave Bow," when he told the story, probably because he thought it sounded cool, but to Roy he had simply been *"Aniséhí,"*—"guardian" in *Dineh Bizaad*, the Navajo language derived from Athabaskan in which, unknown even to his closest friends, Roy still dreamt, sang, and counted.

Formerly attached to Raymond, Roy grew up considering himself a member of the *Ashiihi* clan with the *K'aa' Dine'é* as his *Nalii*, or paternal grandfather's clan. It was understood that he had no mother, and also occasionally whispered that she must have been *Bilagana*, or "English." Roy ignored the white kids at school, except to cajole them into parting with the magazines they sometimes carried around in their backpacks. He would even trade silver and turquoise bracelets or beaded eagle feathers he might have sold at Hubbell's for publications featuring the world's bravest archer, Green Arrow, whom he idolized. And though no one else he knew on the reservation had red hair or freckles on their shoulders—attributes that had earned him the affectionate and deliberately ironic nickname of *átsílí lichíí*, or "little red brother"—Roy didn't truly understand that he was different from his brothers and sisters until he decided that he had fallen in love.

Her name was Marla Dayish, born of the *Todích'íi'nii* clan for the *Hashk'aa hadzohi*. She had a beautiful voice and a challenging gleam in her smoke-colored eyes when she looked at him. She wore her straight black hair long and unbraided, and after thinking it over for a summer, Roy decided he might marry her.

Announcing his plan to his best friend and clanbrother, Hoohimini, Roy expected to be met with admiration, but conceded privately to himself that jealous derision was also a possibility. Never in a million years would he have predicted the look of cold indifference that crossed over Hoshimini's handsome face.

"You are not of our ancestors, *átsílí lichíí*, and you cannot marry anyone."

Roy opened his mouth to protest, but suddenly lost his internal sense of balance. Who *were* his ancestors? Was his mother really *Bilagana*, and did that count—was it really a tribe? Or did it mean that he somehow did belong to the arrogant, sunburned missionaries who would spend hours in Raymond's hogan arguing about whether or not Roy had been baptized and if he had accepted the Lord Jesus Christ as his savior?

Roy looked up at the windy, wide sky where the clouds were racing into the north and suddenly began to run. He meant to go home, to Raymond, but instead found himself heading north.

He ran for hours, until the sun dropped behind *Naat-*

sis'áán and his feet were blistered and bleeding. Picking his way home through the dark, cold and tearful, Roy had stopped thinking about Marla. The desire to touch her hair or press his palm against hers had left his body, replaced by a tight, painful knot in his stomach and a dryness at the back of his throat that he couldn't seem to swallow away.

Walking under the stars of the Arizona sky, he tried to think of something he knew about himself that he could prove. It couldn't be about his ancestors, because he realized that they belonged to Raymond and not to him. He didn't know his true age, or the people who had given him his life and name. Though he liked to boast that he was the fastest runner of all the *Ashiihi*, the truth was that most of the older men could have beaten him if they'd chosen to race. He was a good hunter, but Hoshimini had more kills under his belt, since Roy spent so much of his time lining up crazy trick shots that impressed all of his friends but were never aimed at anything so pedestrian as the rabbits Hoshimini patiently stalked.

Roy stopped to skip a rock across the river that meant he only had to walk two more hours to get home, and frowned to himself. Maybe that was it, maybe it wasn't the hunting, but the archery itself. Maybe all he had to be was really good at hitting things.

He said nothing to Raymond when he finally got back to the trailer that night, even though his *aniséhí* was still up waiting for him, coughing into the dark with the scent of liquor strong on his breath. In the morning Roy asked him for more lessons with a bow and arrow, which Raymond agreed to, his eyebrows arched up slightly in surprise.

"You're already very good," he told him.

"I have to be the *best*," Roy insisted with a determination in his voice Raymond had never heard before. Raymond shrugged and got down his long bow.

For a whole year, Roy ran home after school and practiced archery until dark. He woke up early to complete his chores and stayed up late into the night to finish his homework. Impressed by his drive, one of his teachers at the tiny reservation school he attended checked a book out of the library for him called *Zen in the Art of Archery*.

Roy was reading it on the walk home when he noticed an expensive Jeep parked outside Raymond's trailer. He got closer and circled the vehicle slowly, thrilled with its size and glossy newness. Carefully, he reached out and touched the sun-warmed metal of the driver side door. His *aniséhí* called to him from inside the trailer.

"*Átsilí lichíí*, come in here."

Roy pulled his hand away from the Jeep and ran into the trailer. There, seated across from Raymond on the tattered trailer couch with a warm can of beer in one gloved hand, sat Green Arrow. Roy dropped the book.

"Roy Harper, this is Green Arrow," Raymond said formally. Green Arrow had bent down to pick up the dropped hardback and was grinning at it with recognition.

"You readin' this?" he asked, turning his dazzling smile on Roy.

Roy swallowed and nodded. "I just—just started it . . . sir."

Green Arrow stood up and placed the book on the scruffy chest Raymond used as a coffee table. For the first time in his life, Roy felt ashamed of his surroundings. The trailer was cramped and dusty and uncomfortably hot, and apart from a beautiful wool rug woven by Raymond's mother, they had nothing, *nothing* worth showing their guest.

"Well, I'll tell ya how it ends, and then we can go out and see what you can do. Ready?" Green Arrow placed a hand on Roy's shoulder and bent down close to whisper in his ear. "*Fundamentally, the marksman aims at himself.*" Roy's eyebrows knotted in confusion as Green Arrow rose to his full height again and winked at him. "Got it? Great! You're all set."

Roy turned to Raymond in bewilderment as Green Arrow strolled outside, but the usually calm Raymond looked rattled and hurried Roy out after their guest with fluttering hand gestures and another volley of coughing.

"Hear you're quite a shot," Green Arrow was saying as Roy ran to catch up with him outside. He handed him the most exquisite long bow Roy had ever seen and reached into the quiver on his back to pluck out an arrow. "Impress me."

Roy stared at the bow in his hands, caressing the northern white ash stave with reverence. When he looked up again, Green Arrow was smiling down at him amiably.

"What should I hit?" Roy asked, his excitement mounting.

Green Arrow shielded his eyes from the sun and squinted out at the horizon.

"How about that hawk?"

Roy's eyes went wide. The bird was a tiny dot gliding toward the northeast, nearly a thousand yards away. Roy shook his head. "I cannot kill him. He represents union with Great Spirit, and is my animal totem." Green Arrow's

eyebrows rose as the boy turned to him with utter serious-
ness. "He's telling me to look at who I have become and
to rip out the threads of my self-illusion."

Green Arrow wasn't sure what to say. "I . . . didn't mean
any offense, kid. I just thought it'd be cool to have a tail
feather." He shrugged and started to look for another target,
but Roy had raised the bow and taken aim. Green Arrow
noted with interest that he appeared to be left-handed.

With impressive confidence and strong form, the squinting
boy released the shot. Green Arrow watched his follow-
through before turning to observe the arrow whistle through
the air.

Though he could barely see the hawk himself, it was
clear to Green Arrow after a brief pause in which it looked
like the bird might have been grazed that the animal wasn't
going down. "Nice try, kid, really." He smiled down at the
frowning redhead supportively. The boy was still focused
on the horizon, watching the sky with such intensity that
Green Arrow wondered if he was seeing things. "Good
form, and a nice, gutsy shot."

Without looking at him, Roy thrust Green Arrow's bow
back toward him and began to run in the direction he had
fired.

Green Arrow called after him. "Don't worry about the
arrow! There're plenty more where that one came from!"
Roy kept running, though, motioning finally for Green
Arrow to follow. The crime-fighting archer scratched his
beard and then sprinted after him.

It was a long run, nearly half a mile, but the boy ran so
doggedly that Green Arrow found himself embarrassed
not to follow. Just when Green Arrow thought his chest

was about to explode from the unexpected exertion in the heat of the late afternoon, Roy stopped, a huge grin plastered across his deeply tanned face, and pointed.

There, in the dirt, was the arrow Roy had fired, a perfect hawk tail feather pinned between the arrowhead and the ground. Green Arrow crouched down and pulled up the arrow, astonished.

"You took a single feather off a bird in flight?"

The boy's grin broadened and Green Arrow decided then and there that he liked him. No one that proud of themselves could be all square.

"I told you," Roy said. "Hawk asked me to uncover the truth of who I truly am. So I aimed, fundamentally, at myself, and I told him that I'm the best archer in *Ch'ínílí*."

Green Arrow threw his head back and laughed. Tucking the feather into his vest, he placed a hand on the boy's head and turned to head back to the trailer. "You're thinkin' too small, kid. I'd say you're the best archer in Arizona, and I'd give you the whole West Coast if not for me."

The boy's green eyes were shimmering with pride and admiration as he walked alongside Green Arrow, gazing up at him with undisguised curiosity. "Is it true you can hit a man between the eyes from fifty paces?"

Green Arrow chuckled again. "From a hundred, sure, but I don't go around doing that much. If you want to be a hero, you can't use lethal force. It's important to remember that."

Roy nodded seriously. "How many crimes do you stop a night?"

"Heh. Depends. Two, three, four . . ."

"What's the most? In one night?"

"I dunno. Probably . . . six or so? I like to get my beauty sleep, plus after a while, once they hear I'm out there, you know, who's gonna be dumb enough to try something?"

The kid turned his gaze back toward his trailer and the sparkling new Jeep parked in front of it. "Why do people do things they know to be against the law?" he asked.

Green Arrow stretched his knuckles out in front of him and listened to them crack before answering. "Well, you know, it's got something to do with social inequality and a biased distribution of wealth between the rich and the poor and blah blah blah. I'm actually still kind of studying all that myself. For now, suffice to say that people have some pretty base instincts, and there's a law of averages that leans toward mediocrity. It's only natural that not everyone's gonna come out a cowboy. Uh—I mean a good guy, you know, a white-hat. I didn't mean Indi—um—*Native Americans* are bad or anything . . . That was a bad example, never mind." Roy felt a large, gloved hand come down on his head and muss his hair. "*You* know what I mean," the archer insisted. "Ninety percent of anything is garbage." Roy squinted up at the hero but was no longer sure he was following the man's line of thinking. It didn't seem to matter, though. The archer was talking mostly to himself. "'Cept maybe women. They really seem to come out with better-than-average odds. And beer. You don't run into a lot of *truly* bad beer. Nothing you wouldn't drink if it was free, anyway. But in general, you know—" Green Arrow looked up and seemed pleased to be nearing the trailer. "*What* was I talking about?"

Roy bit his lip and shrugged.

Green Arrow snapped his fingers. "Oh, crime! Right! Yeah, listen, this is important." The archer stopped Roy just outside the trailer, placing a hand on each of the boy's shoulders. "It isn't always easy to do the right thing, but doing the right thing is always the right thing to do. Okay?"

The kid nodded, though he looked confused. Raymond stepped out from the trailer into the sunshine. He was coughing again.

"Well, what do you think?" he asked Green Arrow.

Green Arrow flashed him a grin and a thumbs-up. "He's everything you said he was. The whole southpaw thing's intriguing, too. Be interesting to work with him on optimal form."

Raymond nodded. "He's a good learner. Very adaptable."

Roy was beginning to feel like he should excuse himself when Raymond turned to him. Roy thought his *aniséhí* looked unusually tired.

"And you, Roy? Is your hero what you hoped he would be?"

Roy nodded, eyes wide. He was so excited, he ignored a pang in his gut that was trying to warn him that something was wrong. Raymond had turned back to Green Arrow, his face unusually grave.

"So, will you do this for me? Will you raise this boy into manhood?"

Confused and increasingly anxious, Roy watched as Green Arrow turned to him and gave him an approving once-over, nodding his head as if to the beat of a song only he could hear.

"Sure," he said. "Why not?"

Roy wanted desperately to run to Raymond and throw

his arms around him and beg not to be cast from the Nation, but he worried that he was too old for such a thing. The look of panic on his face must have been evident, though, because Raymond came carefully down the three trailer steps, stopping to cough at the base of them, and then strove to hold the teenager's gaze.

"Your destiny is not here, *átsilí lichíí*. I am sorry. But you will always be welcome in these lands, even if I am not present to greet you."

"*Aniséhí*—"

Raymond coughed again, and then frowned up at the sky. "Wander along the path of long life and happiness, *átsilí*. And may you always walk in beauty."

Roy felt a strange numbness come over his limbs and wondered for a moment if he was dreaming.

"Thank you," Raymond said to Green Arrow. "You have lifted a great burden from my shoulders."

"Glad I could help." Green Arrow turned to Roy and elbowed him playfully toward the Jeep. "Come on, kid. Hop in. You ever seen Star City?"

Roy turned to Raymond, who was smiling at him sadly. He nodded in encouragement. Slowly, Roy got into the Jeep, looking up at the sky for signs. The high air was luminous with twilight, usually one of his favorite times of day, but Roy felt afraid that the approaching night would be too long. Green Arrow started the Jeep, talking a mile a minute, and Roy once again looked over his shoulder at his *aniséhí*.

"We're gonna have fun, you and me. Did that hawk friend of yours tell you you're gonna be a super hero? Well, a sidekick, really, to start—that's what they call 'em in the paper, anyway. You know, like Batman and Robin. It's workin' for them, it'll work for us! Oh, and you can call me Ollie, by the way. Oliver Jonas Queen—that's me. Green Arrow's just . . . when you're heroing, you need to protect yourself and you need a name with some caché, some mystique. I'll have to think of something to call you. 'Red Arrow,' maybe, or . . . nah, that's too obvious. But don't worry, it'll come to me. We'll get you all suited up, too. Yeah, you just hang on, kid, you're in for quite a ride! Say, how do I get out of here, anyway? Guess I just gotta get back on 191. That'll get us over to I-40, right? Oh, did you, um—did you have anything you wanna bring or anything?"

Raymond stopped smiling, seized by a fresh wave of coughing, and Roy turned back around in his seat, eyes glazed as he stared at the dashboard. Slowly he shook his head.

He had nothing.

Arsenal carefully watched the control board in the cockpit as Batman disengaged the auto throttle and began to prepare the Batplane for landing. He was keeping a running list, for his own amusement, of things Batman seemed to be able to do with his eyes closed—such as pilot a supersonic jet—and also trying to soak in as much "how to" knowledge as he could. One of the skills Batman seemed to have down cold was "how to avoid ever ending up in a compromised position that would necessitate your partner taking control of one of your toys," but Roy remained hopeful. There was always the possibility that eventually they'd have to split up, or that Batman would become distracted with a more pressing concern and leave the Batplane or Batmobile steering to his temporary subordinate.

"So where are we?" he asked, squinting out at the pale blue sky and the red-tinged desert sand beneath it. He recognized the only building on the landscape, but wanted to hear Batman confirm their location and their mission.

"Northern Qurac, near the border of Kuwait. I thought you would have recognized the prison."

Arsenal sighed. "There's always the possibility somebody built a new theme casino in Vegas."

Batman's eyes narrowed. "I need you to get any and all information she has on Qurac: current international interest in, displaced commandos from, loose ends, recent inquiries, target status, perception of political climate . . ."

Arsenal didn't see Batman touch anything, but a door opened behind him and an exit ladder began to unfold, leaving half the plane exposed to the sweltering heat of the desert at midday. The penitentiary holding Cheshire loomed just past a barbed-wire gate eight hundred or so meters from the plane.

"I know how to do interrogations," Arsenal snapped, unfolding his lean body from the copilot seat.

"Knowing how to do something and being willing to do it are two separate things," Batman intoned darkly. "Understand that there's a fifteen-year-old boy's life at risk here, and that I'm *counting* on you."

Arsenal stepped out of the plane onto the ladder and eyed the long gate and the distant guard posts with a scowl. "How am I supposed to get in there?"

"You've managed it before. Here."

From the ladder, Roy caught a capped and loaded

medical syringe that Batman tossed to him. He examined it with a frown and then looked back up at Batman questioningly.

"It's an antidote to the toxin she's used on forty-six percent of her recorded poisoning victims. There's an eighty-two percent probability that she can produce this variant with supplies on hand in the prison."

Roy blinked at Batman for a moment and then smiled down at the syringe. "Um, thanks. But the only time she's ever dosed *me* with poison, she used a special slow-acting modification."

"I know. I'll be on extraction."

Roy had an additional protest forming on his lips, but the moment he climbed down the ladder and stepped onto the baking sand, the ladder extension lifted and folded itself back into the plane. Arsenal watched the aircraft door slide shut as cleanly as it had opened, leaving him frowning half a mile from the security gate. He tucked the antidote into his holster with a sigh.

Extraction? How would Batman know when he was ready to leave? Roy was already crossing the sand toward the northwest guard tower when a realization made him groan aloud. Batman would extract him when *Batman* was ready for him to leave, which meant that Batman also had him bugged somehow and would be listening in to his entire conversation with Cheshire.

Roy clenched his jaw, settled into a low crouch, and pulled a pair of compact binoculars from one of his boots. Shading his eyes from the glare of the sun, he focused his view on the Quraci soldier standing rigidly between him and the nearest guard tower. Truthfully, he'd gotten in before by bribing guards he knew from his time with the CBI, but those had been visits he himself had reconned and scheduled. The man he was now watching on the tarmac with the M-16 was not a guy he recognized or felt like chatting up. With a sigh, he counted the opportunities for cover between him and his goal and began to carefully position himself as close to the exterior of the fence as he could get without alarming the unfamiliar sentinel. Pulling a custom-made grenade from a pocket on one of his gauntlets, Roy took aim at a support leg of the northeast tower. He set and then tossed the small time bomb, counted to five, and then used his crossbow to shoot a grapnel up into the northwest tower support beams as the grenade exploded twenty yards away, knocking out one leg of the northeast gun tower.

As usual, his aim held true, and he let the line pull him over the barbed wire fence and onto the face of the tower before anyone had even begun to react to the small amount of noise. Roy clung to the metal beams for a moment, collecting the grapnel and ascertaining that no one had seen or heard him, and then he scrambled up past the armed guard in the turret and onto the very top of the structure as quickly and quietly as he could, finally settling onto his stomach on top of the tower, just four vertical feet from the turret guard.

"Hey," he whispered, assuming that Batman could hear him. "If you get a bunch of gunfire over the wire in the next few seconds, that means I screwed up."

Shifting into a low crouch on top of the tower, Arsenal pulled a pen out of one boot pocket and a small, flat skipping stone out of another. The pen was a matter of foresight, but for the rock he had his daughter, Lian, to thank. It was something she had given him several weeks ago, one of many spontaneous gifts with which she loved to surprise him, this one pressed earnestly into his hand along with the utterance *"ch'al,"* which was the Navajo word for "frog." Roy had been so touched by her generosity and her unadulterated delight in the natural world that he had forgotten to ask her if there was any connection between the word and the object. It was unlikely that she had her vocabulary confused—she habitually and consistently proved herself far smarter than he considered himself—but did she think it was shaped a little like a frog, or had she found it near a frog, or given it to him in the hopes of trading it for a frog? A wave of longing for her presence came over him so fast and so fiercely that he had to bow his head and catch his breath. Even if Lian was the only good thing that Cheshire had ever had any part in creating, it was, to Roy's mind, more than enough to demand forgiveness. He understood completely why Cheshire was evil, but he could not bring himself to hate her. He loved her just enough to know that he would always love her, maybe not even because of what she was so much as what she could have been, what they could have been. He recognized in her the same accident of habitual desertion that had always plagued him; some people were clumsy with objects, others uncomfortable in their skin, but Roy and Jade kept dropping out of places, out of relationships, out of the social contract of predictable futures. Roy and Jade kept losing their destinies.

Roy pulled the pen top off with his teeth and scribbled a quick symbol on the flat of the stone. He recapped the pen and tucked it back into a boot pouch, then rolled up into a low crouch on the tower top and counted the windows along the western wall. Pressing his lips together, he drew in a sharp breath and then slowly exhaled as he pitched the small rock at a narrow, distant space between two bars on a window he knew to be hers.

Fundamentally, the marksman aims at himself.

Life in Star City was not without its joys. The beginning was rough, but eventually things smoothed out. Roy worked harder than he'd ever worked at anything in his life to learn the rhythm and vocabulary of Ollie's life and city, and although it was unclear whether or not Ollie ever noticed his ward's struggle, he was fast to praise accomplishments, and always acted like Roy was joking when the teenager would double-check about what to call a chandelier or a cuff link.

"You never seen one of these before?" he'd ask incredulously, waving around a strange kitchen implement or an odd piece of electrical equipment. If Roy looked truly embarrassed by his ignorance, Ollie would shrug and throw the object casually over his shoulder. "Yeah, I don't know what the hell that is either."

In no time at all, Roy adored him.

And if life in Ollie's mansion was sometimes strained, out on the streets at night they were naturals. Ollie dressed Roy up in a smaller red version of his Green Arrow costume and took to calling him Speedy, sometimes in praise of his archery tempo, and sometimes, Roy suspected, because he couldn't remember his name.

Working off a tip from Batman, Ollie hired a succession

of butlers, all of whom he and Roy managed to scare off within a matter of weeks. They set booby traps, exaggerated the occasional wounds they received, stayed up until all hours, and in general seemed to take tremendous personal satisfaction in their ability to go through household staff like tissue paper.

On Sundays they'd play B. B. King albums and make chili, their recipes always becoming spicier and more byzantine until they were the only two who could stomach their own creations.

They had an Arrowcar and an Arrowplane and later even an Arrowcave, and although Roy never forgot that he was secretly *Dine'é*, he quickly became a master at upper class and street-level colloquialisms, learning to blend into any environment they moved through even more convincingly than Ollie himself.

And Ollie did try. When Roy became soul sick for the music of the mesas, Ollie bought him a drum kit and taught him a few rock and roll licks. When Roy ached to see the sky stretching overhead or feel something other than concrete beneath his feet, Ollie took him camping in the national parks. And when Roy finally found his longing to once again see *Ch'ínílí* and his *aniséhí* overwhelm him, Ollie sat him down on the black leather couch in the living room and poured him a juice glass full of twenty-year-old scotch.

"Yeah, uh . . . Brave Bow's dead, kiddo. He had cancer. That's why he called me to come and get you. He didn't want you to see him fading and he was worried that life on the reservation would be too hard on you, you know, without him. I'm really sorry."

Roy sat on the couch for three and a half hours drinking the scotch, and then he got up, barefoot, and went out for a walk. He couldn't have been alive more than fifteen years, and already he had been orphaned twice. Ollie picked him up eleven hours later just past the Washington State border and let him sleep in the car on the way home. Neither of them ever mentioned Arizona again.

Roy had the strong suspicion that without Ollie to cling to he wouldn't have made it. Fortunately, Ollie had absolutely no sense of age-related boundaries and was happy to take Roy with him almost everywhere he went. It was around that time, too, that as Speedy, Roy was formally introduced to Robin and the other teen "sidekicks" of the JLA. With the exception of Kid Flash, they were also all orphans who had somehow bypassed the bureaucratic hell of state aid and foster homes to end up living under the protection of self-proclaimed super heroes. They were all extraordinary in one way or another, and they were all shouldering psychological wounds the size of asteroids. Almost immediately, they pledged eternal fidelity and tended to make up faster than the grown-ups did when they fought among themselves.

Ollie liked to refer to himself as a "playboy," but there was another significant change on the horizon. By the time another year had passed, Ollie had lost all his money thanks to the machinations of a scheming business partner, and was finding himself increasingly involved with a fellow JLAer. The loss of money didn't bother Roy at all—it actually gave him a way to be helpful to Ollie not previously available to him, like helping him find a new, low-rent apartment in Star City. The woman, Black

Canary, initially threw Roy off by heroing at night in a blonde wig and fishnets, but transforming almost magically by day into an extremely smart and levelheaded brunette by the name of Dinah Lance. Roy liked her, but kept his distance. There was something a little awkward about the age difference between her and Ollie, at least as it related to him and the woman who was rapidly becoming a sort of surrogate stepmother—Dinah seemed closer to his age than Ollie's. That didn't, however, stop Ollie from falling hard—so hard that Dinah ended up pretty much living with them.

That actually suited Roy fine, too. Ollie's relationship with Dinah tended, if anything, to make him stay closer to home. It was Ollie's friendship with Green Lantern Hal Jordan that proved problematic.

Ollie was on fire about social injustice. The loss of money—and the privilege and status that came with it—seemed to wake something up in him. Hal was having his own problems, and instead of going easy on his friend, Ollie came down on Green Lantern hard.

"He's takin' orders from little blue men from another planet!" Ollie told Roy as he rushed around their small apartment throwing socks and cans of stew into a large backpack. "I mean think about that—*from another planet!* What about *this* world, man, what about what's goin' on *right here*? I mean, really, what are we doing? We dress up in costumes and these bad guys dress up, too, and we beat the crap out of each other on rooftops, and for what? What does it really all mean? We really think we're *helpin'* people? I'm punchin' out Rainbow Archer and meanwhile, *right on the street where we live*, there's this woman—Macy from next door, you met her?—she's trying to feed four kids on a welfare check because she had to drop out of high school and help out her alcoholic mother when her dad got thrown in prison for a crime he didn't even commit and couldn't support the family anymore, and now she can't get a job and this is on my block, you know. Her kids are hungry *on my block*, but me, I'm too busy fighting Red Dart or Bull's-Eye or whoever to just open my eyes and see what's really going on! And Hal, he's even worse, man, he just has no clue. So I'm gonna show him, I'm gonna show him America—the *real* America, Speedy, warts 'n' all. We're hittin' the road!"

"How is that gonna help Macy?"

Oliver stopped and thrust a finger in Roy's face. "It starts with seeing, really *seeing* what's going on around you. You need to change your consciousness before you can change anything else."

Roy said nothing more, and within fourteen minutes, Ollie was out the door. Roy looked around the ratty little apartment, bewildered, and then heard his mentor calling for him from the street.

"Speedy! Speedy, come to the window, I gotta tell ya something!"

Roy felt his chest expand with hope as he went to the living-room window and forced it open. He stuck his head out and grinned down at Ollie, who was standing in the middle of the sidewalk staring earnestly up at him.

"Hey, listen, I just want you to know—if I ever called you an 'Indian,' kid, I'm sorry. That wasn't right. It's 'Native American,' and that's important, because this used to be your land, and we took it from your people without even understanding where we were. Well, I mean, not *your* people, not the *Irish* or whatever you are biologically but . . . *you* know what I mean. So . . . so peace, okay? Be proud. And keep on truckin'!"

Roy watched as Ollie hopped into his beat-up blue Ford and took off for parts unknown. Then he turned from the window, leaving it open behind him, and wandered around the apartment frowning in confusion. He was completely alone, and instead of exhilaration, the freedom made him feel distinctly nauseous.

Cheshire was sitting on her unmade bed, knees drawn up to her chest, when the small rock came hurling through the window of her cell. She frowned, stretched her long legs, and moved to retrieve it.

On the rock, which was small and smooth and flat, someone had drawn a simple, almost iconic arrow. Cheshire smiled at the simplicity of it and went back to her bed, a disobedient flood of anticipation spreading through her belly.

She swallowed but otherwise remained calm as an actual arrow shot through the bars of the same window and implanted itself into the security glass that covered the interior wall of her cell, pulling a tight grapnel line through with it. She watched with her back to the window as the line bobbed up and down slightly, registering weight. And then his warm voice, soft and unbearably familiar, was at her window.

"Hey, Chesh."

"Arsenal." She wasn't ready to face him, to see him, and so she stayed where she had been most of the evening, on the threadbare mattress, admiring the spiderweb cracks his arrow had punctured into the glass wall.

"Glad you got my note. I'm always a little afraid I'm gonna shoot you in the head one of these nights by accident."

"You should have just told me to duck."

His voice became indignant suddenly. "I did! You got the rock, right?"

She turned her head to glare at him where he was crouching outside her windowsill, and was glad she was sitting down when her eyes met his. They were as green as the pine trees he loved to tell her about, and utterly unguarded. She didn't know how he could stand to walk around like that, with every emotion passing across his face as visibly as the shadows of clouds. She supposed he was lucky that there weren't more people like her in the world, people who took the time to read every last one. "Yes, with the arrow! To announce that you were coming. Last time you came to the front—how does that tell me to duck?"

"It was pointing down!" He sounded exasperated and she was about to protest that he couldn't possibly have known that the picture would still be pointing down when she went to retrieve the stone, but just then she remembered that it had been. She had righted it immediately without thinking. She rose to her feet.

"You counted how many times it would spin on its way through this window?"

"Of course." There was no cockiness in his voice, just a slight impatience. Cheshire moved to the window, wrapped her hands around two of the cool steel bars, and pulled herself up with all the strength in her arms to bring her face close to his. She heard him catch his breath and then he leaned in as she had known he would. She pressed her lips against his and closed her eyes to take in his scent and feel the rough sensation of his bristled jaw against her cheek. Slipping her tongue past his teeth, she let herself, for the briefest second, be transported back in time to a place where no bars separated them.

Except for a heavy exhale that escaped from his nose, he was quiet when at last she pulled away from him and dropped back down to the floor. "I assume this isn't just a conjugal call?" she prompted, turning her back to him again to run her fingertips across her lips in an impulsive attempt to seal the kiss more firmly into them.

She could hear the laughter in his voice when he answered.

"Oooh, that reminds me. Will you marry me?"

"No," she said lightly, though a slight smile of pleasure betrayed her otherwise faultless restraint. "Stop asking."

"Okay. Not why I'm here anyway. Say hello to Batman."

"Hello, Batman." Cheshire's tone remained calm, though her eyes had narrowed and her shoulders pulled back as she glanced around the dimly lit cell. "Where is he?" she demanded, turning back to her lover.

Still crouching on the windowsill, Arsenal shrugged. "Damned if I know. But he sent me here to ask you about Qurac."

"Qurac?" Cheshire's eyes narrowed farther in annoyance and she stared at Arsenal challengingly. "I have nothing more to say about whatever may remain of that worthless country."

"I know." Arsenal's voice had softened again, and

Cheshire knew that he felt himself the pawn of a much stronger force. Left to his own devices, he would ignore the topic entirely. It was the one subject on which they most violently disagreed. "And it's not that he even really thinks you'll have anything necessarily, we—he just has to cover his bases."

Cheshire sat down on the bed again, drawing her hands carefully into her lap and turning her face from her lover's again.

"Chesh—" There was compassion in his voice, compassion and concern, and it set her teeth on edge.

"Just ask your stupid questions and get out," she said calmly. Again she heard him sigh and shift slightly on the sill.

"I don't know, just—anything. You know, current displaced interest in, international commandos from, loose inquiries, recent target status, perception of political climate . . . just tell me everything you know."

Cheshire refused to look at Arsenal as she drew her knees together and sat with her back perfectly straight, her voice a detached monotone. "I know that their rising political star, the hope for a true democratic future for Qurac, was the young Muslim Amin Bin Hatim Abdul-Hakam, eldest son of current President Hatim Abdul-Hakam. Amin— and his mother, I believe, as well—were killed during my attack on their country, though I assure you I had no particular interest in him. Hatim himself, who had been a mid-level adviser to the ruling autocrat at that time, rose in political prominence after that attack. Obviously, he was heavily aided, and certainly financially sponsored, by the United States government and their interest in controlling the Middle East. Though the majority of Quracis are pleased with their new alleged democracy, there are of course still plenty of displaced mercenaries who would love to seize power there, and also two or three separate religious factions who feel underrepresented."

"Do you know who those displaced mercenaries are?" Arsenal asked from the window. "Any major players?"

Cheshire paused for a moment and then continued in the same resentful monotone. "No, but I'm sure the Department of Defense does. Why would anyone contact me?"

Arsenal's eyes narrowed slightly and he cocked his head, but Cheshire rushed on.

"Look, Hatim is not well respected by the Middle Eastern people in general, but he does enjoy support from key representatives around the globe and could reasonably be assumed to be under the protection of the United States."

Cheshire paused and tucked a stray lock of long black hair behind one ear.

"As far as I know, Hatim's relationship with and intentions toward America have been and will continue to be utterly benign, and although no longer a cesspool of unaffiliated mercenary terrorists, Qurac remains a largely useless political entity except for its geography and its oil. I believe this very week the ports of Gotham City are expecting a shipment directly from Qurac—the first since the bombing, I'm sure. At one point President Hatim himself was scheduled to travel on that ship but ended up having to send it ahead for trite matters of scheduling with which I can't possibly be expected to concern myself."

Roy's eyes narrowed.

"Interesting how you say 'the bombing,' like it just happened all by itself."

Cheshire said nothing in response, so Arsenal exhaled and continued.

"What's on the boat? Is it just an oil shipment?"

"Better than that. I believe it's a prototype for a new oil refinement process developed by the Quracis. They're sharing it with the U.S. as a sign of sycophantic political alliance or something along those lines." Cheshire frowned at Arsenal in annoyance. "C'mon, Roy, don't you ever read a newspaper?"

Still perching on the window ledge, Arsenal grinned sheepishly and shook his head. "Get all my news online. When I remember to check the blogs, that is. So let me get this straight—as we speak, Qurac is shipping a major scientific advance to the United States for free?"

"Nothing's ever *free*, darling."

Feeling overheated and restless, Cheshire rose from the bed, but kept her back to Arsenal at the window.

"I'm sure they expect military protection or some sort of key political alliance in return, but yes, as far as I know, Quraci and U.S. relations have never been better, largely owing to President Hatim's influence. And I've heard nothing about anyone in what you would call the 'supervillain community' express any interest in any of it, though my ties to said community are obviously severely compromised here."

Cheshire heard Arsenal shifting on the narrow confines of the sill again and without looking could tell that he was trying to get in closer, trying to wish away the bars that separated them. For the millionth time, she thought how foolish and how very charming he was, and for the millionth time, unbidden, the corners of her mouth rose in the barest intimation of a smile.

"Jade, are you okay? I mean, is there anything I can do to make you more comf—"

Cheshire interrupted him coolly, pulling her unruly mouth back down into a frown. "Of course, Qurac was once home to the meta-human terrorist group, the jihad. The Suicide Squad—who, in my experience, have an annoying habit of not living up to their name—destroyed their base years ago, but I suppose they would constitute a serious threat if they've re-formed. Beyond that, it's hard to say."

She dropped her head and spoke in a quiet, more intimate voice that made his throat ache.

"Trouble starts in strange places. It could be any little thing."

They were both silent for a moment, and then a strange electronic buzz drew her attention back toward him. Her eyes widened as she watched him begin to draw a pocket arc cutter across the bars at her window, carefully severing them where they met the base. Unsure of his intentions and wanting to mask the little bit of noise he was making from any roaming prison guards, she continued speaking.

"Even back when they *were* a threat, your friend Superman made my job easier by destroying much of Qurac's military capabilities in a fit of pique shortly before I bombed the place. And as you also know, I did so not because Qurac was of any interest to me, but rather because it was of no interest to anyone."

She cast another glance up at him but he was still absorbed in severing the window bars. She continued with increasing nervousness.

"I suspect that has not changed much, though they've shifted from an annoying potential threat to an annoying imperial subordinate, widely understood to be at America's beck and call. It is difficult for me to imagine what interest or danger the country could possibly represent to your Batman."

Arsenal continued working with the arc cutter as he answered her.

"No, it's—we're not worried about Qurac, we're worried *for* them. The president's other kid was shot at in Gotham, Batman thinks by Deathstroke. We're trying to figure out who hired him, you know—who'd put out a contract on a fifteen-year-old kid."

He broke through the last metal bar and began to lean one shoulder into the frame, obviously intent on popping the entire structure out.

"I am sure Batman will figure out any connection between—what are you *doing*?"

He had managed to completely detach the bars and was holding them in one hand as he dropped into her cell. Standing less than three feet away from her, he rested the frame of bars against the cell wall beneath the window and tucked the arc cutter away in his holster, next to something that looked to Cheshire's narrowed eyes like a stun gun.

"Look, I know we're on opposite sides of the law and that I'm more than a little screwed up and you're more than a little crazy, but together, we're all that Lian has. I just—I think about you all the time, Chesh. I wish—"

Cheshire threw her hands up in exasperation and took a step back from him toward her bed.

"You think about me because you are raising our daughter, that is all!"

She could feel her eyes begin to flash dangerously.

"And as for your wishes . . . your wishes are irrelevant, as are mine. Surely you understand at least *that* much by now."

He continued moving slowly toward her, his approach controlled and sensuous, one gloved hand reaching out for hers. "Tell me anyway. Tell me what you wish for, I wanna know."

Jade stopped with the back of her legs against the metal bed frame and let him come close, taking a deep breath and finally smiling down at his boots softly, her body centimeters from his and undeniably aroused by his closeness.

"Roy . . ." She imagined his face as she spoke, every emotion that would pass across his handsome features. "I wish I'd gone with you that time in Sendai. I wish I could be with you, raising our beautiful daughter and watching her grow. I wish I could be good, like you, and I wish I'd never heard of Qurac. But most of all . . ."

She raised her dark eyes to him slowly, slipping her hand, finally, into his. He closed his hand around hers instantly, all the indomitable passion and optimism of his heart communicated through the strength of his grip. She struck fast, swinging her forearm around into his stomach and pulling him down, hard, by the hand. He grunted and went immediately down to one knee, pulling his hand away from hers to catch himself. With both hands free, she grabbed up fistfuls of the ginger-tinted highlights on the back of his lowered head and slammed his forehead as hard as she could into the metal bed frame below the mattress.

". . . Most of all I wish you'd stop being such a sentimental idiot."

She reached into his holster and pulled out the arc cutter and the stun gun as he slumped down, face first, onto the floor of her cell, and then she snatched up the discarded grapnel rope still hanging from the wall-implanted arrow.

Moving quickly, she frowned at the bars he had left propped against the wall of her cell and then up at the unobscured view from her window, wondering why he couldn't have come at night. After one last glance at him over her shoulder, she leapt up onto the window ledge and began to climb down to her freedom.

After cleaning the apartment from floor to ceiling in a burst of nervous energy, Roy made himself some chili and ate it in front of the TV. To his great relief, Dinah came by looking for Ollie, a bouquet of day-old flowers tucked under one arm.

"Did you do this?" she asked Roy, admiring the clean orderliness of the apartment. Roy nodded and did his best to sound casual as he offered her some chili. Dinah wrinkled her nose and shook her head, but continued to look around the tiny living quarters with obvious approval, finally washing and peeling the label off a used spaghetti sauce jar and arranging the flowers in it before placing them on the small, lopsided table in the kitchen.

"Well," she said then, dropping her hands to her sides in a gesture of resignation, "guess I'd better go find him."

Roy dug the fingers of his left hand into the bicep of his right arm. "You're gonna find him and bring him back, though, right?" he asked her huskily.

She smiled at the low pitch of his voice and then shrugged lightly.

"Eventually, I guess, if he wants to come back. I can think of worse things to do than follow him and Hal around the country a little, though. Betcha they'll be in trouble by sundown."

Dinah's smile broadened and she playfully made guns with her thumbs and index fingers, brandishing them up at the ceiling.

"Might just be needin' some lil' lady to sweep in and rescue them."

"You could stay here," Roy blurted out. He had meant to tell her that neither Ollie nor Hal needed any help, but instead he reached out and grabbed her by the wrist. Dinah's eyes narrowed and her posture tightened. Roy immediately released her.

"If you wanted to, I mean. Like, *mi casa es su casa* just . . . just so you know."

Dinah put her hands on her hips and frowned down at the young redhead.

"Are you hitting on me, Roy?" she demanded, one corner of her lipstick-stained mouth curling up mischievously.

To do so had hardly even occurred to Roy, and yet suddenly it sounded like a good idea, like maybe the best idea anyone had ever had. He shook his head "no" but continued staring at her, trying to imagine what she'd look like without her clothes on, how warm she might feel. If he couldn't get Ollie back, and if he couldn't make Dinah stay, was there some other way not to feel so alone?

Dinah left less than an hour later after packing a small bag and changing into her Black Canary outfit.

"You're gonna be okay here, right?" she asked Roy once she was already halfway out the door. Roy nodded, because it was the only possible response, and Dinah smiled at him, waved, and then was roaring off on the motorcycle she used for heroing without glancing back.

Roy listened to the sound of the bike engine until he couldn't hear it anymore, and then a glance at his drum kit gave him an idea. He walked to a downtown music store and perused the local bulletin board, carefully tearing off the phone numbers of bands looking for additional members. He went back to the apartment with four numbers and no contact names, so he started dialing and simply asking "Yeah, did you want a drummer?" when someone picked up. There was no answer at the first place, the second guy said he already had someone on drums, and an older woman, who told him "Oh, you want my son, he's not in right now," answered the third number.

The word "son" spoken by a woman sounded so profoundly exotic to Roy that he kept her on the line longer than he had any right to, asking her dumb questions about her son's schedule just to hear her talk about him. There was a warmth in her voice when she said the kid's name—Matthew—that fascinated Roy. By the time he said good-bye she was under the false impression that Roy and Matthew went to school together and had invited Roy over for dinner. Roy knew he wouldn't go, but he cherished the invitation.

The fourth number rang for a while and then a young man who was probably in his early twenties answered. He spoke extremely rapidly and laughed a lot, though not with condescension. They talked about the kind of music they liked and songs they could do covers of, and the sound the guy was after for his band.

"Sure, man, come on over," he told Roy after he asked to play the drums for the guy. "Sounds like we're in the same groove. Bring your kit."

Roy hadn't realized he'd have to bring his drum set anywhere, and he fretted briefly over transportation logistics after hanging up the phone. He'd told the guy, Mark, that he'd be over within the hour, so after debating his ability to carry his drums on a bus, he found himself staring at the orderly key rack Dinah had installed above the light switch plate in the apartment's small, rounded front hall. He grabbed the key to her cherry-red '65 Mustang convertible, the car she only used in her civilian identity, and silently steeled himself against the guilt pangs of his own conscience. Raymond had always taught him that nothing belonged to anyone, and Ollie seemed to believe that everything belonged to him, so Roy tried to tell himself that somewhere between those two philosophies lay an excuse for him to borrow something of Dinah's without asking.

By the time he was unloading the drums at Mark's, though, he had made a decision in a slowly rising tide of quiet anger that surprised him; the next time he was cast out from or abandoned in a place in which he had sought shelter, it would be because of something he had actually done.

An expressive-faced, long-haired Asian guy who introduced himself as Quon came out to help Roy move the drums into Mark's carpeted, musty-smelling basement. Mark had bad skin and an abundance of manic energy that only served to make Roy calmer—neither of the young men asked Roy how old he was, which was fortunate since he wouldn't have been able to tell them. He accepted the beer Mark handed him and passed on Quon's offered cigarette. Then he sat down to play.

He started with a showy warm-up, demonstrating some brushwork and riffing on a little prepared etude on the snare, took a quick eight bar solo to show off his technique, and then settled in to an easy rock groove that he quickly sped up at Mark's urgings. Quon stood up, cigarette dangling from his mouth, and picked up his bass, joining Roy without looking at him. Mark was yelling at them from the couch.

"No, you guys—it's too laid-back. Faster, man, faster!"

Quon glanced at Roy over his shoulder, making eye contact for the first time, as they worked together to establish a faster rhythm. Mark jumped up, waving his hands.

"Wait, wait, stop, hold on—I got it."

Roy and Quon stopped playing as Mark rifled through a nearby desk drawer and pulled out a small brightly colored plastic container with a grin.

"How about we put some rock into this jam?"

Quon set his bass guitar down and moved to sit on the couch beside Mark, who was using a razor blade to arrange white powder into thin lines on a large hardback Fake Book.

"You ever used, Roy?" Mark asked without looking up from his task. For the second time that day, Quon's dark eyes met Roy's, a slightly mocking smile poised on his lips.

Roy shrugged. "No, not really."

In his head he heard the high-pitched shriek of a diving hawk, saw the talons ripping into the flesh of his face, smelled the scent of burning sage, and felt an ancient rhythm pounding into his chest through his feet, through flapping wings and beating drums and the churning chant of the Blessing Way.

Yo yowa lana ya na'eye lana heya 'eye
Yo yowa lana ya na'eye lana heya 'eye, holaghei . . .

"Well, actually," he continued, closing his eyes and shaking his head without realizing he was doing so. "Peyote once or twice, but only in ceremony."

When Roy opened his eyes, the mockery in Quon's expression had vanished entirely and Mark had jumped up, arms opened, to lead Roy to the coffee table.

"Peyote!? Damn, man, you're hardcore! Sit yer butt down! You gotta check this stuff out!"

Now darkness
He comes upon me with blessing
Behind him, from there
He comes upon me with blessing
Before him, from there . . .

Roy sat down on the rug across from the couch and leaned over the coffee table as Mark pushed the Fake Book toward him. Mimicking Quon's actions of a moment before, Roy pressed one nostril closed, shut his eyes, and breathed in the blessing of darkness with no thought of ever reaching dawn, afterglow, sun, Turquoise Boy, Corn

Kernel Girl, or any of the honored gods sung about in the rhythmic verses of the Blessing Way.

Arsenal waited, flat on his face, until he heard Cheshire leave the small cell through the window. Then he sat up, rubbed his forehead with a frown, and loaded a second grapnel line into his crossbow.

"Bats," he whispered, "I'm going on a little field trip. Hold off on extraction until my plan fails and I need to bail out, okay?" He was losing the conviction that his partner in the field could actually hear him, but figured it was worth a shot.

A glance out the opened cell window confirmed that Cheshire had descended to the concrete beneath the complex unnoticed and had begun making her way stealthily south. Arsenal shot for the roof and climbed up quickly, hoping to trail her from above. As he had expected, she ran into her first guard between the north and south cell blocks. He readied his crossbow and held his breath as he watched her from three stories overhead. When Cheshire used the nonlethal stun gun she had taken from his holster to knock the guard out, Roy exhaled and lowered his bow.

"That-a-girl," he whispered. "Let's keep this friendly . . ."

She dispatched two more guards in a similar matter, and although Roy felt bad for them having to endure even that much, he knew it was a lot better than what she would have come up with on her own. Silently he thanked the Coyote, the spirit of mischief, for the hints of resourcefulness and kleptomania in her that had made him so certain she would steal the stun gun.

He trailed her all the way to the third and last building

on the compound, which was smaller than the other two—the warden's office, he guessed, and perhaps the medical infirmary. He jumped down to the building's lower roof and then dropped farther to hang off the south side eaves, concealing himself from the view of the southern guard towers. He tucked his legs behind him to keep his feet from dangling over the frame of what appeared to be a large garage door of some kind, and tried to use the muscles in his legs as well as his shoulders to hold himself in place. The arrangement was less-than-perfect and took a great deal of upper arm strength, but Arsenal assumed he wouldn't have to remain there for long. He was wrong. Cheshire did not emerge from around the side of the building as he had expected she would, and after a solid five minutes had gone by, Roy began to worry.

Had she veered off due east where he couldn't see her? That wouldn't make any sense . . . she'd have to contend with one standing guard tower in addition to the one he had compromised that was probably still attracting a good deal of attention. He would have seen her if she'd doubled back or made the straight break for the south fence that he was anticipating . . . was she somewhere inside the C block building, and if so, to what end?

With his forehead throbbing and fatigue setting into his shoulders, Arsenal was about to give up and report his disastrous failure to Batman when he heard the unmistakable commotion of soldiers discovering the injured. Roy did not speak Quraci, but deduced that a small roaming foot patrol had come across one or two of the guards Cheshire had kayoed with the stun gun. He got quick confirmation of his infirmary hypothesis as every man available rushed to help get the unconscious guards to the medics, who were clearly inside the building he was clinging to, and was surprised when the garage door beneath his position reeled up to let a large military ambulance roll out of the building.

Of course! Chesh would never go for something so mundane as using arc cutters on a perimeter fence and making a run for it! She must have known that injured soldiers were treated off base and was probably already hidden away in the ambulance, waiting to be driven out of the compound.

Without time to think through the consequences of his actions, Arsenal let go of the eaves and dropped down onto the top of the moving ambulance. Though he landed in a crouch, he was immediately forced to go flat on his stomach, facedown as he clung to the roof of the speeding vehicle. He was just becoming confident about his grip when he realized that if the ambulance continued to approach the compound exit, in less than twenty seconds he would be fully visible to the south tower guards. He cursed silently for a second and wondered what he had ever seen in this woman he was about to get killed attempting to pursue.

He fantasized about shooting an arrow into the roof of the ambulance and running a line down the back of the vehicle so that he could somehow climb beneath it, but quickly rejected the plan as being both too difficult to set up from his present position and too likely to result in a seriously unfortunate case of road rash. Besides, climbing around on moving vehicles was not what he was really good at. What he was really good at was hitting things.

With a sigh of resignation, Arsenal rolled over onto his

back, aimed his crossbow at the guard in the southwest tower, and fired. The second the arrow left his bow, he reloaded and turned to aim at the guard in the southeast tower before the guard in the southwest tower had hit the turret floor. Both were clean shoulder shots that disarmed the guards and knocked then back away from their viewing posts without causing severe injury, but that didn't mean that they weren't painful. Arsenal was still feeling bad about it when the ambulance slowed down at the compound gate, nearly throwing him from the top of the van. He rolled back over onto his stomach just in time to catch the roof of the ambulance in one gloved hand, but lost the crossbow in his effort to remain aloft. His heart was beating too fast and he was more amazed than pleased to find himself still clinging to the ambulance roof half a mile up the road, where all the penitentiary checkpoints had been safely passed.

Roy quickly discovered that the problem with drugs was not that they obliterated your memory and reason, but rather that they kept promising to do so and never quite delivered. The amphetamines gave him nervous, surging energy, but did nothing to address the psychic exhaustion perpetually hanging like a boulder from his neck. Cocaine smoothed the omnipresence of time into an exhilarating, candy-colored, kinetic blur of a tunnel, but it always dumped him out at the other end feeling spent, disconnected, and shaky. LSD he avoided altogether after one disastrous run-in that brought him face-to-face with a hideously distorted version of his already too-aggressive spirit guide; hawk feathers spewing from his panicked throat as he fought to cough them up, and the obsidian-sharp talons sinking deeper and deeper into his gut while everyone in the room—had there been anyone in the room?—laughed and turned their backs on him. XTC got mixed up in his head with the first girl who had shared it with him, leaving him with a tactile memory of her fingers tracing the freckles on his shoulders and a lingering uncertainty about whether the drug resembled the intimacy of sex, or sex resembled the intimacy of drugs.

Alcohol slowed his brain into a meandering, golden, muddy river, but left his critical awareness standing right on the opposite bank to hurl stones into his pooling obliv ion every time the current tried to take him somewhere. Pot filled his limbs with restful, warm air, but then snaked around in his brain the second he was still, whispering invectives and threats. Combos left him spinning, bad trips left him cowering, and good hits left him shaking for more.

Mark, the lead guitar player and lead singer in his band—they were called Great Frog, though Roy couldn't remember where they got the name or what it was supposed to mean—was concerned that he couldn't find the right flight pattern for his young drummer.

"Man, I don't know *what's* gonna get you high if you keep leveling out so, you know, *low*."

It always startled Roy when someone mentioned "getting high." He was only trying to get parallel with the ground, just up to where he could lie flat on his belly and not be a bother to anyone, let them walk across his back if they needed to. In the beginning he didn't show much initiative, just took what was offered, maybe encouraged the offerings. The first time Great Frog got paid for a gig, he was content to surrender his share of the money to Quon, who promised to come back with something "grade A." Looking back, Roy could never remember how much money it was, or how long Quon was gone, or if there'd been any additional discussion of it beforehand. But for the rest of his life, he would remember when Quon got back; that was to become the clearest, hottest, most intense, trustworthy memory of his whole unreliable life.

"Holy crap!" Mark shouted from the next room. "Holy crap, man, you actually got it!"

Roy, sitting on the musty green carpet of Mark's basement with his back against the tattered couch, opened his eyes to glance at Derek, the second guitarist, who had joined the band only two weeks after he had. Derek gave Roy a sleepy smile and pushed a small fall of sandy curls off his forehead before rising to his feet with a stretch and a yawn. Mark bounded down the stairs clutching a small paper bag and stopped in front of Roy's drum set with an eager gleam in his eye.

"Lighter!" he demanded. Roy, who had already been drinking and was coming down from a speed ball, just watched him, but Derek patted down his denim jacket as Quon appeared at the bottom of the stairs just in time to flip the requested lighter to Mark with a big grin and a thumbs-up gesture. Derek was sent upstairs to fetch a spoon from the kitchen while Mark lit a black column candle and moved it over to the dilapidated coffee table in front of the couch. Quon was pulling a medical syringe out of his jeans. Roy sat forward with interest.

"Smack, man," Mark told him eagerly. "Heroin. *This'll* get you high, I goddamn guarantee it!"

Roy watched as Derek returned with a silver tablespoon and Quon and Mark began fussing over the powder with obsessive attention as they used the candle flame to turn it into a boiling clear liquid that was eventually drawn into the syringe through a cotton ball Mark had stolen from his mother's bathroom cabinet. Roy was surprised when Mark turned to him first, but he did not object. Quon reached over and rolled up Roy's right sleeve as Mark came to crouch beside him, offering the syringe like a tribute.

"Anywhere?" Roy asked, feeling strangely languid and compliant.

"Get the vein," Quon instructed, his dark eyes investigating Roy's exposed arm. He leaned across the coffee table to press on the soft inside of Roy's elbow, his black hair swinging into his eyes as he exposed a thin blue line on Roy's arm. "Like you were gonna draw blood—there." He pulled the syringe out of Mark's hand, tapped against it with his index finger, and handed it carefully back to Roy.

Roy stared at the exposed vein on his arm for a moment, the possibility of self-harm coming seriously into his thoughts for the first time. And then with a slow smile meant to convey indifference, he slid the needle into his flesh.

"Oh, uh," he heard Mark mutter. "If you have to throw up, try to hit the bathroom, okay, man?"

Roy pushed the syringe plunger, unsure what he was hoping for.

The heat rushed up his arm, across his shoulder, and then spread through his stomach like a blossoming flower. He groaned and closed his eyes, letting his head loll back on the couch seat. From what sounded like miles away, he heard

Quon's quiet laugh, but there was no desertion in it, no disdain. Roy felt his entire body relax as he was sure it had never relaxed before, waves of warmth lapping over him as for one brilliant instant every fear and hurt and shame and doubt shattered inside of him, flying outward, past his skin, in a brilliant shower of painless crystal shards. Roy wept with elation. His mother's hands reached into his skull and gently wrapped strong, soft fingers around his brain, painlessly freeing it from the spinal cord to let it float unfettered—he could smell her, sink into her utterly, perfectly contained within her embrace, perfectly protected. His cheeks burned with the pleasure of it. He couldn't remember the word for her, though, and he started laughing as he chased it. Would Raymond know? Ollie? He couldn't find them, but he felt no alarm over their absence. He was standing at a crossroad of infinite possibility, and all roads led to shelter. He was so sure of it that he imagined every dusty pebble under his feet and counted every star above his head—he never wanted to go in. As long as he knew there was somewhere safe to go, he would stand forever in the brilliant, cold wind, in the gorgeous dark, breathing deeply, so deeply, so alive that he could barely contain it, could not contain it—understood, as he had understood so long ago, that life did not begin or end within the parameters of his flesh, that he was a child of the universe, sewn seamlessly into the grand weaving of life, the very fabric of being. He was wide-awake, and wanted, and he would never sleep again.

Amá.

Mother.

Amá . . .

Roy opened his eyes and knew the room he was sitting in too well. It was not where he wanted to be. He closed his eyes and his hand at the same time, trying fruitlessly to capture the feeling, the word—to keep it, make it stay. And then he realized he had it, the word, and he couldn't forget it, no matter how desperately he suddenly wanted to. He had it, but it was empty, meaningless, and his muscles ached from lying on the floor, and the rug smelled bad, and the enduring certainty that had visited his blood only seconds before was illusory, was fading, was already gone.

Cheshire hid in the back of the ambulance under the gurney until she had counted seven thousand revolutions of the tire. She managed to take out the Quraci army EMT with the stun gun without moving from her position, and then pushed the gurney forward in order to leap out and dispatch the attendant medic and the armed guard. She glanced at the patient, but he was both unconscious and strapped to the gurney, so she let him be, turning her attention instead to a small metal supplies box that she used to smash in the window separating the ambulance back from the driver.

With lights and siren still in full effect, the ambulance pitched off the main road suddenly as Cheshire pressed the stun gun against the astonished driver's neck and zapped him where he sat. She crawled through the small opening, ignoring the cuts the shattered glass left on her hands and the back of her legs, reached across the unconscious driver to open the driver side door, and used both legs to kick him out of the cab. The ambulance was careening toward a rocky mountainside when she finally took control of the steering wheel and calmly brought the vehicle under control, leaving the lights flashing on top of the cab but silencing the blaring siren.

When first abducted from the prison, she had put all her energy into identifying the voice of her captors and tracking the location to which they brought her. They had pulled a heavy canvas bag over her head, effectively blinding her, but she had excellent hearing and an extraordinary sense of direction, and gave her full attention over to the task of memorization. Turning the ambulance to the east, she continued off road for three miles until she came to an abandoned aircraft hangar standing at the base of the same mountain range into which the ambulance had nearly plowed. She shut off the ambulance, let herself out, and walked around to the back to lock the medical bay from the outside before proceeding to investigate the hangar.

Once inside the dark, empty shed, Cheshire felt sure she was in the right place. Dust drifted up from the cement floor into infrequent shafts of light created by splits and tears in the tin structure frame, and the choking heat was exactly as she remembered it. To be positive, she spoke out loud into the high-ceilinged, vacant chamber to test for the distinct echo pattern she had noticed during her captivity.

"Hello."

Her own voice bounced back to her as it had during her brief internment. She was just turning to commence a methodical investigation of the space when another voice cut her fading echo short.

"Hey."

She whirled around to see Arsenal leaning in the doorway, covered from head to toe in dust and smiling at her softly. His crossbow seemed to be missing and a dark bruise on his forehead attested to her recent assault.

"You followed me!" she spat out, realizing the obviousness of the statement the moment she uttered it. In the half-light of the hangar, his eyes were gleaming with insolent pride. If she'd been capable of summoning lightning bolts, she would have smote him where he stood.

"You can't seriously think you've earned a 'get out of jail free' card, babe, or that I'm stupid enough to spring you without a reason." He spoke calmly and added a gentle shrug. "I got the feeling there was something you were hiding from me and figured I'd let you show me if you weren't gonna tell me." Still leaning against the door frame, he looked around the hangar with quiet curiosity. "So what is this? Where are we?"

"That's what I'm trying to figure out," Cheshire answered with a hint of anger still heating her voice. "I *was* contacted about the Abdul-Hakam assassination, if 'contacted' is the right word. Four army officers, one thug, and a private translator abducted me from the prison and brought me here. They wanted to know everything about how I had managed to steal the Russian warhead I used to bomb their country. I can only assume they did not have access to my debriefings." Without pausing, she glanced at him sideways and let her features settle into a frustrated frown. "Why do you *constantly* put yourself in situations where I have no choice but to hurt you?"

Roy flashed a grin. "Maybe I like it." Then, just as quickly, his expression mirrored hers, darkening into a frown. "Who were they, Chesh? Why were they questioning you?"

"I told you, I don't know." Cheshire looked around the empty hangar with a sneer. "My guess is it had something to do with the shipment I told you about—not so much the refinement technology itself as the timing of a Quraci ship docking in an American port. *You* do the math. Mostly they were interested in information on President Hatim. Discriminating information, for which they were willing to pay me, threaten me, cajole me, and smack me around a little." She looked up into Arsenal's eyes then, her brows slightly knotted. "These were Quracis, Roy. It's amazing that they did not kill me. I felt sure they would try, but I happened to have the information they wanted, pointed them in the right direction—and then that was it, they returned me to the prison."

Arsenal was frowning. "You said you gave them what they wanted? Dirt on Hatim?"

"I have no reason to protect him." Jade smiled slowly as she answered.

"What did you tell them? I mean, about Hatim. What did he do?"

He shifted his weight slightly from one booted foot to the other and Cheshire found her eyes wandering from his chest down to his thighs. Her smile widened.

"Roy, your naiveté really is one of your most charming qualities. As secretary of defense, he helped engineer the arms deal that allowed me to steal the nukes in the first place. His security policies at the time were, shall we say, conveniently lax. You know it's just physical, what we share, don't you?"

Arsenal's eyes flashed dangerously. "Don't change the subject, this is serious. You're accusing the current president of Qurac of being complicit in the bombing of his own country!"

"I'm not accusing anyone of anything, lover. I'm stating a fact. Two of them, actually. Acknowledge the other one."

Roy frowned. "That our bond is physical? That's where we really connect, yeah. But I have feelings for you, despite telling myself not to." He tore his gaze away from her to let his eyes comb the empty room. "Why did you want to come back here?"

"To track them, and kill them if I could. Whoever these monsters are, they're connected. Getting a prisoner in and out of a military penitentiary is no small feat. It takes a lot of skill or a lot of cachet . . ." Cheshire's eyes narrowed and she took a single step toward Arsenal, enough to get him to look her in the eye again. "Are you going to take me back to jail?" she asked.

"Me?" Arsenal straightened up to his full height and regarded her quietly. "I don't know, Chesh. I don't think so . . ."

Roy hadn't seen Ollie in slightly over four months (though, characteristically, Ollie would later insist that it was only one) when Green Arrow dropped in through the ceiling of Quon's attic apartment in Chinatown. Green Lantern was with him, using his alien power ring to convey them safely through the roof in a large green bubble, upping the element of surprise and avoiding any structural damage to the building. Ollie's left arm was in a sling, and it was clear to Roy that the heroes were not paying a social call.

Quon and his friend Samuel panicked, assuming they were about to be busted, as Roy froze on the window seat where he'd been perching, all the blood draining out of his face. He'd wished every night for Ollie to come back, but had never imagined that they wouldn't just run into each other one day at the apartment. Though the three boys were actually waiting for their friend Chucky to come back with a score, Roy still felt that he'd been caught red-handed. All his righteous anger and excuses evaporated like sweat, leaving him mortified and cold. For the first time since he'd met him, he was wishing Ollie away.

Ollie, hotheaded as always, was threatening to send Samuel to jail by the time Roy finally raised the courage to step up behind him.

"You plan to lock me up, too, Green Arrow?" he asked numbly, unsure whether the cramps in his gut as he stared at his mentor's back were from shame or the early stages of withdrawal.

Ollie whipped his head around to confront his ward.

"Speedy! I can't say I'm surprised to find *you* in this hole!"

"You're . . . not!?" Roy was perplexed. Was this an indictment, or some kind of admission of guilt on Ollie's part, some tiny understanding of the potential consequences of abandonment? Just for a moment, Roy let himself imagine Ollie throwing his arms around him, telling him that he'd missed him and would never leave him alone again, that everything would be okay. *I'm sorry, Roy. You're a good kid. I'm here to help you now . . .*

"Nah," Ollie continued, leaning in close. "When you

vanished I knew you had to be on the trail of the baddies! I figured you were playing undercover agent!"

Vanished? Roy hadn't been at the apartment for several days, but he'd hardly vanished. Ollie was the one who had dropped off the face of the earth. What did he think Roy had been *doing* the whole time he was gone?

The answer was obvious, and it made Roy's shoulders stiffen. Ollie hadn't been thinking about Roy at all.

"Sure," he answered quietly. "Secret-operator Speedy— that's me. I ought to try out for the funny papers . . ."

"Had any luck . . . I mean . . . have you learned who's *behind* the narcotics racket?"

Ollie had placed his hand on Roy's shoulder and Roy realized with a pang of guilt that he was trying to protect Roy's "undercover" identity within the drug ring. For a second, Roy wondered why he wasn't who Ollie thought he was—the kind of kid who would fill his spare time tracking down criminals by infiltrating their inner circles. The thought of getting closer to the supply line only made him hungrier for another hit.

"Not yet." He wished Green Lantern would use his ring to make the floor disappear beneath his feet, wished Quon would pick up one of the weapons his father had mounted onto a display rack on a nearby wall and shoot him where he stood.

"*I* can show you!" Quon, from the doorway, was insistent. Green Lantern was standing stoically behind him, blocking his and Samuel's exit, as Ollie turned toward the Great Frog bassist. "I don't dig my habit, man! I wanna see the pushers behind bars!"

Violence swelled in Roy as he watched Quon and

Ollie. He doubted Quon's sincerity, which made him worried for Ollie and Hal, but at the same time, he experienced a terrible swell of jealousy as Quon so easily stepped in where he himself had failed.

"You can locate them for us?" Ollie was asking.

Quon was resolute, eager to please. "No problem!"

Roy was about to protest when Ollie turned toward him again, once more placing his good hand on his ward's shoulder. Roy wanted to ask what had happened to his left arm, wanted to know where he and Hal had been, what they'd seen. He wanted to know how they'd ended up tracking down drug dealers in Star City, but he couldn't make himself stop shaking long enough to form a question or a warning.

"You're looking pretty pale, fella!" Ollie was saying. "No need for you to come along . . ."

Of course there isn't! Roy thought hotly. *There's never any need for me anywhere!*

"Sit tight, I'll give you a play-by-play of the action tonight."

Roy nodded slowly, a tremendous headache thundering through his skull as he struggled to kick his brain back into high gear. Quon, under duress, might take them to Browden's suppliers, men Roy had met only once. The suppliers were rash, violent, and well connected . . . Roy wouldn't have gone anywhere near them if his need had not become so intense. As it was, his life had become a full-time compromise between inescapable external risk and deliberate self-destruction. That first night, heroin had delivered him into a new landscape of concord and relief. His need to get back there was physical as well as emotional, every cell in his body equally committed to return. *Ch'ínílí* was just a heartache, Ollie's mansion a promise unfulfilled, but heroin felt like home. He would never get warm, never get *right* if he couldn't get back there.

That door, though, had locked behind him after the first trip—even shooting up daily for the past three weeks he hadn't come near that initial bliss. Somewhere in the back of his foggy head, he knew that his efforts to return to the belly of the beast were pitiable and doomed, but he felt he had no choice. Finally, after seventeen years of searching, he had found a place where he belonged.

And he had been cast from there, too.

"Anything you say, Green Arrow," he mumbled.

Green Lantern used his power ring to create a bubble large enough to carry himself, Green Arrow, Quon, and Samuel, and then the heroes left the same way they'd come in, defying physics and leaving no trace of their presence, except maybe for Roy himself; useless and left behind.

He patted the pockets of his brown leather vest— Ollie's vest, actually, but one he had taken a liking to—for change before heading out to see if he could beat Hal and Ollie to the airfield where Quon would probably take them. He wasn't sure how much they understood about the world they were about to find themselves moving through. A room full of users too sick with need to see straight was one thing, but the suppliers never took the drugs they distributed and would not be so easy to quell. If Ollie got hurt . . . Roy put the awful thought out of his head and forced himself to hurry. Just because Dick had sent him home early from the past three Teen Titan cases he'd tried to assist with didn't mean he'd stopped being a hero. Just because he was slowly killing himself didn't mean he'd stopped caring about the people he loved.

Out on the street, Roy realized he had a serious disadvantage. Hal could fly and fashion lifts of green light to take Ollie with him. Roy didn't even have a car. He'd left his drum kit at Mark's and hocked Dinah's Mustang months ago. He'd have to take the bus.

On the ride across town, he thought about Ollie and felt another hot wave of embarrassment. Maybe it wasn't too late. Maybe he could get clean before Ollie ever even noticed anything was wrong. Of course, that would mean getting Dinah's car back, and the stereo and the TV set and—Jesus, had he really done this?—the leftover G.A. arrows he'd traded for drugs. Squirming on his vinyl-covered bus seat, Roy pressed his fists against his eyes and tried to keep himself from sobbing. He knew he was in over his head and no matter how hard he tried, he couldn't think of any way to set things right. The despair filled him like muggy air, permeating his every pore and making it hard to breathe. The only thing that kept him from curling up right there in the back of the bus and never getting up again was his determination to help Ollie and Hal.

He got off at a stop in front of the private airstrip where Browden had sent him once to make a pickup. Cop cars were already racing toward one of the hangars, which was not a good sign—if Green Lantern was still on his feet, he would have been able to take any number of suspects into custody without assistance. His head throbbing in protest, Roy ran to intercept the police, pointing them toward an office on the other side of the airfield, a tip they accepted gratefully.

The scene inside the hangar was as he had feared. Quon and Samuel were nowhere to be found, but Ollie and Hal were both out cold on the tarmac, covered in powdered heroin.

Roy had seen Ollie unconscious before, but the stillness of the large body, so animated in consciousness, always disturbed him. Realizing that Green Lantern was their best hope for a quick exit, he knelt beside Hal and gave the unconscious hero a brisk backslap across the face.

"Snap out of it!"

Green Lantern mumbled something nearly incoherent about being warm and comfortable as Roy tried to heave him to his feet.

"If you don't use your power ring to fly us away, we'll all be rotting in jail soon! I faked out the police, but they won't *remain* faked, G.L.!"

Still looking groggy, Hal swayed unsteadily on his feet as Roy pressed him against one of the hangar walls for support. He couldn't believe how clearly he was thinking suddenly, the need to help and impress Ollie suddenly stronger, even, than the jones that was gnawing its way up his spinal chord from his stomach to his brain.

"I'll bet you *can't* make the ring work!" he taunted, trying to goad Hal into action. Hal protested blearily and pointed his ring at the far wall. As Roy understood it, the alien gift was powered by Hal's imagination, forming in tangible green light anything Hal could visualize. And there, at least forty feet tall, a new Green Lantern shimmered into being, this version sickened by the heroin, twisted and hideous, a slavering, hungry monster that grabbed Hal and Roy and the still unconscious Ollie in his disfigured gloves, intent on devouring everything in its path. Roy was transfixed by the image, recognizing his own incurable famine in Hal's manifested inner demon. Still heavily dosed, Hal finally managed to protect himself, Roy, and Ollie in a simple green bubble that floated them back to the apartment, but Roy shivered during the entire ride back, trying to picture what he might look like if he could make a projection of his own sickened psyche with Hal's ring. Hal had only been dosed the one time, but Roy had been using for months. Would the inner Speedy be forty feet tall, or one hundred, or large enough to crush the entire city? Or would he be withering away, a tiny thing, less than a centimeter in height, roaring and stamping his minuscule feet until Ollie lifted a boot and squashed him like a bug?

Once on his own couch, Ollie groaned back into consciousness and complained vociferously about how awful he felt while Hal sat across from him pondering why anyone would ever voluntarily use anything so awful as heroin. No one seemed to notice the shape the apartment was in. The drawers in Ollie's room were still open from when Roy had rifled through them looking for loose change and valuables to sell. The sink was overflowing with dishes from the few times he'd eaten. His room was blanketed wall to wall with discarded clothing, including his Speedy uniform and some of Ollie's clothes that he'd worn in his mentor's absence and failed to return. The bathroom was a jumble of mildewed towels, urine and vomit stains visible around the toilet rim. The living room was still covered in the pillows and blankets he'd dragged from the two bedrooms when the band had crashed on his floor the previous weekend. Dust covered every visible surface and half the electronics were missing, pawned for drugs.

Roy did his best to tidy up as the two super heroes moaned in the living room, but it was largely hopeless. Fortunately, Ollie wasn't in a critical mood. When at last he did stand up, it was to compliment Roy for having rescued him and Hal. Roy didn't want his secret anymore. If he had saved them, he wanted to be saved right back.

"I still don't understand why people want to poison themselves with heroin . . . pills . . . the whole sick bag!" Hal reiterated.

Roy sank down onto an ottoman beside him and tried to unlock his tongue.

"Maybe I can throw some light on the reason, G.L." It was hard to tell if Ollie was listening or not, but Roy could tell he had Hal's full attention, so he continued. "Say a guy has someone he respects, you know—looks up to. Like an older man. And say the older man leaves . . . chases around the country and gets involved with other people, kind of ignoring his young friend. Then, the guy might need a"—Roy faltered, knowing no words for his pain—"a substitute for that friendship, for feeling *included*, you know? And he might see it in smack . . ."

He snuck a sideways glance at Ollie, worried that he was being entirely too obvious, but Ollie was already back on his feet heading toward the door.

"Gee, Speedy," he said, laughing. "All your tale lacks is violin music! I'm touched." He turned to Hal with a wink. "At least, my stomach is. Because every time I hear a sob story I almost lose my lunch!"

Hal peered over his shoulder at Roy one last time,

frowning softly, but followed Ollie out the door without saying anything. Roy didn't know if they were off to chase after more bad guys or if Ollie was just walking Hal out, but he could already hear his words to Hal ringing in his head, becoming increasingly insufficient and absurd. It had been over twelve hours since his last hit and the pain was becoming unbearable. Flushed with heat, sweating and sick, he remembered the resolution he'd made on the way to Mark's house the first time he'd played with Great Frog and realized it was less foolish than he had initially assumed. His destiny was catching up with him again, he could feel it. Ollie was home but no more present than he'd been when he was gone. This time, if he was going to be cast out again, at least it would be because of something he had actually done. Maybe that was the blessing of darkness . . . one dismal chance to master his own fate through active self-negation.

Roy got out his works and sat down at the kitchen table to prepare the fix. He had just finished pulling the liquid drug into the syringe when he heard Ollie's footsteps in the living room, his voice cheerful and gregarious.

"Speedy! I'm gonna cook up some of my special 'scorch your mouth' chili! Can I interest you in a bowl?"

Roy remained seated at the kitchen table, shaking, knowing that it was in fear of Ollie's reaction and not just because of his withdrawal. He rolled up his left sleeve, tied off, and felt Ollie's shadow fall across his back.

"Oh, dear God!" Ollie gasped, sounding more shocked than Roy ever remembered hearing him before about anything. "You *are* on drugs! You're really a junkie!"

"Who did you *think* I was talking about?" Roy replied quietly, lifting the needle.

Ollie's reaction was immediate and, in some small way, Roy told himself, protective. Still dressed in his Green Arrow uniform, Ollie backhanded Roy right off the kitchen chair, shouting in anger and fear.

"You're a lousy junkie!" Ollie was raging. "No better than the *rest* of those sniveling punks!"

Roy lost the needle and hit the cold kitchen floor with a mixture of relief and desperation.

"If that's the way you see it, Arrow." He felt the sting of the blow throbbing on his jaw and ducked as Ollie hurled the small vial of heroin at the wall behind him. "Go ahead, hit me!" Roy prompted from the linoleum. "Maybe that'll make you *feel* better!"

"Maybe you're right!" Ollie fumed, throwing a plate he had grabbed randomly from the washboard. Roy struggled to get back on his feet.

"Want to do it again? Or have you proven to yourself that you're stronger than us weaklings?" Roy knew he was provoking his mentor but he didn't care. Ollie's anger was terrifying and fiery, but it was also focused and interactive. Roy knew how to fight. He'd fight all night if it would make Ollie stay. "A big man like you doesn't need drugs, does he? You get high on your own self-righteousness!"

"Shut up!"

Roy was on his feet, ready to weather another blow, but instead Ollie hugged himself suddenly, pulling his good arm over the injured one as he reined in his physical temper. He turned his head sharply away from where Roy was standing. "I'm not *interested* in *excuses*! I'm not interested in *you*! Not anymore!"

Roy found himself leaning against the doorjamb for support, staring out into the small round entryway, his back to Ollie, whose back was to him. The heat that had been eating him alive died out, leaving him suddenly freezing and unendurably sober.

I'm not interested in you. Not anymore.

"Just . . . get out!"

Roy realized his mistake immediately. So he'd had a hand in it this time, he'd actually done something that warranted the abandonment. It didn't make him any less alone.

"Don't worry," he managed, forcing himself not to look back. "I'm going."

He made it out into the street and two blocks east before the withdrawal took him again, driving him to his knees. He couldn't figure out if he was too hot or too cold, his guts burning while he shivered and started dry heaving into the gutter.

Somehow, he made it back to his feet, wandering blindly, moving just to move. He decided he needed to get back to Chinatown and dedicated his entire being to that single purpose. Twice he found himself staggering in the street, car headlights bearing down on him seconds before a deafening squeal of brakes, a blasting horn, and an angry voice sent him racing to the far curb. He began to talk to himself, singing the Blessing Way in a dry, flat voice, struggling near tears to remember all the words.

"*Neya*, now, Darkness, *'iya* . . . He comes upon me with blessing, *wo* . . . Behind him, from there, *ye, Sa'ah naaghéi* . . . He comes upon me with blessing, *wo* . . . Before him, from there, *ye, Bik'eh hózhó* He . . . He . . ."

When the neon signs ceased to be readable, he realized he had made it to Chinatown, but could no longer remember why he had wanted to go there. He had begun to scratch at his arms somewhere around midtown and now looked down to see his freckled flesh raw and bleeding.

He hated the freckles.

"He comes upon me with blessing, *wo!* People, my relatives, *yowa lana,* I have come up on blessing! People, my relatives, *ya,* blessed, *na'eye l ana heya 'eye, holaghei!*"

He stepped back into a trash can and fell over backward, smacking his head on the brick wall of an alley that smelled like urine and stale beer. His hands began to tremble violently and he realized he wasn't going to be able to get back up. The will that had carried him to Chinatown had to be utilized—all of it—to accomplish a negative. There was nothing he had to do anymore except *not* take more of the drug. He curled up into a ball on the cold cement and promised himself that if he could just get through the night, nothing else in the entire rest of his life would ever be quite as bad again.

"I don't know, Chesh. I don't think so . . ."

Arsenal watched Cheshire carefully, aware that she was about to bolt. Outside, the desert sun continued to beat against the tin hangar; inside, it almost felt like a sweat lodge. Even Cheshire—whose temperature generally ran subnormal, her skin enchantingly cool whenever he put his feverish hands on her—was perspiring as she watched him and calculated her odds of escape.

"That's right," she murmured, frowning. "You won't

have to take me in. You already told me, you're working with a partner."

"Correct."

It seemed to Arsenal that Cheshire retained her composure, but he could feel himself jump slightly as Batman's rough voice suddenly echoed through the hangar. It gave him a headache even trying to think about how the Dark Knight had found them.

Batman stepped out of the shadows and squared off with an increasingly tense Cheshire.

"Where did you send them to collect evidence against Hatim?"

Arsenal watched as Cheshire glared at Batman warily.

"The paper trail in Abu Dhabi would have been obliterated by the explosion, so I suggested that they track the arms deal back to a former Soviet agent working out of Yekaterinburg. I did steal the warhead, so there would be no reason for the Russians to lie about the initial deal that made that possible. Evidence disgracing Hatim is easy enough to find if one knows where to look, though I also mentioned that it would not be enough to legally indict him. That did not seem to concern them."

"Is that when you gave them the contact protocol for Deathstroke?"

Cheshire's frown deepened and she stuck her chin out at Batman accusatorily. "What are you talking about? Deathstroke never came up. That was an entirely different occasion."

"Did your contact know about the ship leaving Qurac?" For the life of him, Arsenal couldn't think what that had to do with anything, but Batman sounded very serious when he asked.

In response, Cheshire gave him a single nod.

Arsenal crossed his arms in front of his chest and tried not to look bewildered. "You were abducted more than once?"

"No," Cheshire snapped. "Of course not." Her posture changed, stiffening as she wiped a bead of sweat off her forehead with the palm of her hand. "I'm not going to tell you anything else unless you promise you won't return me to that hellhole of a prison."

Batman moved so fast Arsenal couldn't track it. One minute he was standing two feet in front of Cheshire, and the next minute he was behind her, executing an expert choke hold. Cheshire struggled fiercely but couldn't free herself.

"You're a prisoner of the nation of Qurac," Batman said quietly into her left ear. "Your fate is out of my hands."

As Batman held her, Cheshire turned her eyes to Arsenal, a hint of pleading in them. Roy swallowed and looked down at his boots.

"I strongly suggest you continue to answer my questions," Batman continued.

"Go to hell," Cheshire whispered back hoarsely.

There was a quick struggle, most of it obscured from Roy's view by Batman's cape, and then suddenly, as Batman continued to hold her, Cheshire slumped forward in his arms, held upright only by his strength.

Arsenal felt panic beating inside his chest like hummingbird wings. "What happened!? Why is she—!?"

"Antidote," Batman instructed. Roy heard the metal click of cuffs and then Batman hoisted Cheshire the rest of the way up into his arms, moving to cuff her ankles.

"*Now*," he growled as Arsenal continued staring at him in confusion.

Roy shook off his shock and snatched the poison antidote out of his gauntlet as he ran toward Batman. He pulled the cap off with his teeth as he ran, spit it out on the dusty floor, and then stopped in front of Batman with a frown. The only accessible flesh was Batman's strong jaw and something wouldn't let Roy plunge a syringe into Batman's face.

"Not me, her!"

Batman had Cheshire in wrist and ankle cuffs, but managed to turn her left forearm toward Roy, displaying the bleeding fingernail slash she had apparently inflicted upon herself. Arsenal didn't hesitate to plunge the syringe into her right bicep, pumping the antidote under her skin.

"Why would she do this?" he agonized, more to himself than to Batman.

"Don't fool yourself into thinking it's anything more than a desperate attempt to rearrange the odds in her favor," Batman answered darkly. "It would be much easier for her to escape from an inexperienced medical team post-treatment than from us."

"But what if no one got to her on time? She could die!"

Batman answered quickly and with so much conviction that Roy felt his shoulders relax. "Not on *my* watch."

The Dark Knight began carrying Cheshire back out toward the ambulance as Arsenal stood in the middle of the hangar, catching his breath. He realized that Batman had anticipated Cheshire's reaction to being recaptured before Roy had even gone in to speak with her, which meant that he'd also guessed that Roy might attempt to break her out.

Arsenal exhaled slowly, squared his shoulders, and turned to follow his interim partner out of the hangar. He could still feel his heart pounding and knew it would be difficult to regain physical equilibrium in the heat. Sweat trickled down the back of his neck, soaking the armor that clung to his back.

Batman always seemed to know what people were going to do a solid fifteen moves before they themselves did. Stepping out into the blinding Quraci sunshine, Roy wanted to ask him for more practical advice. Forget his proclivities in battle and interrogation—what Roy wanted to know was what would finally become of his own broken heart.

He couldn't remember Green Lantern finding him in the alley behind the trash cans, and only vaguely recalled trying to explain to Hal why, in his case, warnings about the risks involved in drug use had fallen on such deaf ears. His answer had been a good one according to Hal, encompassing the societal failures of war, racism, corporate greed, and indeed the entire generation gap, but all Roy remembered telling him was that the Star City drug runners operated from the south shore off a boat called the *Lady Billie*.

And he remembered Dinah standing in the doorway of a residence he hadn't even realized she had; a warm, orderly one-bedroom apartment that she welcomed him into without hesitation after Hal literally dropped him off on her doorstep.

Closing the door behind Hal, Dinah looked Roy up and down and then cocked her head to one side.

"Um, forgive me if this isn't entirely the best timing, but . . . you wouldn't happen to know where my *car* is, would you?"

Roy tried to swallow but found his throat had gone so dry that the attempt was painful.

"I . . . hocked it," he confessed, his voice low and whispery. "I'm really sorry."

"Oh, my God," Dinah spoke energetically and her real-ness made Roy want to cry. In her own home, she was far from the abstract love interest of his dashing guardian, she was a dynamic, unpredictable stranger who Roy wished he had the right to say he knew. "What did you get for it!?"

"Uh . . ." the question took Roy by surprise but he wracked his brain for the answer as he groped toward her living-room couch. "It was, you know, for drugs. But like . . . eight hundred? If you converted it back to cash?"

Dinah let out a disbelieving gasp, one fist resting against her hip. "It was in *mint condition*. Did you even *bargain*?"

Roy had been moving toward the dark red couch; a solid, soft focal point not too far off in the distance. Finally laying a hand on the back of it, he noticed its color was picked up by horizontal pattern lines in a small Navajo saddle blanket being used as a throw rug on the floor in front of it. Her living room smelled like jasmine. Tears began to run down his face.

Dinah's tone softened. "I'm sorry . . . this is kind of embarrassing, but . . . Green Arrow, um, Oliver . . . he always calls you Speedy. I'm afraid I don't actually know your real name."

Roy was shaking so hard with withdrawal pain he could barely speak, but continued to make the effort with the intention of honoring her kindness.

"S'okay," he stammered. "Not sure—he does—either." Without deciding to, he slumped down on the rug and ran his hand slowly across the woven wool. "It's Roy. Roy Harper."

Dinah crouched down next to him, peering into his face and then, seeming to deem him safe, gently pushed a fall of red hair off his forehead. "How can I help you, Roy? You look really . . . sick."

Roy dropped his head between his knees and tried to ride the waves of nausea swelling over and over again in his stomach. The addiction was relentless, mocking his resistance with whispered promises of relief and infuriated, terrorizing threats delivered to his nervous system simultaneously.

"Only—two ways to h-help *me*, lady," he gasped, trying not to be transported back to *Ch'iníli* by the intensely familiar smell of the rug beneath his shins. "Get me more heroin . . ." The very word on his tongue made him shiver. "Or *shoot* me."

Dinah rocked back on her heels and folded her arms around her knees as she regarded him shrewdly. "I see. But I'm afraid I don't approve of drugs *or* guns. Are there any other options?"

Roy wanted to bury himself in her suddenly and didn't know how to get past the boundary of his own crawling skin. He needed her warmth but had no idea how to reach it. Crouching six inches from him, she might as well have been fourteen galaxies away. Having a new desire bruise on the surface of the already too-dominant need for drugs was more than Roy could bear.

"Forget it!" he roared, turning away from her, angrily swiping at the tear that had been leaking from his eyes since the first moment he had seen the rug. "Just leave me alone! Don't you *get* it? You *can't* help me! *No one* can! No one *will*! *No one ever will!*" Roy felt his voice catch in his throat and realized his face was getting wetter, the despair still building in him, releasing in an angry flood. "No one ever will and I didn't do anything wrong! Ask 'em! Ask my *parents* what I did! Ask *Raymond!* Any of the *Dine'é*!"

Feeling his insides dissolve into hot liquid, Roy groaned, struggled to his feet, and lurched toward Dinah's kitchen. Grabbing the counter for support, he started to dry heave uncontrollably into the sink.

"Ask *Ollie!*" he gasped once he finally stopped retching. He was so furious and so terrified that discharging the words felt just as unavoidable as the heaves. "Ask Ollie! Ask Ollie what I did to deserve being—being—" The chills that were still prickling through his back and shoulders tortured his tender stomach with shivers he couldn't control, but at the same time heat was flushing through his face and circling his skull in a tight, burning band. His sweat felt oily to him, dense and noxious.

He stuck his head under the faucet and turned the cold water on full blast but could not find relief. After a few seconds, he shut off the water and pressed his shaking hands to his face. "Something's wrong with me, Dinah. Something gotta be wrong. I'm untouchable, I'm worthless, I—"

The shivering finally forced him to his knees below the sink. Dinah had followed him into the kitchen and knelt down beside him again. He turned to her, sobbing.

"Can you *see* it!? Is it *visible*? Some kind of *force field* or *warning sign* or—?" Gently, Dinah placed a hand on his shoulder, empathy evident in her warm blue eyes. "Why does everyone keep *leaving* me!?"

"Oh, honey . . ."

He felt her arms circling his shoulders and threw his own gratefully around her neck, falling against her helplessly, unable to stop sobbing.

"And now . . . now I *did* screw up. And I have to—*beat* this—*alone*. I *have* to." Some of Dinah's dark hair had fallen over Roy's head, forming a soft curtain, and his burning forehead was pressed into one side of her perfumed neck. "Hafta—show *Ollie* I can—be *good* enough . . ."

Dinah had begun to gently rock him, and he closed his eyes tightly as he clung to her on the floor, giving himself over to the gentle rhythm of her swaying body.

"It's okay, Roy," she said softly. "It's okay . . ."

"Everyone lets me down," he whispered into the warm, yielding flesh of her throat. "I just get *thrown out* again and again and again and no one's ever gonna stay when I *need* them. No one ever stays and I'm just so scared if I *try* again, I'll—I'll—ah, God, *please*—"

He struggled back up into a sitting position suddenly, placing his sweaty hands against her cheeks and forcing himself to meet her eyes despite the physical pain that the simple act of intimacy cost him.

"Dinah—puh—please . . ." That they were practically strangers meant nothing. Shuddering in her arms, he tried to piece together what he knew about her, but had to give up. It was just a collection of details: her fishnet stockings and blonde wig, her martial arts prowess, her beautiful apartment, her cool car that he'd hocked for not enough drug money, her willingness to let the teenage ward of her boyfriend into her home in the middle of the night and sit with him on her kitchen floor while he detoxed . . . What he needed was her warmth, her sympathy, her humanity. With the last leap of faith he thought his tattered spirit could bear, he tried one more time to find a safe place to land. " . . . Help me . . ."

"You're going to be all right, sweetheart," she murmured into his hair. It made Roy cry even harder, because he desperately wanted to believe her, but could no longer imagine how what she said could ever possibly come true.

Cheshire was conscious and asymptomatic for poisoning by the time Batman and Arsenal got her safely back to the prison. She was given a new room with increased security—a fact Roy felt slightly guilty about since he was the one who had actually compromised her initial cell—and was refusing to speak with anyone. She looked angry and, more unusually, tired.

Arsenal stood outside the steel doors of her cell watching the back of her head and flexing his jaw. Batman had felt confident enough to approach the Quraci military directly while returning her to incarceration, and the obvious pain and hatred displayed in the faces of the guards when they handled her made Roy's throat tighten.

They had every right to hate her. She'd killed over a million people and there were very few individuals who would even argue in defense of her life. Roy was smart enough to know that some of his feelings for her were a matter of transference, but that didn't make them any less painful. The ways in which she had been forsaken in the raging river of life were so unmistakable to him that he couldn't stop forgiving her for the horrible places in which she'd finally washed up.

"I'm sorry," he said finally, turning to leave.

"What are *you* sorry for?"

Her back was still to the door of her cell, but her voice was soft and clear. He turned toward the small barred window that allowed him to speak to her and pressed the palms of both hands against the steel door.

"I'm sorry that . . . that I can't save you."

"Save me?" She turned to glare over her shoulder at him. "Save me from *what*, Roy? This prison? The final judgment of the Quraci people? Myself?"

Roy swallowed and held her gaze. "Yeah, all those things. And also, I guess, from the moment when I'll have to leave."

"Oh, my God." She rose to her feet, astonishment animating her cool features. "How do I make you leave *sooner*?"

Roy shook his head. "Like it or not, me and Lian are the only two people on this planet who give a rat's ass about you, Chesh. And I think . . . no, I *know* . . . that no one can survive without someone else watching their back— or at least, you know, seeing them with some kind of recognition and compassion, authenticating their experience of themselves. And I just wish I could keep doing that for you . . . that's all."

He started to step away from the door again but she came at her side of it fast, teeth bared.

"You're wrong!" she shouted, pounding the cell wall with her fist. "Naive! No one's *ever* had my back and I've survived. I'm still here! I'm still here whether you see me or not!"

"You sure?" He stepped away from the door and frowned to himself for a moment before inhaling deeply and turning toward the cell-block exit. "It was nice to see you, Jade," he said quietly, without looking at her. Then his green eyes were searching her face again, as if memorizing it, and though she wanted to turn away from his gaze she forced herself to return his stare with studied indifference. A maturity she wasn't familiar with tightened the lines of his face as he turned away from her for the last time and walked down the hall to the guard.

She was turning back toward her new cot when she noticed a small piece of glossy paper on the barred ledge of the door window through which they had spoken. She understood what it was before she reached for it, but picked it up to examine nonetheless.

It was a small photograph of Lian, her dark hair pulled back in a ponytail, one flowered, purple plastic barrette holding additional bangs off the right side of her little face, the bridge of her nose sprinkled ever so lightly with freckles despite the tea-stained tint of her perfect skin. Her eyes were dark and wise and looked so much like Jade's own that there was no mistaking the connection. The girl's smile, though, was her father's; an open, friendly, self-satisfied grin. She looked, even to Cheshire, like a happy, well-adjusted, intelligent young girl, someone who it would be a pleasure to know. Cheshire crumpled the picture up in one hand and tossed it toward the cell room's sink.

She managed to ignore it for forty whole minutes before she felt compelled to pick it up again and smooth it out. Carefully, she tucked it under her pillow.

Roy stayed with Dinah for two and a half weeks, sleeping on her couch, sweeping her hardwood floors, doing the dishes, and spending at least four hours a day outside so that she wouldn't feel exasperated by his presence sooner than he could bear for her to ask him to leave. She never actually asked him anything of the sort, instead providing him with clean towels and a spare key and remarking lightly once or twice that he was better company than she had expected. They ate dinner together and sometimes watched movies on her small black and white TV at night, avoiding talk of drugs, Ollie, or the vigilante heroing she still crept out to attend to every night. She would wake him up in the mornings bundled up in a thick, sky-blue robe, excited to tell him over coffee about the strange dreams she had during the little bit of time she had slept. He would make her breakfast while she read the paper, and tell her Navajo stories and legends after dinner on the nights she didn't rush out the second it became dark. When Roy finally decided to leave, it was because he was beginning to understand just how badly he wanted to stay.

Speechless with gratitude, he simply whispered "thanks," kissed her on the cheek, and let himself out after breakfast much as he had done on all the previous days. He had been gone for over six hours by the time she found his spare key and the offering he had left on her bedside table: a beautiful, elaborate dream catcher he had secretly made for her during his long afternoons in a park a few blocks from her building. Dinah was stunned by the gift, both because it was gorgeously crafted out of items he had managed to coax from the hidden natural world of Star City—vine maple twigs, woven pine needles, the centers of black walnuts meticulously carved into thin, gleaming beads, and snowy white egret feathers he had somehow found near a local estuary—and because he had obviously worked on it for days without any knowledge whatsoever of the rich, inveterate tradition of little boys leaving magical found objects for their mothers in spontaneous expressions of appreciation and adoration.

Roy figured he was clean by his twentieth birthday, but he couldn't quite be sure. What he did know, irrefutably, was that it had been nineteen days since his last hit, and that the desire for another one was never going to go away. He applied the entire force of his will toward avoiding that particular temptation and let the rest of his life just drift.

He worked on and off with the Teen Titans, but they knew about his drug history and frequently treated him with cautious suspicion. Grateful not to be ejected outright, he didn't care. When Robin frowned and told him he'd better sit a particular case out, he merely shrugged and left their headquarters.

Great Frog he quit outright, and Hal helped set him up with a government job with the Federal Drug Enforcement Agency, which soon led to work at the Central Bureau of Intelligence and the government-run Checkmate, where he worked as a sharpshooter and a field agent "knight." Roy hated being a soldier, but he was good at it. He was nonchalant and reasonably obedient in the field, having no real opinion about most of the top-secret missions Checkmate sent him out on. The other soldiers enjoyed the lighthearted mischief he arranged for them after hours and took comfort in his unflappable calm, though stories did circulate about his prior drug use and the absurd rumors that he had once been a super hero. Most of the men in Checkmate would have called themselves his friends, but Roy called them merely friendly. He made it a policy never to lie about himself and his history, but he was also an expert at deflecting conversations away from the revelatory. He avoided lethal force whenever possible, and only deliberately killed a man once, under orders from Sergeant Steel, and in an effort to protect another soldier, with a shot no one else could have made. That he had no future and no personal ambitions of his own was irrelevant, even encouraged, by the government for whom he worked. He was slowly sinking into the kind of fraternal anonymity that only soldiers endure, and like the very best of them, he was soon more committed to the safety of his unit than to defense of his own increasingly trivial life. In fleeting moments of self-awareness, he laughed softly to himself, realizing that he was a hero all over again, but now one defined by a valor borne of self-negation rather than self-creation.

By the time he found himself in Japan on an undercover mission for Checkmate in the city of Sendai, he hadn't felt anything genuinely spark his interest in close to two years. That was part of why Cheshire was such a surprise to him. She woke him up.

She was the first thing he noticed when he walked through the door. The suffocating heat of too many people sitting too close, the sweet, sticky smell of steamed bun and pork, and the woman in the corner: long-legged, black-haired, lipsticked, obscenely gorgeous, and alone. He stood in line for food, was pegged as a foreigner and charged too much, paid for it with a sigh, took his tray in large Western hands, and crossed the bamboo matted floor.

"You alone on purpose?" he asked her. "Or is this just another example of there being no justice in the world?"

Watching her eyes sweep over the length of his body, he realized that she was not necessarily Japanese. Though her skin and hair coloring was Asian, she had vivid green eyes, not unlike his, and there was also something European and angular in the structure of her beautiful face. He fought to ignore his jet lag and exhaustion as she smiled slightly and looked back down at her tea.

"No English?" he asked, sitting down in the chair across from her. It was too small for him and he hunched over the table almost comically. Her eyes flashed into his and he felt his smile broadening across his face as his entire body stiffened with interest. "No problem."

Overcome by hunger, he stopped talking long enough to raise his bowl toward his mouth and use the chopsticks in his left hand to shovel rice and spicy beef into his mouth with gusto. She was smiling as she watched him eat.

"Beauty speaks a language all its own," he continued, still grinning, his mouth full of food.

"Oh," she groaned, leaning in closer. "And you were

doing so well. That first line about purpose and justice—
that was pretty good. But 'Beauty speaks a language all
its own'?—I know I'm beautiful. Don't you have anything more interesting to tell me?"

He stopped, stunned by her silky voice and her sophis-
ticated syntax, and then he swallowed, threw his head
back, and laughed.

"Ouch! Two points home team! I guess I should just
crawl off now and go lick my wounds . . ."

"No," she said with a smile. "Let me." Had he ever
truly been in love before, he might have recognized the
feeling right then. As it was, what he recognized was the
potential for calamity.

He had just wanted lunch, and shelter from the rain.
Her exotic beauty and sharp wit were nearly as out of place
in the small restaurant as his red hair and the gun in his
hip holster. He sat back and felt his jaw shift as he watched
her look down at the table and dab at some spilled tea
with her napkin, her long, red fingernails glistening under
the muted light of the ceiling lanterns.

Whether or not she was the woman he had been looking for his whole life, she was almost certainly the woman
he'd been looking for for the past three weeks.

When she looked up again she was frowning, and Roy,
staring hard, guessed that she'd just arrived at the same
conclusion. The woman had to know she was being
hunted. She put her hands down on the table suddenly,
tapping her talonlike fingernails against the blond wood
as her eyes darted to the exposed skin of his throat. He
shifted and moved his hand so that it was resting lightly
on his belt, his eyes watching her chest as it rose and fell.

Her eyes were cold.

He didn't blink.

Her breath was held.

He stayed completely still. He wondered if poison hurt like heroin withdrawal, and then whether or not he would be able to bear shooting her at so close a range. He desperately wanted to kiss her mouth, felt he'd do anything just for the chance to press his body against hers. Checkmate wanted her, but so what? They couldn't possibly want her half as much as he did right then. Besides, what were they gonna do if he didn't bring her in right away? Fire him?

There were, Roy realized, advantages to having nothing to live for.

"Okay . . ." he said, and his body shifted again, both hands on the table. He was close and wide open, a reckless gleam in his eyes, and she rewarded his trust by relaxing her hands and sliding forward on her seat slightly, her mouth curling up into a smile. "Lick away."

She led him to a small house, crowded amid many others, in the outskirts of Sendai. It was just one room with a large mattress on the floor, covered in embroidered linen, a dark, lacquered dresser in one corner, and a washbasin in the other, but it suited their purpose just fine. Outside, the rain dripped from the bare, spindly branches of hundreds of zelkova trees and beaded on the still-green leaves of the maidenhairs. They didn't talk, except for groans and shouts and whispers that were sometimes jokes and sometimes prayers. He was confident in his skill and took his time, pleasantly surprised by how powerfully aroused she seemed to be and her utter lack of inhibition. He did everything he knew, and when he ran out of experience and she was not yet fully transported he made things up, just like that, easy as a river by a mesa under mountains. Her body intoxicated him. He would later learn that she had done things he could not even imagine, but that first afternoon she didn't mention them. They had not been amusing and had not pleased her. And what he did—it was, it did.

They had arrived at the small house at two-thirty in the afternoon and didn't come up for air until eleven that night. Lying naked on his back, sweat-drenched and laughing with pleasure and exhaustion, he announced that he was once again starving. She smiled and rose and pulled a green silk dress over her head, not bothering with washing or with underwear.

"Goddamn, you're gorgeous," he sighed from the bed.

"I like your smell on me," she said. "I hope they can smell it outside. Stay here. I will get you food."

"It's the middle of the night. I don't think anyone's makin' goyza anymore, hon."

"You hunger. And I will feed you."

He struggled up to his elbows and regarded her intently.

"Hold on a sec. I'll come with."

"You will stay."

"No, really."

"It is too late for me to be seen outside with you."

"Oh. Well. You sure?"

That didn't sound right to him—Sendai was a fairly modern city with a large student population—but he shrugged and settled back down on the bed. "Okay, don't be gone long. You need any money or anything?"

She turned to him so fast his hand twitched. Her lip was curled into a snarl and her eyes were flashing. "You dare!? You dare!?"

"Hey-hey, whoa. Take it easy. I just meant—"

"You cannot pay for this! You could not afford it! You could not afford me!"

"N-no. Calm down. You misunderstand. The food. I meant for the food."

Her shoulders dropped suddenly and her face emptied of all expression. She had frightened him. Angry, she had reminded him of death—intriguing and unavoidable but something you wanna stay real the hell far away from. Swallowing the apprehension, he scrambled off the bed and went to her, trying to take her in his arms, only to be pushed away.

"What uh—what's your name?" he whispered absurdly, aching to know suddenly, arms hanging uselessly at his sides.

"Jade," she said. And then she frowned at the floor and grabbed her purse off of it, sliding her bare feet into Italian black heels and starting out the door.

"Roy," he said. "I'm Roy."

She turned in the doorway and blinked at him.

"We do not care what your name is."

"We?"

Her eyebrows knotted in agitation and then she pivoted again and disappeared out into the night.

Roy watched the door bang closed and wondered if he'd have to kill somebody before morning.

He stood in the corner behind the dresser, his gun within reach, for what must have been thirty minutes. And what kept going through his head was: *Send goons. Please send goons. Don't make me shoot you. You're a total class one. Way the hell too beautiful.*

Finally, there was a hand on the doorknob outside. Roy grabbed his federal-issue 9mm Beretta and cocked it. The door opened. Roy took aim.

"It is only me," Jade said calmly, without even glancing toward his corner or in any way ascertaining his position. She was carrying a large tablecloth bundled into a sack.

"I hope you still have hunger," she purred, dropping her purse by the bed, kicking off her shoes, and kneeling on the floor. She unfolded the cloth to display several small, covered bowls of food and then pulled her dress over her head, her bare skin gold and glistening in the moonlight.

Roy put the safety back on the gun and stepped out of the shadows feeling a little bit foolish.

"Where'd you get all that?" he asked as he slipped the gun back under his pillow and went to join her on the floor.

"I have a friend." She smiled, looking almost sincere in her happiness. "His name is Takeo. He cooks to calm himself. I suppose he worries too much, so he always has a lot of food. He warmed these for me in his kitchen when I told him of you. You will meet him tomorrow."

"Cool. Well, here's to friends who cook. Now if you just had a friend with a liquor store . . ."

Jade shook her head. "Takeo is my only friend."

"Not anymore," Roy said quietly. He already had his

fingers in several dishes and was sampling them contentedly while Jade laughed. "Mmm. This is great. Like this
Takeo guy already. What's so funny?"

"You hide in the corner naked with a gun, as if I had
one to aim at you. And then you sit on my floor and you
eat food offered to you by one you suspect to be an assassin known for her work with poison."

Roy stopped chewing, his throat tight, hands numb. He
stared at her for a minute, hard. And then he swallowed.
And then he smiled.

"You won't kill me," he told her.

She tilted her head to one side. "No?"

"You like me," he asserted.

"Roy . . ." Her voice was serious, and he crawled across
the tablecloth to get to her, to take her face in his hand.

"What? What is it, Jade?"

"I won't. I won't kill you."

"I would never hurt you . . ."

"I love you."

"Baby, I—"

Her face, so warm, so pained, stretched into a smile
suddenly, then she threw her head back to laugh. "Does
that put your mind at ease?" she cackled as he pulled back
and frowned.

"Oookay. Never mind."

"Oh, my poor, brave white man. Did I hurt your feelings? My poor, dear fool."

"Actually, I'm not," Roy answered curtly.

"A fool?"

"*Belagona*. A white man."

Jade stopped laughing and tucked her legs beneath her

body, intrigued. She bent her head like a child waiting to hear a story, the very picture of innocent curiosity. Roy took another serving of eggplant and tried to let go of his anger. Fine. So she was a bitch. It wasn't like he hadn't had that coming for years.

"You know that old game: cowboys and Indians?" he started. "Well, despite hanging out with the biggest bunch of cowboys this side of the Milky Way, I'm Navajo. *Dine'é.* An honorary tribesman, to be sure, but a tribesman nonetheless."

Unexpectedly, he found himself telling her his history, a story he had never uttered out loud before much less shared with another human being. Raymond, the *Ch'inili* sunsets, Marla, the heroin . . . he told her about everything except Ollie and the secret identities of the Teen Titans. There was something about the stillness of the room, the desire to have more sex but the physical need to wait, that made it possible to really talk. She listened with patience and genuine interest, even curling herself into his arms at one point, her naked back resting against his chest as he leaned against the bureau, the impromptu picnic still spread out on the floor before them. She had reached up lazily behind her to finger the small, silver charm hanging from a leather cord around his neck, and he shivered every time her fingernail scraped against his throat, but did not stop her.

"Your charm has magic?" she asked when he at last fell silent. Looking down at the top of her head, he could see her beginning to close her eyes in the dim light, so physically revealed and unguarded, it made him swallow.

"Huh? Oh. No." He flashed a grin. "Why? Is it bewitching you?"

She smiled back without meaning to, quickly catching herself and pulling her face down into a frown. "Tell me."

"It's just a hawk—my totem. And an arrowhead. And a piece of *Naatsis'áán*."

"*Naatsis'áán*?"

"Navajo Mountain. Some believe that the *Dine'é* are never to leave the mountain."

"And so you take the mountain with you?" She had turned around in his arms and was looking up at him, her strangely green eyes gleaming.

He stared at her hard, then he smiled. And then his smile faded. Swallowing, he slowly held out his hand to her, deeply grateful when she took it. "I don't know why I'm boring you with all this," he said quietly.

"I am not bored," she answered seriously. "I know who you are now, and that you are truly here. You cannot be anywhere else, because there is no place for your heart to return to. You are still lost. You have never fit in anywhere, despite having always done exactly what was asked of you. And then the people who finally take you, they do so because they know you cannot resist. They take you to change you. And when you protest they say see? See? You have no home. And we are your family now. And when at last you change for them, they leave you all over again."

Roy pushed the tablecloth away and led her back to the bed, between the covers where it was warmer. It wasn't exactly true, what she said, but it wasn't exactly wrong either. In fact, it was more right than anything anyone else had ever guessed. And it wasn't a guess. She knew. He knew she knew. Because of where she'd been, what she'd lost. And for the first time that night, despair cast its all-too-familiar shadow over him, tightening its talons into his heart. He knew they were connected—they were outcasts, together. He felt an overwhelming need to protect her—from everything; the people who had hurt her, her solitude, the rain. He knew that they could ease one another's burdens, soothe each other's loneliness in a meaningful way. And he knew that they would never be allowed to. Never.

"Is that what happened to you?" he asked, when her head was resting again on his arm. He had started to lick plum sauce off of her fingers but she pulled her right hand away hastily.

"There are things about my life you do not understand."

"Tell me."

"There are things you do not want to think about."

"I'm a big boy."

Jade frowned and was quiet for a moment, but finally spoke. "I do not have a very good imagination," she admitted quietly, shifting in closer to him. He let his hands wander over her skin and hair as she spoke, tenderly soothing, petting, reassuring her. Occasionally, he would feel her start to roll away from the gentle touches, and then she would relax more fully into them, looking at once bewildered and lulled. It was not difficult to guess that she was rarely touched with gentleness or compassion. "I was thinking it would not be difficult to do anything someone else wanted because I could not think of many things for which they might ask. And I was also without choice."

"Didn't your parents protect you?"

"My parents are dead. An uncle sold me to make

money to buy an oxen. Much more useful than a little girl. To him. There were other men that knew what to do with a little girl." Roy felt her fingernails scratching at the skin of his thighs as her hands clenched and he shifted slightly to avoid their sting.

"You mean you—you were sold into prostitution?"

"I was sold into a dynasty. I belonged to a man who did not like me. There are strange people in the world, Roy. And still I feel envy for those who know what it is that they would like. Some people like power. Some people like a cigar after dinner. Some people like to hurt the things they play with."

Roy swallowed and buried his face in her hair. "Yeah," he said, pulling her closer and tightening his grip around her small hand, which he had reclaimed. "I guess you see enough of that kinda stuff, you have to let yourself get a little hard."

"*Seeing* it is not the problem." Jade took his hand and led it to her stomach. He remembered the strange scars a second before his fingers touched them. He looked up at her face and her eyes were ice.

"No. God, no. Not you. Not you . . ."

"It is a very dangerous world, *Lichíi*. You know that. Sometimes it is better not to be alone. Will you stay tonight?"

"Yeah," he whispered hoarsely, pulling her as close as he could. He was dizzy, confused. "Yeah, of course."

"Things are much better now. I was rescued, and by sixteen I was married, and by nineteen I was free."

"You're . . . um . . . divorced?"

"My husband was an assassin. He taught me mastery

of poisons. He trusted me. He has been dead for many years now."

Roy frowned. That didn't sound so good. Jade continued.

"And I am my own master now. I am very good at what I do."

"Baby, I—"

"A very good assassin, yes. So Jade is no longer lost. Cheshire has much to do. Does that put your mind at ease?"

Roy closed his eyes. Her fingernails rested lightly on his chest.

When her fingers tensed suddenly on his skin, Roy clicked the safety off his gun and pressed the hard, cool muzzle against her temple. Her hand relaxed and he exhaled, another click echoing in the near empty room. He thrust the pistol back under his pillow as she nuzzled against his chest.

"Good night, Agent Harper," she whispered.

"Sweet dreams, Chesh."

"So, was that good for you?"

Arsenal was standing on the roof of the penitentiary without any visual whatsoever on Batman, but he was talking out loud to him anyway, certain he was nearby.

"Honestly, I don't know what you see in her," came the rough reply, less than two feet above where Arsenal crouched. Roy thought he had been prepared for any crazy extraction his temporary partner might come up with, but seeing Batman swoop toward him on a black-winged hang glider with scalloped edges embellishing its thirty-four-foot wingspan was shocking even to him. He prayed he wasn't trembling noticeably as Batman grabbed him without slowing down and pressed him against the harness.

"Good," he countered when he'd caught his breath. "I'd consider you unreasonable competition."

Having reminded himself that he was not—despite all external indications—in actual mortal danger, Arsenal allowed a slow grin to spread across his face. The twilight air felt amazing rushing around his body like a waterless river, and even the minimal cement squares of the prison compound, with its roving beams of stark white searchlights, took on an unexpected aesthetic appeal when viewed from so high above.

"You understand that she's a sociopath?" Batman's voice was surprisingly neutral. Arsenal could not see his face but doubted he would have been able to read it anyway. He let himself wonder if the hang glider was truly the best escape vehicle available to them, considering that they'd just driven up in the ambulance to return her, or if at some very small and undoubtedly rationalized level, Batman found it just the tiniest little bit fun.

"Hey," he replied easily. "You don't call my girlfriend names and I won't say anything about yours."

Arsenal thought he felt Batman's body stiffen above his.

"If you're referring to Catwoman, she is not a true sociopath. Selina knows the difference between right and wrong. She suffers from attachment disorder and takes things she feels she needs. Cheshire is incapable of framing the consequences of her actions ethically. If you don't understand the difference between a thief and a mass murderer, then you may have deductive moral reasoning limitations of your own."

Arsenal smiled quietly to himself. So Batman really *did* like Catwoman—cool.

"What do *you* suffer from?" he asked playfully. Batman didn't have much of a reputation for exercising a sense of humor, but then, how many people were cocky enough to tease him?

"Fools," Batman answered immediately. "But not lightly."

Arsenal's smile broadened. He was beginning to see a little glimpse of why Nightwing so passionately defended his mentor. Everyone knew Batman was scary-smart, but they tended to forget that such intelligence also included common sense, empathy, and the ability to at least fake social graces.

The glider began a controlled descent. As they approached a low bank of the delta flanking one side of the penitentiary, the Batmobile loomed into view. It responded to the proximity of the glider with an automated roof release that exposed the interior seats. At Batman's concise prompt, Arsenal let go of the control bar and was dumped into the passenger seat with relative economy. Batman had the more difficult task of releasing himself from the harness, but with the studied calm of a man who had practiced the maneuver thousands of times—which, Roy realized, was in fact likely—he, too, dropped into the Batmobile, efficiently pulling the glider wings in behind him. Seconds later, the roof was resealed and they were off.

Roy leaned back in his seat.

"Okay, so, other than the fact that I have lousy taste in women—which I coulda told you for free if you'd asked—what did we learn there?"

"That this is personal, and the work of a well-connected amateur. We're looking for an insider, someone close to the Abdul-Hakams, but also someone emotional and inexperienced. That rules out most of the president's military force, members of which were used inefficiently to make contact with Cheshire. Our perpetrator is extremely close to the family, but untrained in military protocol."

Arsenal frowned and shifted to peer at Batman's impassive, masked face. "Now wait a minute—what about those dispossessed Quraci mercenaries Chesh mentioned? Don't we have to eliminate them?"

Batman shifted the car into high gear, passing the occasional civilian car at well over three times the speed limit. "They were never a consideration. Why would a mercenary from Qurac use a hired killer like Deathstroke to assassinate a Quraci national on American soil? It's complicated and expensive and leaves him with a dangerous loose end. It is also all but guaranteed to produce international scrutiny, which professional mercenaries work hard to avoid."

"Okay, but what about a religious angle?" Batman's deductive reasoning intrigued Arsenal, who had leaned forward again without realizing he had done so. "If you're staging a coup, then there's some advantage to having the current president out of town, right?"

"Maybe. But we can dismiss that hypothesis as well. A Quraci striking out for representation or broader political hegemony would not hire an American to vanquish his opposition, much less a former U.S. military officer like Slade."

Arsenal rubbed at the four o'clock shadow emerging on his jaw. "Okay, well let's back up for a second." Out of the corner of his eye he saw Batman nod curtly and felt encouraged to continue. "We do know now for sure that the boy was Deathstroke's target, so Slade clipped him to send a message. But to who?"

"Me."

Puzzlement showed clearly on Arsenal's face. "How do you know *that*?"

Batman turned his glower on Arsenal. "Because it happened in *Gotham*."

Roy's eyebrows shot up and he pressed his lips together to keep from whistling. Turning to glance out the passenger side window, he reminded himself that brilliance and insanity were not mutually exclusive conditions. Living with Ollie should have taught him that much. He ran the heels of his gloved hands absently down the front of his leather pants and wondered if Lian had gotten to sleep all right without him there to tuck her in. She had told him once that she slept better when she knew he was in the apartment.

"Roy."

"That Yekaterinburg lead—that's something, right?"

"Illness like the kind from which Cheshire suffers is often progressive."

Arsenal folded his arms across his chest as he turned to glare at Batman, his green eyes narrowed and his posture stiffening. "What? What are you talking about?"

"You should value any agreeable memories you may have of her."

"Right, *thanks*." Roy's voice was bitter and sarcastic, and he frowned at his stoic driver, jaw tightening.

"And you should ask yourself *why* Slade would accept a contract on a fifteen-year-old boy in the first place."

Arsenal's brows knotted and he watched Batman's profile for a long moment before turning his attention back to the road. Illuminated by the Batmobile's headlights, the highway snaked beneath the wheels of the speeding car, a long black river heading to an ocean Roy could not name.

He was standing in the rain in Sendai, almost unaware of the water that was cascading down his hair and coat. She was standing just inside the pale wooden doorway of their secret place, looking uncharacteristically traditional with her shiny, black hair wrapped up in a bun at the back of her head, her body shifting slightly under a snow-white embroidered silk robe, her eyes dark and wide with something hard to say.

They had been lovers for slightly over three weeks. They had secret names now and secret touches, they had a mutual friend named Takeo who was making up names for their future children and they went to his restaurant every time it rained. She had been sick once and was surprised when her lover tucked her into bed and kissed her forehead and found oranges to bring to her and failed to be angry. He had been sad once and was surprised when his lover leaned her head against his shoulder and kissed his hand and failed to laugh at him. They had told each other things they had never told another living soul, and had refrained from addressing things that were too dangerous to discuss. She had forgotten how to imagine days without him in them, and he was dizzy and dense with the persistent image of her face, the never fading smell of her skin.

"Baby," he said. "Baby, I've got to—"

"Hush. I know. It was always coming. It was always here."

"Come with me, Jade. Come with me."

"Do not be a fool, Roy."

"Together. Together who the hell could touch us?"

"*'Oh, baby, just you shut your mouth.'*"

"This is no time to joke, Jade! I—"

"*'Shhh . . .'*"

"I'm serious here. Can't you at least consider—"

"Changing destiny? There would be repercussions for my disappearance, Roy. Repercussions you could not live with."

"It wouldn't be anyone's fault. I'd—"

"It would not matter."

"But—"

"Do not be naive. Criminals cannot go unpunished. Nor can heroes. Circles must be closed. Better that the innocent suffer than an act remains open to attract angry spirits and retribution. We would be running our whole lives, and when they did not catch us, they would select people here to suffer in our place. They would go after your family and your friends. They would persist with an energy you cannot imagine. And I—you would take me to your country to kill there?"

"You wouldn't kill. You could—you could work with us. The Titans, I mean. I don't think the CBI is gonna be too terribly enthused about this . . ."

"Killing is all I know."

"I'll teach you. It's just a matter of restraint. Baby, please."

"And what would you say, what would you say, lover, if I asked you never to work again?"

"My work is my life."

"Yes."

"I—I'm needed."

"Yes."

"Jade, it's—it's the only thing I'm *good* for."

"Yes."

"Jade—"

"Go, Roy. You are, as you say, needed."

"Jade—"

"I will . . . never forget you."

"Jade!"

"Does that put your mind at ease?"

Arsenal was so disoriented by the time the Batplane touched down in Gotham that he had to work through the likely date in his mind three times. In the space of what was probably actually less than forty-eight hours, he and Batman had left Gotham in the dead of night, flown halfway across the world to toil under the glaring Middle Eastern sun, crossed and recrossed multiple time zones, and finally returned to a Gotham City seemingly untouched by time, sun, or light. All that and Jade, too. Roy saw sunspots every time he closed his eyes, and couldn't stop thinking about a nicely worn set of dark green cotton sheets he had on his bed at home. He wanted to call Lian, just to hear her voice, but had to assume she had once again been put to bed without him.

"If my daughter ends up doing drugs because she felt abandoned by me during her early childhood, I'm gonna blame it on you," he told Batman as they disembarked.

"Lian's too smart to do drugs," Batman answered evenly. Roy had been smiling over the compliment to his daughter for six whole seconds before he perceived the insult to himself. Then his smile widened.

"So where to now, El Capitan?"

They had left the hotly damp darkness of the Gotham night behind to enter into the coolly damp darkness of the Batcave where Batman kept the plane and most of the rest of his equipment, including a gigantic Cray computer that generated so much heat Arsenal could feel it the moment he stepped onto the cave level where it was housed. Large brown bats occasionally flitted by overhead, and every piece of modern, gleaming equipment seemed precariously poised under primitive, jutting stalactites or centimeters away from small, organic drips caused by pooling condensation.

"We'll meet up with Arthur and Garth on the *Herron.*"

Roy nodded, quietly running a gloved finger over the sharp metal edge of a mounted Batarang, and wondered what Ollie and Dick were doing.

PART THREE

Green Arrow clapped his gloved hands together and turned toward Nightwing with a wink. "All right, then," he said with a grin. "Let's go get this bad boy."

Nightwing nodded seriously, a slight frown darkening his features as he scanned the unconscious men on the floor of the bar.

"What do you think?" he asked quietly. "Start at the Daggett Industries building?"

"Oh, where he shot at the kid? Yeah, yeah, sure, that sounds good."

"Might be cops there," Nightwing warned.

Green Arrow shrugged. "Bring 'em on."

Nightwing laughed. "Let's leave the cops alone, okay?" His tone changed, brightening slightly, as if he were deliberately shifting from the role of a leader into something more compliant. "Hey, how'd you get here anyway?"

"Arrow Car. What've you got?"

"My motorcycle. The, um . . ."

"Wing Wheels?"

"Night Bike?"

Green Arrow chuckled. "I like it. You drive."

He followed Nightwing out into the alley behind the docks and watched as the former acrobat leapt effortlessly from the ground to a large trash bin and from there up to a rusty iron fire escape that Green Arrow wouldn't have climbed on a bet.

"I'll be right back," Nightwing called down.

"What? You don't want me to see where you parked?"

Nightwing smiled a little sheepishly. "It's not that. It's just. I can move faster without—"

"—Without the old man tagging along. I gotcha. Go on." He saw Nightwing's teeth flash in the dark in an obvious grin and then the young man was gone, vanishing as expertly, if not quite as spookily, as his mentor.

Ollie stood in the dark between the bar and a warehouse and was glad that he wasn't yet dead. He liked the people he knew, and though he could vaguely remember some sense of building ennui from his young, pre–Green Arrow days, standing in Gotham a little after midnight on a Thursday he could think of plenty of things worth doing. Watching the back of the original sidekick, who also happened to be the adopted son of one of his best friends, wasn't as good as, say, pulling the fishnets off of Black Canary's shapely legs, but it was up there.

He heard the bike before he saw it; a rich, Italian purr that sounded like leashed speed. Then Nightwing was skidding sideways into a showy stop at the mouth of the alleyway, and Green Arrow thought again about how lucky these kids were. Not that he was complaining about his dance card, but the second generation—damn. Ollie thought he'd be amazed if any of these boys spent a single night of their enchanted young lives alone.

"You are *hot*, baby," he said with a wide smile, climbing onto the back of what appeared to be a tricked-out Duccati. Nightwing's head dipped forward in what Ollie guessed was a winsome blush and then they were off, racing through Gotham traffic with the wind in their hair.

"So remind me," Green Arrow shouted toward the back of Nightwing's head. Nightwing shifted slightly on the bike and Ollie felt convinced that he was listening. "You were actually some kinda bonafide circus kid before Bats found you, right? Like an acrobat or something?"

"An aerialist," Nightwing shouted back, nodding. "I did a trapeze show with my parents until they were killed." They hit the Aparo Expressway and Nightwing hunched forward slightly, opening the bike up with evident pleasure. "But what about you? I don't think I know how you got started. What got you interested in archery?"

Every fourth word whistled by Ollie, snatched away by the wind like auditory sales tax, but he understood the gist of the question.

"Imagine you're all alone on a deserted island in the middle of the South Pacific," Ollie hollered, no longer sure he could even be heard but enjoying the recitation nonetheless. "I was just a little younger than you are now, and suddenly I found myself staring death right in the face. It was man against beast, and there were days when I wasn't sure which one I was. But I had one advantage—"

"Opposable thumbs?" Nightwing grinned over his shoulder. Green Arrow punched him in the back of the arm, but Nightwing's smile only broadened.

"Errol Flynn, you little smartass!" Green Arrow cast a glance at the speedometer and loved that Nightwing was cocky enough to be looking over his shoulder while pushing 140 MPH. "He even gave me the bow he used in *Robin Hood*, but that was later. All I had on Starfish Island were wood, rocks, and my own ingenuity. Fortunately, that was enough. See, I'd studied truly fine bow and arrow work in the movies, and I—"

"In the *movies*? You learned archery from watching *movies*?"

"Sure." Ollie chortled. "Isn't that how Bats learned martial arts?"

Nightwing was changing lanes to hit the Robinson Park exit and Ollie regretted that he couldn't see the young man's face. "Uh . . . you know, that was before my time, really, but I'm thinkin' not so much."

Ollie was able to drop his voice as Nightwing slowed down for a turn back onto city streets. "Forget it. I can tell my tale of human grandeur is wasted on you and your plebeian work ethic."

"Well, what about Roy? Tell me how you met him." They slid to a neat stop in front of a red light and Nightwing turned around with an expression that Oliver found almost heartbreaking in its eagerness. "How did you, you know, *pick* him? How did you know he was the one you wanted for your partner?"

"He never told you that story?" Ollie realized that Batman probably rarely chatted with Dick and felt a surge of generosity toward his exotic young chauffeur. He continued as the bike started up again. "I was in his hometown once when he was only thirteen. He lived with the Indians, you know."

"The *Dine'é.*" Nightwing nodded. Ollie sighed and continued.

"Yeah, the Navajo, whatever. Well, that's how he learned archery. He lived with this legendary medicine man, Brave Bow—"

"How do you say that in *Dineh Bizaad?*"

"What?"

"Their language. Roy knows it. What did *he* call him?"

Ollie frowned. Kids didn't know how to listen to stories anymore. "*I* don't know. Not the point. The point is, he was the best archer in the entire Navajo nation, and Roy was the only kid who could keep up with him. They had these fierce competitions—archery powwows, yeah—kids would come from everywhere, all over Arizona, Utah, New Mexico . . . but Roy, he beat 'em every time. Still, what really caught my eye was this day at the bank . . ." Ollie was surprised to feel Nightwing's gloved hand cup his knee and even more surprised when the bike took a fast right turn and leaned so far over into it that Nightwing's foot pegs nearly scraped the asphalt. They came out of the turn fast and clean and Nightwing righted the bike and let go of Green Arrow's leg.

"Sorry," he apologized, without sounding the least bit remorseful. "I just didn't want you to think we were gonna dump."

Oliver shook his head, smiling. "Listen, if Batman trusts you, who am I to give your driving a second thought?"

"Batman's never actually been on the back of my bike," Nightwing admitted. "I'm pretty sure he'd tell me to slow down."

Ollie snorted. "Huh. Then I say go faster. Anyway,

where was I? Oh, yeah—I was making a deposit when these two—no, you know what? It was three. These three guys come in, they're big, and they've got guns. This is in broad daylight, after all, these guys aren't messing around, they're pros. One of 'em gets everyone down on the floor, another starts going from cashier to cashier emptying out the drawers, and the third one, he's taking point at the door. So obviously, I'm about to put a stop to this when I happen to glance over and see this scrappy little Irish-American Navajo kid with this cocky glint in his eye on the floor next to me, and he's got a penny in his hand—just one single arrowhead penny. And before I can warn him not to risk his life—remember, these guys are fully armed—he flicks the penny at the guy keepin' everyone on the floor and hits him *right* between the eyes, so perfect and so fast that the guy stumbles backward into the guy with the cash bag. And then this kid jumps up and runs at the guy by the door and just head butts him over. It was the most audacious thing I'd ever seen! I knew right then *that* was my sidekick, that was the kid for Green Arrow!" Nightwing was pulling the bike up into the delivery entrance zone for the building across the way from the Daggett high-rise, but when he cut the engine and turned toward Green Arrow, his face was aglow.

"That's the coolest story I've ever heard." He dropped the kickstand and hopped off the bike, his features softening under the influence of a quiet, rueful smile. "Man, I wish I'd been doing something that cool when Batman first saw me."

Green Arrow climbed off the back of the bike and gave Nightwing's shoulder a quick, paternal squeeze. "One look into your baby blues and I'm sure he didn't care what the hell you could do."

Nightwing, whose baby blues were at that moment hidden behind his eye mask, nonetheless managed to look so completely shocked that Green Arrow found it necessary to throw in a playful wink.

Thankfully, Nightwing started to laugh, and continued laughing for quite some time.

In the wet, grief-soaked months following his parents' death, Dick had poured his memories out to Bruce in an earnest ritual of capitulation. He had meant to purge himself of the intolerable longing to return to a life he was forced to leave behind, and in his eight-year-old mind, the only possible way of achieving this was to confess to his new, steadfast guardian every last one of his recollections and loves. He imagined his memories as a train track leading back to a place he'd never go again; all he had to do was tell every rail and connector until the old track converged with the present. Then he would be able to get onto the new train, the future, and never look back.

Instead he found that in the telling, every mile traveled became more immediate and less ambiguous, so that in the end his memories burned all the brighter. When he admitted this terrible failing to his guardian, Bruce had nodded seriously and told him that it was impossible to lose something willingly shared. He had spent all that time listening patiently not to help his new ward exorcise his memories, but rather to help him sustain them. "They're yours to keep," he had said, a large hand placed firmly on the eight-year-old's shoulder. "Let them continue to inform who you are."

And so Dick retained it all: the feel of aluminum and chalk on his hands and the smell of hay and elephant manure, the feel of muscles pulled taut in his shoulders as he swung the weight of his body from the trapeze bar into the rarefied air, a thrilling flight he would unfailingly be plucked away from by the strong, offered wrists of his catcher. The taste of bright pink cotton candy and stale popcorn was as easy for him to summon as the vinyl-tent-contained roar of a crowd forty feet below or the flat buzz of an electricity generator humming just beyond the walls of his family trailer. He was intimately familiar with stake lines and tiger teeth, greasepaint, muddy fairgrounds, and the gravel-strewn parking lots of nascent malls. The work ethic pounded into him from the day he was born included two shows a day, seven days a week, for nine months straight every year, and for the entirety of his life, he would never travel anywhere without instinctively noting the nearest laundromat and pay phone.

Richard John Grayson never had to run away to join the circus; he was born into it. His father, John Grayson, was a third-generation trapeze artist and full-blooded Rom "gypsy," while his mother, Mary Chilvers, had started life as the youngest daughter of a prominent New Jersey dentist only to be swept off her feet, figuratively and literally, before her eighteenth birthday.

Dick had heard the story of their meeting many times, and knew that somewhere hidden in the tale was the reason he had never met his mother's side of the family. He loved trying to imagine the argument his mother, then a girl of seventeen, might have had with her older sister, the argument that ultimately sent Mary huffing out of a circus tent in Trenton and into a back lot cookhouse where she had run into his dad.

"I don't know which were more dazzling—his eyes, or the sequins." Dick's mother would laugh as she and Dick's father sat together in the cramped trailer, retelling the story in response to their son's endless prompting.

"Admit it, Mary, it was the cape."

"Well, there is something about a guy in a cape. I'll give you that."

"Especially when you're lost."

"I wasn't lost! I don't know why I told you I was . . . I mean, how lost can you *be* under the shadow of a 283 foot tent?"

"You were a *townie*," Dick would taunt, his small nose wrinkled in distaste.

"But not a virgin," John said, laughing.

"John!"

"What? It was the *second* thing you told me!"

"You called me a 'good girl'!"

"I said that to Dakar! Dick, Dakar offered your mom a beer, I was just trying to defend her."

"You're gonna have to explain to him what that means now."

"Mom, I *know* what a beer is."

"See? He knows what a beer is . . ."

Dick decided, when he was six, that the fight his mother had had with her sister must have been about safety netting.

"I don't see *why* anyone would risk their lives like that when a simple net strung under the trapeze could make them safe!" In Dick's mind, his aunt was a much older woman, with gray hair and round cheeks, despite the fact that in real life she was probably only a few years older than her younger sister, then all of seventeen.

"Because danger is how we know we are alive," he imagined his young mother answering defiantly. For his whole life, he would hear those words in her voice, eventually forgetting that as far as he knew, he had made them up.

His father's side of the family was another matter. During the circus off season, January through March, Dick's father would arrange to catch up with a Kalderasha *kumpania*, or caravan. Every year the group would be made up of mostly the same people, but the meeting place would be drastically different. While the rest of Haly's Circus caught their breath and rested their aching muscles in Gibtown, Dick and his family would use their American citizenship to easily jump continents, enabling them to meet up with their *kumpania* even after a nine-month travel lead time on the part of the gypsies. Most members of the camp traveled more precariously under League of Nations-issued Nansen passports—in Russia one year, Turkey the next, India the year after; they would even sometimes come through Florida and spend the winter traveling around the United States—but this never seemed to stop them from covering vast distances. Playing the quiet, dignified crowds of Pennsylvania or the dishearteningly small shows on the West Coast, Dick would sometimes find himself envying them the unpredictability of their destination. He enjoyed his work and never would have dreamed of shirking his responsibility to the circus, but he longed for contact with the winter caravan the way most boys dreamt of summer and release from school.

Dick loved wandering through the campfires, watching the swaying, voluminous skirts of the women as they cooked and listening for an older man who might be telling *paramitsha*, or gypsy fairy tales, late into the night. Eventually he and dozens of other boys—usually referred to as "cousins," though Dick was never sure if this was literal or not—would crowd together between two large eiderdown *dunhas* spread out on the ground to sleep under the stars while the grown-ups retreated into tents or nearby wagons. The night air was sometimes balmy and sometimes cool, but always filled with the scents of earth or sand, burning wood, coffee beans, and the nearby horses and *kumpania* dogs. When it rained or snowed heavily, everyone would squeeze into the wagons together, and although he missed the fresh air and open sky, Dick secretly loved the warm crush of sleeping human bodies. Less than half-awake, he would smile over both the unconscious late-night embraces and the deliberate shin kicks, happy to be so absorbed by kindred dreamers in the stifling dark. In the mornings he would run with the other boys to wash himself in any nearby river or stream, whether it was raining or not, and to rub sea salt crystals over his teeth before breakfast and the inevitable breaking down of the camp.

On the few times the *kumpania* was assaulted by superstitious locals and well-armed police, Dick was taught to hold his physical anger in check. "Let them make up reasons to hate us," his father whispered to him, a large hand firmly on his shoulder. "Don't give them real ones."

Dick had protested, furious at the unnecessary brutality of the *gaje* and desperate to defend his family and friends. "But if we told them who we were—about the circus and our real passports and everything—wouldn't they leave the rest of the camp alone?"

"Don't tell them anything, honey," his mother had answered, crouching low by the outskirts of the camp. "Let them strike out at their misconceptions, and know in your heart that their hatred has nothing to do with you."

One winter night in Kashmir when he was seven years old, during the second of what would prove to be a four-night celebration prompted by the "rescue of six goats from waste," Dick began dancing on the ice-hardened ground to the joyously drunken singing of the Kalderasha and did not stop moving until well past the break of dawn, even after the last guitar and violin had been carefully tucked away. He ignored those who stopped to watch him but shared blissful grins of camaraderie with the cousins, uncles, and *kumpania* guests who joined him for an hour or two in the graceful, frenzied spins and undulations of his dance. His father came to check on him once, glanced at the position of the moon, smiled, and shook his head with obvious wonder and affection, but did not command him to stop or send him to bed. Dick danced for the black sky and the joy of moving, danced for the dark red stain of morning as it spread slowly across the western horizon, danced for the rising golden sun that at last appeared to lap at the icicle-stillness of the mountains and surrounding snow. He felt lost in something greater than himself, and also conclusively defined. Pulling sleep-strewn hair off her face and stretching in the frigid morning air, his mother at last put a hand on the back of his neck and bade him to be still.

"Aren't you tired?" she asked, smiling softly into her son's flushed face and red-rimmed azure eyes.

"Mom, I'm never tired," Dick answered with feverish ardor. "*Never.*"

Mary had no doubt he meant it, even when, drawing his head in close to her body and wrapping an arm around his shoulders, she felt him sway slightly and then collapse the entirety of his weight against her frame, so that she ended up having John carry him, glowing with contentment and instantly fast asleep, back to the wagons and the warm down quilts.

Green Arrow had noted the shattered window and the shot-out elevator panel and was ready to leave the Daggett Industries' sky bar in favor of one still containing people he might fight with, or at least one that was actually open. Nightwing, however, was busy crouching by the police tape near the window's ruined glass, carefully adjusting the angle on a laser line he had beaming out the building.

"Didn't the police already do that?" Ollie asked impatiently, eyeing the liquor bottles glittering behind the bar, some of which were of excellent vintage.

"They don't know Deathstroke like I do," Nightwing replied seriously, still absorbed in his work. Ollie wondered what it would take to get the kid drunk. Probably not much. Chances were good that Batman had never let him drink, and that he had grown up too aware of his body to enjoy losing control of it.

"Fought him before?" Ollie asked, just to make conversation.

Nightwing looked up at him, his eyebrows expressively arched even under the eye mask.

"Yeah, and also . . ." He paused, frowning down at the bloodstain on the carpet for a moment, and then he looked back up at Green Arrow. "You don't know about Joey?"

Ollie shrugged and paced back over to the elevators. The shot that had lodged itself into the center of the call panel was truly impressive, something he wasn't sure even he could pull off with an arrow. "Doesn't ring a bell."

Nightwing rocked back on his heels and took a deep breath, his shoulders tensing with stress.

"Joey was Deathstroke's son—Joseph William Wilson. Maybe you knew him by his hero name, Jericho?"

Ollie turned to face Nightwing, neither confirming nor contradicting the assertion. The code name did sound familiar, maybe someone Roy had mentioned once or twice.

Nightwing stood up and brushed the palms of his gloves against his pants. Or maybe they were tights. Green Arrow wasn't sure what to call them. Nightwing's entire costume was a skintight one-piece in black and dark blue that ran from his neck to his gloves to his boots. There was no question that it was fire retardant and probably at least partially bulletproof, but it was also more elastic and yielding than most of the armor Ollie saw, and suited the acrobatic former Robin beautifully. Though nothing, Ollie thought, grinning to himself, had ever really been as cute as the little green swimming trunks the kid had worn in his earliest days as Batman's sidekick.

"Anyway, Jericho was with the Teen Titans," Nightwing

continued, referring to a group of young heroes he had worked with and led for years. Ollie liked to think of the Titans as a sort of support group or dating club for former teen sidekicks, but the truth was that they were constantly redefining themselves and had consistently done significant and impressive work, sometimes on a global scale.

"Yeah. Speedy runs that now, right?"

Nightwing shook his head, a slight smile tugging at one corner of his mouth. "Arsenal's leading the Outsiders, sir. It's a different group. Though to be honest, there are a lot of similarities." Nightwing had his hands on his hips and seemed to be lost in thought for a moment. Then he gave in to a smile. "He's good at it, you know. He's doing a really good job. You should be proud of him."

Green Arrow beamed. "Of course I'm proud of him! Look, you gotta get past the *names* of things, kid. What's important is the *essence*. You know what I mean?"

Nightwing moved past Green Arrow toward the building stairwell behind the elevator bank, and Ollie realized they were probably about to head for the roof. He took one last look around the impressive bar, noting how out of place the police tape and investigative clutter looked. The GCPD had left empty Styrofoam cups, chalk, tape, even a Polaroid camera in their wake. Ollie frowned. Even he wasn't that much of a slob.

"Yes, sir. But we agree on names as a way of communicating essence and acknowledgment. It's especially important in detective work, where you wouldn't want to, for example, confuse a toxin with a potentially toxic antidote." Nightwing shouldered open the stairwell door, walking backward for a second to face Green Arrow as he finished his assertion. "Or with former teen sidekicks, where you wouldn't want to confuse a loyal, young orphan with the independent adult and hero he eventually manages to become."

"Ha!" Ollie followed him up to the building's roof, stroking his beard with a thoughtful smile, his green eyes sparkling. "Point taken."

On the roof facing the park, Nightwing was pulling out his grapnel gun and indicating a building across the avenue from where they stood.

"I think the shot came from over there. Let's check out the roof."

Green Arrow nodded and yanked a line arrow out of his quiver, readying his bow. They fired for the designated building together, Nightwing swinging out into the dark the second his grapnel anchored, while Green Arrow took an extra second to secure the back of his line to the Daggett building before grabbing the taut rope in his gloved hands and sliding into the night after Nightwing, hundreds of feet above the city street.

Nightwing was already frowning at the cement rooftop by the time Ollie pulled himself up over the building lip. The rooftop was gravel with a large water tower several feet behind them, and thoroughly unremarkable. "Batman's already been here," Nightwing commented. "But I was right, this is where Slade fired from."

Green Arrow wasn't sure how Nightwing had come to either conclusion, but he stood where Nightwing was staring and squinted at the building across the street. "He hit that elevator panel from here?"

Nightwing nodded, his expression uncharacteristically

grim. "A long time ago, Slade was injected with some kind of military super-serum. Now he has meta-human strength, speed, reflexes . . . even his brain is working at something like ninety percent capacity."

"Great. So all we have to do is work at one hundred."

"Easier said than done," Nightwing replied. "Most of us are set at about fourteen percent."

Green Arrow grinned and elbowed Nightwing. "Fourteen percent *conscious* thought, kid. You're forgetting about internal systems regulation and, way more importantly, the seventy or so percent of our brains habitually sloshing around in the gutter. You can get some good stuff from there, you know."

"You mean the subconscious?"

Green Arrow ignored Nightwing in favor of aiming a suction arrow at the shattered window across the street. If he was going to take on Deathstroke man to man, he might as well know how outclassed he was. He doubted it was as bad as Nightwing seemed to be implying.

He thought about where the elevator panel had been and released his shot. Nightwing had stopped talking and was clearly watching with fascination as the arrow shot through the shattered window and disappeared inside the building.

"Well," Green Arrow prompted. "Aren't you gonna go check it?"

Nightwing's masked eyes narrowed and then a slight smirk played across his expressive face. "No time. We're on a mission, remember? Gotta find Deathstroke." Nightwing pulled his grapnel gun out again and shrugged. "Besides, I know you're pretty good. If you weren't, you wouldn't be Green Arrow."

"Pretty good!?" Green Arrow was stung. "*Pretty good!?* Kid, I order you to go over to that building and check that shot."

"I'm sorry, sir." Nightwing's features had settled into an impassive calm, but Green Arrow knew he was being toyed with. "I want you to feel you can rely on me, but right now I'm bound by previously established orders from my immediate field supervisor."

Green Arrow held Nightwing's masked gaze with his own, his back teeth beginning to grind.

"Batman told you to follow *my* lead . . ."

"Not quite, sir, but don't worry." Nightwing paused with a slight dip of his head that almost certainly disguised a laugh. "My instructions do explicitly require me to accept full responsibility for your safety and well-being during the course of this investigation."

"Accept full responsibility for *this*!" Green Arrow swung a haymaker that Nightwing easily dodged and then, grumbling to himself, jumped back onto the line he had left stretched taut between the two buildings. It took him nearly three minutes to crawl back the way they had come, but it was worth it just to leave Nightwing there on the opposite roof worrying about whether or not to follow him.

During Dick's fourth circus season as a performer, when he was eight years old, his responsibilities were increased exponentially. In addition to his self-appointed job as Senior Official Elephant Visitor and his second year as the elephant trainer's Special Ambassador of Socialization to Minors for Zitka, a two-year-old Indian pachyderm and the circus's newest animal acquisition, Dick was tasked by his mother to begin thinking about new music for their show, asked by his father to take over tipping the electricians in the morning when they plugged the family RV into the circus-supplied generator, commissioned by Mr. Haly to give out ten free tickets and flyers to children his age and younger when they hit venues that were traditionally weak in attendance or underadvertised, and made officially responsible for helping the other circus family kids study basic math, reading, and logic, subjects he had excelled in after the minimal amount of exposure afforded him by contact with the teachers inconsistently hired on the road. For this last service he was to earn a small fee, a prospect that delighted him. His dad had told him he could start saving up for a motorcycle just like the one Nicolai Koshechka rode across the tightrope during the high-wire act.

In addition to these commitments, his role in the trapeze act was expanded to include twice the amount of stage time and, during the finale, the execution of a special quadruple somersault he had been working for the last fourteen months to master. It was a signature move, one no one else in the country had accomplished, and because people were willing to pay just to see it, it elevated Dick's status among his coworkers.

Dick was grateful for the preoccupations, especially when the season got off to a bad start. The principal seamstress lost a baby while in her second trimester and a drunken townie in Pensacola climbed over six warning barricades to get to the cat cages before deciding to share a corn dog with Gowon, Haly's notoriously stranger-shy four-year-old male tiger. Gowon shredded the man's right wrist and thumb, and Haly himself ended up having to miss the first six weeks of travel to stay behind and fight through the legal repercussions. In Georgia, one of the youngest members of the Koshechka high-wire family got caught shoplifting shoes from a local retail store, and animal rights protesters and truant officers were waiting for them by the time they rolled into South Carolina. Dick, along with Juan and Jorge Camacho, Pani Petulengro, and the five younger Koshechka brothers, spent two days in an all-boys school in Bennettsville. By third period on the second day, Juan was making passes at the school nurse, Pani was AWOL, Alexi Koshechka was running a lunch money racket while Yuri sold expired show tickets, and Dick had given a sixth-grader a black eye. The boys were fairly proud of themselves, but Mary scolded Dick later that night back on the lot as he helped her prepare for a midnight dash to the next venue.

"You represent Mr. Haly when you're out there, Richard, and I would think you would know better than to prove a local boy's prejudice about carnies and violence correct by taking a swing at him."

"But he said I was *short*!" Dick protested, incensed.

Mary cast a wry glance at her eight-year-old son. "You *are* short," she sighed. "For a *sixth-grader*. Why didn't you just stay in Pani's class?"

"The third-graders don't get any cool books." Dick shrugged. "In Mr. Lawrence's class we got this huge book called *Life Science* which had mammals and reptiles and fish and biology and cells and microbes and everything! They even had microscopes—in the *classroom*!"

Mary's brow furrowed and she crouched down in front of Dick. "Do you want to stay, honey?" she asked quietly, brushing a stray strand of dark hair off his forehead. "Finish a whole semester of school?"

Dick made a face like she had just suggested he voluntarily spend the rest of the season eating nothing but zucchini and brussels sprouts. "Stay? In *town*?" He narrowed his blue eyes and looked at her carefully. "Mom, are you feeling all right?"

Mary laughed and assured him that she was.

The rain chased them up the Eastern Seaboard, but four enthusiastic, sold-out shows in Philadelphia lifted the company's spirits. Mr. Haly was back with them by then, and they entered New Jersey in top form. By the time they raised the Big Top in Newtown, just a quick boat ride from Gotham City's Cape Carmine, they felt they had outrun the season's early curse. All they were missing was the sun.

It was not unusual to see Mr. Haly taking tense meetings with municipal officials or showing city inspectors around the lot. Dick vaguely understood that there was a safe full of money in Mr. Haly's trailer office that could be used as "social lubrication," and also that many cities housed low-level criminal organizations that considered the circus a company of itinerant grifters infringing on their territory. This knowledge made him attentive to the few times he saw Mr. Haly get truly hot under the collar, but otherwise didn't concern him. He had spent his whole life wheeling and dealing within an almost entirely self-sufficient circus economy, and would not have been able to say with any certainty which of their daily practices might or might not be legal.

Dick was walking Zitka back to her cage after introducing her to an excited crowd of local children when he saw Mr. Haly actually throw somebody out of his trailer. Mr. Haly was red-faced and fuming and the man tossed from the trailer office was bristle-jawed and letting out a stream of colorful cursing that would have attracted Dick's attention even if the initial confrontation had not.

"It's your funeral!" the man shouted as Mr. Haly slammed shut the door to his trailer. "Just remember, accidents *will* happen!"

Zitka flapped her ears, alive to the tension, and Dick murmured to her comfortingly as he leaned a shoulder against her left leg. The bristle-jawed man glared at him for a moment and Dick held the stranger's gaze as calmly as he could. Eventually the man looked away to spit and mutter another low curse. Dick reached up to tug on Zitka's howdah and hurry her along. He sensed that something was wrong but hoped the hostility would dissipate before the second show. Animals and circus owners were, in his experience, both highly susceptible to stress. In a crisis situation, it was usually best to just stick to the routine and keep them both on schedule as much as possible.

Dick saw the bristle-jawed man again right before the parade that opened the evening show. The man was walking hurriedly away from the tent, hands thrust in pockets, his head low, the bright orange glow of his cigarette tip the only light revealing his surly face. Dick tried to point him out to his mother, but Mary was listening for their entrance cue. Before he knew it, Dick was marching out to the center ring with his parents, basking in the enthusiastic greeting of the east coast crowd.

The clown, the cats, the Koshechkas—as usual, the show went by in a frenzied blur. Dick was helping Pani find a misplaced juggling club when he heard the applause for the fire breather that signified the end of the act before his own.

"Gotta go!"

Pani nodded, and then gave a chin nod in the direction of the stage entrance. Dick turned and saw his mother smiling at him.

"Come on, honey! We're on!"

"Don't forget to check with Dakar!" Dick shouted to Pani as he raced toward his mom. "Gowon loves to chew on the clubs, maybe it got into his cage somehow!"

Dick was watching over his shoulder as Pani flashed him a thumbs-up in acknowledgment and then crashed directly into his father.

"Everything okay?" John Grayson asked, chuckling as he pushed his son gently back so that he could look into his face.

"Pani's missing a club," Dick panted.

"And didn't want to call the prop master *why?*" Mary asked with a smirk and a raised eyebrow. Dick grinned, shrugged, and remembered that he wanted to tell them about the bristle-jawed man just as the Big Top plunged into a sudden, dramatic darkness. Everything would have to wait. He began to scamper up the trapeze rigging.

He was already almost at the top, his mom right behind him, by the time a single, hot spotlight picked the M.C. out of the inky darkness. Even though he couldn't see him, Dick upheld his twice-daily ritual of waving to his dad, who he knew to be climbing up the opposite side of the rigging, preparing to take control of the catch bar. Fifty feet away, across the darkness, Dick was sure his dad was waving back.

"And now, ladies and gentlemen, if you would please direct your attention high above the center ring . . ."

Dick stood on a riser, took a deep breath, felt his mother step onto the pedestal board behind him before resting a hand on his shoulder, and braced himself for the blaring glare of lights.

". . . *Haly's Circus* is proud to present . . ."

Dick put his shoulders back, lifted his chin, and plastered a grin on his face.

". . . the *Amazing Flying Graysons!*"

Dick was never sure if the warmth he inevitably felt at the end of this introduction was due to the sudden assault of spotlights or the roar of the crowd. The prepared performer grin instantly stretched into something real and irrepressible as he posed and waved to the cheering multitude below.

"I must now warn the weak of heart among you to avert your eyes! For the daring, death-defying tricks you will witness here tonight are performed *without the aid of a net!*"

Still waving, Dick grabbed the fly bar with his free hand and listened for his dad's prompt—a sharp clap and loud "Huht!"—before dropping his cape and turning his attention to the execution of his first pass, a little act opener that was meant to catch the crowd off guard and get their adrenaline pumping. When he had first begun performing at the age of four, this had been a simple double swing across the rigging to his father's side, but as he grew older and more proficient he began to embellish, first as a way to guarantee the adoration of the audience, but eventually in a slightly mischievous effort to surprise and terrify his parents.

Already warmed up from the first show, Dick grabbed the steel bar in both chalk-kissed hands and swung toward the center of the rigging, his grin widening with exhilaration. He loved feeling the muscles in his entire body tighten, from his shoulders to the arches in his feet, while at the same time some unnamed knot of thrill swooshed up uncontrollably from his groin to his throat. Sensing more than seeing the second fly bar his father threw to him, Dick let go of the first bar, tucked his knees against his chest, clasped his arms around his knees, pitched his weight forward, and spun, weightless, in two tight somersaults before unfurling and grabbing for the pass bar.

"A double already, huh?" He heard his father laugh as he landed on the platform beside him. "Show-off."

Dick barely had time to make eye contact with and beam at his dad before another "Huht!" sent him soaring back the way he had come, this time spinning off the second bar in a tight vertical triple twist before catching the first in one hand. The crowd cheered, whistled, and applauded, tension mounting.

He passed his mom in midair, dreaming of the day when she would trust him with a proper passing leap, and lit onto the pedestal board just in time to turn around and watch her smile at his father, who was hanging by his knees off the catch trap, already swinging toward her. Forty feet below, the audience watched with bated breath as Mary let go of the fly bar and reached for her husband's wrists.

Since John was responsible for the cues and timing of the act, Dick, when not in flight, always kept his attention on his father's face. The physical knot of thrill that had been fluttering in his throat constricted suddenly, becoming cold and leaden before dropping into his stomach as if from a much greater height. Something was wrong. It wasn't even a full frown that passed across John's face, just the shadow of one, his eyes darting from Mary to the stage left guy wire as he registered some slight imbalance in his weight.

Dick couldn't see past his mother's flowing dark hair and so couldn't tell if she noticed, but there wouldn't have been anything she could have done even if she had. She clasped onto her husband's wrists as John clamped onto hers, and in that second of combined weight, the guy wire came apart like a spiderweb, dumping the two flyers, the three-foot-long steel bar slipping out from beneath John's knees like a baton sent twirling high above his head.

"Dad!" Dick screamed, going down flat on the pedestal board and knocking the wind out of his chest as he reached for them, helpless.

He heard the crowd gasp, heard his mother scream, watched his father struggle to pull her close, their arms locking around each other in midair as she tucked her head against his chest and closed her eyes. They plummeted together toward the tent floor.

Dick saw them hit in his mind at least six times before they actually did. Saw, too, a dozen ways they could be saved—somehow, miraculously, he could catch them, or they could go back, go back in time just six minutes and he would throw himself across the bristle-jawed man's back and beat his fists against the man's skull until his father came to pull him off and his mother ran to double-check the rigging. He could've swung out on the catcher bar, just this one time, just to tease his dad, and he would have been practiced enough to notice that the wire was compromised but light enough to make it to the other side in time to warn his dad not to use it. The clowns, they could be running to get the trampoline! Or the audience, someone could tell them to run out into the center ring and they would catch them, they could all catch them! If he could fly, throw a rope, stretch his body below them, and live the rest of his life as a net they would always and forever use from this night on if only, please, if only he could save them!

Trying to make himself close his eyes, Dick saw his mother's skull crack against the ground a second before he heard the thud of his father's body landing beside her.

Dick felt a wave of cold negation take his entire body, his strength collapsing in on itself, but found himself halfway down the ladder before realizing he had decided to climb. He jumped the last ten feet and, ignoring the pain in his left ankle as he hit the hard, dusty floor, ran to the center of the ring and sank to his knees beside their broken, twisted bodies. He grabbed on to his father first, his fingers desperately searching the flesh and muscle for signs of life, and then grabbed his mother's head a second before remembering what he had seen from the platform. He pulled his hands back too late—they were soaked in her warm blood and her face had rolled toward him, expressionless, blood pooling from the back of her skull, seeping around his knees. Her blue eyes were open, staring, but her gaze swept right through him—right through his eyes, which were the same as hers, and right through his heart, which was breaking.

Two inches to the right. That's all Green Arrow had missed by—two lousy inches. Not close enough to jam the elevator system, but still damn impressive. Ollie grabbed the Polaroid camera left behind by the Gotham City Police Department's investigative unit and took a picture. That'd teach Nightwing what "pretty good" looked like.

Ollie sauntered back to the blown-out window and smiled at the developing photo. Squinting across the avenue, he saw that Nightwing was still crouched on the lip of the roof, apparently talking to someone with the use of the comlink he had integrated into his gauntlet, or possibly recording case notes. A sudden sense of uneasiness came over Ollie. Having no actual superpowers had taught Batman and Nightwing to plan out every move and contingency; the same lack of power had taught Ollie to go with his gut. Sometimes experience and instinct proved more valuable than all his training and skill.

Frowning, he turned his back on the window and took a slow look around the room. Nothing had changed. Same blown elevator panel, same small bloodstain on the carpet, same shattered glass on the floor . . .

Green Arrow stuck the photo into his vest pocket and turned around again, taking a closer look at the building from which Nightwing insisted the shot had come. Scanning the horizon, Ollie remained alert. He knew he was a hothead, and sometimes short on patience, but he was not the kind of man to get discouraged by a challenge. Deathstroke interested him, and he was so determined to find him that for a second he thought he must be imagining the hulking, masculine silhouette that suddenly took shape on top of the water tower directly behind Nightwing. It was a strong surge of alarm that finally convinced Ollie that his eyes weren't playing tricks. The maniac was taking aim at Batman's former ward, and Nightwing, who could usually sense a cold sneaking up on him from last week, appeared completely unaware of the danger.

Ollie readied his bow, grit his teeth, and after less than a second's reflection, drew an armor-piercing arrow from his quiver. If everything Nightwing had been saying was true—and Ollie had no reason to doubt that it was—Deathstroke would shrug off a normal arrow and potentially dodge an explosive one, which would be bad news for anyone or anything nearby. If Deathstroke evaded the armor piercer, nothing bad would happen to anyone else, but if it did hit him, he would know he was in a fight he couldn't ignore.

Aiming and firing an arrow was as fundamental to Ollie as breathing—deep, meditative breathing. It was all a matter of muscle memory and flow, of letting go of ego and recognizing the interconnectedness of all living things. He could hit Deathstroke because he *was* Deathstroke. Nothing real stood between them. The muscle, bones, skin, air, and space that separated them were all illusion. What was real was Green Arrow's intent to reconnect himself with truth as it was manifest over *there*.

There.

The arrow flew from his bow high above the busy avenue, cleaving the darkness between him and his target. When the arrow was within centimeters of Deathstroke, both Nightwing and Deathstroke seemed to notice it simultaneously. Following the trajectory of the shot, Nightwing glanced up at where Deathstroke was hovering above him, noticing him for the first time. Though he knew he could not have seen such a detail from such a distance and in such darkness, Ollie just knew that Deathstroke smiled.

The shot would have hit him, Ollie was sure of it. But at the last possible second, Deathstroke brought his arm down sharply and sent it ricocheting off course. It was a rare human being who would parry an arrow with his bare hands. Ollie felt a spark of admiration, and then his alarm intensified.

Deathstroke leapt off the water tower at Nightwing with superhuman agility. Nightwing just managed to dart out of the way, forced down into a low roll. Ollie watched as Nightwing attempted to get back up on his feet, but Deathstroke was faster, coming at him with a vicious straight punch that Nightwing just barely managed to dodge.

Across the avenue, Ollie's heart raced. He wanted to sail over the rooftops and pull Deathstroke away from Nightwing with his own two hands, but he knew Nightwing was better trained in hand-to-hand combat than he was. He had the advantage with ranged weapons, so that's what he'd use. At very least, he could provide a distraction and give Nightwing time to get away.

A volley of multiple arrows would provide more coverage than Deathstroke could easily dodge, but might also put Nightwing at risk of getting hit. Ollie chewed his bottom lip in frustration. The explosive arrows were still out, for the same reason. Fire was not something he liked to play with in crowded urban areas, but gas was a possibility—even if Nightwing didn't have time to get his rebreather on, Ollie could drag him to safety once Deathstroke had been subdued.

As Ollie deliberated, he watched Deathstroke and Nightwing continue to fight. It was a strange, full-contact brawl defined by feigns and evasion, and yet both of them kept circling back in the first chance they got.

Ollie set another armor-piercing arrow, deciding that he might have better luck while Deathstroke was distracted by Nightwing. A "pretty good" archer wouldn't have risked the shot, but Ollie reminded himself that he was Green frickin' Arrow, and he wasn't running around in tights for nothing.

Aiming at Deathstroke, he shot another arrow across the avenue. And then another. And yet another. Every time, Deathstroke managed to dart out of the way at the last possible second. Ollie had decided to try a three-arrow volley of concrete-penetrators after all and was readying the shot when Deathstroke managed, by sheer force of strength, to knock Nightwing off balance. As Nightwing teetered on the edge of the rooftop, Ollie fired—but not at Deathstroke. He aimed his arrows at the building side, firing as fast and as accurately as he could.

Deathstroke gave Nightwing another hard shove and then watched dispassionately as Nightwing lost his footing and plummeted over the edge of the roof. Ollie watched with the sound of his heart beating in his ears. In midair, Nightwing contracted his body, pulling his feet up over his head and changing the free fall into a dive so that he could see where he was going and get his bearing. He seemed to notice the arrows immediately and reached out to grab on to one with nimble, confident fingers. Though the arrowhead had burrowed into the concrete in the side of the building, the shaft began to buckle under the unexpected addition of Nightwing's weight. Ollie readied three additional arrows, but Nightwing had already swung off the first shaft as if it were a monkey bar. Ollie fired anyway, trying to give Nightwing an exit off the building, but much to his chagrin, Nightwing executed a perfect handstand on the second arrow shaft before pushing off of it with all his arm strength, reversing his fall and bounding back up onto the roof.

"What are you doin'!?" Ollie knew Nightwing couldn't hear him, but he shouted anyway. "That was a perfectly good escape route!"

Nightwing was already reengaged with Deathstroke, down low in a sweep kick trying to knock Slade's feet out from under him. Deathstroke bounded backward, looking more amused than threatened, but Nightwing wasn't giving up. Ollie decided he'd have to get closer.

Using his bow as a makeshift rappelling huit, Ollie zipped across the line he still had up between the two buildings, finally climbing up onto the roof less than four feet away from where Nightwing and Deathstroke continued to fight.

Positioning himself at the building's northwest corner, Ollie tried four more times to hit Deathstroke. Though he was shooting from a much closer range, Green Arrow still couldn't manage to hit him. And Nightwing's indefatigable energy wasn't helping—Deathstroke would gamely dodge a few of Nightwing's strikes and then turn the table on him, forcing him back. As a martial artist, Nightwing was creative and adaptable, never settling into a conventional pattern. Most of the hand-to-hand fighters Ollie knew, including Batman, tended to have strong stylistic preferences. Batman, for example, usually held the midground and paired soft, redirecting parries with hard-style hits. Though trained by Batman, Nightwing was considerably more acrobatic and fluid, often changing styles in mid-attack; darting back and forth between high and low evades, hard and soft offensives, fundamental parries and elaborate dodges. Ollie never had any idea where he was going to be next.

Deathstroke, on the other hand, used a very pure, military judo technique augmented, Ollie figured, with whatever melee weapon happened to occur to him. His unpredictability stemmed from his superhuman agility, speed, and strength. A leaping roundhouse, Deathstroke style, involved a booted foot coming at Nightwing's head at seventy miles an hour from twelve feet above, and would usually be followed up by a sword strike or grenade lob.

"Must be fun at parties," Ollie muttered to himself before trying once again to hit the flashing blue and orange of Deathstroke's costume. The mercenary wore a full head mask, half in blue and half in orange, the dividing line running vertically down his face. Only the orange side appeared to have an eye slit and the hood was apparently cloth . . . two flowing ties occasionally fluttered behind him. Like Nightwing, Deathstroke wore thick gloves and boots over tight, body-fitting armor. Unlike Nightwing, he also had a *katana* and a broad sword strapped to his back, a machine gun slung over one shoulder, a handgun holstered on his thigh, a hunting knife sheathed at his waist, an ammo bandolier slung across his chest, and a smaller ammo belt fasted over his bulging left bicep. Ollie had no doubt that there were even more weapons hidden in his gauntlets and boots, and wondered how pissed this guy was that Ollie's boy, Roy—who sometimes had a crossbow on him, at best—was running around calling himself Arsenal.

After another flurry of archery shots, one of which Deathstroke nearly managed to swing Nightwing into the path of, Ollie gave up with a frown and glanced around the roof impatiently. With a grimace, he aimed a punching glove arrow at one of the three support legs holding the water tower in place and pulled back on the bow with everything he had.

Nightwing averted Deathstroke's attempt to fire on him with a full body slam and was in the process of flipping over the mercenary's back when the lukewarm water burst across his back and shoulders in a liquid explosion. He had the strange sensation of treading air, and then was slammed down onto the roof by a force much stronger than gravity, winded and soaking wet.

Deathstroke didn't fare much better. Hunched over to avoid having his face connect with one of Nightwing's boots as the young gymnast scrambled over him, Slade heard but did not see the water tower crashing down just to his right. The water was rushing over his head before he could lift his face to track it, and although he managed to leap away from the worst of the deluge, he wasn't fast enough to keep from getting drenched.

Ollie shouted from the roof rim, standing safely behind the flood. "If you two are done with your pissing contest, me 'n' the kid have a few *questions* for you!"

Nightwing wiped the water from his eye mask and bounded back up onto his feet, frowning over his sloshing boots, as Deathstroke turned to Green Arrow. Ollie realized that even close up, there was no way to read the guy's expression under the full face mask, but once again felt sure that the son of a bitch was smiling.

"You know everything I know," Deathstroke answered. His voice was cultured and rich. "Except the compensation."

The mercenary turned to Nightwing then, his back to the Emerald Archer. Ollie took the sight of Deathstroke's back as both an insult and a challenge and drew a fresh arrow from his quiver.

"Five million—half up front, half on completion. Supposed to collect directly from the big guy."

Ollie fired the arrow. Nightwing rolled to dodge a feigned lunge. And Deathstroke disappeared, sopping wet, into the darkness.

Dick remembered the aftermath of his parents' death with surprising clarity. There had been a stretch of motionless time as he crouched by their bodies, drowning and lost in a black sea of grief, but eventually he got shakily up on his feet and reached in his heart for the only bar still swaying anywhere near his consciousness: vengeance. He clamped on to the idea of finding the bristle-jawed man with all the concentration of a seasoned aerialist. Instinctively, he knew that revenge was the only thing that could ever carry him safely back to any kind of pedestal board.

He turned around and faced pandemonium. The audience was already out of their seats, some of them standing stock still and whispering to one another with pale faces as they craned to get a better look, others hurrying small children out the tent exit, visibly shaken. The circus performers were rushing into the center ring, many of them skidding to a stop when they saw Dick turn toward them with his bloodstained hands and tear-stained face. There was a strong smell of sweat and lions, and then Dakar was kneeling before him, pulling him close.

"Oh, God, Dick . . . Are they . . . ?" He pulled back and fixed Dick with a sorrowful stare. Dick nodded, trying to swallow, the tears springing into his eyes all over again. Dakar's mouth trembled, but then he seemed to bite down on his reaction, reaching out to smooth Dick's dark hair away from his face. "Don't you worry, little man. We're your family, and we'll take care of you, okay?"

Dick nodded and let himself feel the warmth of the embrace offered by his father's best friend, but then he pushed away from the lion tamer and asked, in a small croak, for the police.

Dakar frowned, but stood up and took Dick's hand. He led him through the center of the tent, past sobbing performers and horrified roustabouts, many of whom reached out to squeeze Dick's shoulder or touch his head as he passed by. Dakar stopped him briefly in front of Pani and his family. Like Dick's father, they were Rom, but *Lowara* rather than *Kalderasha*. Being from different tribes and *kumpania*, the Graysons and the Petulengros had never traveled together in the winter, but during the circus season, the two families were inseparable. Pani's mother, father, and three older sisters were keening and tearing at their hair and clothing in unguarded displays of gypsy grief as Pani stepped forward and offered the traditional Rom prayer to the dead, his small, dark head hung.

"John and Mary, *akana mukav tut le Devlesa*."

Pani's family wailed the same prayer, and Dakar offered it in English.

"John and Mary Grayson, I now leave you to God."

Dick, however, would not say it. He was not ready to give them up, not with their murder unavenged.

"Police," he whispered again when Dakar turned to him questioningly. Pani's mother and father moved in tearfully to kiss the top of his head, and then Dakar continued to lead Dick through the crowd.

The circus had its own security, and those men, along with Mr. Haly, were already in a conversation with uniformed members of the Gotham City Police Department by the time Dakar was finally able to assist Dick out of the tent, past the disorderedly crowd.

"Excuse me," Dick said quietly to their backs. Dakar frowned over the scene, squeezed Dick's shoulder, and moved to Mr. Haly's side when he caught the quarrelsome tone of the roadies. The conversation was heated, too heated for accidental deaths. "Excuse me!" Dick repeated, louder.

"Just a minute, son," one of the policemen said, turning to glance at Dick over his shoulder and then immediately turning back to Creighton, the man responsible for assembling the trapeze rigging.

"Where would I even *get* acid?" Creighton was protesting.

"That's their son," Dick heard Mr. Haly quietly acknowledge.

"I saw who killed them!" Dick shouted, tugging on the policeman's sleeve. His hands left bloody prints on the dark blue fabric.

The policeman turned around again, brown eyes wide. Dick continued.

"That guy, Mr. Haly—the one you threw out of your office after the first show. I saw him coming out of the tent!"

The policeman looked interested, his bushy blond eyebrows shooting up over his glasses, but another one of the officers was arguing vehemently with Creighton and after quickly asking Dick to stay still for a moment, the policeman brushed at his thick graying mustache and turned back to his fellow officer to try to defuse the argument.

Dick turned back to the tent with a miserable, frustrated frown and saw a man standing in the shadows just past the ticket booth wearing a costume he had never seen before. It was dark and frightening and animalistic, but Dick felt no fear as the figure motioned to him. He looked over his shoulder at the still-arguing policemen and walked past the ticket booth around the corner of the tent. For a moment, he didn't see the man who had beckoned to him, but as his eyes adjusted to the dark, he saw a flash of a strange, long cape and followed it around yet another corner.

Behind the tent but just out of sight of both the trailers and the fairway, Dick nearly crashed into the mysterious stranger, who had stopped there to wait for him. The moment Dick came close to him he sensed the man's intensity and power. Strength and purpose radiated off of him with such clarity that Dick knew it must have been at least partly intentional. The man was tall and covered from head to toe in his strange, dark costume, which included two sharp animal ears on the top of his head and the black flowing cape Dick had followed. There was a black bat emblazoned across his chest, and his eyes, disguised by a cowl, were ghostly white slits. He wore heavy, dark gloves and boots, and only the skin of his strong, clean-shaven jaw was exposed, his mouth set in a hard, thin line, inexpressive. In the language of circus imagery, he was dressed as a shadow, a villain to be vanquished by an appointed hero wearing glittering red sequins and a bright white satin sash. But Dick knew that there were no acts in Haly's Circus incorporating such a character, and also that the man was not a performer. To the grief-stricken eight-year-old boy, he looked like a personification of vengeance. Though Dick recognized many elements of the man's costume, the sum was something altogether new; thrilling and serious. The young aerialist shivered slightly, wishing he still had his own cape.

"Dick," the Bat-man said. His voice was dark and resounding, and it didn't strike Dick as at all odd that the demon knew his name. Dick had wished for him, after all, willed him into being with his determination to see the murder of his parents avenged. "You say you saw someone suspicious?"

Dick told him the story about the bristle-jawed man, everything he'd overheard and every time he'd seen him. As Dick spoke, Batman gently took Dick's small hands in his own much larger, gloved ones and used a corner of his cape to wipe off the blood. Dick was a little bit frightened by him, but the fear excited him. He told the man about Creighton and how carefully he always checked the rigging, how the police had said something about acid, and how that would explain what had happened to the guy wire.

Batman listened attentively, and when the boy was done speaking, he put a hand on his shoulder.

"Listen to me carefully, Dick . . ."

Dick nodded. In the ten minutes following his parents' death, the only things that had made sense to him were Dakar's embrace, the wailing grief of the Petulengros, and the dark, mysterious Bat-man.

"You're a material witness. That means you know things that can help put the man who murdered your parents away in jail. You say that after he argued with Mr. Haly, the man noticed you and made eye contact. Chances are he's looking for you even harder than you're looking for him. Though normally I would advocate that someone your age turn to the police for help, in this case I'm concerned that the criminal organization behind this murder has access to the police department and will work diligently to see you silenced. We need to find a safe house for you, a place you can stay where no one will think to look for you. Do you understand?"

Dick nodded again, though an idea was beginning to form in his head. A cold wind blew across his shoulders.

"You're going after him, aren't you? The man who murdered my parents."

The stranger nodded and then, after a brief but noticeable hesitation, put a hand on Dick's shoulder.

"I'm Batman. I work to keep Gotham City safe, and to make sure criminals are held accountable for their crimes. I promise you, I will not rest until I capture the man responsible for the murder of your parents."

"I'm coming with you." Dick clearly saw Batman's surprise, and his hesitation. With an eight-year-old's instinct for malleable borders, Dick sensed that no matter what Batman answered, his suggestion was not entirely out of the question.

"I . . . can't allow that. However, I do know a place where you'll be safe. One of the policemen here is an acquaintance of mine. With your permission, I'll have Captain Gordon make arrangements on your behalf and escort you to the home of a Gotham citizen I know to be trustworthy. Do you have any surviving relatives?"

"I don't know," Dick answered honestly. Batman raised an eyebrow and Dick continued. "We don't see my mother's family. I've never met them, and I don't know whether or not any of them are still alive or where they might be. My father's legal parents were alive last winter, but they're not his biological parents. We're Rom, and sometimes when people marry and have children young, an older couple goes to record the birth for them. Plus we use different names sometimes. So I have a family, at least on paper somewhere, but not the way you mean."

Batman's eyes narrowed and he gave a single nod. "I'll look into the matter for you."

"No one will mind if I go live with you," Dick insisted. He almost added "as long as you promise to take care of me," but decided that he didn't need to. He was already sure that Batman took care of everything, whether he had promised to or not. Standing alone with him in the dark, feeling the cool night air on his shoulders and neck, Dick felt strangely comforted. For maybe the first time in his life, he had found an adult who seemed to understand the things in his heart and didn't tell him that he was being silly, or argue with him about what was or was not possible. For maybe the first time in his life, he had found someone who seemed to live, as he did, utterly in action.

"You've been very helpful." Batman's voice was serious and completely without condescension. "I promise I'll contact you when I know more, or if there's anything else you can do. For now, I need you to go back to your friends and wait for Captain Gordon."

Dick turned and squinted over his shoulder, but was too far behind the tent to see anyone up front. When he turned back to protest, Batman had vanished.

He stood for a moment alone on the circus lot, and then decided to put his faith in Batman's directives. He hadn't been told to wait and do nothing because he was a child, after all, he'd been told to wait and be safe because he was a witness. And just as Batman had promised, the police officer with the glasses and soft gray mustache came to Dakar's trailer a few hours later to retrieve Dick and take him to an "undisclosed location." Dakar seemed unhappy about letting Dick go, especially with a policeman, but at Dick's insistence he relented, hugged the boy warmly, and told him to come home soon.

As the police captain drove him across a bridge in an unmarked car, Dick had the sinking feeling he might never be back. He wished he had thought to say good-bye to Pani, and Zitka. The policeman was mentioning that he had a daughter just a few years older than Dick, but Dick wasn't really listening to him. Streetlights illuminated the dashboard in an inevitable, rhythmic pattern that reminded Dick of being very young, on a train, watching his mother's smiling face as the window of their train compartment sent patterns of light and dark flicking across her features. Dick tried to make sense of the idea that he'd never see her again and felt panic threatening to rise up from his throat. Quickly, he refocused his thoughts on the bristle-jawed man, and stared out the window counting telephone poles until he was calmer

Eventually the policeman turned and drove through the open gates of the largest private home Dick had ever seen; a gleaming white mansion at the end of a circular drive, perched high above craggy cliffs that led down to the Atlantic Ocean. Even in the dark, and as exhausted as he was, Dick understood that the house was what his mother would have called "old money," sumptuous and refined. She would have told him to be on his best behavior.

Before the police captain could even ring the bell, one of the heavy, double front doors was opened by an older man in coat, tails, and bow tie. He was lean and impeccably groomed, with a pencil-thin mustache and a dignified bald spot. His black shoes were so well polished that, looking down, Dick actually thought he could see his reflection in them. He was pretty sure this was the richest man he had ever met, and all at once felt shy.

"Good evening, Alfred," the police captain said. He had a way of speaking that was both reassuring and grave.

"Captain Gordon, how nice to see you." The man paused and then leaned down slightly, his hands on his knees, thin back curving. When Dick glanced up at him, he was rewarded with a slight smile. The man's brown eyes seemed very warm, and he spoke kindly. "And you must be Master Richard." The smile faded from his face, replaced by a look of sincere sympathy. "I am so terribly sorry for your loss, young sir."

"Thank you," Dick answered in a whisper.

"Won't you gentlemen please come in?" The man spoke with a soft, pleasant accent that Dick recognized as European, probably British.

In response to a gentle push from the police captain, Dick stepped into the front hall, which Alfred would later tell him was properly called the Great Room. The ceilings were easily forty feet high, and a winding marble staircase to the left led up past a visible landing. To the right was a sort of living-room area with a fire blazing in a fireplace so large Dick could have slept in it, and fresh flowers were handsomely arranged in porcelain vases on every end table. The police captain took a seat on one of three supple white couches and refused, as did Dick, Alfred's offer of a drink.

"I'm afraid I've got to get back to the station and catch up on some paperwork," Captain Gordon sighed. Dick was busy counting the fist-sized crystal droplets dangling from a chandelier the size of a small elephant.

"I'll summon Mr. Wayne directly, then," Alfred replied. He gave a crisp nod of his head and left the room.

"Big house, huh?" Captain Gordon smiled, watching Dick spin slowly in the center of the room, taking it all in. Dick turned to the policeman with wide eyes and spoke in a stage whisper.

"That guy's *loaded.*"

Captain Gordon chuckled. "Oh, no. Alfred is the butler here. Mr. Wayne is the one with the money."

Dick was about to ask what a butler was when he heard Alfred entering the room again, another man, presumably Mr. Wayne, following briskly behind him.

"I'm sorry to keep you waiting, Jim," Mr. Wayne announced. The police captain was getting to his feet, offering Mr. Wayne his hand. They shook.

"No, I'm the one who should apologize. It took us a long time to clear the scene in Newtown. I didn't mean to keep the boy up this late."

Mr. Wayne turned his attention to Dick, and Dick had a strange feeling that he'd met his host before. The man was tall and commanding, with dark hair and striking, angular features. As he crouched down in front of Dick to look him in the eye, Dick decided he didn't know him after all. He'd never seen anyone with stone-gray eyes before. The color was unusual, and Dick liked it.

"I lost my parents, too, Dick." The man spoke with an artless candor, as if he and Dick had known each other for years. "I won't say I know how you feel, but if you ever want to tell me, I'm sure I would understand."

Dick appreciated the offer, but he was restless and damp with his own unreleased tears. He knew that only action would keep him afloat. He was aching to run somewhere, or hit someone. To speak softly with a stranger about grief would undo him. He would drown instantly in his anguish and terror, drown in that pool of blood on the circus tent floor. Silently, he ground his back teeth together and offered Mr. Wayne a solemn nod.

"My name is Bruce," the man said, when it was clear that Dick was not going to respond. There was a pause and then, still gazing directly into the man's eyes, Dick realized he had to speak.

"I'm Richard John Grayson, but everybody calls me Dick. I'm with Haly's Circus." He paused and then added, as an afterthought, "Sir."

Bruce nodded. "I saw you perform tonight. You're going to be staying here for a few days while the police investigate what happened to your parents."

Staring into the man's eyes, Dick almost told him about Batman. But something in his gut warned him not to mention his personal vengeance demon while a police officer was nearby.

"We will do everything in our power to make your stay here a comfortable one," Alfred assured him, moving to stand behind Mr. Wayne.

Captain Gordon stepped forward and handed Dick a business card, which Dick accepted and nervously began folding into smaller and smaller squares. "You're in good hands here, Dick. Call me if you need anything. I'll be back to check on you in a day or two."

The men said good-bye to one another, Dick thanked Captain Gordon for the ride, and then Alfred closed the front door and turned to smile gently at Dick. Bruce was still standing in the living room, watching the young acrobat carefully. Alfred moved closer and placed a hand on the boy's shoulder.

"I wasn't sure if you would have had a chance to eat, Master Dick, and so I took the liberty of preparing a light repast."

"Thanks." Dick was feeling a little more confident with the policeman gone, and spoke more clearly, looking up from the richly detailed oriental carpet beneath his shoes. It wasn't that the captain hadn't been nice, it was just that as a Rom and a circus kid, Dick was naturally wary of law enforcement. He decided to put the minds of his hosts at ease. "I'll try not to be any trouble, and I don't think I'll be here very long." His face, which had been drawn and sullen all evening, suddenly took on its customary level of animation. "Can I tell you guys a secret?"

Alfred seemed to suppress the twitch of a smile, but Bruce nodded seriously. "Of course, Dick."

Dick turned so that he was facing both of them, then he spoke with quiet earnestness, his warm blue eyes sparkling.

"I don't know if you've heard of him, but *Batman* is working on this for me. He's gonna catch the guy who killed my parents."

Bruce and Alfred exchanged significant looks over Dick's head, but Dick barely noticed. He turned to the fireplace and tossed Captain Gordon's business card into the crackling flames.

"Dad," he whispered, "Mom—*akana mukav tut le Devlesa.*"

"Thanks for the shower." Nightwing frowned at Green Arrow, taking his boots off one at a time to shake the water out of them.

"That wet hair thing really works for you, kid. You look like the cover of a romance novel."

"I look like an idiot. You couldn't think of any way of stopping him that wouldn't trip me up, too?"

Green Arrow lost his patience, turning on Nightwing with sudden savagery. "You're supposed to be the level-headed one around here. What the hell were you *doing*? You spend an hour telling me how dangerous this Death-stroke character is, and then when we finally run into him, you don't do any of that distance and evasion stuff you've been preaching. No, you go after him like a rabid dog and you complicate every single one of my shots in the process!"

Nightwing, who had displayed such hot-tempered tenacity in physical confrontation only moments earlier, showed none of that moxie in verbal argument. Instead, he shifted his weight uncomfortably, looked down at the building rooftop, and spoke quietly.

"I'm sorry. When I'm fighting with Deathstroke close-range, it takes all my concentration. I didn't mean to jam your offensive."

Ollie snorted and, on a whim, gave Nightwing a sound shove. As he expected, the young vigilante immediately came to life, eyes narrowing, posture flowing into a defensive stance. Ollie stepped back and chuckled, gesturing for a truce.

"You give 'pushover' a whole new meaning, Bat-boy." Nightwing cocked his head to one side, confused, and Ollie continued. "Lucky for you, I was thinking ahead. Got a tracer on that creep."

Nightwing's masked eyes went wide. "You put a tracer on Deathstroke?"

Ollie beamed proudly and pulled a tracking device out of his quiver. "That's right. The old man's got your back."

"Damn!" Nightwing turned away from Green Arrow, looking agitated as he opened the small computer embedded in his left gauntlet. Ollie frowned. "I got one on him too, there's no way he'll miss both of them."

Green Arrow brought his tracker close to Nightwing's gauntlet and they silently compared the signals. Both blinking lights were heading in the same direction on the respective maps.

"So far so good." Nightwing shut his gauntlet comlink and turned to Green Arrow with new resolve. "Let's follow yours."

Green Arrow nodded and began rappelling down the side of the building toward Nightwing's bike. Nightwing followed close behind.

"So what did all that 'compensation' jazz mean? Who's the 'big guy'?"

"I'm not sure." Nightwing, either to show off or to save time, had forgone a line down to street level in favor of hopping down from one window ledge to the next in a zigzagging diagonal. "That could mean President Abdul-Hakam's bodyguard, who's awfully burly, or the president himself. Or someone prominent we don't know about yet, a major baddie, or even, I don't know, someone who's just . . . big."

Ollie snorted. "Thanks, Detective. That really narrows it down."

Nightwing shook his head with a sigh. "Narrowing it down is what comes next."

Ollie felt his boot touch cement and released his line. Nightwing bounded down behind him.

"Well . . ." Ollie pulled his line free and began winding it back up so he could stick it back into his quiver. "The good news is that whoever the 'big guy' turns out to be, if he's the one who's supposed to finish supplying payment for that kid's assassination, then he's the one who ordered it, right?"

"Maybe." Nightwing had moved farther into the shadows to start his bike. "Unless he's an uninformed financier, or someone who's being framed."

"Oh, for God's sake." Ollie listened to Nightwing push up the kickstand and start his bike. "Just tell me who to shoot."

He heard Nightwing laugh from somewhere behind him, then the headlight of the motorcycle cut into the darkness. Nightwing pulled the bike forward and Ollie hopped onto the back and consulted his tracker.

"He's heading west on Commerce."

"Let's review our objectives." Nightwing twisted around slightly in the driver's seat, addressing Green Arrow over his shoulder. "Deathstroke's not easy to defeat, as you just saw. We know he's the one who took the shot at Dabir Abdul-Hakam, but we also know he was hired to do so by someone else. Batman and Arsenal are looking into that, and Aquaman and Tempest are guarding the boy. So all we have to do is clarify the information we got from Slade, and keep him from getting another chance to hurt Dabir. Are we on the same page?"

Ollie had not looked up from his tracker. "He's *still* heading west on Commerce."

Nightwing gave an exasperated sigh and lifted his foot up as the bike started moving. "Fine. We'll go west on Commerce. But just so you know, there's a ninety percent chance we're being led into a trap right now."

Ollie looked up from the tracker with a slight nod. "That's why I always wear clean underwear, kid."

They drove in silence for a while, except for Green Arrow's occasional directions as he tracked Deathstroke's signal. They seemed to be heading toward Chinatown. The signal stopped moving at Englehart Boulevard, so they stashed the bike a reasonable distance away and hit what Nightwing liked to call the rooftop express.

"Hey, you never finished telling me about Death-stroke's kid," Ollie prompted as they closed in on a small Chinese restaurant that smelled of lemon chicken and fried rice. Ollie heard his stomach rumble and realized it had been over ten hours since he'd last eaten.

"Joey, yeah." Nightwing, intent on Green Arrow's tracker, failed to disguise the look of grief that passed across his face. "He was really . . . I mean, I love all my friends, but Joey was special. He'd gotten his throat slit by the Jackal early on—some kind of kidnapping thing Slade apparently couldn't prevent—and he couldn't talk, but . . . I don't know, in some ways he was the clearest communicator I ever met." Frowning at the rooftop he was standing on as if he could see through it into the restaurant, Nightwing motioned Green Arrow toward the back of the building. When he spoke again, he was whispering. Green Arrow knew they must be close to their quarry. "His power was amazing, he could literally inhabit you—you know, his body would just fall into a kind of trance, and he'd take over yours completely, and at that point he could talk or do pretty much anything in your body that you could normally do." Nightwing paused and turned to look at Green Arrow with obvious fervor. "Can you imagine that? Literally getting under someone's skin like that?"

Green Arrow smirked. "I prefer the old-fashioned way."

Nightwing shook his head, his masked eyes still wide with awe, and then turned his attention to the small loading area below him and just behind the restaurant. "Anyway, we were battling Trigon—the demon lord, you've heard of him?"

Green Arrow shook his head. "You kids sure get around."

Ollie was joking, but Nightwing's jaw had tightened, his mouth pulling down at the corners. "That fight was personal, too. Trigon, in addition to being probably the gravest threat to the planet I can think of, is the father of one of our members. So we were giving it our all, and somehow Joey released his own energy and ended up possessed with Trigon's. From that moment on, he was dead set on destroying the Teen Titans."

"We have a lock." Ollie was enjoying Nightwing's story—demons and betrayal and spiritual possessions—but he hadn't forgotten about the case they were actually working. He was standing three feet from the building's rear, and his tracker clearly indicated that Deathstroke was in the building, directly underneath where he was standing. "Are you gonna insist on a plan or something?"

"Me?" Nightwing relaxed into a smile. "How about we plan on beating him into submission?"

"Now we're talkin'." Green Arrow was about to leap off the rooftop into the back lot when Nightwing stopped him. He had his gauntlet computer open again and did not look pleased.

"Hold on. My tracer's still in motion."

Green Arrow tensed impatiently. "What's that mean? He stuck it on a stray dog? Who cares?"

Nightwing leveled a sober gaze at him. "How'd you get yours on?"

"With an arrow, of course. It's a sticky. Just has to side-swipe him and it'll attach to his side or his upper arm or whatever." Green Arrow folded his arms across his chest, green eyes twinkling with pride. "Invented it myself, based off of close observance of weeds."

Nightwing nodded. "Okay, no offense, but he probably noticed yours first. I got a chance to plant mine while I was in close. It's in the middle of his back, hard to reach even if he does notice it."

"First of all, I'll be offended whenever I feel like it." Ollie was frowning, and he glanced down at his tracker again, then pointed to a man in his early thirties who had just stepped out from the back of the restaurant to light a cigarette. "Second of all, who the hell is that, and why is he wearing my tracer?"

During his eighth evening as a guest at Wayne Manor, Dick let himself out the window of his second-floor bedroom, jumping toward a nearby oak and catching a sturdy branch with both hands. He didn't realize he was smiling as he slowed his fall with a graceful double spin, and was frowning again by the time he dropped lightly to the soft, perfectly mowed lawn of the mansion.

Without the aid of a net!

Dick shivered and pulled a cap out of the front of his jacket. There was no one to notice or stop him as he began to sprint across the lawn. The entire Gotham suburb of Bristol was empty and quiet. He'd have to remind Bruce to get a dog.

If he ever made it back.

He was a polite enough child to feel awful about leaving Bruce and Alfred without so much as a good-bye, but he knew they would have tried to stop him. They had to, it was their job. And they'd really been very nice to him. He had wanted to get a chance to thank them. He wouldn't have minded staying if things had been different. Alfred was one of the coolest guys on the planet, and although he hadn't gotten to know Bruce Wayne very well, the billionaire's sheer size thrilled him—there was something about his remote host that he trusted implicitly. Someone had killed his parents too, after all. And in the same way that Alfred always knew exactly what to say, Bruce had a way of saying nothing that made perfect sense. They had both seemed lonely to Dick, and he had been hoping he could help. He had a child's endless desire to be useful, and a child's nearly flawless ability to tell the good guys from the bad guys. Bruce and Alfred were good guys; mountains of contradictory evidence couldn't have convinced him otherwise. But eight-year-old Dick Grayson didn't have time to hang with the good guys just yet.

His life had crossed paths with a bad guy.

He reached the manor gates slightly short of breath. The city was down the hill. He remembered from when the policeman had driven him here, and besides, it was only logical. With one apologetic glance back toward the mansion, Dick began to run down the paved road. He hadn't even had time to leave a note, and grown-ups worried so much.

Sorry, Bruce.

The wind felt good against his face as he ran, but a rumble in his stomach reminded him that he was about to miss supper. They'd have it in the dining room again, probably. Just Bruce, and Alfred standing behind his chair. They wouldn't even talk.

Sorry, Alfred.

And he doubted he'd make it all the way downtown before dark. It was one of the things he could remember his mother telling him, teasing him gently, although he hadn't understood the joke: "You're too pretty to be in the city alone after dark. But then, so's your father." Dick curled his fingers around the orange toothbrush in his jacket pocket.

Sorry, Mom.

He just prayed he wasn't already too late. He should have done more sooner. He'd left it in the black-gloved hands of the scariest guy he could find. And although he was certain that Batman had been doing everything he could, and still was more than willing to help him if he could find him, he'd heard only slightly less than a million times from his father's own lips that if you want something done, you have to do it yourself.

He heard the amused, rich voice again as he raced down the hill, like it was right in his ear, or a permanent stain in his blood. "Listen to me, Dick, I'm serious. I may not know everything about this crazy world, but what I do know, I know hard. You're gonna hear this so many times you're gonna stop hearing it, ya know what I mean? But it's the best advice I can give you: if ya want something done, ya gotta do it yourself. You know what that really means? It means every man on the planet is a complete dolt compared to *my* son. It means no stuntmen. It means you doubt yourself and you're dead. It means pass on the glory and you might as well *be* dead. Remember that, and life's a cakewalk. Life's a damn cakewalk . . ."

Dick's eyes had started to tear as he continued to run. He told himself it was from the cold.

I'm sorry, Dad! I'm so sorry . . .

It wasn't just luck when four hours later, in a part of the city that was so much colder and darker and dirtier than Bristol it might have been on a different continent, Dick actually found the man he'd been looking for. Tony Zucco, after all, had also been looking for him. And although an eight-year-old boy running around the Gotham Bowery showing a Wanted poster of a man he hoped to find wasn't unheard of, one brave enough to walk up to prostitutes and into bars and pool halls was uncommon.

For his part, Tony Zucco was already packed and ready to leave town. The cops were bad enough, but somehow he'd become the sole pet project of Gotham City's masked vigilante, and he wasn't ashamed to back away from a showdown with *that* freak. Still, if he could eighty-six his one and only material witness before hitting the highway, so much the better. Every single one of his associates was under orders to point the kid toward his hideout, and to call him the minute the brat started getting close. And since Tony Zucco had considerably more associates than Dick Grayson, it wasn't really so hard to get his hands around the back of the kid's neck before dawn.

"Well lookey here!" The boy squirmed with all his might, but Zucco wasn't about to let him go. "The one that got away! Nice of you to drop by. You don't really think I won't kill you just 'cause you ain't shaving yet, do ya, kid?"

"Let go of me!" Dick demanded. "I'll *kill* you!"

Zucco laughed. He'd never actually killed a kid before, but he was really looking forward to it. Especially this one. They were alone by a row of condemned tenements lining the bank of the Sprang River in a neighborhood infamous for its lack of cops and civic-minded citizens. Suddenly, everything was going his way.

"You and what army, Peewee?"

"You killed my parents! You *killed* them! Why? *Why!?*"

"Why? Why not? You know somethin', junior? I don't even remember. Somethin' about insur—OW! HEY! Muther-a—!" Involuntarily, Zucco flexed his hands, allowing the boy to slip from his grasp. Pain was burning through his leg. The brat had somehow managed to twist and kick, hard, at his shin. "You little . . ."

"Police!" Dick shouted, loud and more angry than scared. "*Police!*"

Zucco spun wildly, shaking with adrenaline. There was no one in sight. Well, that was just about enough of that! Sneering in anger, he pulled a small black handgun from an inside vest pocket. The kid saw it flash in the streetlights and looked angrier yet. With a snarl of indignation, the eight-year-old charged at the gangster like a quarterback. Tony Zucco gasped as the small, bent head connected with his gut. It didn't really hurt, but it did knock him over. He grabbed a fistful of the boy's thick, dark hair as he went crashing down, and the kid rolled with him. The gun fired wild, missing them both.

"You little—" Zucco had the boy by the hair, and he pulled his head up as soon as he was balanced on the gravel, recocking the gun with one hand and pressing the still-hot muzzle against the boy's temple as the kid, sobbing with frustration, attempted to pulverize him with a volley of powerful but mostly misguided punches. "I don't know if you're brave or just stinkin' crazy, kid! And I don't frickin' care!"

"Die!" Dick was screaming between his sobs, swinging as hard as he could, over and over again. "*Die!*"

"*Dick!*"

Zucco whirled the gun in the direction of the voice just as a tight eight-year-old fist connected with his jaw, snapping his head back. Zucco fired again, then roared in anger as a hard metal object flew out of thin air to knock the gun painfully out of his hand.

Tony Zucco didn't seem to mind that he had lost his gun. He was ready to kill Dick Grayson with his bare hands. The man and boy were locked in mortal combat, both blind with rage, struggling at the lip of the river, unyielding.

Out of the corner of his eye, Zucco thought he saw a dark shape moving quickly toward them when the guardrail suddenly snapped, causing him and the boy to lose their purchase on the slippery cement rim of the waterway. Still tangled in fury, they plummeted together into the ice-cold waters of the Sprang River.

"Get offa me you crazy brat! I'm gonna drown you! I'm gonna frickin' drown you!"

Dick coughed desperately as his lungs filled with water.

He flailed wildly, trying not to panic, less concerned with staying afloat than with somehow sinking the man who thrashed in the water beside him.

"I *hate* you!" he hollered when he had coughed up enough water to speak again. "*Help*," went through his mind, and also "*drowning*," but what he continued to spit out was a litany of fury. "I hate you! I hate you! I hate you!"

"I'd be saying my prayers if I wuz you, clown boy!"

". . . *Hate* you!"

He saw Tony Zucco's face, wet and enraged and sneering—stringy, sparse hair flattened against his reddened forehead. And then he felt an irresistible pressure against his head and neck and he had to close his eyes because the salt was stinging them and he was once again fully submerged.

Don't breathe! he commanded himself fiercely as he reached up to try to pry away the large hand that held him captive. His lungs were about to burst and as hard as he tried, he couldn't free himself from the murderer's grasp. *Don't wanna die!* Fear began swelling up for the first time in his chest. *Not now! Not like this!*

And then the thought that followed, unmediated and genuine, nearly broke his heart as reality rushed up behind it, twisted and gruesome. Under the inky black waters of the Cape Carmine Bay, Dick Grayson's lips, blue with cold and lack of oxygen, parted in frenetic entreaty. He called out for help, for comfort, for defense, for mercy, for warmth, for God.

He called out for his mother.

The sob that followed sucked too much water down his throat. "Batman . . ." he thought, a second before black pain exploded in his head. From the oxygen-rich height of another world, Tony Zucco leered with satisfaction as the young boy's body finally went limp under the powerful, submerging pressure of his hands.

"That'll teach you ta mess with—"

Zucco would never be able to explain what happened next. One minute he was there, treading competently enough in the freezing water and not even upset by how far out the current had already dragged him, and the next minute his face was split in pain, blinding fire spreading in a blaring line beneath his nose as the world went dark and wet, full of chills and salt and throbbing agony.

What the hell happened to the air? Zucco struggled against the intense desire to grab his nose and wail in torment just long enough to find the water's surface again and indignantly cough up his share of seawater.

What the hell happened to the kid?

Something shot past him in the water, fast and intrepid, like a shark. Zucco recoiled instinctively and turned around to make sure it wasn't coming back. That's when he saw a demon rising out of the water to grab the body of the drowned boy. Without so much as a glance toward Zucco, the Batman tucked the boy under one arm, careful to keep his head above water. Then he began swimming for shore faster, Zucco knew, than humanly possible. Without a second thought, Zucco began to swim in the opposite direction as fast as he possibly could.

Dick was aware of nothing but coldness and water and a darkness so total it blurred the lines between him and the world he was trying to swim back to. He thought he heard a deep voice tell him not to struggle, and then rocks were being dropped on his chest and a hot, insistent wind was locked around his mouth and trying to force its way into his lungs. Confusion gave way to a sudden liquid certainty. His eyes opened and he coughed up what felt like four lungfuls of water, not at all surprised to see Batman kneeling over him.

"Batman," he whispered hoarsely. "Batman, we've got to—"

"Quiet."

Dick struggled up to a sitting position, clutching at his chest to try to shove back the pain that washed through him, and scrambled angrily to his feet.

"Zucco, he's—"

"Gone. You . . . fought well. But we lost him."

"No!"

Batman rose to his feet and stood still while Dick spun himself in every direction, desperate for a glimpse of his nemesis. The Cape Carmine dock was utterly bare except for him and Batman and the watery outline of where he had lain. Comprehending how close he'd come to death again, and also how close he'd come to getting Tony Zucco, Dick shook with a final burst of adrenaline. Turning to the man who had saved his life, he began beating on Batman's gray-and-black-clad torso with his fists.

"No! We *couldn't* have lost him! We *couldn't* have! Why'd you let him get away!? Why? *Why!?*"

Batman said nothing as the small, wet child hammered against his chest, exhausting himself finally and falling against the vigilante with a hiccup of despair. Shifting imperceptibly, Batman radioed the Batwing. When its shadow obscured the moonlight and a gentle hum signaled the possibility of boarding, Dick Grayson pushed himself far enough off of his hero's chest to blink up at the strange object in the sky, his blue eyes sparkling with curiosity.

"Where're we going?" Dick asked, swaying somewhere between exhaustion and relief.

"Home," Batman answered. He detached the long, flowing cape from the mask that covered his head and neck and draped it carefully around Dick's shoulders. Dick pulled the cape more tightly around himself, lulled by the sudden warmth, and smiled sleepily up at the man who was frowning down at him.

The smoker who had emerged from the small Chinese restaurant was looking up at Nightwing and Green Arrow, somewhat alarmed. Nightwing frowned at Green Arrow's tracer, frowned at the smoker, and then, offering a brief shrug in answer to Green Arrow's inquiry as to his identity, leapt off the two-story roof, landing in a crouch a few feet away from where the man stood.

"Let's ask him."

"What happened to the beating-someone-into-submission plan?" Green Arrow tried not to sound disappointed as he followed Nightwing's lead, bounding off the building and into the small back courtyard.

Glancing back and forth between the two costumed heroes, the would-be smoker panicked and turned toward the back door of the restaurant as if planning to bolt. Green Arrow calmly sent an arrow at a diagonal through the doorjamb, effectively rending the exit useless.

"*Salaam alaykum*," Nightwing said formally.

The man answered haltingly and Green Arrow decided that maybe he wasn't Chinese after all.

"*Kaif hal ak.*"

"We're associates of Deathstroke," Nightwing continued smoothly. Green Arrow decided to stand behind him and look tough, since the kid seemed to know what he was doing. "Didn't he tell you we'd be coming?"

The young man shook his head slowly, keeping his mouth firmly shut.

Having spent three seconds standing still, Green Arrow grew bored and stepped in front of Nightwing to begin patting the man down. "I'm sorry," he apologized, "I'm terrible with names. Let's see here . . ." He produced a wallet from the young man's back pocket and flipped it open to reveal his driver's license. "Salah? Am a pronouncing that right?" He flashed the license at Nightwing, but noticed that Nightwing had shifted so that he was now standing behind Green Arrow, looking tough. Green Arrow grinned and threw Salah back his wallet. The man caught it, blinking rapidly.

The back lot was small and dirty, surrounded by a worn chain-link fence and finished with a narrow concrete walk that led four feet from the back of the restaurant and then stopped abruptly, haphazard patches of grass surrounding it on three sides. One naked bulb over the door was attracting frantic moths above Salah's head, and littered cans, plastic bags, and cigarette butts were strewn everywhere. It was, Green Arrow thought grimly, a pretty good place for a fight, but poor Salah was definitely out of his league.

"He was just here though, right?" Nightwing asked

Salah, stepping forward again. He and Green Arrow didn't seem to be able to get their good cop/bad cop routine down and were slowly settling into something closer to an Abbott and Costello routine. "Deathstroke?"

Salah was clearly nervous, but also steely-eyed and defensive. As if to prove his indifference to their presence, he lit his cigarette and took a long drag. Nightwing and Green Arrow exchanged glances. The kid had almost managed to keep his hands from shaking. Almost, but not quite.

"He was, wasn't he?" Green Arrow threw his hands up and turned away, pretending to be hugely offended. "And he didn't leave any instructions for us? After we came all this way?" He turned to Nightwing with a mock frown. "Well how d'you like *that*?"

"What *did* he say?" Nightwing asked Salah, keeping his tone conversational.

Salah took another drag on his cigarette and squinted at the heroes through the smoke.

"He said you were the reason he couldn't complete his contract," Salah said smoothly. Standing less than a foot behind him, Green Arrow could clearly see Nightwing's posture tense even before Salah called for reinforcement. "Burhan! Ghazi!"

From his peripheral vision, Green Arrow caught the movement of two additional figures shouldering their way out through the restaurant's back door, and was already snatching an arrow from his quiver when he heard his partner's calm warning.

"Gun," Nightwing said, and was then a blur of movement rushing toward the assailants.

Green Arrow fired at the man to Salah's left—Burhan, he decided arbitrarily—just in time to knock a large Smith & Wesson out of his hand. Burhan gurgled in pain as he found his right hand attached to the door frame by Ollie's arrow. Nightwing had already leapt over Salah and was tearing through the reinforcement muscle rapidly filing into the restaurant's stockroom, which left Salah and the man to his immediate right for Green Arrow.

Green Arrow already knew that Salah wasn't armed from when he'd patted him down for his ID, but the man to his right, Ghazi, who must have been at least seven feet tall, produced both an automatic assault rifle and an ugly smile.

Drawing blindly, Green Arrow found himself loading a grapnel arrow into his long bow. It wouldn't have been his first choice, but Ghazi was already tearing up the dirt and weeds by his feet with rapid-fire shrapnel and there was no time to switch out arrows. Frowning at the restaurant rooftop, Green Arrow fired over Ghazi's head and grabbed on to the trailing grapnel line with one gloved hand, winding it around his wrist to truncate the line length while rolling sharply left to avoid a fresh burst of fire from the assault rifle. The millisecond he felt the arrowhead burrow into the roof, he grit his teeth and tugged on the shortened line. Ghazi followed Green Arrow's trajectory with the muzzle of his gun, releasing intermittent bursts of fire as the archer's boots left the ground and came flying toward him. Green Arrow realized in midair that there was a very good chance he'd get sprayed by gunfire as he closed the distance between himself and the shooter, but if there was one thing nearly two decades' worth of heroing had taught him, it was that even the most boneheaded move demanded full commitment once execution had begun.

His right boot connected with Ghazi's face with a satisfying crunch the exact same second that one of Nightwing's sharp, shiny Batarangs flew into the back of the gunner's neck in the chaos of the badly-lit stockroom. The assault rifle clattered to the cement steps leading from the stockroom down to the small back lot, and Ghazi's beefy hands grabbed Green Arrow's ankle as his eight-foot frame rocked backward. Green Arrow released the grapnel line and tried to roll with the remaining momentum, but the newly disarmed gunman would not release his hold on his assailant's ankle. They fell back together, toppling onto several of the storage-room lackeys already laid flat by Nightwing's offensive.

"'Scuse me, but I've grown rather attached to that," Green Arrow snarled, attempting to pull his ankle free. In response, Ghazi tightened his grip on the archer's right leg and clamped his jaws onto Green Arrow's foot, boot and all. Appalled, Green Arrow elbowed his slavering captor in the groin as hard as he could, but Ghazi only bit down harder until Ollie was convinced he could feel the man's molars breaking through the leather of his rather expensive boot. "Get *offa* me, you lunk!"

Though he didn't have time for a thorough head count, and Nightwing had kicked out the one naked bulb in the cramped storeroom so that only the dirty light from the kitchen filtered in to illuminate the fray, Green Arrow sensed at least eight other guys intently fighting Nightwing, and that wasn't including the four or five the former Boy Wonder had already taken down. Green Arrow could see flashes of his spirited partner emerge from the darkness: a leg low on the floor sweeping somebody's feet out from under them, a solid haymaker careening forward out of a shadowy corner, even an occasional booted foot impossibly high overhead, smashing into some unfortunate thug's ear or jaw. On his worst day, Green Arrow could easily handle a room of eight or ten all by himself—a fact that made his predicament with Ghazi all the more intolerable. It was like fighting a pit bull. Batman's kid would think he was a total loser if he didn't shake this one guy— big as he was—and get back into the fray. And God only knew what Ghazi's unorthodox fighting tactics were doing to his footwear.

Green Arrow tried to think back to the last time he'd fought a pit bull and realized that he never actually had— in fact, he thought they were fairly nice dogs who suffered mostly from bad reputations and inexplicably stupid owners. Still, if one *had* latched itself on to his foot, he'd probably kick it. Yeah, kick the side of its head with his free foot, that's what he'd do. And since Ghazi, at nine feet tall, was about thirty times the size of the average pit bull, Green Arrow decided it wasn't overkill to begin beating him over the head with the stave of his bow as well.

"You okay?" Nightwing's head popped out of the gloom behind Green Arrow's left shoulder where he was suddenly crouching. Concern tinged his voice.

"Got 'im right where I want 'im, kid," Green Arrow replied tersely. He thought he heard Nightwing laugh, but then—miracle of miracles!—the pressure on his foot slackened.

Green Arrow pulled his boot free from Ghazi's jaws

and bounded back up on his feet, ignoring the sharp throb of pain in his right tendon. His bow was in his left hand but he didn't care. More than anything, he felt like hitting the guy in front of him, even if he *was* ten feet tall. Ghazi had barely gotten up on to his own feet when Green Arrow planted a powerhouse straight shot dead in the center of his opponent's nose. Blood gushed over Ollie's green glove, but Ghazi failed to look fazed. That didn't surprise Green Arrow, though. When facing an eleven-foot-tall guy, it was reasonable to expect he wouldn't feel much pain.

With one last elbow to the throat, Green Arrow flipped backward twice, putting enough distance between himself and Ghazi to draw on him again. This time he reached straight for the punching glove arrow and loaded it with relish. Ghazi was already rushing toward him, snarling like a rabid beast, ignoring the blood still pouring from his nose.

"Keep comin'," Green Arrow murmured, grinning. Nothing wrong with a little convergent impact. He released the arrow and watched with satisfaction as it flew the remaining four feet between him and Ghazi, smacking Ghazi hard in what was left of his nose. To Green Arrow's great satisfaction, Ghazi stopped and swayed slightly, looking more confused than hurt, and then pitched backward, slamming the back of his head against the cement floor of the storeroom.

"You see that!?" Green Arrow looked around for Nightwing and caught sight of his partner's balled fist as he dealt a clean undercut into the solar plexus of one of the last storeroom thugs standing. "That guy was twelve feet tall!"

Nightwing smiled and then dodged out of the way of a thrown hunting knife. "He was a big boy, all right. That's why I left him to you."

Hands on hips, Green Arrow glanced over his shoulder and noticed that Burhan had managed to pull the arrow out of his hand, but then had seemingly passed out from the pain. That left Salah, unarmed, standing in the dirty back lot, shaking. Green Arrow walked up to him with a friendly smile and smashed his forearm into his throat.

"Sleep tight."

"Hey," Nightwing called. Green Arrow whirled back around to face the dark storeroom, loading his bow as he turned, but Nightwing had the last standing guy by the front of the shirt. "Did you leave anyone conscious?"

Green Arrow smiled and shook his head. "These boys are afraid of the sight of blood."

"Okay, then." Nightwing slammed the man he was holding against the storeroom wall and got up close into his face. "That means it's show-and-tell time."

Sauntering toward the storeroom, Green Arrow chuckled. "That means he shows you his fist and you tell him everything you know, buddy."

Nightwing was toe to toe with the guy, danger radiating off of him like a scent. All at once, he was making even Green Arrow feel a little nervous, and Ollie figured it was one of Batman's intimidation tricks. The man Nightwing was pinning against the wall was literally shaking, but also seemed strangely dignified and aloof.

"Kill all of us," he said in heavily accented English. "You will have stopped nothing."

Nightwing threw a wallet he had fished off the guy to Green Arrow, who caught it with ease. "And what is it we're trying to stop?" Green Arrow asked. He stood behind Nightwing and squinted at the contents of the wallet. " . . . Mr. Ehsan Ghazi?"

"The independence of Qurac," Ehsan answered with obvious contempt.

Ollie rubbed his beard in confusion and turned to Nightwing with a frown. "Isn't Qurac a democracy? I mean, I'm no whiz at global politics, but I'm pretty sure there's a pop song about that."

"I thought you guys were just lackeys for Deathstroke," said Nightwing, turning back to Ehsan. Green Arrow hid a smile. Nightwing thought no such thing, but it was a good way to step on Mr. Ghazi's pride and get him to clarify information he might not otherwise volunteer.

"He works for *us*," Ehsan hissed.

"As what?" Green Arrow asked. "Minister of Voter Registration Confirmation for Stateside Quraci Expatriates?"

Ehsan stared, hard, at Nightwing's boots, refusing to answer.

"I'm just kidding," Green Arrow said with a friendly smile. "I know he's an assassin, and I know all you guys here couldn't possibly have been expected to take down a fifteen-year-old boy by yourselves. I'm just wonderin' what killing him has to do with Qurac's democracy since he's not an elected official or anything. You understand that part, 'Wing?"

Nightwing shook his head. "I don't understand that part."

"Yeah," Green Arrow continued. "We don't understand that part. Maybe you could educate us."

Ehsan looked up into Green Arrow's eyes suddenly, his frown deepening. "The death of Dabir Abdul-Hakam was ordered by our leader, and is but a small part of our plan."

"Uh huh." Green Arrow was nodding his head, but the expression on his face was doubtful. Nightwing continued to pin Ehsan against the storeroom wall, ignoring the faint groans of Ehsan's colleagues on the floor, some of whom were slowly and painfully regaining consciousness. "And when this great plan is all accomplished and everything, who is it we're gonna give credit to?"

Ehsan's dark eyes lit on Nightwing. "You can call us the *Mutawwiin.*"

Nightwing was frowning, clearly lost in thought, so Green Arrow took it upon himself to kayo Ehsan with a sharp uppercut to the left temple. Ehsan slumped against the wall, and then fell to the floor as Nightwing released him and turned his attention to Green Arrow.

"What'd you do *that* for?"

Green Arrow shrugged, frowning back at his younger, temporary partner. "We're done here, ain't we? And we got another tracer to catch up with. Let's just call in the CBI or somebody and get outta here already." Ollie turned his attention toward the empty kitchen and gestured to a collection of pots still boiling on the industrial stove. "That or grab some Kung Pao chicken. That fight with the thirteen-foot giant made me a little peckish."

Nightwing sighed and examined the tracer display on his gauntlet. "Target two is still moving, but I feel like there's more to know here. '*Mutawwiin*' is a Saudi Arabian term for the Committees of Public Morality, though now that I think about it, the word itself literally means 'volunteers,' or 'the obedient.' But I'm unaware of any such group in Qurac."

Green Arrow gestured impatiently toward the bodies littering the floor. "Well, there's your problem, kid. They're not in Qurac. They're here!"

Nightwing walked to the back door and shot a grapnel line up at the restaurant's roof. "Go ahead and call this in," he told Green Arrow. "I'm gonna feed the cell name to Batman."

Green Arrow nodded and watched as Nightwing used the grapnel line to disappear into the humid night. Then he began to look around the storeroom for a pay phone. "Hey," he said, gently prodding the unconscious form of Ghazi with the toe of his boot. "Any chance you got a quarter?"

Dick was only eight years old when Batman unburdened his soul to him, confessing all his secrets in a quiet, measured tone. By that time, Dick had already traveled by wagon through winter-silenced fields under a moonless sky. He had held his breath under a canvas tent nearly three hundred feet tall and waited for the hot blast of a spotlight to pick him out of the imposed oblivion. He had stared out the windows of trains as they barreled through underground tunnels and slept in the back of trailers during generator failures and blackouts, but nothing he had ever seen was quite as dark as the cave. It wasn't only the absence of light. The cave *felt* dark and cool and damp. It defended its darkness and kept little corners of it alive even after Batman wired it for artificial lighting. There were times when Dick closed his eyes and opened them over and over again, trying to be sure of the difference.

Even standing in the circle of firelight cast by a single white taper, Dick was aware of the darkness as a living thing. He imagined it watching the flickering candle flame with amusement. He was also aware of the jagged rocks that surrounded him and the precipice less than twenty feet to his left. Most of all, though, he was aware of the man standing in front of him; the man with the voice like hot granite, wearing the mask of a demon. And he was aware that he was not afraid, even though the only element missing from the nightmare was blood. He was not afraid, and he was not asleep. And the man and the candle and the cave walls and the darkness . . . all of it belonged to him. He was as rich as he could imagine being.

Mirroring the man on the other side of the taper, Dick raised his right hand.

"Swear that you will fight against crime and corruption, and never swerve from the path of righteousness."

Dick's answer came from the bottom of his gut. "I *swear* it."

Batman held Dick's gaze and then he nodded, satisfied. He didn't say anything else. Dick slowly smiled, basking in the enormity of what he had just done. Batman had, at various times, referred to it as a ritual, a ceremony, and an oath, but Dick understood its true nature. It was not merely a pledge between the two of them, though certainly that element existed and was the one that Dick complied to without hesitation. If Batman had told him to walk off the edge of the precipice he would have done it, if only to feel the rush of falling interrupted by the hot, solid presence of Batman plucking him out of midair. His faith in his new guardian was absolute. And that's how he knew, too, what the oath really meant. It was a challenge to fate itself; a conscious rejection of destiny. It was a little prayer that told God he didn't have to worry about them anymore, because they were taking matters into their own hands. They were no longer merely orphans. They were apostates.

"Let's go over the rules one more time." Batman said "one more time" in a way that made it clear Dick should expect to hear the rules a minimum of three times a week for the next nine years of his life, but he didn't mind. He was good with rules, at least the memorizing and reciting them part; following them sometimes proved a little trickier. But if there was anyone he could fall in line for, it was Batman.

"Out on those streets, my word is law. You follow my orders without objection or hesitation. Ask questions in the car or in the cave—never in front of a civilian or enemy. We work in secret: our identities, our tactics, our limitations; none of these can be known outside these walls. There may be times when I can't explain my actions, even to you, but I promise that your safety will always be of paramount importance, as is the safety of every citizen of Gotham, even the criminals we fight." Batman paused to look into Dick's face and seemed to see nothing to dissuade him from continuing. For Dick's part, he felt he was all but bursting with compliance. He admired every detail about the man in front of him and had no trouble imagining a life devoted to exceeding his every expectation.

Batman continued. "Your training will be intensive. It will also be incessant. In addition to physical conditioning, I will need you to master numerous skill sets ranging from analytical thinking to Zen meditation. Some of these will challenge your natural aptitudes, but there are benchmarks I will have to insist that you hit. However, it is critical that none of this interfere with your academic development. School is your primary responsibility, and I expect you to perform there flawlessly. At the same time, you must not draw undue attention onto yourself. Organized sports and other competitive endeavors are no longer permissible. Once you're at a brown belt level in any one of the nine martial arts we will be studying this year, fighting with civilians will not be tolerated."

Dick was momentarily distracted by the leathery-winged flight of several large brown bats, but a slight shift in Batman's posture reclaimed his attention.

"I also need you to know that not everyone is cut out for the work I do. There's no shame in that, and you will remain in my custody regardless of your performance here. If you are anything less than one hundred percent committed out there, though, you become a liability to me. Do you understand?"

Dick nodded, but he was slightly thrown. Somehow the very mention of the word "shame," even when brought up in a reassuring context, made him aware for the first time of how much there really was to lose. Batman didn't say the final thing, the definitive rule, but Dick knew what it was. It took all of his effort not to make Batman say it to him out loud even though he understood that it was the sort of thing that would always remain unspoken between them. It really should have been rule number one: *Don't die*.

Dick already knew he could survive. He had knelt in the nadir of death and gotten up again with every hair on his head in place. But shame . . . Dick didn't understand why the concept chilled him so deeply, as if it had already burrowed somewhere under his bones. Facing criminals twice his size, dodging gunfire, diving from the top of seventy-story buildings; all of that sounded kind of fun. But the idea of Batman being *disappointed* in him . . . in that one moment in the cave, Dick instinctively knew that nothing could ever be more threatening to his survival. The idea was so frightening and overwhelming, he had to stop thinking about it all together. He took a deep breath and exhaled slowly.

"So," he said brightly, when his voice was once again steady. "What am I gonna wear?"

"You think we're gonna get to fight another terrorist cell?" Green Arrow had talked Nightwing into letting him drive the tremendously fast motorcycle while Nightwing rode on the back, navigating them toward his tracer. Nightwing had rigged Green Arrow with a comlink headset so that they could actually hear each other over the roar of the bike.

"The *Mutawwiin* aren't really a terrorist cell—not in the way you mean. They've never participated in international terrorism before. They're more like an independent political party in Qurac, though if you remember Qurac's history, that doesn't necessarily mean they're well-behaved diplomats. Batman has access to the Batcomputer on the Batplane, so he's still looking into them."

Green Arrow interrupted with a snicker. "You said that all with a straight face, didn't you?"

Nightwing frowned and continued. "In the meantime, I think it's fair to assume that their arrival here is in some way associated with President Abdul-Hakam's visit. They've been very vocal about their dislike of him."

"Do they dislike him enough to take a shot at his boy?"

Nightwing squinted down at the tracer in his gauntlet and then gestured to the right. "Deathstroke seems to think so. Why else would he lead us to those guys? Maybe they're who hired him. Head east here."

"East. Check." Green Arrow took an unnecessarily sharp turn, enjoying how well the bike handled. Nightwing didn't protest. "But you still think there's a chance that Deathstroke's son has something to do with this, right?"

Nightwing sounded startled. "What?"

"You know, 'cause he turned evil and all."

Green Arrow couldn't turn to look at him, but he felt Nightwing's posture slump slightly behind him.

"No. No, that's not what I meant. I guess I didn't finish that story, did I? Joey's not behind this. Joey's dead."

"Oh, uh—sorry 'bout that, kid." Green Arrow reached around to pat Nightwing on the knee. "Listen, nothin' to be ashamed of. He went after your team, you had to stop him . . ."

Nightwing shook his head. "I don't kill. But Slade does. And he—"

The bike screeched to a halt suddenly, sliding sideways forty feet before it came to a dead stop. Nightwing, assuming the worst, was already crouched on the back of the seat, ready to grab Green Arrow and bail, but Ollie still had control of the bike.

"You're tellin' me Deathstroke killed his own kid?"

Nightwing swallowed and nodded, slowly climbing back down into a proper sitting position on the back of the bike. "His first son, Grant, died in his arms. He was a victim of experimental inorganic meta-enhancement at the hands of the H.I.V.E. When Joey was corrupted, Slade stabbed him through the heart." Nightwing glanced down at his gloves and noted that his tracer had stopped moving. He looked up at Green Arrow with knotted brows. "Slade Wilson is a very complicated man, Ollie. He's dangerous and predatory and I have to consider him one of my foremost enemies. But you have to believe me, Deathstroke lives and works by a code of honor. He's been through so much—I don't know if you noticed that he only has one eye, but the other one was shot out by his wife, who's also dead now . . . He and I have always had a wary respect for one another and I know his failure to kill that fifteen-year-old wasn't accidental. Like Batman said, he wants us to be involved. He wants us to solve this case. Slade doesn't believe in using kids as pawns. I just can't believe he'd accept a contract on a teenager. In his own way, he's trying to prevent this crime."

Green Arrow was quiet for a moment, frowning down at the asphalt beneath the bike wheels. Then he raised his right boot to show Nightwing. "That guy back there, the twelve-foot giant I took down? He bit me."

Nightwing looked confused. "Uh . . . I'm sorry . . . what?"

"The terrorist, the *Mutawwiiny* guy. He tried to bite through my boot."

Nightwing opened his mouth to reply and then closed it again, utterly lost by the unexpected turn in the conversation. Green Arrow continued grimly.

"What I'm sayin' is, no one does anything thinking it's the wrong thing to do. The road to hell is paved with righteous dumbasses and all that jazz. I don't care if Deathstroke thinks he's stoppin' World War Three, he clipped a fifteen-year-old boy and he led you and me into a room full of animals armed with M-16s and bad teeth. Don't let your guard down just because you think we're all working together on this one. Deathstroke's got his agenda, the *Mutawwiin* have theirs, and we've got ours. We didn't get shot back there, and that's good. But one of those guys tried to bite my foot off." Green Arrow tapped on the tracking device in Nightwing's gauntlet. "Next time, it might be your head. Just remember that."

"Okaaay . . ." Nightwing blinked at Green Arrow's quiver as Green Arrow turned around in the driver's seat and started the bike back up.

"Do you need *medical* attention?" Nightwing asked the question gingerly, as if he was really asking whether or not Ollie needed psychiatric help.

"No."

"D'you need a new pair of *boots*?"

"Maybe."

"Okay, then. We'll, uh . . . we'll be sure to take care of that. Keep heading east. Looks like the tracer stops near the south side of Grant Park, City Hall District."

"Right."

"Fashion District's just north of that if you want to look at footwear . . ."

"You can shut up now."

"There're some great leather shops along Moldoff."

"I don't wear leather anymore. Got my own skin, don't need to sport someone else's." Green Arrow glanced at Nightwing over his shoulder with a grin. "Glad to hear *you're* up on the leather scene, though."

Behind his mask, Nightwing's eyebrows shot up and then he quickly frowned down at the tracker in his gauntlet. "We're almost there," he said curtly.

Green Arrow chuckled.

In the beginning, it was fantastic. Dick had needed a hero, and a hero had emerged. He knew complete fulfillment.

Dubbed Robin, the Boy Wonder, Dick wore a bright green short sleeved shirt covered by a brilliant red tunic, green gloves, boots, and shorts, and a canary-yellow cape that flowed just past his waist. A black domino mask hid his eyes and a bright yellow armored "R" was stitched over his heart. The code name was born of several elements: his red-breasted costume, his love of the hero Robin Hood, and his rejuvenating facility for inspiring hope in a man who mostly inspired fear. The one newspaper to catch sight of him racing across the Gotham rooftops called him a "laughing, darting ray of sunshine," and the crooks that sneered at his size when they met him in the urban nights quickly learned to fear the force of his undercut and his indomitable will. He used a slingshot in place of the heavier Batarangs that Batman wielded and scampered up and down the city skyscrapers with unrivaled skill and obvious delight. With Batman at his side, Dick felt invincible.

Maybe the very best part, though, was that Batman

seemed to need him, too. As much fun as he had with Bruce camping and studying and hosting the occasional cocktail party at Wayne Manor, Dick understood immediately that the other face, the mask, was his mentor's real one. Batman was who Dick Grayson knew and loved.

But Batman was rigid and uncompromising, especially with himself. He did not allow for much levity in his life and was often consumed by the cases he tracked. Having assigned to himself responsibility for every living soul in Gotham City, Batman triumphed in each battle he waged and yet still managed to be fighting a war that he consistently lost. It was simply not possible to save everyone, but Batman went out each night anyway, over and over again, not because he thought he could make it all better, but because he knew that without him it would be much worse.

Robin, on the other hand, went out every night because he wanted to be with Batman, and because he thought it was fun. And although this never changed the determination with which Batman approached his duties, it certainly made his nightly obligations easier to bear. Sometimes Robin could even make him smile.

It was more than anyone else had ever been able to do.

They were bonded, too, by their grief. Dick never forgot the first night he saw Bruce in distress. Dick didn't know what had upset him, but he'd never before seen his guardian as he was that night; brows high in grief, fists clenched, moving swiftly out of the house in his civilian clothes without a word to anyone.

"Where's he going?" Dick struggled in Alfred's arms as the butler moved to hold him back. It was pouring rain outside, all of Gotham drenched in gray.

"To the grave, no doubt." Alfred's reply was calm but tinged with sympathy. "Tonight is the anniversary of his parents' death. It can be a . . . difficult time for him. But I assure you that he will return in a much more civilized state."

Dick broke free and went racing out the front door after him. Alfred called for him but his voice was quickly lost in the rain. Water was everywhere, soaking Dick's clothes and hair, running off his face and down his neck. His feet were heavy and hard to lift as they stuck and slid, and his sneakers filled with mud. But he could see Bruce only ten or so yards ahead, already on his knees before the looming headstone of Thomas and Martha Wayne, head bent in misery. Dick ran faster than he'd ever run before.

"Bruce! Bruce!"

The lightning cracked and filled the sky with white light. Dick knew he couldn't be heard over the thunder. He continued up the hill, panting and stumbling for footing in the slippery grass, his breath puffing white clouds of heat into the freezing Gotham air until at last he reached him.

Without thinking, he threw himself across his mentor's back, clasping his arms around his throat and burying his face into the back of the man's warm neck.

"I'm here," he said, holding him as tightly as he possibly could. His feet rose just off the ground as he clung to Bruce's neck. "I'm here and you're not alone!"

Bruce turned and grabbed Dick in his arms, moving him like a tiny doll until he had him pressed against his chest. Dick's small feet were in the mud again, he was standing on his tiptoes between Bruce's knees. Bruce cupped the back of his head with one large hand and pressed it against his massive shoulder.

After a long moment, Bruce rose and took one of Dick's hands in his own.

"Come on," he said. "It's cold out here. Let's get you inside."

From that moment on, Dick understood the true nature of their partnership.

His first case required him to go undercover as a newsboy to break up an extortion racket, but soon he and Batman were fighting costumed criminals like Two-Face, Penguin, and the Joker, many of whom arrived in Gotham specifically to test their mettle against Gotham's Dynamic Duo. Though Dick's natural athleticism and aptitude for combat were obvious, Batman hadn't exaggerated about the intensity of his instruction. Dick's circus training served him well; he had no problem catching sleep during the odd off hours and seemed to have absolutely no interest in what his peers called "hanging out." He was happiest when fighting at Batman's side, but also took evident pleasure in his crime-fighting studies, devouring the material Bruce set up for him and constantly asking for more. Though he was uncomfortable attending school, he did so to please Batman, and although it made Bruce and Alfred uncomfortable, he slowly but surely teased them into the only social configuration he recognized: a family.

Bruce, who had trained himself in his late teens, seemed fascinated by the idea of working with so young a subject and frequently spoke to Dick about the tremendous advantage he would have if he continued working and training into his adult life. "Imagine knowing everything I know by the time you're twenty, and still having thirty good years in front of you."

Batman made such proclamations with discernible pride, but Dick didn't like to think about the future. The present was perfect. So perfect, in fact, that somewhere in the midst of his schooling and crime fighting and martial arts training, not to mention chess and music-appreciation lessons in the kitchen with Alfred, chemistry and forensic instruction in the lab, and applied probability algorithms in front of the giant Cray computer Batman was programming in the cave to hold criminal databases and assist in civic monitoring, Dick decided he didn't want his parents back. It wasn't that he didn't love and miss them. He just felt like he had collided headfirst with his true destiny and that anything that might threaten it—that might take him away from Bruce—was dangerous and unwelcome.

There was, of course, no real chance of his parents rising from the graves Bruce had appointed them in Newtown to wrestle their son back to his life at Haly's, but Dick felt his secret desertion of them like a shameful wound in his heart. He had finally found a way in which he would certainly disappoint his mentor and began to worry incessantly that Bruce would find out; detect it lurking in his heart or somehow read it written across his face. Bruce had lived without his parents for more years than Dick had been alive, but every gesture he made was dedicated to their memory and to the undying hope of avenging their meaningless deaths. Dick had dreams of pushing his own parents off the trapeze pedestal board and waiting for Batman to come and rescue him.

"It is perfectly natural to blame one's self for catastrophic events quite out of one's control." Alfred spoke reassuringly when Dick confessed to having nightmares about complicity in his parents' death. "Indeed, developmentally, a young man of your age is incapable of framing the world in any other context." In response to Dick's confused frown, the Wayne Manor butler added a comforting pat on the shoulder and a mug of freshly made hot cocoa. "In some ways, it might seem less frightening to believe one's self capable of egregious sins than to acknowledge one's utter powerlessness in the face of fate."

Dick blew across the face of the steaming chocolate and wrinkled his nose at the butler in protest. "But Bruce says we control our own fate."

Alfred smiled placidly, sprinkling a few miniature marshmallows into Dick's mug. "I suppose both things are true. One cannot control the events of the world, but nothing in the world can control one's response to those events save one's self."

"Ugh." Dick put a hand to either side of his head as the butler smiled again. "That totally makes my brain hurt."

"Do not fret so over your dreams, Master Dick. The unconscious mind is always working on practical problems in an emotional environment. Dreams can be a source of great insight, but they can also be expressions of residual anxiety or indigestion." Alfred bent over the kitchen table so that he was level with the boy's shockingly bright blue eyes. "I dare say, if they were still alive, you wouldn't really wish your parents harm now, would you?"

"Uh, no." Dick's voice was somewhat muffled behind the mug as he took a long swallow of hot chocolate, his eyes darting away from Alfred's. He didn't know how to explain to the thin English gentleman in front of him or the brooding billionaire upstairs how much he already loved them, how he couldn't think of anyone he wouldn't kick off a cliff to keep them safe and close.

He put the cup of cocoa down and looked up at Alfred seriously. "I'm gonna be a really good hero," he swore. "I'm gonna do everything Batman says and I'm gonna study really hard and someday, I'm gonna save *everyone*."

"I have no doubt that you will," Alfred said with a gentle smile.

"I'm serious."

Alfred stood up straight and met the twelve-year-old's eyes. "I know."

The second tracer led Nightwing and Green Arrow to a security apartment building off Andru Street just east of Old Gotham.

"We're going in, right?" Green Arrow was standing by the buzzer panel out front, peering in through the partially glass door for signs of a doorman or security guard.

Nightwing, who was quietly eyeing the fire escape on the west side of the building, nodded. "Yeah. Our guy's on the fourth or fifth floor. Lemme just—"

Green Arrow smiled at Nightwing and dragged his elbow up one row of buzzers and down the other. "Pizza!"

Nightwing jumped back from the building stoop into the shadows of the west alley and frowned at his cheerful partner.

"Ollie! Who orders pizza at three in the morning!?"

Green Arrow shrugged and shouldered in the door as a buzzer signaled the electronic unlatching of the bolt. "Crime fighters?"

Nightwing sighed and shook his head. "Well, I'm going up, I'll meet you in there."

Green Arrow held the door open with his boot. "Aw, come on, Wingster. What do you got against the front door?"

Nightwing was already scrambling up the side fire escape, but he paused to stick his head around the corner of the building and scowl at Green Arrow. "There's a security camera in there, for one thing."

Green Arrow peered into the harshly lit lobby, tugged at his beard with his right hand, and then pulled, loaded, and fired his bow with astonishing speed. "Not anymore," he replied with a grin. Nightwing rolled his eyes, even though he wasn't sure Green Arrow could see the gesture behind his eye mask, and continued up the fire escape.

The bars that covered the windows along the bottom of the building were no longer utilized by the time Nightwing climbed past the third story. The west window of the fourth-floor hall was covered in flaking white paint that came off on Nightwing's gloves to show spiderwebs of rust running across the frame. It opened outward only three inches, not quite enough for Nightwing to slip through. He loosened the screws by the lower sash in case he needed a fast exit later, then headed up to the fifth floor where a hastily replaced glass pane lifted easily out of its casing.

Less than half the lights in the hallway were in working order, but Nightwing stayed close to the wall out of habit, occasionally frowning down at his tracker. The trace he'd put on Deathstroke had been still for the past forty minutes, but Nightwing didn't truly believe that it was still on Slade, much less that Slade was peacefully sleeping a single floor beneath where he stood. The elevator engine whirred to life several feet away, and Nightwing ducked down into a carpeted central stairway before realizing that it was probably just Ollie being too lazy to take the stairs.

Nightwing moved stealthily down a single flight of stairs, then peered out into the fourth-floor hallway, which was more brightly lit than the fifth had been. He fished a small electronic device out of his right gauntlet, listened for the elevator to arrive and open on the lower floor, then snapped the device onto the plaster overhead, positioning it carefully against the side of the closest ceiling light. Crouching in the stairwell, he activated the night-vision setting in his eye mask while an electromagnetic breaker cut power to the central hallway lighting and the elevator controls. He smiled as he heard Green Arrow's quiet footsteps approach him from the lower landing.

"You can see in the dark, can't you?" Green Arrow was whispering into the radio link, but Nightwing motioned for him to get down and stay quiet. He pointed at an apartment door just to the right of the stairwell marked 4E and indicated that they should move up into the hallway and flank it before utilizing it as their point of entry. He was about to signal that the south window could be used as an emergency exit when Green Arrow frowned at him and flapped his own hands around meaninglessly in the air, apparently unfamiliar with standardized hand signals for close-range engagement operations. "First of all, I can barely see you," he whispered, annoyed. "Secondly, I think the door buzzing trick probably gave away our imminent arrival. And last but not least, *what*?"

Nightwing exhaled slowly and then stood up and gestured to the door again. "Fine, Arrow. Just go knock. Maybe we'll get really lucky and wake Deathstroke up from a doxylamine-enhanced REM sleep and he'll let us in and make some tea and tell us everything we want to know."

Green Arrow snorted. "Don't be ridiculous. You don't really think Deathstroke's behind that door, do you? Personally, I'm hoping for another branch of the terrorist cell, and it's only sporting to give 'em time to load."

"Man, I just can't wait to write up this case report for Batman."

Green Arrow strode up to the door marked 4E and jiggled on the handle. "Eh, quit whining and come pick this lock for me."

Nightwing obeyed, and had the lock jimmied in under four seconds. Green Arrow finally quieted down as the door swung open into a dark one bedroom apartment. He hung back to examine small items in the living room while Nightwing silently followed his tracer signal into the bedroom.

"I've got good news and bad news." Nightwing reappeared in the apartment's small living room holding a lightweight men's nylon jacket. Green Arrow turned and put down a decorative glass paperweight he'd been idly holding.

"The good news is, our guy's not here." Nightwing produced his tracer from the jacket's left pocket and flashed it toward Green Arrow, who nodded. "The bad news is, our guy's not here. He's definitely too small to be Deathstroke, though, and obviously a smoker. There's a stack of Arabic newspapers on the bedside table in addition to a half-finished cup of sweetened coffee. The bed's tousled but unslept in—like he read on it or watched TV or something—and I found the jacket hanging in the closet, though it's still damp under the arms from being recently worn in this heat. No sign of a female or roommate, and I've got a hunch this guy is military—there's an orderliness to the bedroom that suggests someone used to keeping personal belongings in a small, close space. Bathroom confirms that. Very minimalist. We need to know why Deathstroke thinks this guy is important, so we could wait here, or split up and—"

"He went out for cigarettes."

"Sorry?"

Green Arrow lifted a brimming ashtray off the coffee table and kicked over a small mesh garbage can that was completely empty except for several burnt-out matches and a used-up, crumpled pack of smokes. "Smoker, like you said. Cigarettes. Betcha can't find a fresh pack anywhere in this dump."

Nightwing flashed an approving smile. "Good! So we wait?"

Green Arrow put the ashtray back down and started walking toward the kitchen. "Let's see what our soldierboy's got to eat. I'm starvin'."

Nightwing hesitated in the dark living room, looking concerned. "Ollie, we don't know much about this guy. What if he hears you messing around in there and comes in armed or something?"

"Don't worry, kid." Green Arrow flipped on the kitchen light, causing Nightwing to recoil and throw an arm over his eyes while he fumbled with his eye mask to turn off the night-vision lenses. When he could see again, Green Arrow had several cupboards open and was grinning as he cheerfully opened a can of beans. "I'll make enough for three."

The real trouble started in Japan. The Dynamic Duo survived countless attempts on their lives and thwarted attacks on Gotham and her citizenry nightly for years. Disagreements between Batman and Robin passed quickly, as did Dick's insecurities. He was the perfect partner for Batman—Alfred knew it, Batman knew it, and truthfully, so did Dick. When he stopped being anxious about his tremendous good fortune he began to be grateful for it, and in his gratitude he was inspiring.

In time, the community of super heroes grew, and so, too, did the habit of working with a younger teen "sidekick." As the first and most experienced of these, Robin was a natural draw for his burgeoning peer group. By the time he was thirteen, he was the informally but unanimously elected leader of a teen super hero group called the Teen Titans. Though the group grew in size as Dick grew in age, initially it was him, Kid Flash, Wondergirl, Aqualad, and Speedy, the teen sidekicks of Batman, the Flash, Wonder Woman, Aquaman, and Green Arrow respectively. When they weren't saving the world (which was happening more often than their grown-up guardians imagined), they functioned as a sort of teen-hero support group for one another, their relationships slowly evolving and deepening until they understood themselves to be family.

Most of the Teen Titans regarded Batman with terror-tinged awe. All of them admired him, but none of them could understand how Dick could bear working with someone so dark and autocratic. What they did understand was the unqualified nature of Dick's loyalty to his mentor, and the tremendous skill and competence the relationship had apparently conferred on him. In some ways, it would have been easier on Dick if his friends hadn't learned so early to stop questioning him about his relationship with Batman. By the time Dick himself started questioning it, there was no one to talk to.

Bruce arranged the trip to Japan for Dick as a tribute to his ward's growing mastery of the martial arts. Dick was sixteen. Hearing Batman acknowledge that he was running out of things to teach Robin about hand-to-hand combat was such an unexpected honor it knocked the air out of Dick's lungs. He was thrilled to be getting a chance to study with one of Batman's original teachers, and was immediately aching to make both senseis proud. He promised Bruce he'd be on his best behavior and learn everything he possibly could. Packing, he realized how much he had missed traveling and let himself become excited about the adventure of visiting a country he hadn't seen before.

It wasn't until Alfred dropped him off at the airport with a slightly dimmed glow in his kind brown eyes that the reality of being away from Gotham began to sink in. Dick found himself telling Alfred that he didn't need to go, that he knew enough to keep helping Bruce and that was all that really mattered. Alfred forced a smile and told him not to be silly. Dick dawdled at the gate, tried to call

Bruce at his office from the airport pay phone fourteen times, and finally boarded the plane with a sinking heart.

Four hours into the flight, Dick realized what was wrong. Batman had sent him away. Batman would be working alone for the whole two months that Dick was supposed to be in Japan and he hadn't seemed the least bit concerned about it.

Batman didn't need him.

Dick's eyes dilated and his heart began to race. He put down the book he was trying to read when his hands started shaking so badly his eyes couldn't follow the print on the pages. Two flight attendants, convinced he was having an air-travel-related panic attack, plied him with water and maternal cooing, but Dick, who had been piloting a supersonic jet regularly since he was fourteen, couldn't catch his breath long enough to reassure them. His mind had seized on to a single word that seemed to hold his entire fate in its balance, and more than anything he needed it explained to him, needed to be sure he understood its definition. He thought back through the 218 passengers he had instinctively counted on his way to his seat while boarding and remembered that one of them had been carrying a law book. He jumped out of his aisle seat and headed for the five-foot-eleven, 165 pounds, brown-haired and hazel-eyed Caucasian male in 18b.

"Excuse me, sir. I'm sorry to bother you, but are you by any chance a lawyer?"

The man blinked up at the unusually handsome teenager frowning down at him and patted the empty aisle seat next to him. "Uh, yeah. Yes. I—I practice contract law for Madison and Brinn in Gotham." He stuck out a hand, which Dick accepted and shook. "Peter Boustani."

"I'm Dick."

"What can I help you with, Dick?" Peter still looked somewhat startled, but Dick was too preoccupied to notice. He rarely took note of the impact his charisma and intensity had on the people around him.

"Can you explain the term 'ward' to me. Like, what it means to be someone's 'ward'?"

Peter loosened his collar slightly as he answered. "As in 'ward of the state'?"

Dick shook his head. "No, like someone's ward specifically. Like you're a ward of a particular person."

Peter swallowed, squared his shoulders, and got his professional poker face back on. "It's pretty much the same idea, really. A ward is a minor or incompetent person placed under the care or protection of a guardian or court—a guardian, it sounds like, in your case. If you're a ward that just means you're in someone's legal custody, that's all."

Dick's brows furrowed and he began to fidget with his own fingers. "But you said a minor or incompetent person . . . so, if I'm someone's ward now, what happens when I turn eighteen?"

Peter smiled and nodded. "Well, assuming you're competent—which you very much seem to be—you'd be automatically emancipated. In Gotham, at least, eighteen means you're of legal age. You'll be a free man."

"And my guardian . . . ?"

Peter shrugged. "Doesn't really have a legal responsibility to you from that point on. If there's a matter of an inheritance of something, I could look over the paperwork for you, or—"

"No, uh, that's okay." Dick stood and started to move back into the aisle, then offered his hand again and shook Peter's firmly. The cabin pressure was starting to hurt his ears. "Thanks. That's all I needed."

Taking in the teenager's pale complexion, the lawyer looked concerned. "Are you okay, Dick?"

"Yeah, I, uh—thank you. Thanks."

But Dick was not okay. Japan was torment. The dojo Dick attended was top rate, but Dick, during that time, was not. The sensei ordered him into longer and longer sitting meditation sessions, concerned with what he deemed "homesickness and a restless, grasping spirit." Unable to quiet his racing mind, Dick tried to follow the sensei's instructions and just let his thoughts flow through his mind without assigning value to them, but found that he could not detach. Despite a lack of supporting evidence, he had completely convinced himself that Bruce would throw him out of the manor and the Batcave the literal moment he turned eighteen. He oscillated between anxiety and despair and felt the sensei's frustration with him mounting.

"You are perhaps the most naturally gifted fighter I have ever had the honor of instructing, but you are unfocused, Grayson-san. You cannot truly master your body unless you also master your mind."

Dick didn't tell the sensei that it was really his heart that was out of control.

During the seemingly endless hours on the *zabuton*, Dick tried to think of how he could remain valuable to Bruce past his eighteenth birthday. His mind was more creative than he had previously realized. During one two-hour meditation he imaged himself as Bruce's legally adopted son, as his business partner at Wayne Enterprises, and as an adult sidekick working by his mentor's side forever. None of the scenarios seemed likely. Could he grow up to be Batman's best friend, his equipment developer, his lieutenant, his enforcer? What did Batman need? By the time his brain started entertaining the idea of growing up to be a super-villain menacing Gotham City just to keep Batman entertained, Dick got up from the meditation cushion with a grunt of self-disgust and began beating on the dojo's heaviest punching bag until the sensei came and insisted on a walk around the lake bordering the school grounds.

"Shall I send you home, Grayson-san?"

Dick kept his eyes turned toward the water and let one hand brush against the low-hanging ginkgo branches they passed. "No, sir. I—I know I'm screwing up, but . . . I can't go home 'til I get in right. I can't go home . . . disgraced."

The sensei nodded and they walked together in silence for a while. Dick noticed how unfamiliar the tree-filtered sunlight felt on the back of his neck and wondered how much of himself he'd already lost to the night.

"That which you cling to is already gone." The sensei's words stopped Dick in his tracks, but the sensei kept walking and Dick hurried to follow. Was it true? Was Bruce already something he had lost? He didn't think he'd be able to bear that, though he couldn't quite say why. An image of his mother's face floated into his mind suddenly and Dick stopped and swallowed, staring at the tree roots that rose up from the soil and the blanket of fallen golden leaves beneath his feet.

"You mean my parents, don't you?"

The sensei stopped and turned to the teenage boy with an enigmatic smile. "I mean that somebody taught you how to defy gravity long ago, but you choose to remain shackled to the ground. You are free as soon you decide to be free."

Dick kicked a small pebble into the lake and hid a shy smile. "I bet you say that to all the students."

"Only the ones who can fly."

Dick stared at the lake and the sensei stood beside him, also looking out over the water.

"I think I might be doing everything for the wrong reasons," Dick confessed. "Just more and more I have these . . . weird thoughts."

"The surface of the lake is easily disturbed," the sensei said slowly, still turned toward the water. "A rock, the breeze, the rain, a fish coming up from underneath . . . We see waves here sometimes, and mud clouding the depths from our view. But at its center, the lake remains unchanged. If you were to swim out to the middle and sink to the bottom and sit there for a hundred years, you would hardly notice the changes in weather or the passing of time."

Dick decided it wouldn't be polite to mention that anyone sitting at the bottom of any lake for a hundred years wouldn't notice anything at all due to the fact that they'd be totally dead. Except for maybe Superman.

"Your thoughts are the surface of your mind: windy and wild. At your center, your core, below your orphan nightmares and your gypsy heart, you are not so easily swayed."

Dick frowned to himself and turned to meet the sensei's eyes. His teacher was watching him with careful attention.

"I can teach you to fight from that place, Grayson-san. But whether or not you choose to live from there is up to you."

Dick's brows knotted. "What if I don't? I mean, what if I'm *not* a lake? What if I'm more like a river, or—or a waterfall?"

"Moving water is good for stirring *chi*, it can bring much energy. But a soul that cannot be still is a soul that loses itself over and over again trying to attach to the impermanent. There may be moments of great joy and great grief, but peace will be elusive. When you grasp too tightly at water, all of it slips through your fingers. If you yourself are the waterfall, then you are always falling from a great height; falling in love, falling in line, falling into disarray, falling apart. Falling off the wagon, falling to your knees, falling short of perfection, falling into place . . ."

The sensei trailed off and Dick stood up straighter, raising his eyes from the reflection of the clouds in the water to the actual clouds overhead. "Yeah," he said quietly. "That sounds about right."

By the time Mahbi Bin Thawab Almihdhar got back to his apartment, there was a masked man dressed as Robin Hood sitting at his dining-room table enjoying a large bowl of chili and a glass of cold grapefruit juice while another masked man in a skintight black and blue unitard crouched on the arm of his couch, casually flipping through his record album collection.

Seeing them, Mahbi immediately dropped a small plastic grocery bag on the floor and lifted both hands in the air.

"Take anything! I am not wanting any trouble!" Mahbi's accent was thick and recognizably Quraci. The man in green smiled at him reassuringly as the man in black magically disappeared and then reappeared behind Mahbi, gently closing the apartment door behind him.

"No worries," said the man in green. "We're the good guys. I'm Green Arrow and that's Nightwing. There's some chili on the stove, though I gotta warn ya, this batch is a real scorcher! Those chilies you had in the crisper could make a grown man weep."

Mahbi stared at the man in confusion and then flinched as Nightwing handed him the grocery bag he'd dropped on the floor. "You are sent here then by Cheshire?" Mahbi asked nervously.

Nightwing and Green Arrow exchanged glances.

"No," Nightwing answered, still blocking the door. "But we can help protect you from her if you tell us everything you know about the attempt on Dabir Bin Hatim Abdul-Hakam's life." Mahbi shifted his weight toward his bedroom and was immediately stopped by Nightwing's gloved hand on his shoulder. "I unloaded the gun in your bedroom closet, and also the one under the couch. Sorry, but Green Arrow here already had his boot bit earlier this evening and we're trying to exercise a little caution now."

From the table, Green Arrow nodded in agreement. "Yeah, and my skinny buddy here won't eat anything until he knows he's not gonna have to fight anymore tonight, so do him a favor and pull up a chair."

Mahbi stayed rooted in his entryway for another long minute, then sighed and carried his bag into the kitchen. He tried not to be unnerved by Nightwing's careful observation of his every move as he put away a pint of milk and pulled out a fresh pack of cigarettes. Green Arrow smiled as he watched him light up.

"It is Safwan he who sends you then, yes?"

Another frowning glance was exchanged between the two masked men. "Safwan Qusti," Nightwing said, clarifying for his partner. "President Abdul-Hakam's military adviser and bodyguard." Nightwing's frowning face turned toward Mahbi. "Is *he* the one who wants Dabir killed?"

"I need to be knowing who sends you."

"We're independent contractors." Green Arrow took a long swig of the grapefruit juice he'd obviously liberated from the refrigerator, then turned his full attention on Mahbi. "Trust me, you don't want to meet the guy *we* work for. We're here because the merc who took a shot at that fifteen-year-old kid planted a tracer on you that we had originally planted on him, so now we gotta figure out what he thinks you know that we need to know."

"In other words"—Mahbi turned to Nightwing, hoping he would make more sense than his companion, Nightwing smiled—"we'd really appreciate it if you'd answer a few questions for us."

Mahbi leaned against the refrigerator and continued smoking his cigarette. "Yeah, okay. I am not involving anymore. What are you wanting to know?"

"Who's trying to kill—"

Nightwing interrupted Green Arrow, cutting him off mid-question. "Start by telling us your involvement in all this. How do you know these people? Cheshire and Safwan?"

Mahbi shrugged and flicked ashes into the metal sink. "Every person in Qurac know Cheshire. Her she blow up our country, yes?" Mahbi took a final drag off his cigarette, then ground it out in the sink. "I am with military and later trained by Safwan. For private guard, you know? For president? But Safwan, he not like me. He say I am not good, not good for private guard. He say this to many. Is okay. We go back to base. Not as much money, you know, but still we have job. I work for prison."

Green Arrow belched, pounded his chest with his fist a few times, excused himself, and waved for Mahbi to continue. Nightwing was constantly in motion, pacing the small apartment, but never took his eyes off Mahbi.

"So that is why I am contacted. Because my information is there in the files of Safwan, and because I am working for prison. I am asked to assist in special project, in interrogation of Cheshire off grounds of the prison. That is all I did, and all I know. I assist in moving her from cell to airport hangar, and guard her while she is answering questions. Then we take her back."

Green Arrow got up from the dining-room table and began to clear his chili bowl and juice glass. "Who was askin' the questions?"

As Green Arrow approached the kitchen, Mahbi exited from it, moving toward his living-room couch with an uneasy look on his face. "It was Abdul-Hakam."

Nightwing's masked eyes narrowed into thin white slits. "And what was he asking Cheshire? What did she say?"

Mahbi took a seat on the edge of his own couch, his posture tense and hunched. Green Arrow was in his kitchen removing his archery gloves, preparing to wash his own dishes. "He is asking for evidence connecting the president to arms deals that are same that later let Cheshire her steal the bomb she used against Qurac. She confirmed this, showed him to what he need. That is all. Later I hear he visit her again in prison. She give him a contact protocol for mercenary you speak of, this Death-stroke. But I am not there for that."

Nightwing, who was making Mahbi nervous with his restless pacing, came to perch suddenly on the arm of the couch. "So President Hatim Abdul-Hakam goes to Cheshire to see what she knows about his participation in an earlier arms deal and gets her to tell him how to erase the trail that leads to him? That makes a sort of sense, but it still doesn't produce any motive for anyone to want to kill Dabir."

Mahbi turned from the vigilante doing dishes in his kitchen to the one crouching like a gargoyle above him on the couch and shook his head. "No, is not right. Is not *Hatim* Abdul-Hakam who goes to Cheshire. It is *Dabir*. Dabir is who calls to me for this mission, and Dabir is who speak to Cheshire about evidence against Father, and Dabir is who she is giving contact protocol for Death-stroke. Not Hatim. It is Dabir."

Once back from Japan, Dick did not confess his new fears to his mentor. Batman watched him perform the martial skills he'd learned at the dojo without comment, then unceremoniously incorporated him back into the nocturnal work flow. Dick wanted to ask what life had been like in his absence, but was afraid to hear the answer. It was obvious that Batman had everything under control. The cases had been solved, the villains vanquished, and the innocents rescued without him. Dick felt a terrible, anxious distance growing between them, but if Batman noticed anything, he kept it to himself.

Once again following his mentor on their nightly rounds, Dick convinced himself that Batman's demeanor had changed as much as his own. Batman was sending him off to retrieve evidence and subdue rising threats on his own with greater frequency. The jokes and terrible puns that used to make Batman smile now seemed only to annoy him. The orders Batman barked at him increased in frequency and specificity exactly when they should have been dwindling. Most alarmingly, the fights between them became so ugly and heated that there were nights when Dick willingly chose to be away from him. It was a choice he could not have imagined even contemplating prior to his time abroad.

The first serious quarrel was about Catwoman. Dick, already ordered away from the fight by Batman for reasons that he thought were trite and suspicious, watched the cunning jewel thief toy with his mentor with narrowed eyes. By the time Batman finally came back without her, Dick's back teeth were grinding.

"You let her go, again?" It was an accusation more than a question.

Batman frowned. "She gave me the location of the merchandise. I'll return it to the museum in the morning."

"So she can steal it again tomorrow night?" Under his

green Robin gloves, Dick balled his fists. "Great. That's just great."

"You want me to arrest her for a rectified crime?"

Exasperated, Dick kicked a loose piece of gravel off the top of the rooftop upon which Batman had forced him to wait. He knew Batman hated it when he fidgeted, but the anger building inside of him demanded physical release. "That's usually how it works, isn't it? You commit a crime, you go to jail. It doesn't matter what happens to the stuff you steal. You pay for the *act* of thievery, not the value of the items you stole."

Batman had already turned his back on Robin, and was moving purposefully toward the edge of the rooftop. "Come on. We have better things to worry about. Killer Croc is loose in Robinson Park and the Penguin's expecting an arms shipment in through Port Adams early this morning."

Dick exploded. "Exactly! And you just now walked away from a chance to get Catwoman out of our way for good! For, like, the billionth time, by the way." Dick knew he should have stopped when he heard Batman turning back to glare at him, but he pressed on recklessly, some part of him wanting the confrontation, wanting to force a response out of Batman—any response. "What do you wanna bet we end up having to chase her all over town again later this week? Or is that what you're *hoping* for?"

Batman stared at Dick coldly. Dick wanted to shove him, or kick him. He wanted to fall at his booted feet and beg not to be cast aside. He wanted to go after Catwoman himself and beat her until she begged to be thrown in jail.

He wanted to storm away from his mentor and never come back.

"If that's what we have to do," Batman finally answered, "then that's what we'll do."

"Yeah, but—"

"Are you finished?"

It was clear to Dick that "yes" was the only answer Batman would accept. He pressed his lips together and looked away. Batman read the gesture as suitably submissive and threw a grapnel line down toward the Batmobile without further comment.

They said nothing in the car, though Dick was full of questions he didn't know how to ask and frustrations he didn't know how to express. When they finally cornered Killer Croc, an expert wrestler with razor-sharp teeth and tough, scaly green skin, Robin launched a forceful offensive without waiting for his mentor's orders, eventually kayoing Croc, but also earning Batman's wrath.

Batman said nothing while they tied up Croc and anonymously contacted the police. Even though he was wearing gloves, Dick had busted two of the knuckles on his right hand while driving a straight punch into Croc's teeth and was rubbing the injured hand distractedly. Once back in the car, sweaty and breathing hard, he was caught off guard when Batman grabbed his hand with uncharacteristic roughness and ripped off the glove to examine the injury. Robin winced, as much from surprise as from the sudden sting, and Batman dropped his hand again with a sneer of disgust.

"What did you think you were *doing* back there?"

Robin blew a strand of damp hair off his forehead and

frowned. He'd known better than to expect praise or gratitude for defeating Croc, but he wasn't prepared for scorn either. "I took him down, didn't I? What's your problem?"

Batman's anger became something almost tangible in the cockpit of the Batmobile; a hot, suffocating growl that smothered the air and the small distance between their two seats. "My *problem* is that you could have gotten yourself *killed!*"

Every instinct in Robin's body told him to back away, so he sat forward, pressing into Batman's space, ignoring the throbbing in his knuckles as his hands once again clenched. "By Croc?" he scoffed. "Please."

"By anyone!" Batman was actually shouting. Robin could smell his sweat; see the stubble on his jaw. The cockpit felt hot and close. "Do you have *any* idea how much time I spend thinking about ways to protect you? How much *harder* this job is with your safety hanging over my head?"

"Then why do you *bother*?" Robin let his own voice raise into a shout, his resolve every bit as forceful as Batman's.

Batman ignored the question, proceeding down his predetermined path of reprimand. "*Anyone* out here could kill you at *any* time, and you *know* that, Dick!"

Robin crawled halfway over the parking brake to close the remaining distance between them, even though it was already too slight. He couldn't really see Batman's eyes behind the night-vision lenses in his cowl, but he glared into the white slits anyway. "Yeah? So what if they *did*?"

The response was so fast and so unexpected that it threw Dick off balance. Expecting to be shaken, or maybe even hit, he instead tumbled back into the passenger seat as the Batmobile roared forward, the air in the cockpit going ice cold even more quickly than it had superheated. Batman, less than an inch from his face less than a second before, now seemed remote and untouchable in the driver's seat as he piloted them back toward the manor, white-knuckling the steering wheel, teeth grit. He didn't look at Dick once, or utter a single syllable. Dick felt a slight panic flutter in his throat and kept still, his stomach aching with tension. He couldn't remember Batman ever driving faster, not even in bona fide emergencies, and when they finally squealed to a stop on the rotating vehicle pad in the Batcave, Batman didn't even have to reach across Dick to open the passenger side door. He did it with a button; a single, unseen tap that disabled the seat belt Dick should have been wearing and swung open the door on his side. When Dick didn't move, Batman uttered two words, still without looking at him.

"Get out."

Dick faltered, remaining in his seat, his own anger dissolving in the face of Batman's furious disappointment. "Bruce, I'm sorry. I didn't mean to—"

"*Out!*"

Dick got out of the car slowly, subdued and miserable, his shoulders hunched. When he spoke, his voice was rueful. "Really, nothing's gonna happen to me, I promise. I'm okay. You've taught me never to—"

"We'll discuss this *later*."

The Batmobile peeled out of the cave at the same breakneck speed with which it had entered, leaving Dick frowning thoughtfully at his little green Robin boots.

He knew they would never discuss it again. Batman could not speak rationally about the possibility of his side-kick's death. Slowly, Dick exhaled, removed his mask, and raised his head.

It wasn't "I love you."

But it was something.

"So let me get this straight." Green Arrow stood on the roof of Mahbi's apartment building, frowning at Night-wing as the younger man crouched nearby entering more data in the miniaturized computer set into his gauntlet. "The kid ordered his own murder?"

"That's what it sounds like."

Green Arrow was indignant. "What the hell would someone do that for!?"

Nightwing looked up at him with a slight frown. "It's just a complicated form of suicide, isn't it? Or some kind of cry for help." Nightwing's eyes narrowed but stayed locked on Green Arrow's face. "You know, like running at police with a gun in your hand. Or . . . taking heroin."

Green Arrow threw his gloved hands up in the air and turned his back on Nightwing with a grunt as the young man rose. "All right, all right! I'm the worst guardian in the world. When does this end with you kids? Speedy already punched me for it once, and it's not like I stuck the needle in his arm myself."

Nightwing shook his head, frowning as he stared at the cheap roofing material beneath his boots. "It might help if you stopped calling him Speedy," he muttered through clenched teeth.

Green Arrow ignored him until Nightwing started moving back toward his bike. "Where're you goin'?"

"Back to the docks," Nightwing answered with a shrug. "Check in on everyone else?"

"Unh uh." Green Arrow folded his arms across his chest and shook his head.

Nightwing raised an eyebrow in amusement. "You got a better idea?"

"Yeah!" Green Arrow began striding away from Nightwing, not because he actually knew where he was going, but because he wanted to make the younger vigilante follow him. It worked. "Were you napping when Deathstroke mentioned he'd already collected two and half million buckaroonies?"

"No." Nightwing allowed a slight smile. "I believe I was *bathing* at the time."

"Well, dry your ears out, kid. We gotta go get that money back."

Nightwing looked genuinely surprised. "We do?"

Green Arrow had reached the end of the rooftop and turned to face Nightwing, hitching his thumbs into the belt he wore over his green tunic. "Absolutely! Otherwise we're just . . . condoning paying someone for murder."

Nightwing's brows furrowed but he was still smiling. "Actually, I think we'd be condoning accepting money *not* to murder someone in this case."

"Whatever." Green Arrow waved his hands impatiently. "He can't keep that cash."

Nightwing thought for a moment and then began to slowly nod. "Okay. Okay, you're right." He turned back toward the direction he'd first been heading, and Green

Arrow realized he was going for his bike. "But first things first: Dabir is still a danger to himself and possibly to others, and his safety is our primary concern. Once we've got that whole situation under control, we can go after Death-stroke again, but we're not gonna go cowboy on him this time."

Green Arrow wasn't sure what "going cowboy" meant to Nightwing, but he nodded his agreement while stroking his beard. "What, uh—what *are* we gonna go?" he asked as Nightwing threw a Batarang across the street in preparation for diving off the rooftop.

Nightwing, grapnel line taut and boots on the very edge of the building's rusting ornamental gutter, grinned at Green Arrow over his shoulder. "We're gonna go posse."

Green Arrow smiled as Nightwing dove gracefully off the top of the building, almost instantly swallowed by the thick, dark shadows of the alleyway beneath him. After tying a line onto an anchoring arrow, Green Arrow shot it into the brick wall across the alley and swung after him.

He still wasn't entirely sure what "going posse" was, but he didn't want to miss it.

PART FOUR

Garth was supervising his infant son's wide-eyed examination of a sugar starfish when he heard the powerful swimming strokes of the former King of Atlantis approaching from the east. He gently removed the starfish from his son's eager hands and replaced it with a smooth piece of abalone shell that Cerdian could teeth on to his heart's content, then cast a glance at his wife, Dolphin. She had clearly also heard Arthur's approach and turned to Garth with a reassuring smile. Cerdian—usually simply called Ian—squealed with delight when a school of flashing silversides preceding Aquaman shimmied around, through, and past the young family, barely bothering to alter their course to avoid colliding directly into the Atlanteans. And then Arthur was there, radiating strength and majesty as he floated before Garth, a slight, affectionate smile warming his sea-blue eyes.

"Well, hello there, shrimp," he chortled to Cerdian, running his right hand over the boy's still-tender head. "You're growing like a yellow fin, aren't you?"

Dolphin had swum forward to hug Arthur and he returned her embrace with more familiarity than Garth felt was necessary. He was frowning when Arthur finally turned to him, though the former king seemed not to notice.

"We have a guard mission in Gotham Bay," Arthur announced authoritatively, not bothering with additional small talk.

"We do?" Garth was slightly caught off guard. He was used to aiding Aquaman, but not used to being asked by Aquaman to do so.

"A favor for Batman," Arthur confirmed with a nod. Garth's eyebrows shot up in surprise. "Well, really for Green Arrow," Arthur clarified, "on Batman's behalf. Deathstroke attempted to assassinate the teenage son of Qurac's current president and we have to guard the boy while Batman figures out who ordered the hit."

Garth's eyes had narrowed slightly with interest at the mention of Deathstroke's name. "I'd love to help catch Deathstroke, but honestly, Arthur, what do you need me for?"

Arthur shrugged lightly. "Arsenal requested you. And Nightwing's on the case as well. Additionally, the boy and his father are staying on a Coast Guard ship, the USCGC *Herron*. It's a large area to secure and I could use an extra set of hands."

Garth was about to protest that Aquaman frequently singlehandedly secured the entire Atlantic Ocean, but the mention of his former Teen Titan cohorts had piqued his interest. He had recently lived with Dolphin and Cerdian in Titans Tower but hadn't had a chance to visit with Roy and Dick for quite some time. He was still musing over the oddity of being requested by Roy when Dolphin glided forward and, lifting Cerdian into her arms, inserted herself between Arthur and Garth.

"Well, Ian and I will be just fine on our own for a day or two." The comment had been directed toward Garth, then she turned toward Arthur with a beatific smile. "So of course you may borrow my husband, as long as you promise to bring him back in one piece."

"Don't I always?" There was no evident humor in Arthur's expression, but Garth assumed he was joking.

"Do we have any leads on Deathstroke?" he asked.

Arthur's shoulders raised in an elegant shrug. "Green Arrow and Nightwing are on that one. You and I are just supposed to keep the target alive."

Garth's mouth had begun to twitch in amusement.

"Did you just say Green Arrow and *Nightwing*? Don't you mean Green Arrow and *Arsenal*?"

Arthur answered impassively, though Garth was sure he knew what his ward was getting at.

"They switched. Arsenal's with Batman at the moment."

"Oh, I'm so in!" Garth's smile had broadened and he turned to Dolphin to kiss her good-bye. "Sorry, honey, I can't miss this one."

Dolphin grinned back at her husband.

"Be careful—*you* could get stuck with Batman, too."

Garth chuckled, kissed his son on the forehead, and placed a hand on Aquaman's shoulder.

"Never happen. *Right?*"

Arthur grinned at Garth, shot a quick wink to Dolphin, and took off at a speed of ninety-seven knots, which he knew Garth could keep up with, instead of his usual one hundred.

Garth swam until he was keeping stroke beside Aquaman and felt a rare sense of tranquility settle over him. He was enjoying being a father and, for the duration of their trip out to the USCGC *Herron*, at least, could imagine that Arthur might have enjoyed it, too.

There were no voices in Garth's earliest memories. The stories he later heard about his family just prior to his birth and during his early infancy sounded noisy and riotous: the murder of his father, the King of Shayeris, at the hands of his own palace guards, his pregnant mother's subsequent banishment to Atlantis and the throng of superstitious Atlanteans who then came to tear her newborn son from her arms, exiling Garth from Atlantis when they confirmed that he'd been born with purple eyes—these events must have been filled with shouting, curses, maybe even anguished cries and tears. All Garth could remember, though, was the distant song of whales and the steady pulse of tides.

When friends asked him, much later, how he had managed to survive for so long on his own as a baby in the ocean, Garth had no answer for them. He knew his memories of that time were imperfect, but he was aware of no panic in them, no life or death struggle. It was as if he had lived in some kind of magical chasm, weightless and integrated in the timeless dark of deep water.

That he may have lived in a realm of magic was, in fact, quite possible. The great sorcerer Atlan, father of Aquaman, later showed great interest in Garth's life and developing potential. Garth often wondered if the sorcerer hadn't also been present in those early days, actively protecting him and maybe also lulling any memories of distress.

Aquaman's story made even less sense to Garth. He insisted that he had found Garth as a young boy of about eleven while swimming near Mercy Reef. In Arthur's version of the story, the King of the Seven Seas had been wandering the ocean with his sea patrol—a large group of fish and other sea creatures with which he often traveled—when his cetacean friends had alerted him to the child. The moment Arthur approached him, Garth had thrown himself into the sea king's arms and confessed to being terrified of fish. Garth vaguely remembered telling such a lie to schoolmates later in his life—it sure beat "victimized by successful Idylist propaganda that led to his being judged inferior by the superstitious Poseidonians and left to slowly die" as an explanation for why he had been cast from Atlantis—but he couldn't imagine why Arthur would perpetuate such a ridiculous story. When he countered with memories of playing with eels and octopi and whales, Arthur asserted that such games had all been part of a desensitization program he'd designed to help alleviate Garth's fear of his aquatic compatriots. That part, Garth had to admit, almost made sense. It was difficult to imagine any other reason for Arthur to have been so carefree and playful in their earliest days together; sometimes all but impossible to believe that there had even been a time before Arthur had accepted the Atlantean crown. It was an all-too-brief period in their lives marked by wild adventures and familial intimacy.

Sometimes Garth thought the whole thing must have been a dream.

He did remember first meeting Arthur at Mercy Reef, where he had, indeed, been living alone. The Atlantean's blond hair had shone in the sun, and his smile had promised companionship and protection. Unable to recall any thoughts in his head at that time, Garth did remember the urgency in his young limbs as he swam toward the ocean's greatest defender, the man who had dedicated his whole life to protecting the seas and everything in them. Perhaps he had somehow sensed that his continued survival depended on reaching him.

Whatever the truth, Garth refused to be tortured by it. Whether they were real or not, his memories of those first years of life were soothing and still. When he couldn't sleep at night—which often occurred when he tried bedding down on the hard, pointy, suffocating surface world—he would lull himself with a gentle rocking motion, imagining his body suspended in an endless flow of cool salt water. The taste of raw seaweed was as comforting to him as warm milk seemed to be to his surface-dwelling friends, and he never corrected them when they occasionally spoke of idyllic childhoods he knew they hadn't had.

It was just as well, Garth figured, that he had forgotten some of the earliest hard stuff. There were plenty of dark memories from later in his life upon which to reflect.

"Were you happy as a child?"

"*Excuse* me?" Garth and Arthur had been swimming together in relative silence for over an hour when Arthur suddenly raised what to Garth seemed to be a very strange and out-of-the-blue question. "What d'you mean?"

Arthur sighed and flipped over into an elegant backstroke, making eye contact with his grown-up ward. "I don't know . . . just . . . was your life good? When you were younger?"

Garth narrowed his purple eyes. "You mean when I was a baby and left for dead at Mercy Reef because of the color of my irises? Or the two years you dressed me up in little blue swimming trunks and let me swim around with you patrolling the oceans and fighting pirates? 'Cause that was actually a lot of fun. But then, you could mean the time after you accepted the throne and moved me into a palace bedroom the size of a gulf while you started chasing after Mera? Or when you helped me cheat my way into a surface-dweller school in Scotland, mostly so that you could leave me there all day?" Garth felt his jaw tightening but continued. "Because I *know* you can't be asking about that day you decided to try to kill me to save A.J.—"

Arthur's entire countenance darkened and his blue eyes flashed dangerously. "He was my *son*." His voice was regal and thick with grief, and Garth wished he could be surprised to hear him so distressed by the subject so many years after the baby boy's fate had been sealed. But he wasn't surprised, because he was still angry, too.

"I know," Garth snapped. And then through clenched teeth, "Believe me, I know. I got that message loud and clear." He maneuvered around a high sea cave covered with red-and-white-striped spider crabs. "He was your son. And I'm just some kid you felt sorry for."

Arthur stopped swimming and turned to face Garth

with his most censoring frown. "You have a son now. You know how it feels to—"

"I know how small and dependent he is, and I know that's true of *any* child. Would I do anything to save Ian? Of course I would. But I hope that in doing so, I would never let any *other* child feel that he was worthless and . . . and *inferior*."

Garth felt a tremor pass through his body as he uttered the most hateful word he knew. It was what the Atlanteans believed of him because of the color of his eyes. He was thought to have been bad luck, and also physically, emotionally, and mentally inferior to those around him, a prejudice not easily nullified by even his most heroic deeds. He'd save the ocean a hundred times over before he was eighteen, but still the Atlanteans watched him with displeasure and superstition. Though his friends in the Teen Titans were not affected by Poseidonian xenophobia, they were all surface-dwellers who had a difficult time reconciling his talents and courageous nature with his life-threatening dependency on water. The bigoted Atlanteans, the gingerly sympathetic Teen Titans, and the too-often indifferent Aquaman were the sum total of self-esteem builders available to the young Idylist as he grew up. The one person who had ever truly believed in him, a beautiful, spirited young Poseidonian named Tula, whom Garth knew to be the enduring love of his life, was strangled to death by one of Aquaman's enemies off the coast of New York when she was still a teenager. Was he *happy* as a child? Garth glared at the man swimming beside him and put on a burst of defiant speed when Arthur stopped to frown at his communicator, then shot up toward the ocean surface to answer the hail.

"Go ahead, Batman."

If there was frustration in Aquaman's voice, Batman ignored it. "Orin, forget about the *Herron*. I need you and Tempest on a Quraci ship called the *Hijra*. It's scheduled to dock in Port Adams this evening. Don't let it into the bay."

Arthur glanced at the sun and determined that it was already late afternoon. "What's going to be on it?"

"I don't know." Batman's voice was foreboding. "Possibly mercenaries working for a Quraci resistance group known as the *Mutawwiin*. Possibly something worse."

Arthur nodded. "And as for coordinates . . . ?"

"Unknown."

"All right, we'll find it. I'll contact you with more information."

Batman cut off the communication without additional pleasantries, but Arthur was probably the one person in Batman's life who truly didn't mind his habitual abruptness. When it came to getting things done, Arthur was usually in favor of the streamlined approach, as well. He dove below the surface once more, caught up and then passed his former ward without a second thought.

School, for Garth, had been an intellectual pleasure and a physical torment. Arthur assured him that the prestigious Scottish junior school was filled with the sons of diplomats and royalty, and that it prided itself on the ability to make special accommodations for the needs of individual students. Initially, Garth had felt hopeful. It was, if nothing else, an excuse to get out of the stuffy palace and away from the cloying intimacy that Arthur so freely shared with his new wife, Mera. It didn't take long, however, for Garth to realize that the "special accommodations" he needed went far beyond what any other student required.

Though Arthur was careful to explain Garth's bodily needs to the academy staff, it was up to Garth himself to enforce them.

"He's got specialized, sievelike pores in his skin that act as minute gills," Arthur clarified to a dazed-looking school administrator. "They're full of blood capillaries set in minute membranes able to extract oxygen from water passing over the pores." Arthur stopped to make sure that much had sunk in before continuing. Garth noticed that no one was taking notes. "When he's topside, Garth breathes by extracting oxygen from inhaled air with vestigial lungs in his thorax. That's good for about an hour, but the carbon dioxide filtering system's imperfect, and after about an hour without water, he'll begin to suffocate."

The administrator nodded and guaranteed Arthur that all would be well. Arthur smiled regally, nodded once, and winked at Garth as he strode out of the office.

"Good luck, Minnow," he said. "Be good."

Garth watched Arthur leave and then turned back to the school administrator. Though it took every ounce of courage he could muster, Garth decided to clarify the hydration issue himself.

"So, that'll be okay, right? That I have to go swim every hour?"

Garth noticed that his voice sounded quieter on land than it normally did underwater, but was surprised when the administrator ignored him completely. After an awkward moment, the administrator scooped several files off of his large, heavy desk, turned to Garth with a friendly smile, then politely asked Garth to follow him to his first class.

Nervous and uncomfortably warm, Garth obeyed, following the man down a long marbled hallway with classroom doors on either side. Passing what the administrator called "the lavatory," Garth almost gagged as the scent of fresh bleach and undiluted urine permeated his senses. It was so strong that he was amazed the administrator didn't react to it, but the man in front of him didn't even slow his step.

After another few feet, he again turned to Garth with a sociable smile and indicated a row of doors on the west wall.

"Just head right in through the green door there. You'll stay with Miss Pine's class until we can properly evaluate your academic skills."

Garth stared hard at the three doors closest to where the administrator was gesturing, but as far as he could tell, they were all gray.

"Don't be frightened," the man said kindly, moving closer to place a hand on Garth's shoulder. He gently pushed him toward the door to the left.

The first thing Garth saw when he entered the classroom was a tank full of tropical fish. It seemed odd to him that a school so near the North Sea would have a tank full of fish culled primarily from the waters off of South America and the Caribbean. He was still staring at them, wondering if they were as homesick as he was, when he heard the murmurs of his fellow students begin to rush at him from all directions. He remembered something Arthur had told him about sound traveling very differently on land than it did underwater and forced himself to take a deep breath, even though the warm, stale air of the classroom was far from calming.

The teacher introduced him as "Aqualad" and, noticing his eyes on the fish tank, asked him if he could name the inhabitants.

Garth concentrated on speaking as loudly as he could, pushing his words carefully out toward the other students as they sat, wide-eyed, watching him from their desks.

"Angel fish, gold crescents, black mollies, sumatra barbs, white clouds, blue gouramis, and scissor tails."

Miss Pine nodded, smiled at him, then pointed to an empty desk to her left.

"Excellent, Aqualad. Thank you."

Garth was relieved to take a seat and spent the next several moments trying to make sense of the location of sounds in the room. There were students seated in front of him, behind him, and to either side, but he found he couldn't track the direction of their voices without turning to look for the speaker. It only took him a little while, though, to connect the sound of his classmate's voices to their personal scents, allowing him to turn toward them appropriately when they spoke.

Reassured by this improvised sensory adaptation, Garth settled in to his seat more fully. Miss Pine was lecturing about Scottish history, and Garth listened interestedly for what felt like an entire half tide. He was pleased to discover that several of his classmates were addressed by unusual titles that, though not quite as strange as "Aqualad," did range from "young Laird of Kildrummie" to "your Imperial Highness." Though he received a consistent flood of curious glances, Garth began to have the feeling that he might fit in amid his varied classmates.

Then, as Arthur had warned him it would, Garth felt his throat begin to tighten.

Though Garth knew he should raise his hand and ask to be excused, he couldn't quite manage to interrupt his teacher. He told himself that recess must be close, that he just had to hang on a little while longer. He was sure that if he said something, Miss Pine would frown at him and say, "Yes, Garth, we know. I was just about to excuse you." He told himself he'd count to ten, then ask. He told himself he'd count to twenty.

By the second time he had counted to one hundred, he was panting, wheezing, and pale. His initial reluctance to interrupt the classroom proceedings had grown into full-blown dread. What had moments earlier felt like a scary thing to do now felt impossible. Garth doubted he even had the strength to raise his hand. He began trying to calculate the exact distance from his desk to the nearest body of water, the river locally known as the Firth of Forth, only to realize that his faculties were leaving him.

Expecting to begin thrashing or convulsing uncontrollably, Garth instead found himself growing increasingly weak and still. It felt as if the particles of his body were being slowly torn apart, then evaporating into the endlessly recycled air of the classroom. Garth dropped his eyes, instinctively honoring the seclusion of death. He had no idea how much longer he then stared at the edge of his desk, waiting for the bell to ring. When at last he heard it, it was a sound from a thousand leagues away.

"Garth, do you need a glass of water?" he heard his teacher asking worriedly.

The next thing he was aware of was the sting of chlorine on his skin and in his eyes. Head pounding and fingernails blue, Garth broke through the surface of the school swimming pool, rubbed his purple eyes, and quickly assured everyone that he was fine.

"Look, everybody! A whale!"

Rashid was beaming as he pointed out toward the break line of Port Adams.

President Hatim scowled at his nephew. "Don't be ridiculous, Rashid. There are no whales in Gotham Harbor."

Dabir strained his neck to look, but was hurried along by Safwan, who walked closely behind him. The four of them were surrounded by LEDET guards as they were escorted off the USCGC *Herron* and led toward the empty dock that would soon berth the *Hijra*. Several press members and a couple of news vans were on hand for the important event, as was Gotham City's Mayor Hull.

Dabir was surprised when their party was stopped suddenly by the *Herron*'s Combat Information Center Officer, who whispered something to the chief LEDET officer. The officer, in turn, addressed President Hatim.

"I'm afraid there may be a slight delay with the *Hijra* docking, sir."

Safwan moved in front of the president with a frown.

"What *kind* of delay?"

The LEDET guard scratched his ear, looking a little sheepish.

"We're having some unexpected difficulties clearing

the harbor breakwater. There's going to be a slight holdup concerning port entry."

Safwan's expression grew darker as he folded his arms across his muscular chest.

"What *kind* of holdup?"

The LEDET officer met Safwan's eyes, but looked like he wished he didn't have to.

"Whales, sir. A bunch of them just showed up right at the edge of the bay. Currently, they're blocking harbor access."

Rashid grinned, triumphant, elbowing Dabir in the ribs.

"See? I told you I saw one!"

President Hatim's eyebrows raised in surprise.

"Are they dangerous?"

The LEDET officer shook his head.

"Unlikely. But they're big. And for whatever reason, they don't seem to want to let any ships into the docking bay."

"So what is our plan?" Safwan failed to look amused.

"We're going to continue down to the docking site anyway and hope for the best. The mayor is already there, you can let the press get a few shots of the two of you together while we wait for the situation to clear up."

Hatim nodded and the procession started up again, continuing toward the designated pier.

Three blocks from the dock, the Batplane used its silent VTOL system to touch down on the roof of the Mason Department Store building. Partly obscured from view by the shadow of the towering J&L Technologies high-rise above it, the location worked as an efficient rendezvous point for Batman and his self-elected assistants.

Green Arrow and Nightwing were waiting on the rooftop as Batman and Arsenal disembarked. Batman was debriefing the group before his boot tip even touched terra firma. Nightwing hid a slight smile.

"I've already sent Orin and Tempest out to stop the *Hijra* before it docks at Port Adams. We know the *Mutawwiin* have had control of the ship since it left Qurac and that their goal is to create an international incident between Qurac and the U.S. that can be attributed to President Hatim Abdul-Hakam." Batman turned toward Green Arrow, his cape sweeping behind him in the setting sun like a cloak of night. "Green Arrow, I need you and Arsenal to secure that pier. If anything or anyone does manage to get by Arthur and Garth, you two keep it from getting any farther." Arsenal looked vaguely relieved as he crossed the roof toward Green Arrow, who nodded to Batman that he understood. "Nightwing," Batman concluded, "you're with me."

Green Arrow grinned at his grown-up ward as Roy approached him. "Guess you pissed him off, huh?"

Arsenal offered Ollie a smirk as he threw an arm around his shoulder and turned him in the direction of the fire escape that would take them down toward the harbor. "Me? Nah. We had a great time. He's just saving Wingster from having to listen to any more of your Zen psychobabble."

"Oh, hey, tell me something." Green Arrow stopped Arsenal at the bottom of the fire escape and thumbed up toward the Batplane. "How come Bats keeps calling Aquaman 'Orin'? I thought his name was Arthur."

Arsenal chuckled and continued toward the pier, Green Arrow quickly catching up with him until they were walking in matching strides. "Aquaman is his hero name, Arthur Curry is his human name, and I think Orin is his dolphin name or something."

"His dolphin name?"

Arsenal shrugged. "Yeah, you know, from when he was raised by the dolphins and crap. Just like I've got my hero name, and my English name, and my name in *Dineh Biz—*"

"His *dolphin* name?"

Arsenal sighed. "Anything you wanna throw in your quiver? 'Cause we don't know what we're walking into down there. How's your inventory?"

"Do you have a dolphin name? I want a dolphin name!" Green Arrow's emerald eyes were twinkling with excitement. "Can I get a dolphin name?"

"Sure." Arsenal pulled out his shades and slipped them onto the bridge of his nose as he crossed the large boulevard that ran along one side of the docks. "I'll be sure to push you into the water first chance I get, and you can go talk to the dolphins about it yourself."

The most cherished memory in Garth's heart was also the most anguished. Her name was Tula, and he had known her forever and for far too short a time. Her windy dark hair and deep blue eyes did nothing to hide the sunniest disposition Garth had ever encountered, and the very first moment his lips had touched hers (though she would have been quick to point out that it had actually transpired the other way around), Garth recognized her as the other half of him. She was strong-willed, popular, vivacious, and unshakably brave. She was everything Garth would have been if he'd dared, but it was enough—more than enough—to adore, defend, and encourage her.

Tula had grown up in the same royal palace in Poseidonis that served as Garth's home once Aquaman peacefully succeeded her guardian, King Juvor. Garth often wondered what small, dull thing his life would have become had she not approached him soon after his fifteenth birthday to proclaim her adoration and plant a kiss on the lips he had parted in wonder. When she smiled, he could feel pleasure bubble up his spine like the heat from a thermal spring. She often claimed that the highlight of her day was making him blush.

That the ocean covered seventy-one percent of the earth's surface sounded to Tula like a challenge. There was no adventure she would shy away from, no corner of the sea she would leave uncharted. Garth frequently found himself led astray by her, figuratively and literally out of his depth. More than once she would turn to him with a giggle—usually surrounded by hungry sharks or electric eels or distrustful, sun-mad pirates—and admit that she wasn't quite sure where they were. But they always made it back home eventually, and at a deeper level, Garth began to realize that home for him was, quite simply, wherever she happened to be.

For her own part, Tula seemed equally comfortable in Garth's world. When he continued to hang out and work regularly with the Teen Titans, Tula quite cheerfully joined him. Garth had mixed feelings about the team. On the one hand they were good friends who, like him, had been saved from orphanhood and other tragic abandonments by real-life super heroes rather seriously lacking in real-life parental ambitions, but on the other hand the Titans were also all surface-dwellers who couldn't help but think Garth weak and somewhat defective when they were constantly forced to work around his hourly need for rehydration.

There were no specific rules barring "girlfriends" from Teen Titan missions, but neither were there any precedents for inclusion. Tula took this all in stride, charming each and every member of the team, roundly scolding them when they were at all slow to make provisions for the physical needs of their Atlantean members, and patiently lecturing them on Atlantean physiology until the Titans were every bit as impressed by what she and Garth could do to ensure their safety as they were skeptical about what they must do to ensure theirs.

Basking in her assertiveness, Garth did little to confront his own inherent shyness. For years it didn't seem to matter, and then as suddenly as a shift in the breeze, Tula's smiles turned to frowns and she began complaining that Garth treated her too much like a "pal" and not enough like the love of his life she hoped herself to be. Garth was just on the verge of figuring out how to rationally explain the obvious absurdity of this misconception when Tula began smiling at another young Atlantean, Mupo, who seemed to be every bit as eloquent around her as Garth was tongue-tied.

Though Roy told him he was nuts to give up so easily, Garth decided to finish his education in Scotland. He left Tula and Arthur and the Titans and enrolled in the Academy boarding school, picking a dorm just a stone's throw from the North Sea. In many ways, that brief time on his own proved invaluable. He learned to express his opinions, study his options, and value his unique cultural heritage. He also learned not to sacrifice his own well-being to timidity or social fear, and not to apologize for his differences or needs. It was a necessary solo adventure, a rite of passage he could not have left incomplete. And yet only one year later, he would count every single one of those days spent without Tula as unforgivable wastes. Why had he been floating in the freezing air when he could have been swimming with her?

As a hero and protector of the seas, Garth lived with the threat of death every day. Hardly a month went by without someone he cared about winding up missing, hurt, or miraculously snatched from the jaws of death. The most common responses were to become hypervigilant, like Robin, or completely inured to danger in all its forms, like Speedy. Garth hovered somewhere in the middle. He didn't want to be like Arthur, who responded to any threat against his wife or biological child as a personal attack by the gods, rabidly sacrificing anyone or anything in his path in his efforts to get them back. But nor could Garth bring himself to accept endless occurrences of menace and violence as the norm. Though heroic to his core, there were many days when Garth would have preferred not to be a hero.

Still, after completing his schooling, Garth found himself back with the Teen Titans, and Tula. He found her sitting in the common room of the newly built Titans Tower, talking and laughing with the others as though she herself was a member. Her hair was wet from a recent swim, and when she turned her eyes to him, her smile instantly melted all the nervous tension and awkwardness that might otherwise have lingered between them.

"Ooh! Stop the party!" she said, laughing. "My wet blanket's back!"

Her sparkling blue eyes never left his.

Garth had meant to say hello to his friends, to comment on the new tower, to ask about their latest adventures. Instead, he walked steadily toward Tula, alive to his own body in a way that felt both unfamiliar and absolutely right. She was twisted around on a small yellow couch, and he bent over the back of it to press his lips to hers, just as she had pressed hers against his so many years before. Her tongue darted past his teeth like a kissing gourami's, and he closed his eyes, completely lost to his surroundings. All he could hear was the beat of his own heart, Roy's amused chuckle coming from somewhere across the room, and Dick's purposefully cleared throat. By the time he opened his eyes again, he and Tula were alone in the large den.

"Hi," he said, after catching his breath.

"Hi, yourself." Tula grinned, her face still tilted temptingly toward his.

"I, uh, I passed all my A-levels." Garth spoke quietly and he couldn't tear his eyes from hers.

"Of course you did." Tula's nose wrinkled bewitchingly. "You're a genius. But are you smart enough to be done with this reclusive stage of yours? I've been pretty lonely."

"I'm done," Garth said quickly. "I'm totally done."

"Good."

Tula's smile swam up closer in his vision and then her

lips were pressed against his again. He almost fell over
the back of the couch trying to get his arms around her
shoulders. Tula caught him, laughing, and began to rain
tiny kisses all over his face. Garth smelled Dick's presence nearby and looked up just in time to see him outfitted
in his Robin armor, gingerly clearing his throat again.

"Aqualad, Aquagirl? Sorry to interrupt, but our alert
system just picked up some probable H.I.V.E. activity just
off the shore of Sydney."

"On our way, O valiant team leader," Tula answered
with a grin.

Garth blinked at her.

"Aquagirl?"

Tula shrugged, jumped up, and pulled him off the
couch.

"Aqualass just sounded a little too . . . I don't know . . .
beverage-y? You know, like, 'Aqualass, official beverage
of the Swiss ski team!'"

Garth shook his head but did not let go of her hand.

"No, I meant—when did you join the Teen Titans?"

"Just now, lover. Anyway, come on. I want to show you
the docking bay—we've got built-in ocean access this
time!"

Thinking back later, Garth wondered if he should have
protested; insisted, somehow, that she stay safe and protected in Atlantis. She never would have allowed it, though,
and since he often thought of her as twice as brave as he
was, what right would he have had? The other Titans
didn't seem to mind, and Garth knew that Dick, in particular, would never have let someone join in the missions
without careful evaluation of their skills. The first time he

almost lost her, Garth begged Tula to sit the next battle out, but by then she considered the Titans her friends as much as he did and was unwilling not to help when her schedule allowed.

When the Crisis came—an interdimensional catastrophe that threatened the very fabric of the universe and necessitated daring sacrifices on the part of every living hero—Tula was right by Garth's side, and he couldn't have imagined it any other way. By the time they found themselves battling with the villains Chemo, Black Manta, and Killer Shark, the threat of individual death had been subsumed within the larger framework of worldwide annihilation. In every fight every hero gave their all, and it was generally understood that they would either finally triumph or all go down together.

Garth later told himself that was why he hadn't been more alarmed when, while fighting with Black Manta, he had turned to see Killer Shark attempting to choke the life out of Tula. During a fight, a glance over one's shoulder showed nothing conclusive. One millisecond a teammate would have the advantage, during the next they might be momentarily overcome. Crises were averted and new dangers revealed continuously; the rule when fighting on a team was to end the threat in front of you, then help someone else if intervention still looked necessary. There was never time for second-guessing.

Garth's second glance revealed Killer Shark swimming rapidly away. That should have signaled a probable triumph on Tula's part, but something made Aqualad turn the rest of the way around to face Aquagirl. It was then that he noticed she was caught in the middle of a large pool of toxic chemicals and acids Chemo had previously dumped into the New York harbor.

Tula was drowning.

In what felt like one tortuously extended moment, Garth risked his own life to free her, then raced with her unmoving body in his arms toward Poseidonis. Once she was delivered into a medic's care, there was nothing he could do but wait. Arthur's wife Mera tried to comfort him, but Garth held on to the unchallenged principle that Tula was a true hero, and that true heroes always managed to pull through in the end. Secretly, too, in some unspeakable part of his heart, Garth felt he deserved Tula. He had lost his parents, his heritage, his throne and his childhood. The ocean owed him love.

When the end finally came, it was no comfort whatsoever that Tula was not the only true hero to break this unspoken law. Many heroes fell, and Garth grieved for all of them in turn—at least, as well as he was able. The loss of Tula so completely shattered his heart that every future sorrow seemed nothing more than a pale shadow flickering across a stone wall the sea had long since ground into sand.

Tempest's frustration with Arthur had faded as it always eventually did, and he watched the dolphins leaping back and forth over the bow of the oil tanker *Hijra* with admiration. They were so graceful and strong, and he had no doubt that Arthur meant it when he referred to them as some of the smartest creatures on earth. That he had cetaceans doing recon for him made Arthur something less than a slouch himself.

"What are they saying?" Tempest approached the former King of Atlantis after Aquaman had conferred with one of them. Aquaman communicated telepathically, but the dolphins had been answering him in a cheerful series of whistles and clicks.

"It's an army," Aquaman said gravely. "Armed, and somewhere between eighty and a hundred of them. I'm also being told they smell wrong, which might mean we're dealing with metas."

"Then let's do it right here," Tempest answered, his purple eyes glistening. "While we still have one big, wet advantage."

Aquaman nodded his agreement and turned his attention toward the harbor. Tempest was halfway up a rope trailing from the ship's stern when he saw what his partner had done. The largest blue whale bull he had ever seen was rushing the boat like a torpedo. Tempest hopped onto the deck anyway, confident that he could hold on, or at least dive off safely.

The mercenaries on the ship were not expecting the aquatic broadside, but they were expecting something. Tempest was throwing a few overboard when he noticed between ten and fifteen bounding from the deck straight into the air. They were dressed in black Nomex armor from head to toe and seemed fitted with specialized jet packs.

"They've got fliers!" Tempest called out to Aquaman.

"We've got archers!" Aquaman called back with confidence.

Tempest smiled and turned his attention back to the chaos his presence and the whale's swipe had inspired on deck. Taking advantage of a wave formed off the port side by an aggressive tail slap from the still-belligerent bull whale, Tempest used his mystical powers to freeze the water that shot above the deck of the ship. The ensuing chunk of ice dropped down on a helicopter four *Mutawwiin* mercenaries were running toward, shattering the copter blades and effectively grounding the mercs. Garth was still alarmed, though, by the sheer number of soldiers and the caliber of their weaponry. The mercenaries who had been running for the copter turned their black-masked faces toward Tempest and opened fire.

A quick glance over the stern confirmed that Aquaman was testing the swimming abilities of another four or five armed mercs, but Garth felt anxious that they weren't working quickly enough to turn the odds in their favor.

Leaping up on the starboard balustrade, Tempest turned his attention to the docking bay, where he could see a volley of arrows flying up from the pier. Moving quickly to dodge the spray of machine-gun fire, he dove over the starboard side and headed toward the sea floor as quickly as he could.

It was clear from the pier that the suezmax was under attack, but Green Arrow and Arsenal were more concerned with the humanoid figures flying toward the pier at a rocket-fueled rate.

"Incoming!" Arsenal was shouting to the lingering press hounds more than to Green Arrow, but Green Arrow had his own ideas about crowd control. As Arsenal took down three flying *Mutawwiin* meta-soldiers in quick succession with his crossbow, Green Arrow shot a small fog bomb into the civilian crowd on the pier, obscuring the

Abdul-Hakams, Mayor Hull, most of the Coast Guard officers, and the press from the view of the arriving mercenaries.

"Now they'll just target us," he explained to Arsenal as he turned back to face the water again, notching his bow.

"Great plan, G.A." Arsenal's tone was facetious, but Green Arrow knew that Roy would not for one second take his eagle eyes off the hostile targets.

"What d'you say we net a real catch?"

"At forty degrees on the count of three," Arsenal agreed. He grinned as he looped one corner of the net Green Arrow offered him over the arrowhead already loaded into his bow, and glanced toward his mentor for the countdown.

"Three!" Green Arrow bellowed with his usual lack of patience. Both archers fired in perfect unison, a wide wire net spreading out between their arrows. Four of the *Mutawwiin* fliers were trapped in the net midair, instantly dragged backward into the water as the arrows continued along their trajectory.

"D'you ever miss the good old days, Speedy?" Green Arrow was reloading as he grinned at Arsenal.

"Sure," Arsenal answered with a roll of his eyes. "But then I know it's time to hit an N.A. meeting."

Back out in the breakwater, Tempest reached the ocean floor and squinted up at the belly of the suezmax. His purple eyes flashed with the gathering red-tinged mystical power he had finally claimed as his birthright and he stretched his arms up toward the *Hijra*. Slowly at first, and then with greater and greater speed, a whirlpool began to grow under the oil tanker, the tip of the vortex seeming to point directly to Tempest's heart.

The suezmax made a loud, groaning sound as it struggled against the circling current, and then it began spinning in tighter and tighter circles, losing its purchase on the swirling water surface as irresistible centrifugal force began to pull it under. Tempest was concentrating so hard on controlling the whirlpool that he didn't hear Aquaman's approach until the sea king was swimming beside him, looking at once impressed and irritated.

"You trying to make me sick?" he said with a frown. A glance in his direction confirmed for Tempest that Aquaman was, in fact, a bit pale.

Tempest smiled with a light shrug. "Hey—not my fault if you don't know to get off a sinking ship."

The entire first deck of the *Hijra* was underwater, so Aquaman swam back up to protect the disoriented *Mutawwiin* from fatal drowning as their ship continued to sink. Tempest used his control over water to slowly turn the suezmax upside down before carefully righting it and once again setting it afloat.

On the docks, Safwan struggled behind the unexpected screen of smoke with the attendant Coast Guardsmen to pull Hatim, Dabir, and Rashid to safety.

One of the officers had run ahead to secure a military car and was waving them down the pier while another team covered the mayor.

"What is happening?" Hatim cried.

"The *Mutawwiin*!" Safwan glanced over his shoulder and then turned back to herd his charges toward the waiting armored car. "They've got an invading meta-human mercenary army on our ship!"

"But that will start a war!" Hatim sounded frantic.

"The Americans will think that I am attempting to start a war!"

"That's probably the whole point," Dabir mumbled very quietly, pulling his hand away from Safwan's angrily.

"And there are super heroes!" Rashid added, breathless with excitement. "Real-live American super heroes, fighting to save us!"

Rashid stopped, craning his neck to try to get a better look at the action behind them on the pier, forcing Safwan to turn around and grab him. Safwan had his hand around Rashid's arm when another explosion of smoke stung his eyes and obscured the car.

"Rashid!?"

"I'm here, Safwan!"

Safwan tried to clear the smoke with angry waves of his free arm as Rashid coughed behind him. When Safwan could see again, the LEDET guards were standing with the door to the black military car open, staring at him expectantly. Safwan snapped his head around to confirm that Rashid was still behind him and then glared at the LEDET guards and the car with incensed disbelief.

Hatim and Dabir were nowhere to be seen.

Years of grieving for Tula eventually taught Garth to hold his happiest and warmest memories of her as the definitive ones. Though he could never force himself to forget the image of her hands clawing at her own throat in panic, or the terrifying stillness of her pale, dying face, he refused to let himself dwell on them. As quickly as he could, he would replace such thoughts with recollections of her engaging, compliant body pressed against his, or the startling beauty of her dark, laughing, all-knowing eyes.

So it was with all the dead. When someone urged him to remember someone as they had been in life, Garth was always ahead of them. He could hold his feelings of loss and abandonment at bay while nurturing his fondest memories of those whose souls had been freed. It was the living he found less easy to forgive.

Among these numbers, it was his mother, Berra, and Aquaman himself who gave Garth the most trouble.

Berra was not someone he had to deal with on a regular basis, and so he did not, though not dealing with her took up an inordinate amount of energy. He had discovered her name and his own at the same time, also learning that she had not been innocent of perpetuating the gross Shayeris misinformation campaign that had cost him his childhood in Atlantis.

From what Garth could discern, his mother had actively worked to keep him from learning the truth of his own past. Her concern seemed to rest on the belief that her son's fate was closely tied to that of her late husband's brother, Slizzath, an Atlantean of such great evil and powerful sorcery that it was better to sacrifice the life of her own son than allow the uncle any ingress.

To Garth, the tale was full of unknown characters and indefinite threats. The wizards, the birthrights, the politics—he couldn't focus on any of it because he was too busy searching the story for proof of his mother's love for him, or at least some understandable justification for his banishment from her life. It was impossible for him to imagine that Slizzath's dark ambitions could possibly be any greater than his own ravenous need to be claimed. He wrote Berra off as part of a life he had never known and made no further attempts to contact her.

Arthur, however, was the wound that would not heal. Garth forgave him constantly, both for the unintentional small physical and psychic injuries, and for the occasional broader, more ambiguous cruelties. There was usually a way out of persistent resentment: Arthur was distracted, or overstressed, or unwitting. Garth tried to concentrate on the good times they had shared before moving to the palace of Poseidonis. He tried to remember the first time he had seen Arthur's smile and found it so full of acceptance and warmth. Over and over again, however, Garth's mind betrayed him. When he thought of Arthur, he thought of his eyes: blue, cold, murderous, and completely without mercy. It was an image he could not will himself to forget.

The transition to the palace had not been easy. Arthur had been swamped with his new royal duties, and the Poseidonians regarded Garth with suspicion and disdain—both because of the color of his eyes and, Garth suspected, because he had no official title, no easily explained connection to Arthur's life. Though beautiful and wildly devoted to Arthur, Mera, Arthur's new bride and queen, hailed from a distant, other-dimensional water world, and Garth was not the first or last to wonder if perhaps the move to Atlantis had left her just the tiniest bit unstable. By the time Arthur Jr. was born, Garth felt less like a third wheel than an anchor on a bicycle. If it hadn't been for Tula and his adventures with the Teen Titans, Garth would have spent those years essentially friendless and alone.

He forgave Arthur for all of that.

And there was nothing but forgiveness on his mind when he was forced by the evil machinations of Black Manta to face Arthur in battle for the life of baby A.J., who had also been captured and was being held in a small capsule slowly filling with air. It was at least a year before the Crisis, and although a recognizable enemy, Manta was not yet someone Garth was single-mindedly devoted to tearing apart with his bare hands. Tula was alive and well and thankfully absent, and Manta had, in Garth's mind, made a fatal mistake in bringing Aqualad and his mentor together. Instead of fighting one another, as Manta wished, they would combine forces, defeat him, then save Arthur Jr. It was the obvious thing for two heroes to do.

Grabbing the trident offered to him, Aqualad moved forward to face his mentor in the arena. Aquaman's chest was heaving and as he pointed his own Trident at Aqualad, his expression was bleak.

"Aquaman?" Aqualad's voice was tentative as he searched his mentor's face for some hint of cooperation, some sign of a plan. Would they turn on Manta at once, or pretend to fight one another long enough to free baby A.J. before taking out his captor? Would one or both of them pretend to be injured to lure Manta into a false sense of security, or should they retreat to some strategically superior ground before launching an offensive?

Aquaman's eyes were as cold and dark as an oceanic subduction zone.

"I'm sorry, Minnow." He spoke in a low growl. "But that's my son up there." Aqualad scrambled backward as Aquaman surged forward with his trident in an unmistakable attempt to end his sidekick's life. "My *son!*"

Aqualad's heart sank. It was true that Aquaman was not his real father—in some ways, they were more like brothers, or even just good friends. But Garth counted on

Arthur just the same, and in that moment the look in Aquaman's brooding blue eyes held no spark of affection, loyalty, or even recognition. Aqualad could not avoid the reality of his own superfluousness. He had always understood that Arthur would sacrifice anything for Mera or A.J.'s safety: his kingdom, his crown, his dignity, his riches . . . the list was nearly endless. And yet the fact that he himself was on that list had somehow never crossed Garth's mind. Why someone with so much power and passion would fail to extend his nepotistic largesse to include a boy he'd shared his home and resources with for years was a painful mystery to Aqualad. He was shocked to find that in the face of true peril, their indelible bond washed away like driftwood.

Aqualad nearly dropped his trident. All this time, he had been putting his faith in a lie.

It didn't matter that Aquaman ended up not killing him. Garth could not remember feeling lonely during the time he had spent on his own at Mercy Reef as a young boy. But he knew that he would never forget the devastating certainty of utter isolation communicated to him that day in the arena by Arthur's narrowed eyes.

Maybe there was a condition worse than inferiority. Aqualad swam away from his mentor feeling disillusioned, defenseless, and completely unclaimed.

The last thing Dabir remembered seeing was two super heroes and a harbor full of whales working together to keep the *Hijra* from docking while two others stood on the edge of the pier shooting arrows up at flying *Mutawwiin*. Nearly a hundred mercenaries had been intent on swarming the Gotham port, and four men had been holding them back. Safwan had been pushing him and his father toward a car, and then there had been an explosion of smoke, and . . .

"Hello?"

Realizing he was seated in a dark room with his hands tied behind his back, Dabir felt a flash of fear, and then became angry.

"Hello? Is there anyone here? What do you want!?"

Furious, Dabir pulled at his bound wrists and nearly upset the chair.

"Be still." The voice that reverberated from the darkness was the least human Dabir had ever heard. Just the sound of it set his teeth on edge and sent a cold tremor racing up his spine.

"Deathstroke?" Dabir's voice sounded more frightened than he'd meant it to as he called out into the dark. Suddenly a hot light bore down upon him. His breath caught in his throat as he turned his head away, transported in time for a moment back to the horrible flash that had torn his country apart at the seams.

"Where is the evidence you have against Hatim Abdul-Hakam?"

Dabir slowly opened his eyes to find that although hot, the light glaring down on him was not lethal. Instead of standing in the middle of a decimated souk, he found himself tied to a chair in what appeared to be an empty warehouse.

"What?" he asked meekly, more than a little disconcerted.

"The evidence you found against your father. What

and where is it?" The voice was relentlessly dark, even in the brightened room, and Dabir had no idea where it was coming from. It seemed disembodied, and at the same time closer than it should have been.

"I . . . I found the Russian copies of a weapons trade agreement. If Dad hadn't been trying to procure nuclear warheads for Qurac, Cheshire never would have been able to steal them."

"What do you think will become of those papers?"

Dabir's anger returned in a hot flush. "They'll be found in his stateroom on the *Herron*. And together with the fact that *his* ship just invaded American shores, I think some people will be pretty mad!"

"As mad as you are?"

Dabir clamped his mouth shut and began to grind his back teeth.

"How did you first make contact with the *Mutawwiin*?"

"Cheshire." Dabir hissed the name in a sickened whisper, staring sullenly at the floor. "I used some guys who used to train with Safwan to get her out of prison long enough to question her about the weapons sale documents." Dabir looked up, thinking he had heard a gasp behind him, but no one emerged from the darkness. Turning his attention back to the floor, Dabir continued. "I told her about the *Hijra*, that it was going to America, and asked if there was anyone who could help me use it against my dad. She told me how to get in touch with the *Mutawwiin*, and they said they'd take care of everything."

Dabir stopped talking and listened as hard as he could, but there was no audible evidence that anyone was in the room with him. Fighting hard to hold back tears of frustration, and with a slight hysteria building in his chest, he continued more rapidly.

"But we were supposed to be on that ship. I was supposed to be able to make sure it was just me who got hurt, and Dad would be in trouble for coming into port with those guys but . . . it wasn't supposed to be like this! When I found out I wasn't gonna be on the ship it still seemed like it might be okay, because Dad would tip somebody off—you know, call for help and get busted with these guys before they reached port or something. But then Dad changed his plans and he wasn't gonna be on it either and I tried—I tried to call it off, but they just laughed at me! I even went back to see Cheshire in the jail and she told me it takes a mercenary to stop a mercenary and told me how to get in touch with Deathstroke. I think she thought I could hire him to kill the *Mutawwiin*, but I hired him to kill me instead. And I got half the money to him and told him to get the other half from my dad after I was dead so that everyone would think my dad did it—ordered someone to assassinate me, you know—and then he'd be disgraced! But he missed me! The stupid idiot missed me and everything's totally wrong!"

Despite his best efforts, Dabir started crying. Hot tears of confusion and shame began to run down his cheeks. Spoken aloud, his plan sounded raw and ill conceived, even to him. Wherever he was, and whomever he was talking to, he prayed they'd kill him soon.

"You want to punish your father for purchasing weapons for Qurac?"

"They killed my mother and Amin!" Dabir was shouting suddenly, using rage in an attempt to fight back grief.

The incorporeal voice intensified along with him, speeding up its inquisition as he sped up his answers, spitting them out in fury.

"And that was your father's fault?"

"If he hadn't—if he hadn't been shipping those weapons . . ."

"Cheshire wouldn't have been able to steal them? She couldn't have stolen them any other way?"

"We were supposed to be at the beach!"

"It's his fault that she chose Qurac to bomb? Not the dictator who ruled there at the time, or the mercenaries who used it as their haven?"

"He sent them! He sent them to the capital! My brother and my mother, it's *his* fault they were there! He told them to go! He *told* them!"

"Dabir—"

"I should have died instead! It should have been me. Not Amin. Me!"

All of the lights in the warehouse came up, but Dabir was crying too hard to bother looking around. His heart felt as wounded and desolate as Qurac after the explosion; a barren, ruined organ radioactive with anguish and guilt. With his chin against his chest, Dabir began to rock back and forth in his chair, eyes tightly closed to squeeze out the endless tears. He needed Amin desperately, and Amin was entirely unreachable, permanently burned from the face of the earth. "It should have been me! It should have been me . . ."

He felt someone with nimble, gloved hands undoing the ties at his wrists and then his ankles and caught the scent of his father's expensive *oud* in the air. Suddenly he was in the president's arms, his father kneeling on the floor beside his chair and pulling him fiercely up against his chest, crying right along with him and calling his name.

"Dabir, my son, my boy . . ."

"Daddy! Dad, I'm so sorry . . . !"

"Not your fault, my son, it was not your fault . . ."

"Why can't Amin be here? Why can't I remember the sound of Mama's voice?"

"We have lost too much. Dabir, Dabir . . . we must not lose each other!"

After Tula's death and Arthur's betrayal, Garth spent more time with the Titans, aiding Aquaman dispassionately when called upon but otherwise avoiding the politics of Atlantis as much as possible. Having been appointed ambassador to the U.N. representing Poseidonis, Aquaman's need of Garth's assistance lessened considerably, and Garth made no effort to rekindle their partnership. He spent his time fighting in, recovering from, or anticipating heroic emergencies, one twisting into the next in a seemingly endless whirlpool of worry, pain, adrenaline, and gallantry. The period ended abruptly during a vicious battle with the Wildebeest Society; one moment, Aqualad was on the coast of Long Island fighting a losing battle alongside Titans West member Golden Eagle, the next, Garth found himself rising slowly up from a pool of deep oblivion to a vision of Tula's sun-bright smile and the faraway sound of Arthur's sonorous voice.

"Hey, Minnow. Welcome back to the land of the living."

The vision of Tula faded as Garth's purple eyes fluttered open. Arthur was sitting quietly beside a bed Garth didn't remember lying down in and his walrus friend Tusky was brushing eagerly against his arm. When he spoke, Garth's voice felt dry and reedy.

"Where am I?"

"You're safe," Arthur answered as Tusky swam happy circles around his bed. "We're in the Hidden Valley, where the faith healers have been praying for your recovery for days. Nice to see that their prayers haven't gone unanswered."

Garth's throbbing head spun with questions. Why was Arthur there? How had he ended up back with the Idylists?

"Golden Eagle? Is he—?"

"Sorry, son. We lost him. The Wildebeest strangled him to death before you even hit the ground. We thought we were going to lose you, too. You've been in a coma for several months—S.T.A.R. Labs did what they could, but things were touch and go. Nightwing eventually contacted me to see if I could help."

Garth wanted to turn away and revive the image of Tula that had so vividly filled his eyes only seconds before he had opened them, but he struggled to stay awake and kept talking in order to fight back a tide of grief. Every time he woke from a dream of Tula, the realization of her absence crashed over him with the renewed ferocity of a tidal wave. The question he most wanted to ask Arthur was unutterable, so he stuck with the mundane.

"Why did you bring me here?"

"The medics in Atlantis are still swamped with injured from the war. The Idylists here consider you their prince— I knew they'd do everything they could to make you well."

Considered him their prince? Garth *was* the prince of

the Idylists, as an earlier exploration into his past had finally revealed. Arthur knew that the unsettling story of the regicide of Garth's father and subsequent banishment of his mother led to the even more distressing realization that the former Queen Berra was very much alive, and had done nothing for over eighteen years to find her son or in any way aid him in discovering the truth about his past or birthright. Garth had asked Arthur repeatedly if it was true that Berra had played an active role in concealing the truth about his heritage and even, possibly, in leaving him to die all those many years ago. Arthur had never suggested anything to the contrary.

"Is *she* here?" Garth asked bitterly. The question felt desperately important to him, though he honestly didn't know what he wanted the answer to be.

"Your mother?" Arthur clarified, taking Garth's clenching jaw for a yes. "No. But I'm sure she wishes she could be."

Garth realized that he wished so, too. Not because of the inconsolable ache of loneliness in his gut and the intrinsic need to feel worried over and loved, but because he felt he could have asked Berra the one question he could not quite voice to Aquaman.

Since when do you give a damn whether I live or die?

Nightwing wound the rope carefully around one wrist and then looked up into the rafters of the dockside warehouse. Batman nodded to him and he quickly bounded up a pile of crates to stand by his mentor's side.

"Will they be okay?" he asked softly, glancing down at the tearful Quraci president and his anguished son.

Batman nodded. "A LEDET team is on their way. I've recommended grief counseling in addition to any legal actions that might be taken."

Nightwing handed Batman the tightly wound ropes and glanced in the direction of the pier outside. "And everybody's all right out there?"

"Orin and Oliver were able to get everything under control."

Nightwing cocked his head ever so slightly, continuing to stare at Batman expectantly, one eyebrow slightly raised

Batman turned his back on Nightwing and frowned down at Hatim and Dabir, who were still weeping together. The father and son were sharing their grief, depending on one another to validate the painful realities constructed in their hearts. "At least, that's what I told Garth and Roy to let them think."

Watching the back of Batman's cape, Nightwing smiled, satisfied.

"Oh, hey, Batman?"

The Dark Knight turned to Nightwing impassively.

"Do you have time to help me with one more little thing?" When speaking to Batman, Nightwing's voice took on a quiet, deferential quality noticeably different from the assertive tone he otherwise used.

Batman did not hesitate to answer him. "Of course," he said evenly. He was not surprised when Nightwing, though a young man of twenty-six, beamed at him as if he'd just agreed to take him to the circus or attend a school play. Batman had always meant to spend more time teaching Dick to better hide his feelings, but in some ways, it seemed a shame to train out such an infectious grin.

For a long while, it seemed to Garth that his life existed only as a twisted challenge to death. He'd been out of his coma for less than three months when he found himself bleeding out in the middle of the Atlantic, hundreds of miles from the safety of Poseidonis. It was no comfort at all to see Aquaman wounded nearby, or to note the absence of Charybdis, the enemy who had attacked them. Vision clouded with the red of his own blood, Aqualad smiled faintly, thinking of the fabled whirlpool nymph-daughter of Poseidon and Gaia that the burly self-defined terrorist had apparently named himself after. It might have been interesting to die in an actual whirlpool, an entity so fearsome and deadly as to warrant its own personified myth. To die at the hand of this modern-day Charybdis would just be insulting.

Tula seemed to think so, too. She swam in slow, careful circles around Garth, gently tending to his wounds. Garth tried to watch her through the crimson haze of the surrounding water but kept finding his eyes closed despite his intention to follow her every move. His eyelids were so heavy, and the pressure from the ocean depths pressed painfully against his chest.

Except, Garth corrected himself, *for the fact that I'm not really that far from the surface and—oh, yeah—Tula's dead.*

He felt Tula's warm hand brush against his cheek and woke up several hours later in Poseidonis with Aquaman's friend Dolphin hovering worriedly over his bed.

Everything was clear to him. Of course the figure in the water hadn't been Tula.

She had been Tula's reincarnation.

Despite Dolphin's warnings not to, the moment Garth was strong enough to swim out on his own he returned to the site of his latest near-death experience in search of the woman who had nursed him.

"*I* nursed you!" Dolphin protested. "And I hauled you and Aquaman back here so that you could get proper medical attention!"

"Uh huh," said Garth, already planning his swimming route. "Thanks."

He didn't expect anyone to understand. The possibility of finding Tula, or even a new being somehow possessed of Tula's spirit, was worth every risk, even the risk of disappointment. He had tried hard to continue bravely on without her, but it just didn't work. A certain amount of grief had been acceptable, even expected, but eventually society—both Atlantean and surface world—had demanded that Garth, no matter how bereaved, "move on" with his life.

Move on where? He was missing an entire half of himself. Tula hadn't just been his love; she'd been his purpose and his path. Moving across the Atlantic in search of her gave Garth the first experience of truly living that he'd had in years.

In retrospect, he realized that should have tipped him off to the inevitable proximity of disaster. Maybe he was courting it by then. Maybe his ardent desire to find Tula was really just a secret wish for death.

There was no Tula at the other end of the ocean, but the

creature Garth did find was nearly as mesmerizing. There *had* been a woman ministering to his injuries—he saw her darting in and out of shadows the moment he approached the waters in which she'd saved him. First he glimpsed her flowing, dark hair and foreboding eyes, then a silver-gray flash of a tail. She was some kind of mermaid—half woman, half shark. Garth took after her like a sailfish.

"Wait!" he called. "I need to talk to you!"

His rush forward seemed to alarm the merwoman, who darted away with astonishing speed. If Garth hadn't been trained as an underwater crime fighter, he never would have been able to keep up with her. As it was, her avoidance only strengthened his resolve to catch up with her. The faster he swam, the harder she worked to evade him, and the more determined he became in his pursuit. Her low voice was tinged with urgency and alarm when she finally shouted for him to stay back.

Garth was thoroughly intrigued.

"You saved my life," he insisted. "Please, let me thank you!"

The light reflecting in the merwoman's black eyes seemed to go hard and flat. Garth's body was aching to pull up close to hers, but she was frowning at him darkly over her shoulder, glaring with contempt and racing away from him into increasingly less familiar waters.

"Stop following me!" she demanded.

"Tell me your name!" he called after her.

She said nothing which—Garth was only slightly ashamed to admit to himself—meant that her name actually could be "Tula," even though by then he had half stopped believing in any connection between his lost love and this bewilderingly hostile rescuer he'd taken it upon himself to pursue.

"I'm Garth," he offered.

For a brief second, the merwoman stopped, facing him from a safe distance away.

"And I am not someone you need to know," she stated flatly.

By the time he learned that she was called Letifos, Garth had already followed her halfway across the world, been captured by members of her sullen and intolerant race, and sentenced to death for the mere act of trespassing on their territory.

Crucified and facing a lethal vortex that even Letifos's people seemed to find alarming, Garth was so horrified that he forgot to take comfort in the fact that this, at least, would be a death worthy of the Charybdis of myth.

Forty minutes later, Aquaman pulled himself out of the polluted waters of Gotham Harbor and up onto the rocks at the northernmost point of Sullivan Island. He saw no sign of Batman or Nightwing, but trusted that they'd meet him at the appointed location. Tempest was right behind him but seemed disinclined to get out of the water, doing backstrokes near the shoreline. Aquaman climbed up on the highest boulder he could find, unhindered by the dark or the slippery moss clinging to the black rocks.

"Well?" Batman's voice came from Aquaman's immediate left. Aquaman was practiced enough not to be startled by it, he was still impressed by Batman's ability to so thoroughly hide his scent and hulking form.

"As you suspected. There's one submerged exit large enough for a small water craft."

Batman, leaning out of the shadows enough to make himself visible to his friend, nodded. Aquaman caught Nightwing's scent signature close behind him. "You know what to do," Batman said.

Aquaman nodded and turned back to the bay before diving elegantly off the high boulder. Already in the water, Tempest plunged back under the surface. Almost instantly, all traces of the water-dwellers vanished.

Back on the rocks by the breakers, Batman turned to Nightwing, who opened up his comlink. "Nightwing to G.A., do you copy?"

Green Arrow's cheerful voice came clearly through the electric static in Nightwing's ear. "Gotcha loud and clear, kid. We're good here, 'cept for a small, grounded biplane with strictly interior access."

"Ten-four." Nightwing was about to close down the connection when he heard Arsenal's voice from slightly farther away asking Green Arrow what had just been said.

"I don't know," Green Arrow answered with his usual lack of patience. "Just stick to your post, I'm pretty sure we'll get to shoot something soon."

Nightwing smiled and closed the communication channel. "They're ready," he told Batman. "But there's a small plane inside they can't get to."

Batman nodded and began to move forward, knowing that Nightwing would follow him.

On top of an abandoned research center some fifty feet away, Arsenal lay flat on his stomach peering with a pair of binoculars through a large, central skylight. Green

Arrow was seated across from him, frowning at a small, inaccessible airplane hangar attached to the main building. The area around the deserted lab was surrounded by tall cypress, white pines, and overgrown shrubbery. After a short while, Arsenal lowered the binoculars, rolled over onto his back, and stared up at the patches of starry night sky visible through the highest tree branches. He sighed contentedly. "Now *this* is my idea of a stakeout."

Green Arrow turned his head to glance at him, then glimpsed up overhead at the stars. "Funny," he said, mostly just to say something. "After surviving on my own in the wilderness of Starfish Island, I've seen enough open night sky to last me a lifetime. But you—even after livin' on a reservation all those years, you still can't get enough of it, huh?"

Arsenal smiled up at the stars. "What were you there— like, two weeks?"

Green Arrow snorted indignantly. "Two *weeks*? I was stranded there for months! I couldn't even tell ya how long, kid, 'cause there were no clocks or calendars or—"

"Butlers?" Arsenal interrupted, stretching out his lean frame with a relaxed, almost impudent recklessness. It was clear to Green Arrow that the young man was enjoying himself at his mentor's expense.

"You don't know what it's like to be alone," Green Arrow replied curtly, rising to his feet to brush off the back of his tights with obvious irritation.

Arsenal rolled back onto his stomach and glared up at Green Arrow with his jaw clenched and his green eyes flashing. "Just how oblivious *are* you?" he snapped. Green Arrow turned to face him, surprised by the steel in the younger man's voice, as Arsenal pulled himself up into a crouch. "Seriously, I'm askin'. 'Cause the nonchalance and the non sequiturs and the constant exaggerations all have a kind of charm. But the complete annihilation of other people's realities, Ollie? That's not so cute. And I, for one, am *done* with it." By the time he finished speaking, Arsenal was on his feet on the second-story rooftop, his gloved hands balled into fists.

"What are you talkin' about, Speedy?" Green Arrow's expression was one of genuine worry and incredulity as he stared at his former ward across the skylight, but Arsenal only pressed his lips together and looked away.

"Nothing," he said with an exhausted finality, his shoulders lowering slightly. And then, in almost a whisper, "Forget it."

Green Arrow frowned and looked down through the skylight into a large, dark den. He was rubbing his beard as he looked up again, his eyes, hidden behind a small mask, carefully searching Arsenal's face. "Is this about that whole trip I took with Hal?" he asked quietly, his voice low.

Arsenal crouched down again, eyes glued to the skylight. "Ooh, you think?" he shot back sardonically.

Green Arrow crouched down across from him, still trying to make Arsenal meet his eyes. "That was a long time ago, Spee—er, Roy." The use of Arsenal's proper name earned Green Arrow the eye contact he'd sought. "I wish I could say I'd do it differently now, but it seemed to me like you were old enough to take care of yourself. I didn't want to . . . you know, *insult* you by leaving you with a babysitter or anything. Maybe I shoulda taken you with me, but who would wanna travel all around the country in a crummy old pickup with their old man?" Green Arrow was smiling again, and if not for the physical distance between them, he would have elbowed Arsenal playfully in an attempt to snap him out of his brooding.

Arsenal's posture and expression had softened, but his voice, when he answered, sounded sad and almost wistful. "Almost everyone I know, G.A. And that's a fact."

Green Arrow wasn't sure how to answer, but was saved from having to figure it out by a loud crash from inside the building they wore guarding.

"Showtime," Arsenal said, rising to his full height in order to aim a heavy stone arrowhead at the center of the skylight.

"Time to go posse!" Green Arrow agreed with a grin. He turned his face away from the glass of the skylight as Arsenal shattered it, then leapt through the newly formed entrance with a loud "hee-haw!"

Inside the research center, Deathstroke smiled darkly as he evaded Nightwing's kicks. "I'm flattered by all the attention," he quipped. "But really, I'm not the bad guy this time."

"You're bad enough for me," Nightwing answered, landing a spinning back fist on Deathstroke's muscular left shoulder. Deathstroke didn't notice the Batarang hidden in Nightwing's gloved hand until Nightwing used the brief contact to slice off Deathstroke's bandolier.

Deathstroke had been backing toward the central den of the science station, but upon hearing the shattering of the skylight and Green Arrow's spontaneous battle charge behind him, reconsidered. "And you brought your little archer friend again, as well?" Nightwing had to duck as Deathstroke suddenly reversed direction, using a nearby side table as leverage to keep himself out of reach of Nightwing's long legs while drawing a *katana* from a scabbard on his back and swinging it toward Nightwing's head. "How thoughtful."

Nightwing leapt up to get his feet out of the way of a low *katana* swipe, and Deathstroke used the opening to roll under Nightwing and pop up just past him. Nightwing managed to turn in midair, throwing his Batarang with practiced precision the moment his boots touched ground. "He's heading to the subbasement," he reported into his comlink as the Batarang cut through a single cable near Deathstroke's waist, liberating the retreating mercenary of both an automatic machine gun and a heavy broad sword he'd attached to the back of his costume. The Batarang returned to Nightwing's waiting hand as two of Deathstroke's most fatal weapons clattered to the ground.

Deathstroke didn't slow down until he had opened the interior bay door of the subbasement docking station to discover that the area around his small submersible craft was already partly flooded. That had to mean that the exterior access flap was already partly opened. Deathstroke figured it might have been Nightwing's entry point into the science station and waded gruffly into the overflowing docking bay to get access into the craft.

Though his senses were all well above average, Deathstroke had not been actively monitoring for underwater threats, and was caught off guard by the strong Atlantean hand that grabbed on to his ankle and pulled his footing out from under him. Slipping beneath the docked submersible, Deathstroke caught sight of Tempest forcing the exterior access gate all the way open a second too late. Aquaman was already on him, and Deathstroke was smart enough to know that even his superhuman reflexes could not be expected to even out his chances against two heroic water-breathers if he were to let himself be pulled all the way into the bay. Struggling to maintain contact with the belly of the submersible craft, Deathstroke let go of his *katana* and had been stripped of his thigh holster and waist-sheathed hunting knife by the time he had hold of the rudder.

Deathstroke, in an effort to escape Aquaman's relentless pummeling, was about to attempt scrambling into the submersible craft through a rear exhaust system when he felt the temperature of the already cold water around him swiftly drop. Glancing around to catch sight of Tempest, Deathstroke witnessed the former Teen Titan using some form of ancient Atlantean magic to freeze the water around the bow of the craft. Kicking at Aquaman with all of his strength, Deathstroke propelled himself back toward the subbasement entrance, then brought all of his prowess and concentration to bear on narrowly escaping the docking bay altogether. Aquaman smiled grimly as he watched the super-powered mercenary flee back toward the warm, dry interior of the science center.

"We're done here," he said assertively, still watching Deathstroke's retreat. When Tempest didn't answer, Aquaman turned around and swam out of the docking bay. Tempest was nearby in the water, watching him quietly with his unsettling purple eyes. "I have business to conduct at the U.N."

Tempest nodded, but still did not speak. Aquaman frowned slightly, nodded toward him one last time, then turned and swam east, back out toward the ocean. Tempest did not fully relax until Aquaman was out of sight.

Back in the science station, Deathstroke was dodging a volley of arrows as he crossed the central room on his way to the hangar. One of the archers was shooting from inside the compound, the other from the roof through the broken skylight. Deathstroke knew enough about Nightwing's allies and associates to correctly identify them both, and though he would have loved to take either Green Arrow or Arsenal down a peg, he decided not to confront the unpredictable combination of former Teen Titans and current Justice League members. If Nightwing, Aquaman, Tempest, Green Arrow, and Arsenal had all decided to come for him, it was well past time to retreat.

Once past the rain of arrows, Deathstroke made it to the hangar without interruption. He was ensconced in the cockpit of the biplane and starting the preliminary engine check when his normally agile mind finally seized on to the obvious. They had split up intentionally in an attempt to wear him down and corral him. And they would not have let him get as far as the hangar unless—

"Hello, Slade." Batman's voice sounded like ice water hissing over hot gravel, and it came from directly behind Deathstroke's right ear. Deathstroke let out a slow, aggravated breath and relaxed his posture in the pilot's seat.

"Batman," he acknowledged. He did not resist as Batman deftly handcuffed him, but he did allow for a small, ironic smile. "And five assistants. Don't you think this is kind of overkill?"

"Definitely," Batman agreed, skillfully slipping a tranquilizer dart past Deathstroke's armor to pierce the left side of his neck. "But it was a nice way to spend some time with the kids."

Underneath his cowl, Deathstroke's smile broadened. As his eyes began to close, he let himself remember Batman's boy and his own son, Joseph, laughing together in Titans Tower, teammates and friends. Though mute and wholly unable to produce sound from his throat, Joey had possessed a beautiful, silent laugh, his blue eyes twinkling with visible crescendos of warmth as his slender body shook with mirth. In Slade's memory, Joey—a talented artist and musician born into a family of scrappers—was attempting to paint Nightwing's portrait while Nightwing amusingly and absolutely failed to remain still, finally giving into his own impulse for motion and entertaining Joey with a series of increasingly energetic and improbable poses. It was a scene from what felt like another life, but Deathstroke wondered if it wasn't somehow at the core of his failure to kill Dick Grayson every time he had the chance. He couldn't kill *both* of those laughing young men. That was too much blood for anyone to have on their hands.

Deathstroke struggled momentarily to clear his head, then surrendered to the recollection: Nightwing, with his acrobatic grace and irrepressible energy. And Joey, sweet Joey . . . Slade's own fallen angel, all curly blond hair and wide-eyed innocence. What would it hurt to indulge the memory, just for a minute or two? There would be time enough to free himself once the sedative wore off.

Garth never spoke to anyone about the time he spent in the other dimensional magic realm with the wizard Atlan.

In his memory, the place was timeless and full of light, almost like a dream. He wasn't even sure how he had gotten there, or where "there" was. But he knew that he trusted Atlan, who promised that he'd been watching over the young Idylist for all of his life.

"Am I dead?" Garth asked him, shivering with the memory of the flesh being torn from his bones.

"Aqualad has died," Atlan informed him, "so that Tempest may be born."

Learning how to freeze, heat, and manipulate water with innate mystical powers he hadn't known that he possessed was heady for Garth. Hearing someone speak authoritatively about his past, his family, and even his future, though—that was manna.

"Yours is a great destiny, son of Thar," Atlan assured him on more than one occasion. "Far from inferior, you are to one day become the most powerful wizard the seas have ever known."

By the time Garth left the magic realm, he could almost believe in Atlan's prophecies. The great wizard had provided him with new powers, clarified links to his own history, and even, just by being who he was, a renewed connection to Aquaman.

Garth would always be grateful to Atlan for being his mentor and friend, but he adored him for being Arthur's father. It was in that role that Atlan brought Garth into Aquaman's family with a warmth and finality that the King of Seas, despite his best diplomatic efforts, had never managed to establish.

"You are beyond such concerns." Atlan frowned when Garth tried to explain his appreciation.

"No," Garth insisted, shaking his head as his purple eyes glimmered. "Belonging to a family? Having an excuse to stay connected to the people who helped shape your understanding of yourself?"

Garth stopped to concentrate on the task the older wizard had assigned him, the creation of a small whirlpool in a sea of calm. He smiled as the water started spiraling at his behest, as if the movement had always been there, just waiting to be freed.

"Trust me, Atlan. No one's beyond that."

The following morning, seated in a booth at the Dockside Diner with half a cup of hot coffee in front of him, Dick looked up from a copy of the *Gotham Gazette* to see Roy grinning down at him.

"Hey, man! Join me for breakfast?"

Roy slid in across from him while rubbing the stubble on his unshaven jaw. "You buyin'?"

Dick chuckled. "Sure." He folded the paper and put it down on the table between them, allowing Roy a glimpse at the front page.

"Where's the story about the war we stopped?"

Dick opened the paper again and handed Roy the finance section. "B4. *Quraci Shipment Comes in as Planned; heralds new age for U.S./Quraci relations.*"

Roy scanned the article with evident disbelief, his green eyes narrowing. "You gotta be kidding me! That's it!? What about the whales in the harbor and the suicidal kid and the—the flying guys with M-16s?! I shot twelve of them! Nobody saw those guys!?"

Dick offered a soft shrug, seemingly untroubled. "Never happened. And we all live happily ever after."

Roy slapped the paper back down on the table in disgust before extending his arms over the booth back to either side. "I do not get paid enough for this crap."

Dick laughed. "You don't get paid at all."

"What can I get for you guys?" A petite, blonde waitress in her early twenties with frosted pink lipstick and four pairs of earrings approached the table with an order tablet in hand. She did nothing to hide the appreciative once-over she gave both young men as color rose from her throat to her cheeks, a fact that Dick evidentially missed altogether and Roy rewarded with a slow smile and a quick wink. The waitress dropped her pad, retrieved it with bit lip and fluttering hands, and just managed not to hyperventilate as she wrote down Dick's yogurt and banana muffin order and Roy's request for steak and eggs.

As she refilled Dick's coffee and brought Roy a fresh cup, Dick smiled at his red-haired friend fondly.

"You know, it was kind of cool hanging out with Ollie."

Roy abandoned a lewd observation he was just about to make concerning the waitress and turned to Dick with a smirk.

"What'd you two talk about?"

"All kinds of stuff. His boots, Joey, you . . ."

Roy's eyebrows knotted skeptically

"You mean *you* talked about me and he pretended to listen."

"No. He told me how he first met you and everything. He was really proud, it was totally cool."

"Was it the archery contest or the bank robbery story?" Roy's voice was unquestionably strained and he was stabbing his fork at his placemat senselessly, but Dick just rubbed a hand against the back of his own neck and continued with complete sincerity.

"The robbery! Man, I just don't know if I would have had that kind of poise at that age. I mean, the first time Bruce saw me, I was on my knees bawling my eyes out."

"No." Roy shook his head, frowning, and pointed his fork tines at Dick. "The first time he saw *you*, you were flying through the air with the greatest of ease. You were working. At eight years old. As a professional frickin' trapeze artist." Dick smiled almost shyly and then snatched the fork out of Roy's hand with accomplished speed. Roy surrendered the utensil and continued. "And the first time Ollie saw me, I was living in a trailer in the middle of the Arizona desert dropping a book on the floor in shock over the fact that Green frickin' Arrow was sitting on my guardian's twelve-year-old couch."

"What, you mean the bank thing came later?"

Roy sighed. "*What* bank thing? There was no bank thing, Wingster. I mean, there were lots of banks, later, when we were running around imitating you and Batman like some kind of crazy cover band. But the whole thing about me impressing him with my savvy crime-fighting skills the first time we met on the Navajo reservation? Dude, please. Where was I gonna find a bank much less a bank robber?"

Dick's face crumbled in disappointment as he carefully replaced the stolen fork on Roy's napkin, lining it up precisely with the butter knife. "But what about the arrowhead penny and the three guys with the guns and—?"

"Oh, we're up to three now? Nice."

Dick was incredulous. "You mean he's *lying*?"

A tight smile flickered across Roy's face. He put an elbow on the table, unintentionally upsetting Dick's meticulous place setting. "With Ollie we don't call it lying so much as . . . *embellishment.*"

"So, wait—what about *his* origin story? The thing about Errol Flynn and the man and beast battle and—"

"He fell off a boat." Roy snorted, annoyed. "He was on a party cruise, he got drunk, he fell off, he ended up on some island and learned to hunt until the Coast Guard came and gave him a ride back home. And then he waltzed into his mansion and looked at his piles of money and thought, *Hey, I think I'll be a super hero!*" Roy's face darkened and he turned away from Dick, muttering to himself. "*Hell, maybe I'll even find a kid somewhere! Sure, why not? . . .*"

Dick took a sip of coffee and tried again. "Well, your *Dine'é* guardian, though, Brave Bow—"

"—*Raymond*—"

"—He was the best archer in the Navajo nation, right?"

Roy shrugged. "He was pretty good. I was better."

Dick frowned and placed his hands flat on the table in exasperation. "Well, how'd you learn?"

"I dunno. I just . . . did it. A lot. It was . . . something I was good at. Way not a big deal."

Dick looked crestfallen as the waitress brought them their food, the smell of cigarette smoke fresh in her hair. "That's just . . . I feel so *disillusioned.*"

Roy smiled wryly, pulling his paper napkin out from under the silverware and dropping it into his lap. "Welcome to my world, amigo. Welcome to my world."

"Here you go, guys. One yogurt with muffin, one steak and eggs. Is there anything else I can get for you?"

Roy looked up at Dick from under a few untamable strands of red hair, waiting for Dick to jokingly request world peace, usually his favorite diner order. But Dick just smiled up at the waitress warmly, nearly melting her knees. "We're good here, thanks."

"Against all odds," Roy muttered with a wry smile, cutting into his steak.

When the waitress finally left their table, Dick leaned forward slightly across it, his blue eyes flashing.

"It is kind of incredible, isn't it?"

Roy answered with a mouth full of meat.

"What? That we survived this long?"

Dick lifted his spoon and stared at it thoughtfully.

"Yeah. I mean, it's no surprise that we're alive, I guess, considering who had our backs. But that we're . . . I don't know . . ."

"Reasonably lucid?" Garth winked at Dick, who grinned up at him and scooted over on the vinyl booth seat to make room.

"Hey, Gillhead." Roy nodded.

"N.A. Boy," Garth teased back. "Oh, Cerdian asked me to ask you to bring Lian over for a play date soon."

Roy washed a bite of steak down with a gulp of hot coffee.

"Sure, I'll just grab her scuba gear."

Garth considered freezing Roy's coffee, but turned to Dick instead.

"Oh, I hope you guys don't mind, but I invited Arthur, Bruce, and Ollie to join us. I just didn't feel like we had enough 'together time' running that case." He turned his head to include Roy in his assertions. "I mean, maybe the six of us should team up more often. I think we all learn so much every time we're with the old guys. If we're really lucky, maybe they'll ask us to take back our old sidekicking jobs!"

Dick and Roy both froze, midbite. From the coffee station, the waitress looked over longingly just in time to see all three striking young men erupt into loud peals of laughter.

ABOUT THE AUTHOR

DEVIN KALILE GRAYSON grew up in the San Francisco Bay area and currently resides in Oakland, California. After earning a degree in English Literature from Bard College, Devin was working at a normal day job and taking post-graduate writing classes at U.C. Berkeley when she read and fell in love with her first comic book. She has worked for DC Comics ever since, in 2000 becoming the first woman to create and write a new Batman series. Recent work includes the creator-owned mini-series *Matador*, monthly writing on *Nightwing*, and *Smallville: City* for Warner Books.

LAST SONS

ISBN: 0-446-61656-7

By Alan Grant

SUPERMAN. MARTIAN MANHUNTER. LOBO.

Interplanetary bounty hunter Lobo is a notorious maverick. Happily wreaking havoc as he brings in his prey, he cares little who his clients or targets are—even when his latest quarry is J'onn J'onnzz, Martian Manhunter of the Justice League of America. Suddenly Lobo finds himself confronting . . . Superman. Cogs in the machinations of a powerful artificial life-form, these three aliens, the sole survivors of the planets Krypton, Mars, and Czarnia, have only one thing in common—they are the last of their kind. . . .

LAST SONS

Available wherever books are sold.

HELLTOWN

ISBN: 0-446-61658-3

By Dennis O'Neil

BATMAN. LADY SHIVA. RICHARD DRAGON. THE QUESTION.

There are a lot of unanswered questions about Vic Sage, the Question: how he spent—or misspent—his youth; and how he came to be a journalist in the country's worst city. This story will solve these mysteries, retell and embellish some tales already told and tell a new tale of how Vic, with a bit of help, brought some measure of serenity to a truly dreadful place. From his first meeting with Lady Shiva, where he was almost killed. To training with Richard Dragon, the best martial artist in the world (except perhaps for Lady Shiva and Batgirl). And how Batman, while threatening his life, also saved him, this story will finally provide answers about the Question. Who he is and what he did.

Available November 2006.